RUNAWAY

BY

EDWARD D. CASEY

resoNation

RESONATION PRESS & MEDIA
NEWNAN, GA

Cover illustration by Paolo Libunao
email: np.libunao@yahoo.com.ph
website: www.paololibunao.deviantart.com

Maps and schematics by Edward D. Casey

resoNation press & media
5 Woodmoor, Newnan, GA 30263
www.resonationpress.com

First Edition: August 2010

The characters and events in this book are fictitious, but are based on historical figures. Please see the appendices of the publication for specific explanations. Any similarity otherwise to real persons, living or dead, is coincidental and not intended by the author.

Library of Congress Cataloging-in-Publication Data

Casey, Edward D.
Runaway / Edward D. Casey – 1st ed.
p. cm.
ISBN 978-0-9828491-0-1
1. Fiction Science Fiction General 2. Fiction Religious

To Amy and Emma
The two great joys of my life
and my inspiration.

Special Thanks to:
David, Jeremy, Mom, and Ron
for ongoing encouragement as I wrote Runaway.

Special Thanks to:
Julie, Kevin, Susan M, Susan R, and Robert
for extrodinary editing help.

Thanks to:
Alesia, Ben, Beverly, Bob, Cindy,
Dave, Deborah, Dianne, Dr. O, Gene
Jacki, Janet, Jeff, Jerry, Jill, Jimmy,
John, Kelly, Kenny, Kerry, Lori K,
Lori N, Lynn, Mark, Matt, Michael,
Rebecca, Russell, and Scott
For invaluable test-reading and production feedback.

And many, many thanks to numerous others who have
encouraged me along the way.

The Star King

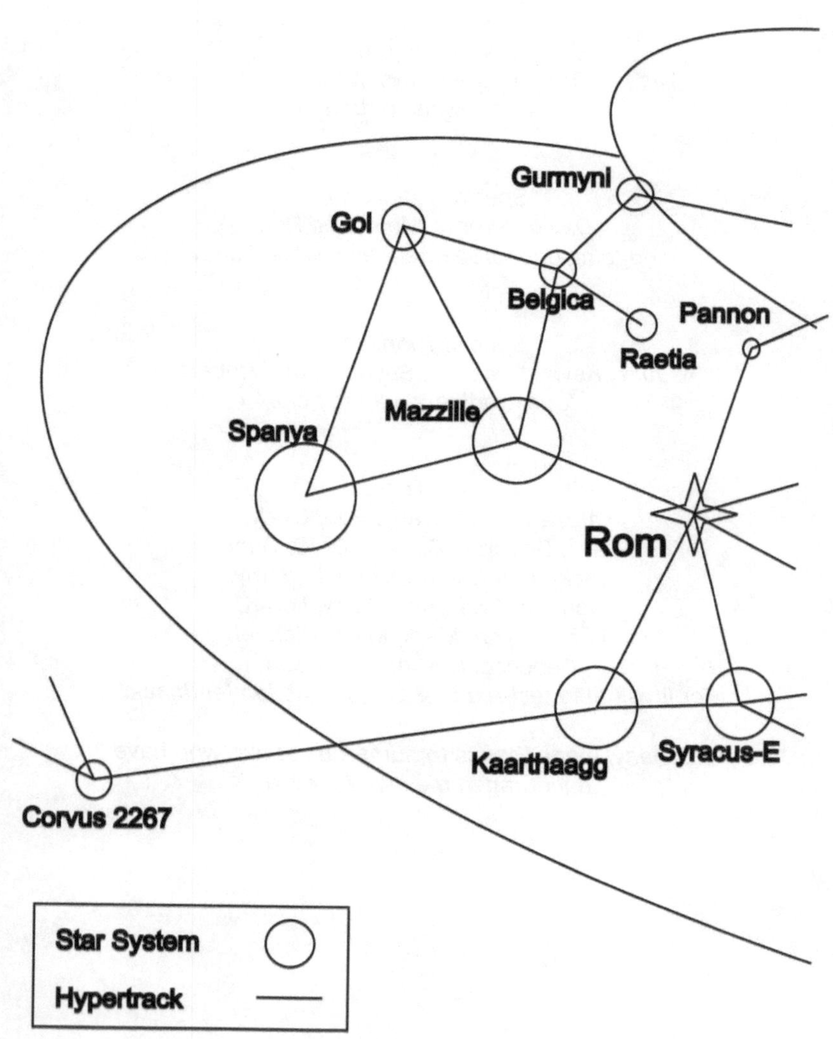

dom of Rom

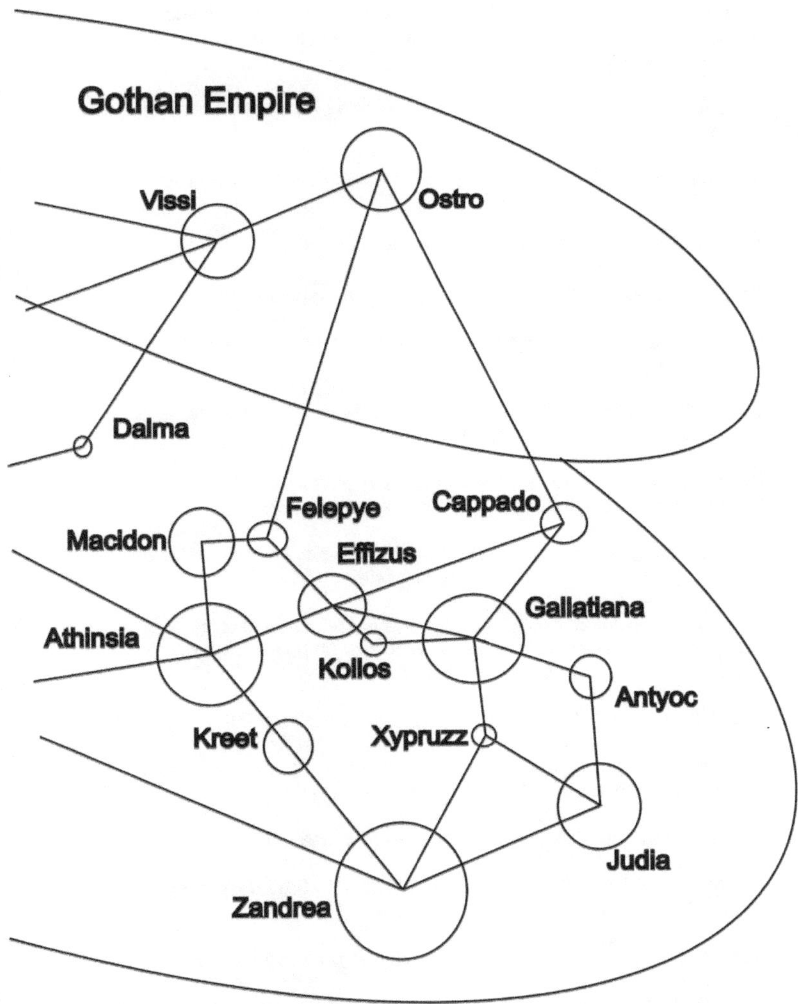
Gothan Empire
Vissi
Ostro
Dalma
Felepye
Cappado
Macidon
Effizus
Gallatiana
Athinsia
Kollos
Antyoc
Kreet
Xypruzz
Judia
Zandrea

Cast of Characters

(pronunciation - gender/age)

Aiolos (Aa-ee-oh-los – M/19) House slave of Deme Trius at Effizus.

Aquyia (Ah-kee-ah – M/29) TENT manufacturer at Effizus. Husband of Prazella. Part-time employer of and follower of Pol at Effizus. One of the leaders of the ekklesia of Effizus.

Apphia (Aff-ee-ah – F/37) Wife of Filymon and mother of Chipus, living at Kollos.

Aristachus (Ar-rist-ah-cuz – M/34) Follower of Pol under house arrest at Rom.

Artimiss (Art-e-miz – F/N/A) Patron goddess of Effizus.

Chippus (Chip-us – M/10) Son of Filymon and Apphia.

Delis (Dell-iz – F/44) Exotic metals exporter based at Tavium, Galatiana. Shipping partner with Filymon.

Deme Trius (Dem-ee Tree-uz – M/51) Idol exporter and smuggler based at Effizus. Shipping partner with Filymon.

Demas (Dee-maz – M/16) Follower of Pol at Rom. Part of the "Fearsome Foursome" including Phroditus, Tychicus, and Yaunmarck.

Epaphras (Ee-paa-frass – M/23) Pilot for Filymon. Follower of Pol at both Effizus and Rom. Leader of the ekklesia at Kollos.

Filymon (Fill-ee-mon – M/39) Owner of the *Wander Wide* cargo ship based at Kollos. Husband of Apphia. Father of Chippus. Owner of Seamus/Onesimus. Employer of Epaphras.

Gaius (Guy-uz – M/46) One of Pol's lieutenants at both Effizus and Rom.

Halcyon (Hol-ky-on – M/40) Owner of a fishing lodge on Kollos. Once romantically involved with Apphia and at odds with Filymon.

Justis (Jus-tiz – M/61) Owner of the house Pol uses while in Rom.

Kaanntaana (Kan-tan-ah – F/92) Ship's doctor of the *Rreennzeestt*, a slave ship based at Kaarrthaagg.

Kepheus (Kee-fuz – M/64) Neighbor of Filymon and Apphia at Kollos.

Liam O'Neil (Lee-am M/44) Geologist and planetary surveyor. Father of Seamus and husband of Lisa.

Lisa O'Neil (F/45) Biologist and planetary surveyor. Mother of Seamus and wife of Liam. Mission commander of the Corvus 2267 survey.

Lukaas (Loo-kaz - M/54) Doctor and friend of Pol.

Löwin (Low-win - F/77) Snowcat from Vissi, Gothan Empire.

Onesimus (Oh-niss-ee-muz) - see Seamus O'Neil.

Phroditus (Fro-dye-tuz - M/17) Follower of Pol at Rom. Part of the "Fearsome Foursome" including Demas, Tychicus, and Yaunmarck.

Pol (Pall - M/52) One-time inquisitor for the Judian state religion, but now known as a mystic for a small-but-growing sect of those who worship Yeshua. Travels throughout the Star Kingdom as a missionary and trains others to do the same.

Prazella (Pra-zell-ah - F/29) TENT manufacturer at Effizus. Wife of Acquia. Part-time employer and follower of Pol at Effizus. One of the leaders of the ekklesia of Effizus.

Rastus (Ras-tuz - M/41) One of Pol's lieutenants at both Effizus and Rom.

Rado (Ray-doh - M/48) Slave trader and captain of the *Trouveur* based out of Mazille.

Seamus O'Neil *(Shay-muz* - M/14) Son of Liam and Lisa O'Neil of Derry,
Ireland. Also known as Onesimus (Oh-niss-ee-muz)

Tem (M/31) Pol's lieutenant and protégé at Effizus and Rom.

Thunderblade (N/A/34) Robot toy of Seamus originally belonging to Liam.

Tychicus - (Titch-ik-uz - M/17) Follower of Pol at Rom. Part of the "Fearsome Foursome" including Demas, Phroditus, and Yaunmarck.

Tyrannus (Teer-ran-uz - M/46) Owner of an educational center in Effizus.

Yeshua (Yah-shoo-ah - M/???) A Judian religious reformer who rose to prominence 25 years previously. He reportedly possessed miraculous powers and claimed to be God. Out of jealousy, the established religious council of Judia arranged for Yeshua's murder. Hundreds of his followers later reported him resurrected, holding to these claims even to their own deaths. The basic tennent of Yeshuaism is that Yeshua's perfect life, blameless death, and miraculous resurrection is a sustitutionary act of God to provide forgiveness of sins for all who believe.

Yaunmarck (Yawn-mark- M/19) Follower of Pol at Rom. Leader of the "Fearsome Foursome" including Demas, Phroditus, and Tychicus.

Zaannddaarraa (Zand-ar-ah - M/116) Captain of the Kaarrthaaggian slaver, *Rreennzeestt.*

The Fernão de Magalhães

and research cutter

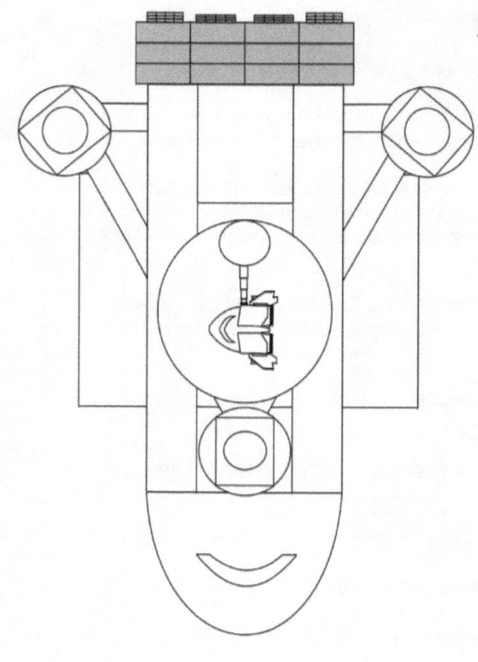

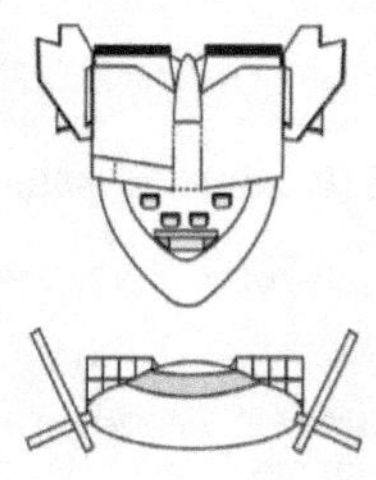

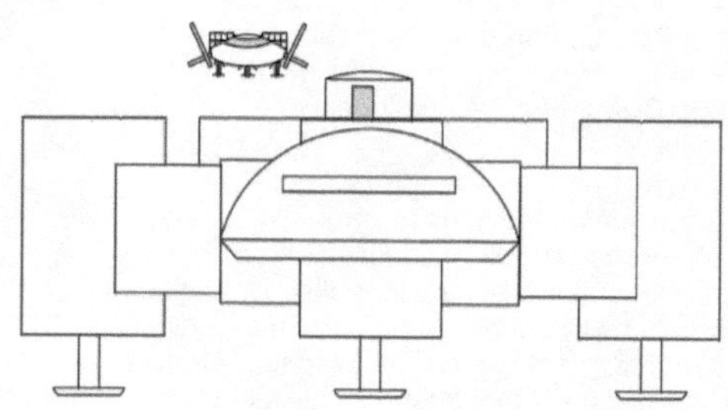

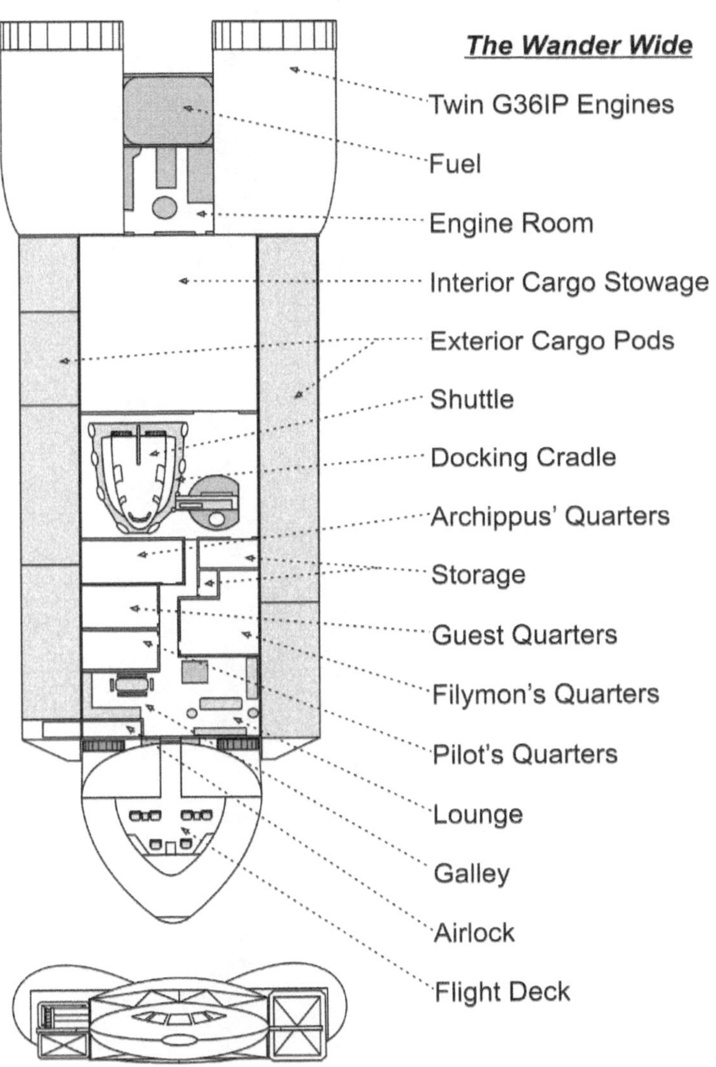
The Wander Wide
Twin G36IP Engines
Fuel
Engine Room
Interior Cargo Stowage
Exterior Cargo Pods
Shuttle
Docking Cradle
Archippus' Quarters
Storage
Guest Quarters
Filymon's Quarters
Pilot's Quarters
Lounge
Galley
Airlock
Flight Deck

ONE – FAR AWAY

"YOU NEVER LET ME DO ANYTHING!"

If the three-room research cutter of the deep space survey vessel *Fernão de Magalhães* had hinged doors to slam, the entry from the central corridor to the research lab would have crashed through the jam and flung through the room. Instead, the sliding door whispered shut, the only satisfaction it brought to fourteen-year-old Seamus O'Neil was how it cut off his mother's shrill voice in midsentence: "I don't know why we let you talk us into bringing you alo—"

To make up for a satisfying slam, Seamus took advantage of the null gravity of the corridor, pitched forward, and hammered his feet into engine access panel. A loud *clang* echoed in his ears as he careened toward the flight deck.

"Ow," he whimpered as he ricocheted off the floor and crashed into the far doorway. As the door recessed into the bulkhead it pinched the skin on his forearm and took a few hairs with it. "Blast it!" he snarled, then tumbled into the gravity zone of the flight deck, clattering to the floor. Angry enough to scream, he glanced back down the passage to the lab. Thankfully, it was empty of witnesses. At least the human kind.

"You really should work on your entry," a voice announced.

"And you should work on your exit!"

A foot-high black and chrome robot sat perched on the back of the pilot chair of the small spacecraft, looking at Seamus vacantly. Honestly, Seamus wondered why he didn't just shut the dumb thing down. Not only did Thunderblade say the most irritating things, he was old – his father's well-worn boyhood toy. His only slightly redeeming quality was he could convert into an old-fashioned helicopter. It was cool to watch the first thousand times, but now Seamus thought of him more as an irritating kid brother who he'd rather have anywhere else but here.

"I take it, that – as I predicted – your parents would not allow you to take one of the *Fernão de Magalhães'* service pods out for a joyride?" What the robot lacked in facial expressions, he more than make up for with his voice.

Seamus sneered. "They said it was for emergencies only."

"If you are bored, you could run another flight simulation?"

"I've done all the sims a million times! I've even upgraded a few to make them interesting. Besides, I've got to move this freighter full of boredom to—"

"SEAMUS! Move this ship to ring 43... NOW!" Even though his mother's growl came through the intercom, it sounded like she towered over him.

"Yes, your worship," he muttered under his breath.

Seamus plopped down in the seat as Thunderblade nimbly leapt to the copilot's chair. With a flick of a switch the canopy above them charged, flashing into transparency. Instantly, the sparkling rocky plane of Ring 42 materialized, the icy chunks orderly floating as if on some calm, invisible river. Beyond, looming above them almost like a streaked blue sky, was Corvus 2267-F, the system's largest Jovian gas giant, faintly illuminated by the distant yellow sun.

Seamus had left the flight systems on, so it took only a few seconds to set the coordinates and for the engines to green-light. Slipping on a headset, he keyed the comm. "Live engines in five seconds." As he mentally counted down, he angled the ship away from the rings where the gravity well of the main drive wouldn't disturb those stupid, precious chunks of ice that he had been daily threatened about disturbing.

At zero he gunned it, sinking into his chair with acceleration. Loose equipment – including Thunderblade – clattered to the deck. The forty-third ring of two hundred and sixty-eight zoomed toward them until he quickly brought the cutter to a relative halt.

"SEAMUS ROBERT O'NEIL!"

They had drilled into him how fast he could go. But, technically, they had never spelled out how quick he could get up to that speed limit.

Thunderblade choppered up from behind in 'copter mode, dropping back to the chair as a robot after a whirl of realignment. "The odds of your parents soon arrival is sixty-five to one."

"I bet," he huffed, already rehearsing his response.

The door hissed open. Seamus kept his back turned, but he imagined his mother or father gracefully dropping into gravity, face red and wild-looking. Whoever it was must be standing in the doorway since the door did not close.

"Seamus! What are you thinking?" Dad snarled. "You could have hurt someone! We have all sorts of loose equipment out all over the lab!"

"My relative velocity wasn't over—"

"Don't give me that! Your acceleration rate must have been... arrr, I'm not arguing with you. You *know* what you did!"

"But I—"

"Stop making excuses! We brought you out here to help you make a fresh start, but you're up to your same old tricks as always. You know, you're going to have to grow up. You can't keep acting like this anytime things don't go your way. You need to face up to—"

Seamus spun around, flushed with anger. "Face up? More like rub my face into it! So much for a 'fresh start'."

"You know I didn't mean—"

"Yeah, whatever! You know, Dad, if you don't like my flying then do it yourself!" Seamus snatched off the headset, tossing it to the console, and with a leap he was out of the pilot's chair and flying past his father, weightlessly down the corridor. He caught a handrail and swung into an opening doorway into the living area. The gravity was off so he sailed right through the door.

"Seamus!" his father called, but the door slid shut.

Across the room he soared, crashing into the kitchen unit cabinets. Seamus caught hold of a handle, huffing as he dragged himself toward his sleeping compartment. After pulling inside his 'tent', he yanked the zipper shut on the door, wishing forever it had a lock of some sort.

He was ready to scream, but he focused on breathing deeply. Each heaved breath seemed to shave off enough of his fury to keep it stillborn - barely. After a minute of angry breaths drawn through gritted teeth, he turned to gaze out the tiny porthole to the impossible black outside, a black fitting his mood perfectly.

His sleeping compartment amounted to his room on the cutter, barely a bed, computer station, and some storage space, but it felt more like his own personal coffin at the moment. He felt trapped. He was trapped on this tin can, trapped in this lifeless solar system who knew how many lightyears from home, trapped in his life. He wished he could just get into his own ship and go. It didn't matter where he went, as long as it wasn't here.

He jerked the shade closed on the blackness outside.

No matter what his parents now thought, leaving that school had been one of the best things that had ever happened to him. Boarding schools were for the rich, not the unfortunate sons of interstellar surveyors. Besides, with little else to do besides his schoolwork he had learned how to pilot starships. Not many fourteen-year-olds could say that.

Just as he pulled himself into the sleeping restraints he heard Thunderblade's voice whisper through the door: "Seamus, may I come in?"

Deep down, Seamus knew that over the years Thunderblade had developed algorithms of his moods and personality; that, based off of observable cues like vocal stress, he knew how long Seamus needed to cool down. It was all calculation, but for some reason he found it immensely comforting. Funny, how the one who knew him the best was a toy over twice his age. Thunderblade apparently took his silence as permission to enter – probably the result of statistical observation, as well.

"Your father is now resetting the acceleration protocols for your piloting profile. I am afraid you will not be able to exceed .5 G from now on."

"Oh, yeah? Did he find my other profile?"

"The full-access command profile you created without your parent's knowledge was still intact as of 67 seconds ago."

"Did you tell him?"

"He did not ask and I did not volunteer the information. Your secret command profile for this cutter does not yet meet the criteria of unduly endangering yourself or others, so I am not obligated to inform your parents. The ship's safety restrictions would not allow you to bring harm to the craft or anyone inside, and I calculate the odds of 228 to 1 you will never use the profile anyway. I theorize knowing the profile exists means more to you than actually using it."

"Ah, therapy... and I guess you take it as more evidence that I'm past aggressive?"

"Passive aggressive."

"Whatever."

"Perhaps if you communicated more openly with your parents and limited the emotional content of your discussions, you would be more successful in solving your interpersonal differences?"

"How's this for open communication? You're the most irritating and worthless hunk of metal I've ever seen!"

Seamus waited for the usual comeback, probably the typical about the evidence not meeting criteria. Instead Thunderblade's limited expression went blank.

"Thunderblade? Hello, you in there?"

Seamus was just about to check the robot's power settings when Thunderblade whirled around to the doorway, yanked the zipper open, and scooted through the opening. "Seamus, we are needed at the flight deck immediately."

"What? ...Why?"

As if in response, the cutter's computer announced through the intercom system in a calm, feminine voice: *"Proximity Alert. Unidentified vehicle approaching."*

Seamus froze.

"Proximity Alert. Unidentified vehicle approaching."

He shook it off, kicked off the bulkhead, and zipped through the open flap. In his hurry he knocked into almost every hard surface along the way, and collided into his mother out in the central corridor just as she exited the research lab on the opposite side of the cutter. Some of her long red hair flung across his face.

She braced herself and grabbed him. "Arghh, these cheap ships with only enough gravity for half the ship at a time!"

"Who is it?" he asked as they untangled and swam toward the flight deck.

"I don't know," Mom gasped as she nimbly swung into the gravity zone. "If it's from home, there must be some sort of emergency. A big one." She dropped to her feet and slipped into the copilot's chair, while Seamus stumbled into his seat behind Dad.

"It's... it's not from home," Dad stuttered.

"What?" Seamus asked. A small rotating yellow icon trailed over the canopy above them, growing ever larger as it showed the path of the approaching ship against the ringed planet and stars. Instead of the typical wording and codes printed next to the icon, question marks filled the blanks.

"Everything's different. There's no... no... uh, the identification codes, the – the emissions are—"

Mom cut him off impatiently: "Is it some new class we didn't get specs on before we left?"

Dad turned to her, his face pale and moist with perspiration. "No... everything is *different*. Look, it's big. It's got power signatures I've never seen before and which the computer can't identify. This isn't new. It's a—"

"First Contact?" Mom breathed out. Dad nodded slowly.

Seamus' stomach knotted, then even the knots knotted. A First Contact?"

Mom's whisper became a babble of excitement: "In 68 star systems surveyed, mankind has never found a trace of intelligent life. Not even a hint. We've been out here for six months looking for organic compounds in dried lakebeds and ice, and here life comes to us... in a starship!"

Dad shook his head. "Uh...I'm going to pull up the First Contact protocols."

Mom shook herself. "What am I doing? I've got to get the lab and get some readings!"

As Mom dove through the door, Seamus slipped into her seat, his hands slowly gripping onto the controls. They felt like anchors in the uncertainty. He watched as Dad rechecked the protocols and then keyed in one last command to send long-prepared friendly messages in every conceivable way.

Dad looked over. "Seamus, we're about to make history!"

Something didn't feel right. "What if they're not friendly?"

Seamus' father smiled reassuringly. "They will be. We only send out our best to other worlds. Why would any other advanced space-faring species be any different?"

Seamus glanced up again at the starry night beyond Ring 43. The yellow icon disappeared as the ship came into visual range, now enclosed with a growing yellow box. The visual's resolution was already up to maximum and Seamus strained his eyes to make out the dark shape. It would be upon them in moments, but he couldn't help but to try to make out every detail. With every second it grew and Seamus felt more uneasy. And then it hit him. The ship looked like a predator, a *shark*.

A moment later, he saw a flash just below the alien ship, followed by two brilliant streaks of light hurdling toward them. The computer tracked them, yellow icons blurring in motion toward either side of their cutter. Just as the icons disappeared to starboard and port, Seamus realized they were missiles.

On either side, silent nearby explosions rocked their cutter.

TWO - FLIGHT

Shockwaves from the two boiling orbs of yellow plasma - exploding missiles from the alien starship - crashed into their cutter, nearly sending it spinning. Alarms wailed throughout the ship. It took a few seconds for Seamus' brain to understand what had happened, but only a moment longer to react. He quickly righted the craft, whipped it around, and fired the thrusters in escape.

"Janey Mac!" Seamus exclaimed in shock.

"The message!" Dad shouted, "We must have sent the wrong message for First Contact! I've got to get to the lab!" With that he was out the door. Thunderblade leapt to his place.

"Too slow!" Seamus howled. Then it hit him: Dad had just changed his piloting profile, limiting how fast he could accelerate. His fingers flew over the controls.

"Are you activating your secret command protocol?" Thunderblade asked. "If so I will inform your parents, as I believe you may put yourself, others, or the cutter in danger."

"Me? Put myself in danger?" he cried as another explosion seemed to fill all of space above them. "Look out the window!" Seamus rode the shockwave away from the blast instead of fighting it, diving sharply as it dissipated, and then throttling into a weaving pattern.

Just then an odd guttural howling came through the intercom: *"Waasnoobaa neebaas!"* A glance at the comm system confirmed it came from the alien ship.

"That is not a standard dialect," Thunderblade announced.

"You think?"

Just then the boards lit up full access and Seamus ramped up the acceleration to emergency – four times normal gravity. He had experienced a simulated 4G pull in the training exercises, but this time with the erratic motion and sharp, banking turns, he felt on the edge of losing consciousness. He clinched his stomach tighter to force the blood back into his brain and eased off the acceleration.

Another nearby blast yanked Seamus sideways. The comm roared again: *"Loosnaa waasnoobaa neebaas aazee!"*

"Their firing pattern suggests warning shots so far. I calculate the next attack will be intended to damage the cutter." Thunderblade's calm voice was maddening. "With your present course and repetitive maneuvers, the odds of being hit are one-in-two."

"Then I need to get creative!"

The thought had crossed his mind a couple times already, but he had quickly dismissed it as both dangerous and probably criminal – at least in his parent's eyes. But now it was life or death.

Seamus dove into the ring.

Chunks of ice clattered over the hull and flung off in all directions. Seamus banked hard to stay in the cover of the ring just as another ball of yellow fire ballooned above. A hailstorm pelted them.

"Where is he? I can't see!" Seamus shouted. He felt like a tiger might pounce on him at any moment. Things were happening too fast for him to pilot the cutter, much less to keep up with the alien spacecraft.

Thunderblade keyed the tactical board to shift the point-of-view of the screen. Instead of looking ahead as if through the canopy, the view flicked to the third-person evaluation mode Seamus would normally see after running a simulation. He saw their cutter about the size of a matchbox with the shoebox-sized alien ship racing behind. The alien crashed through the ring – if it could be called one now.

"If we get out of this..." Seamus sliced sideways up through the ring to the topside, trying to limit collisions "...Mom's gonna kill me."

Like an orca bursting through the ocean surface after a seal, the alien ship crashed through the ring after them. Waves of icy debris streaked off, making a quickly-spreading fog. Seamus dove down again, but this time the alien pulled away.

"It would appear the alien intends to straddle the edge in order to limit the cover it provides you," Thunderblade said, as he lit up the outer perimeter of the ring and a course projection for their enemy. In response Seamus arched away in the opposite direction.

"Then let's head back where there isn't an edge." As the cutter flew into the soup of what was once a mighty ring, the alien mirrored the move, muscling back into the ice and drawing ever closer. Seamus wove through the debris, wincing every time the hull rang with a collision. What the alien seemed to easily plow through might very well destroy their small cutter.

As they drilled in deeper, the alien fired again but the shot exploded closer to the alien than the cutter. "Woohoo!" Seamus whooped. "He can't hit us with all this mess!" The alien seemed to realize it, too, and appeared to renew its focus on getting closer than on firing every few seconds.

In the following reprieve, Seamus took a deep breath, feeling his heart slowing and the adrenaline in his system ebbing. As he evaded both ice and alien, he tried to think of what to do. They couldn't stay out here forever. Sooner or later their luck would run out and the larger, more powerful alien would have them. Where were Mom and Dad? He keyed the comm, but no one answered. He was about to send Thunderblade to check on them when he had a sudden thought.

"Could we remotely signal the *Fernão* to lift off that moon and power up for a jump?" He corkscrewed around a large chunk. The fog thinned out as he approached their original position, and he banked to dive under the intact section of the ring.

"Your parents have the codes for remote operations."

"Go see if they can do it. Maybe if we can get the *Fernão* all ready, we can get into the bay and hyper out before they can catch us!"

"Tricky, but possible. I will return shortly."

Just as Thunderblade unbuckled the seat restraints. The screen filled with a roaring yellow.

Blackness.

Spinning.

Alarms.

Pain.

I hate that school... I won't go back!

Seamus' eyes fluttered open. In his blurry vision he could see the representation of their cutter on the canopy screen tumbling through space with the alien nearly on top of them. Just as he reached for the yoke to try to regain control, the ship lurched as if some huge claw had snagged them. The power flickered and the screen died, replaced with the dull red of emergency lighting. Gravity disappeared. Several loud bangs accompanied grinding shudders running through the ship.

Seamus wanted to close his eyes and sleep, but he shook his head, causing a sharp pain to streak down his neck into his left shoulder. He moaned and clicked open his restraints, glad for the absence of the full crush of gravity.

He had to get to Mom and Dad. They'd know what to do.

As he lifted out of his seat, Thunderblade floated past, lifeless. He grabbed the robot but his fingers didn't want to work and he lost his grip. Thunderblade slowly tumbled away into the dark. He turned toward the door. It wouldn't open and he couldn't get any traction to pry it apart.

Clang. It sounded like the main hatch had been pried opened.

Terror filled Seamus' chest, and he swam away from the door, clawing and kicking the air wildly. He had to get away! His fingers caught hold of the piloting yoke and he pulled himself down and under the control board. He pushed in as hard as he could until the yaw pedals jammed into his back.

Sparks flew and the doorway to the central corridor peeled open. Seamus pulled his knees up into his chest, wrapping his arms around them in a tight ball. He dared to peek and instantly drew in a sharp breath.

In the blood-red light, two dark, wavy eels snaked into the room, followed by an enormous creature floating in the null gravity. A deep guttural wail filled the air, vibrating through Seamus. He tried to still his trembling body and only his paralyzing terror kept him from screaming.

A tail whipped around from the larger beast, wrapping around one of the piloting seats. Like a matchstick, it snapped and then was thrown aside. The larger alien then moved closer and Seamus could now see the eels were actually the arms of the creature. One reached up like a hand to the control board just above him. The tail swung around to compensate and brushed over Seamus' toes. Seamus clamped down on his lower lip until he could taste blood.

Another deep moan from the alien and the power returned, lighting up the room and charging the control panel. Apparently, the alien did not appreciate normal lighting, as it quickly bashed two of the light panels. In the dimness it continued to examine the control board above Seamus.

He wasn't sure what to do. The lack of gravity gave Seamus more options in his movements and maybe even bettered his chances for escape, and right now it didn't seem like the alien was aware of his presence. Seamus' muscles were already cramping from his tightly curled position, so if he was going to do something, he needed to do it soon. What would the alien do if it found him? Everything so far seemed to point to violence. Should he surrender? Should he wait, hoping to avoid detection? He shifted slightly to try to see around the creature.

Before Seamus could consider all his options, the tail shot out from underneath the alien, coiling around him. Within moments he was tightly wrapped and hoisted above to look the creature in one if its black, round eyes. Seamus shrieked, but the resulting roar of the beast silenced him quickly.

As the shark-like creature seemed to study him, Seamus found his eyes roaming from one horrible feature to the next. He first noticed the rows upon rows of teeth, like jagged points of glass, lining its large mouth. Just above on either side of his long slick head were two black, expressionless eyes. Gills behind the eyes puffed in the air. Just behind and beneath either gill, the long arm-fins curled away, drawn back as if ready to attack him. Seamus kept very still, trying not to imagine what the jointed spines he first had thought were claws could do to him if the creature struck. Behind the alien's head was a hint of a dorsal fin, which disappeared as the body of the creature flowed into a long, serpent-like tail, the end of which was now tightly coiled around Seamus.

Just as Seamus thought he might try to communicate with the creature, something caught his eye from the corner of the room. A hint of chrome moved and then suddenly whirling blades flew toward them. It was Thunderblade! Seamus knew the blades were designed to be harmless if touched, but the alien didn't know that. The creature tossed Seamus aside with a roar as Thunderblade zoomed toward him. Seamus kicked off the control panel and shot through the doorway, just as the alien's whip of a tail batted Thunderblade away.

"Mom, Dad!" Seamus cried.

Two other aliens poked their heads into the corridor from the living area and the lab as Seamus sailed toward them. Seamus grabbed a handhold and found himself swinging out of the main airlock into a dim, cold cavern - thankfully full of air. As momentum carried him off in a crazy twirl he could see their cutter, warped and burned, crimped inside two crushing claws at the end of amazingly thick cables. And as he spun, he could also see the approaching main airlock of the alien spacecraft.

Seamus figured it would take another ten seconds or so before he'd reach the platform. Just as he began to form a plan, the airlock opened and another alien emerged, swimming in the air like a fish. Seamus could do nothing other than to spin ever closer toward capture in what seemed like a strobe light of terror: alien, cutter, alien, cutter. As he drew near, the alien's arm-fins opened wide to catch him.

Seamus thrashed and kicked, hoping to ricochet off in another direction.

One arm-fin caught his left arm and with a blur of motion, the other grabbed Seamus's throat. He felt the spine-like fingers pierce his skin and within moments the room grew blurry. Seamus shrieked until his cry died in his throat and the dim room went black.

His last whimper before slamming into unconsciousness: "Help!"

THREE – CAPTIVE

For Seamus, waking up felt more like a puzzle coming together than a single point of time. Brief moments of awareness materialized in the groggy black – pale, meaningless moments that meant everything to one so wanting to live. Intermixed were colorful pieces of intense emotion: terror, rage, regret, despair, and powerlessness, along with snatches of memory and future plans. Seamus' starving mind tried to jam these together into a coherent whole, to fit the puzzle together in some sort of meaningful context. A clear picture never emerged. Yet, slowly a collage of impressions, built not of experience but of a deep, primal knowing, surfaced.

The first impression Seamus felt was that of movement. He somehow *knew* he had been carried deep into the bowels of the alien ship through long curving tunnels, dark and damp. The impression of movement extended outward. Somehow he knew the alien ship had left Corvus 2267 and now sliced through the interdimensional soup of hyperspace, occasionally stopping here and there as if searching for something.

In what could have been minutes, hours, or days, another impression emerged, one of being handled by doctors. At times this seemed very hurried and specific, with a flurry of activity around him. Other times it seemed more general and studious. There were many scans with all sorts of equipment with many conversations made over the findings. And then one minute or hour or day they strapped him down and drilled into his head. It was all painless, but he was certain they had put something into his brain. One of his clearest moments had been just after this time when he saw two of the aliens floating above him, their deep bellowing wails sounding more and more like words.

One last impression was how utterly *different* everything seemed. The corridors were too short, the rooms too wide and low. The air was too humid and cool. The lights were too dim and had a blue cast that seemed to suck the color out of everything. The aliens' voices were too loud, and even as they used more words he could still hardly distinguish any difference from one howl to the next. Even in his semi-consciousness every moment felt other-worldly, and it pressed in on him a loneliness he had never experienced before. He was so far from anyone or anything he knew.

♦ ♦ ♦

The puzzle finally snapped together.

Seamus awoke.

His first moments: a pounding headache, hurried glances here and there, deep breaths gulped, heart hammering, and adrenaline spiking. He lay on an oversized bowl of a table in some sort of medical facility with two aliens floating on either side, each with head cocked to regard him with round, black eyes. Seamus' reservoir of terror must have been nearly depleted, as fatigue quickly smothered his fear. He forced himself to stay awake for as long as possible.

An arm-fin of the one on the left snaked out to a control panel, its finger-spines clicking on the shiny surface. The room filled with a series of loud pulses like some sort of blaring Morse code driving the pain in Seamus' head to another level. He could hardly move, but he lifted his hands to cover his ears. When he realized the aliens had adjusted the volume, he pulled his hands away from his ears. The pattern of tones ended and again the aliens cocked their heads to study him.

"What do you want?" Seamus croaked.

The staccato tonal pattern repeated and one of the aliens pointed to a tank of liquid appearing to be some sort of computer screen. A pattern of images materialized in time with the tones. Somehow it looked familiar, especially the humanoid figure near the bottom. And then he realized it was part of the First Contact message Dad had sent. What was that called again? Arecibol?

"I'm sorry, I don't understand it," Seamus whispered. "It's a code." Speaking took so much effort and he felt himself sliding toward sleep.

The aliens seemed to understand him somewhat and the image in the tank changed to something more familiar. It was a movie from the cutter's entertainment library. He recognized one of the actors, but it didn't seem like something he'd seen before. Seamus noticed the aliens studying him and one pointed toward the screen with a low mumbling wail.

"That's a movie. It's something we watch for fun."

If he had the strength, Seamus would have leapt off the table when the first alien repeated him in a low, deep voice: "mooo-veee". Even more shocking, the sound came not from the creature's mouth, but came from the gills on either side of its head. One side made the 'moo' sound and the other 'vee'. The two sounds mixed and echoed inside the alien's enormous toothed mouth.

"You... you can speak? Where's my Mom and Dad?!?"

The alien watched him, his arm fins slowly billowing in the air. It was bluer than the second alien, which seemed a bit larger and more gray in color. After a moment the first alien swam away, retrieving a small device with a screen above a small, divoted button. It returned, handing it to him. Built for these aliens, it was larger than any of the readers Seamus had ever used, but it was also lightweight and well constructed. Seamus looked at the screen which showed a picture of a table in the kitchen of the cutter. The alien pointed at Seamus' mouth and then to the screen.

"Table?"

In response the alien pressed the button. The device repeated in a slightly mechanical voice: "*table*".

"Yes, table."

The alien pressed the button again and the picture changed to one of a chair. At once Seamus grasped they were trying to learn his language. "Chair," he said and pressed the button. The machine repeated the word. Another pressed button and another picture: a plate.

Suddenly Seamus felt angry. Why should he help these creatures who attacked and captured them? And where were his parents? After this flash of emotion, his strength was gone. He wanted to argue, to make a point, but instead he handed the language device back to the smaller, blue alien and closed his eyes. And within moments he had dozed off into a surprisingly peaceful sleep.

♦ ♦ ♦

Seamus awoke in another room. It was small and empty except for two large concave platforms. Seamus pushed himself up from one and instead of sitting upright, he flipped out of the bed, hitting the low ceiling. Stupid, he thought, you'd think he'd been used to zero-G by now. As he floated back down, he felt the slight pull of gravity, maybe something like one-twentieth of standard. He settled in a seated position.

He noticed the computer pad one of the aliens had given him before, sitting nearby. He stared at it for a moment, considering what he should do. Everything within him wanted to hurl the thing against the wall, to shatter it into as many pieces as these creatures had shattered his own life. But then the enormity of his situation overwhelmed him and a cry came to Seamus' lips with such anguish he felt the physical ache of it deep within. For several minutes he relived each moment and entertained every fear, until his body had no more to give. As he calmed, he sat in silence for some time, his body and mind recharging with the absence of thought and motion. And then he reluctantly picked up the pad.

A drinking glass appeared on the screen. "Glass," he said, then pushed the button. The device repeated the name, replacing the image after another pressed button.

"Toothbrush..."

"Spoon..."

"Shirt..."

In time he had gone through an extensive inventory of the cutter, skipping a few of his parent's instruments that he wasn't sure about. The pad then began to picture items together randomly, and within a few minutes Seamus grasped it was searching for "yes" and "no". The device moved on to numbers and mathematical signs, and then began to determine verbs. Seamus actually laughed a few times at seeing a humanoid character trying to accomplish different tasks in ways that would be impossible or at least extremely uncomfortable. The device quickly mastered each lesson and, within what Seamus guessed might have been a couple of hours, it had begun to say complete sentences with little correction from Seamus.

At last Seamus was bleary-eyed and weary of the lessons. Instead of answering the question *"How does a human use teethbrushes?"* he said, "Listen, I'm really getting tired and I'm hungry and thirsty. Let's do this later." The device seemed to understand and switched off. Seamus set it down at the end of his bed and rolled over on his side in mindless daydream.

A few minutes later, just as he felt himself starting to doze off, the door to his room opened. He sat up as an alien glided in, which he recognized as the bluer one. He gasped as it spoke, its two sets of gills echoing in an eerie stereo.

"Oneeseemus using tool is helpful for language understand."

"How? I can hear...?"

"I called Kaataannaa. I is doctor of vessel. I medicine language translate inside Oneeseemus' head."

"Oneeseemus? Is that supposed to be my name?"

"Clan name Onee, boy name Seemus, correct?"

"Well, yes, sort of. My family name is O'Neil and my first name is Seamus. But it's pronounced *Shay-muzz*, not *See-muss*. And you're saying it backw— wait a second! Did you just say you put something inside my head?!?"

"Kaataannaa medicine all vessel take. All more useful when language understanding. More use tool, more helpful for Oneeseemus."

It wasn't a dream! They had drilled in his head! Seamus quickly ran his fingers through his hair until he found small sore spots on either side, just behind his temples above his ears. He looked up at Kaataannaa with horror. Before, hearing the creature speak in his own language had lessened its scariness, but now the panic of being held powerless by alien monsters returned.

What else had they done to him? The creature must have sensed his panic.

"No fear, Oneeseemus. Kaataannaa good doctor. I have many tests of Oneeseemus before medicine."

"Medicine! The word you're looking for is surgery... brain surgery!

"I have many tests of Oneeseemus before brain surgery."

Seamus huffed.

"Oneeseemus is tired and hungry and thirsty and frightened."

"And really angry that you drilled in my head!"

Just then a smaller, greener alien brought a tray into the room and set it down next to Seamus. On the tray were three foil packets, which he recognized as emergency rations from the cutter: macaroni and cheese, orange juice, and spaghetti. Noticeably absent was any knife or other item that could be fashioned into a weapon.

"Oneeseemus eat now and sleep. We will be at Kaarthaagg soon. Oneeseemus need strong and health."

The aliens left and Seamus poked the straw into the orange juice packet. He had never been much of a fan of oranges, but never had juice tasted so good. He tore into the other two packets and only then realized how starved he felt. Despite being room temperature he squeezed out the contents of both packets into his gulping mouth, and then even ripped the seams open to lick the inside of the packaging. With a full stomach, Seamus felt very drowsy and soon he fell into a deep sleep.

♦ ♦ ♦

For several days this pattern continued until the computer pad stopped working. And then Seamus awoke to see two aliens bring a large, furry creature into his room. They gently laid it on the other bed and exited without a word. Seamus sat up to get a better look. It was like a lion of some sort; thin, but much larger than him. It had creamy-white fur and a long rope of a tail. It wore a brown leather skirt around its waist, which made Seamus think it walked upright. And just like a great cat, it seemed to have fangs and claws. He could only guess at that since it was muzzled and all four paws had fitted coverings that reminded him of straightjackets. As ferocious as the lion looked, Seamus found himself wanting to run his hands through its fur while it was still unconscious. He never had a chance.

The tail flicked twice and then it was on all fours, hissing through its muzzle. Seamus scrambled into the corner as the cat glared at him menacingly, crouching to attack. "Help!" Seamus screamed. "Help me!"

The cat wobbled unsteadily and its covered paws slid out from underneath until it collapsed on its belly. Yet even in its weakened state it still looked formidable.

"Help me! This creature wants to attack me!"

The cat studied him for several moments and then spoke in a tired voice: "Stop your cries, cub. I have my wits now. You're no Kaarthaagian, no threat. You're just a captive, as am I."

"But why?" Seamus said, hating the tremor he heard in his voice.

"Slavery, cub. They intend to make us slaves."

FOUR – FRIEND OR FOE?

"Slaves?" Seamus hoped the language translator in his head wasn't working right, but the knot forming in his stomach told him otherwise.

"You heard me, cub." The lion closed its golden eyes for a lingering moment then shifted to a more comfortable position. "And from the looks of it, you'll be a house slave for sure. None of the games for you, unless they need to feed the wild beasts."

Seamus was still frozen against the wall from the cat's fearsome awakening and he could feel his body trembling. As ferocious as this lion looked – even with his mouth muzzled and claws padded – he could only imagine what it would call a "wild beast".

"Tell me, cub, does your kind always plead for help and flee?"

Seamus didn't know what to say. "Well... I didn't know what you were going to do, snarling and all that."

The cat responded with a purring chuckle. "I'm glad at my age I can still strike fear into timid creatures. Maybe I'll survive a round or two in the games."

"Games?" Seamus felt panic brewing in his soul. *Where* was he?

"The circuses, cub. I'd rather fight in the games. Better to fall with honor than declawed and fangs filed down. You—" a flick of the tail in Seamus' direction "—can serve some fat *plebiscite* for the rest of your miserable life."

Seamus' head was spinning. Slavery? Games? Plebiscite? He ran his fingers through his hair, cradling his head as if it were about to explode. He looked up at the cat. "Please tell me where I am! Who are these creatures that captured me? Where are we going? What does all this 'slave' and 'games' and 'plabaskite' mean?"

The cat's ears perked and its eyes widened. "You don't know? How can you not know? What kind of backwater place are you from?"

"I... we've... we've never met life outside of our own world before. Me and my parents are explorers from a planet named Earth. We were doing a planetary survey at Corvus 2267 when this ship appeared out of nowhere and attacked us. And now they've split us up and drilled in my head with this translator and now you're telling me I'm going to be a slave..." Seamus didn't want to cry in front of this cat, so he looked to the floor and bit his lower lip to distract himself.

"Earth... Corvus... I don't know these places." The lion paused thoughtfully. "Your name, cub. What do they call you?"

"Seamus. What's yours?"

"Seamus is your name? Truly?" The cat sounded surprised.

"Yes..."

"A cursed name. You must never speak it or tell another." When Seamus looked up, fiery eyed and ready to snap back, the cat explained, "A slave cannot be known as 'Shame Us'. You would as well be called Thief or Lazy."

"It's my name!" Seamus shouted. "It's all I've got left and I won't give it up! Who cares what they think!"

The cat rose to the same seated position of any cat Seamus had ever seen, tail wrapping around its toes like a blanket. It spoke gently: "To answer your question, my name is Löwin, the mother of seven great warriors who have sired twenty-six. I have experience in these things so heed my words, cub. You best care what they think.

"Let me tell you what is going to happen. We're most likely headed for Kaarthaagg where they are going to sort us into two lots. The first lot will become the gladiators for the games. Only the strong and the fit will go there. The rest of you will go into the second lot to be servants for the plebiscites. And only those who seem fit for that kind of service will be chosen by the traders. The rest - thieves, lazy, the *shameful* - will go back to the games, not as warriors but to be fed to the wild kanailan while the crowds cheer."

Seamus huffed, the cat's words barely denting his defiance.

"At least as a gladiator or a slave you may win *manumission*, you may win your freedom." The cat caught his eye then added, "You'll be a citizen and no one will ever be able to enslave you again!"

Seamus thought about it for a few moments in the following silence. If what she said was true, then it may be his only choice. But still, it was his name. It was all he had left! But he had to survive to escape or win freedom. He looked up. "The sharks screwed up my name and called me Oneeseemus."

"Clever. It sounds like the ancient Athinsian word for 'useful'. But it sounds too Kaarthaaggian. Say it as Onesimus."

"Onesimus," Seamus muttered with a huff of resignation. "What did you mean when you said Karth... karthag..."

"Kaarthaaggian? I believe you called them 'sharks'. They are our captors. Cruel beasts who have lost thier honor, prowling space for those not submitted to the Kingdom."

"To find slaves?"

"Yes, cub. And whatever else they can use."

Seamus stared blankly at the locked door to their room – their cell. "What if we escape?" he blurted. "There's got to be some way to—"

In a blur, the cat leapt across the room, landing atop of Seamus, and firmly planting a strong, covered paw over his mouth. With a hissing whisper through her muzzle, the cat spoke in Seamus' ear: "Quiet, cub! Or we'll both be meat for the beasts!"

The effort seemed too much for the cat. Her eyes fluttered and then she tipped backwards in a slow motion fall. Seamus surprised himself by grabbing a paw and pulling the cat upright before settling her on his own bed. Even accounting for the low gravity, her thin, lightweight frame surprised him.

The cat seemed to quickly regain consciousness, but she kept very still. "The sharks – as you call them – keep poisoning me..." She paused. "It's in my blood and the more my heart pumps the more it overwhelms me." After a restful pause she whispered the next: "There is only one chance to escape and it's on this ship. Kaarthaagg is an ocean world. There's nowhere to run or hide. And when we get there, every slave will be fitted. Escape will be impossible afterwards."

"Fitted? What do you mean?" Seamus whispered.

"Fitted means implanted with a device. I'm not sure about your kind, but on the Gothans, they attach it to our spinal columns between our shoulders."

The thought of more surgery by these aliens horrified Seamus. "Why?"

"To keep slaves in line. The owner is given a controller where they can set the boundaries of where you can go or punish you with electric shocks. They can even set it to kill you if they want. As a cub my pride came across an escaped slave, a Pannonian.

We helped him as we could but at some point we crossed some border or reached some set distance. The wretched creature fell over, writhing like a pierced pentaboar, and then died from electrocution."

Most of Seamus' hope for escape evaporated. He felt stronger every hour, but now the sharks rarely moved him out of his cell. If he only had some sort of chance...

The door slid open.

Two Karrthaaggians entered. One floated high above, holding a long pole with sharp needles on the end. The other swam at normal height and seemed ready for attack with its arm-fins coiled and finger-spines extended.

"Oneeseemus, come out of the cage immediately."

Seamus' heart nearly stopped. Had they been listening? Had they heard him talking about escape? What would they do?

"Oneeseemus, come out now!"

Seamus slowly stood, glancing at Löwin.

"Go, cub!" she whispered.

He walked toward them, nearly tripping over himself in the low gravity. The sharks looked ready for anything and only after he was out in the corridor and the door sealed did they seem to relax. Even then they seemed to watch the cell door more than him. Maybe it was Löwin they feared? From his brief interactions with her, even weakened by poison, Seamus could believe it. If so, maybe they hadn't heard him mention escape. And more importantly, maybe he could use their preoccupation with Löwin to make a break.

"Oneeseemus, we have downloaded the entertainment files from your cutter and have populated the translation matrix. Does our speech sound normal to your ears? Are we using the proper words and sentence structure? The correct verb tense?"

It took a moment, but Seamus recognized the speaker as the doctor, Kaataannaa. "Yes. It sounds perfect." He began to follow the doctor through the ship. The low, circular corridors were dark and looked as cold and damp as the air felt; a normal stride was out of the question. After a few tries Seamus tipped forward on all fours and took long hops in the low gravity. Every so often Seamus caught a glance into an open doorway or down an intersecting corridor, but it took most of his attention to keep from running into something. Of what he did see, nothing looked anywhere near familiar.

"I am pleased by the results. Hearing is the first sense to adapt, but soon you will be able to read all our languages too." As Seamus marveled over this, Kaataannaa continued. "The entertainment files on your cutter are very interesting. Unfortunately, the rest of your cutter's systems appear to have been destroyed."

Seamus recalled his last glimpse of their cutter, nearly pinched in two from the grip of a huge clamp. He'd be surprised if anything still worked.

"I am taking you to our ship's commander, who has some questions for you. It seems our attack upon your cutter was a mistake. We police the uninhabited systems for smugglers and the like. For example the Gothan in your cell is from the other side of the Star Kingdom with no business out here." An arm-fin snaked out. "Here we are." A round door irised open to a nearly empty room.

As Seamus followed Kaataannaa inside, the other shark remained in the corridor, but he hardly noticed. He almost couldn't believe his ears. It was a mistake? A moment later the door reopened and another shark swam in. This one seemed larger than any other and had a greenish tint to its dark skin.

"Oneeseemus, I am Commander Zaannddaarraa. Thank you for meeting with me." Seamus didn't know what to say.

"Uh, sure." He glanced around for the first time to see a large domed room lined with the same liquid-filled tanks used for computer screens he'd seen elsewhere.

"As Doctor Kaataannaa has told you, we attacked your ship in error. I must take full responsibility and apologize." The shark tipped its head up to expose his underside and then floated back down to his normal position. "We've learned from your cutter's entertainment that you come from a culture unknown to us, and we'd like to return you safely to your people."

Seamus was speechless. Was this true? Was this all a misunderstanding?

"In examining your ship it appears the rest of your computer systems were damaged beyond repair, so we have been unable to find your home world. Would you be able to tell us where you are from by looking at a star chart?"

The room was dim enough already that when the tanks lit up with stars Seamus could see them easily. Dozens of points of light were connected with lines, while other stars hung unconnected. Nothing looked familiar.

"Uh, I don't know. I didn't really know all that stuff. We just were going out to Corvus 2267. We slept the trip out there and so I'm not too sure where it was. My parents would know all that. Hey, where are my parents?"

"Your parents were transferred to another ship and are presently out of communications range. Tell me, Oneeseemus, do you see your world here? We are on this *hypertrack* to Kaarthaagg, and this is where we found you, the place you call Corvus 2267. Corvus has three known *hypertracks*. Does your world connect directly?"

"Hypertrack?"

"That is what we call them. I'm not sure what the term would be in your tongue. It is the point where two star systems connect in hyperspace, allowing starships to cross light years in days. Your world must be connected to one of these two hypertracks. Your cutter would take years to travel the distance otherwise."

As Seamus studied the star chart and considered the questions he grew suspicious. "If you're taking me home, why are we heading away from Corvus?"

The shark did not answer immediately and it made him feel uneasy. "We are retrieving your parents from the other ship."

"Then why don't you get the information from them? They are the ones who flew the ship out there." Seamus noticed the finger-spines on the Commander's arm-fins spread out, the tips glistening with moisture.

"The other ship does not have a navigation tank like this one. They can not see what you can see now."

"Well, that should be easy to fix. They know all about the coordinates. I'm sure you all could quickly figure it out."

"It would go... quicker if you would help them."

Something about the Commander's posture and how its arm-fins were drawing back made Seamus feel uneasy. "Sorry, I can't help you."

"You must tell me where your home world is. Now."

Something was wrong. Seamus' voice squeaked: "No. I won't do it."

Suddenly, the Commander's arm-fins exploded with motion, wrapping around Seamus in a lung-crushing grip. His finger-spines extended, arrayed around Seamus' face and beading with poison that burned as it dripped on his skin.

Seamus would have cried out if he could have drawn a breath.

“You will tell me where your home world is! Tell me now or when we get to Kaarthaagg I will turn you over to the Junta who will torture you until you talk!”

“I... don’t...” Seamus sucked in as hard as he could. “know any... thing...”

The shark flung him across the room. “Then you’ll learn what the sharpest spines at Kaarthaagg will do, human!

FIVE – PLANS

Somewhere along the way Seamus blacked out, and when he awoke he found himself back in his cell laying face down on the floor. He groaned as he pushed himself upright, and saw that Löwin remained just as he had left her.

"Are you okay?" he whispered.

"I'm well, cub. Forgive me for not helping you. You were breathing normally, and I'm still very weak."

"It's alright." Seamus winced as he touched his face. It felt swollen.

"Your left cheek is bruised."

"Hurts," he moaned. He felt sore all over for that matter, but it seemed like he was still in one piece. He climbed up on the open bed and leaned against the wall in a seated position. "They wanted to know where I came from, and when I didn't tell them they did this to me."

"I'm sure information about a new world to conquer would be quite valuable."

Seamus' voice sounded as if despair had filled every corner of his being. "Their leader said he was turning me over to someone named Junta."

"The Junta is their ruling council. I've heard stories about them. They will torture you until you tell them all you know. And then you will die."

As her words penetrated his soul, tears tumbled down Seamus' face. "I... I don't know anything!"

"Good, cub. Then your ignorance will save your world."

Seamus glared at the cat. "Great. I feel so much better."

"It will be a very honorable death."

"I've been trying to avoid that all week."

Löwin responded with a purring chuckle. "I suppose that would rule out an offer for me to take your life beforehand."

"What?!?" She looked *serious*.

"It would be a quick, painless death for you, and would lead to an honorable death for me. I don't recall any Gothans remembered for saving a whole world from conquest. The songs to be sung in my honor!"

She *was* serious! Seamus stared at the cat, seeing anew how very alien she was. She lay there muzzled, padded, drugged, and completely willing to somehow take his life and give her own if he asked. Where was he that sharks and lions roamed space, treating life and death so casually?

"I'll think about it," he said, sounding braver than he felt. Actually, having the option made him feel a little bit better in a weird sort of way. Suddenly, Seamus felt very foolish for blubbering like a crybaby. He sat up straighter and wiped his face. He was fourteen, after all.

They sat in silence for some time and Seamus thought about all that had happened from beginning to end. Having learned the true intentions of the sharks, he soon began to piece things together. The first thing he realized was his parents must have erased the cutter's systems. He was no expert on computers, but there was no way they would all have been damaged so severely in the attack. The second thing he decided was his parents weren't on another ship, they were on *this* ship. And they weren't talking either. Otherwise they would have never questioned *him*.

The third thing - the most encouraging thing - was the sharks must not have known about their mother ship. Whatever hypertracks were, the sharks had thought they had used them to travel *in the cutter*. They had never contemplated the cutter might be a service vessel for something larger. That meant the *Fernão de Magalhães* was still parked on that moon. And that meant if Seamus could escape with his parents, and if they could get back to the *Fernão*, they could still get back home!

When he saw her stretch, Seamus crawled over to Lowin and whispered, "Do you think we have a chance to—". He silently mouthed the next: "–escape?"

"I don't believe in chance. You can only prepare. If opportunity comes, then action may follow."

"Yeah, but if an opportunity comes, can we escape and rescue my parents?"

The cat looked amused but remained silent.

"What we will need to do is break out, find my parents, and get to a ship. The sharks said we were on the hypertrack to Kaarthaagg. So all we have to do is go back the way we came. If we can get back there, then I can get us the rest of the way home."

"Can you drop me off at Vissi on the way?"

"I'm being serious!"

"As am I," Löwin snarled. "Foolish cub! You speak as if all things are in your paws, but you don't realize the more you try to hold, the more likely you will drop something!"

"Well, we've got to try!"

"Tell me cub, how many cells are in this section and which holds your parents?"

"Uh... I'm not sure."

"How do you get to the hangar bay from here?"

"I don't know."

"What ships are in the hangar? What is their range? How are they piloted?"

"I... don't... know!"

"Where is this Corvus? How far is it from here? What's the most direct route?"

"I DON'T KNOW!"

The cat did not respond immediately. Then quietly: "That is what you need to learn. Prepare, and if the opportunity presents itself—" a long pause "—*then* we will act. Only then."

Seamus huffed with anger, but as he saw her sincerity, he calmed, finally nodding his acceptance. Löwin seemed tired by the effort and closed her eyes. After a moment he crawled back to the other bed and lay down, trying to control his emotions and to consider what she had said. After an hour he had the start of a plan.

He would cooperate.

The next time the guards came, he would ask for another chance to look at the star map. It should be easy to find out where they now were and where Corvus 2267 was. Then he'd begin talking about his parents, asking how they were and other questions in order to get them to slip up on their location. And then he'd suggest going back to the cutter to see if he could get any of the systems restarted, with the true goal of learning both the route to the hangar and the sharks' computer systems. When all that happened, he could answer all of Löwin's questions. And then they would act. Later, he whispered all of this in Löwin's ear and she agreed it might work if he did not look too obvious in his intelligence gathering.

♦ ♦ ♦

Seamus had no real sense of day and night, but in what felt like the next morning he awoke to the cell door opening. Two guards were there, both clutching the same long, needle-tipped poles. One eyed Seamus, while the other focused on Löwin. Seamus immediately thought of his plan.

"I've changed my mind. I'd like to see the room with all the star charts again, so I can try to figure out my home world."

"No talking. Both of you get up and come out here."

Seamus stood. "Please tell your commander that I've changed my mind. I want to cooperate."

"Then come out here where I ordered you, human!"

Seamus quickly obeyed, keeping an eye on the sharp needles that seemed ready to jab him at any moment. Löwin apparently moved too slowly and Seamus heard the snap of arcing electricity. She let out a muffled yelp, but it seemed she could move no quicker in Seamus' estimation. The sharks remained behind them and ordered them down the corridor.

Seamus had gotten better with his low-gravity hops, and he seemed to move at the sharks' preferred pace. As they rounded a corner, Seamus saw the room where the computer screens with the star charts were located. Hope swelled. Not only would he get to see the maps again, Löwin would too!

When they came to the door, Seamus stopped, waiting for it to open. Without warning what felt like a thousand bee stings exploded on his back, propelling him away from the door and further down the corridor. That shark had jabbed him with that electric stick! "But the star charts! I was going to show you—"

"Quiet!"

Seamus obeyed, moving forward, turning this way and that, until they reached a large door. It irised open to reveal the hangar bay. Seamus had expected joy in learning the route to escape, but the uncertainty of the moment eclipsed any hope.

There was a large ship docked immediately outside that appeared to fill the entire bay, and no sign of the cutter. He was ordered to embark, and there was a moment of complete weightlessness as he crossed from dock to ship. Two more guards met him inside.

"This one is the special package for the Junta," one laughed.

While Seamus tried to understand what was happening, Löwin entered the ship behind him with the two original sharks close behind. "Goodbye, cub. May you live and die with honor."

"What?"

"It was the start of a good plan, only opportunity never came."

It hit him. They were already at Kaarthaagg. It was too late to escape.

"No!" he cried. He turned, only to be knocked to the deck with an electric shock.

"Get up! We've got a special cage for you, coded to go straight to the Junta!"

Seamus couldn't believe what was happening. This wasn't the way he planned! He began to protest, but then cried out through gritted teeth from the scorching sting of another jab from the guards.

He staggered to his feet and stumbled forward as they shoved him through an opening door. A multitude of cries bombarded his ears: high pitched screeches and low rumbles mixing together in so many tongues it sounded like static. And then he realized the odd walls stretching away on either side of the narrow walkway were actually hundreds of cages.

Stacked three stories high from floor to ceiling, the various sized crates were filled with every conceivable combination of shape, color, texture, and size. Hundreds of creatures were here, and somewhere deep down it registered they were all captured beings, bound to be sold off as slaves. Except for him. A fate far worse awaited him and it crashed over his thoughts like a tsunami. It was too late for escape, too late for Löwin to end his life quickly and painlessly.

Another shove and he found himself jammed in a meter-and-a-half square cage, barely large enough for him to move. The door clanged shut, slapping against the bottom of his feet. He roared with rage, wiggling around to look out the cage door. "Let me go! Let me out of here, you filthy maggot!" He slammed the heels of his hands against the door and then stuck his fingers through the lattice of wire in the small window. He shook it with all of his might until the wires cut into his skin.

The overworked translator in his head finally began to catch up with the horrendous choir echoing all around him. Hundreds of voices in as many languages all screamed for the exact same things: freedom, mercy, anguish, and rage, yet something strange pierced through the din. Seamus strained his ears and focused on a few clear voices singing in unison. How could anyone sing in this racket with nothing but slavery or death ahead? He strained even more and just began to make out some of the words.

"Seamus!"

A sudden black and chrome face with glowing red eyes appeared in the window, startling Seamus. He cracked his head into the top of the crate, but the pain was short-lived.

"Thunderblade!"

The small robot gripped one of Seamus' fingers. "Seamus, I do not have much time. The odds of the guards returning are extremely high."

"I can't believe it's you! How? Where have you—"

"Seamus, if you wish to live, listen to me! I am reprogramming the ID system on your container to send you to someplace other than to the Junta. It identifies you as Seamus Robert O'Neil. Please give me another name you will readily answer."

"Onesimus!"

"I am rerouting you to a reputable slave trader bound for the capital city of Rom. I will track your movements and catch up with you there."

The robot turned to leave.

"Wait! What about Mom and Dad?"

"I have no information on them, but I am searching for them as well. I must leave now. I risk everything being in the open."

"One more thing! If you find a Gothan cat named Löwin, try to save her too!"

"I will try."

As the robot ran off Seamus called out, "Thunderblade, thank you!"

SIX - SLAVERY

Seamus couldn't believe it. Thunderblade was alive! And somehow he'd been able to learn a lot about what was going on. He only wished he could have had at least a few more minutes with that incredible toy robot. He had so many questions!

He felt the transport move and within a few moments it became apparent they had left the hangar bay of his captor's ship and were about to drop through the atmosphere to Kaarthaagg. Löwin had told him it was an ocean world and he pictured a blue clouded orb much like how Earth appeared from orbit above the Pacific Ocean. The thought made him instantly homesick.

The ship rumbled and the dull roar of atmospheric drag drowned out the cries of the slaves in the cargo hold. *Slaves*. The thought made him shudder. Yet it was his greatest hope right now. He wondered about Thunderblade's plan. Would it work? Would he be sent as a slave somewhere instead of to the Junta to be tortured until he told all he knew of Earth? If he escaped, how long would it take before they discovered the mistake and came after him?

After a few minutes the ship lurched and bucked, and Seamus pitched sideways into one of the walls of his crate. He braced himself until the worst was over, deciding not to add his own voice to the multitude of cries around him. They must have landed, but it felt different than the soft retrorocket touchdowns or wheeled runway landings he'd experienced before. The ship now felt like it swayed back and forth, and he wondered if this was normal or if there had been trouble with the landing gear.

Just as most of the voices around him quieted, the rumble of machinery and bright light filled the cargo hold. Seamus pressed his face against the window and saw the roof of the ship had opened, revealing a pale, purplish sky filled with yellow clouds. A renewed cry arose from the captives and Seamus soon realized why. Small robotic aircraft swooped over the open bay like flies over garbage. In an orderly procession each craft dove from the swarm to latch onto a single crate, lift it skyward, and speed off in some random direction.

Seamus' heart pounded. Would he be sent to relative safety? Soon enough the crates above him were removed and one of the robotic aircraft dropped to latch onto his crate. He braced himself as it lifted him from the hold. The cargo ship dropped from view to reveal a deep purple ocean filled with ships and floating facilities. As they sped off in a banking maneuver, Seamus could see that the ship he had arrived in also floated in the ocean, moored along with dozens of others around an enormous cargo facility. The thought of floating cities amazed him.

Within a few minutes they flew over a complex of drifting buildings and then over a stadium of some sort. He heard the sound of cheering and pressed into the window to get a better view. The seats were filled with thousands of spectators, but he quickly focused upon a huge snake in the middle of the arena. It moved *fast* in a blur of ocean purple and thin lime green stripes. When he saw why, an icy knot of horror filled his belly. The serpent was in chase of an orange human-like creature that was no match for its pursuer. It ran this way and that, always quickly cut off from an avenue of escape by a scaled coil. The next happened within moments, but it seemed like an eternity. The snake cornered its prey, reared back, and struck in a blur. Seamus ripped his eyes away from the horrible end, but he could not block out the screams piercing through the approving roar of the crowd.

"No!" Seamus cried, throwing himself away from the window and collapsing onto his back.

His crate gently swayed in flight, but he pressed his hands and feet into the walls and ceiling as if it spun out of control. How could he survive in such a barbaric world, a place where sentient beings were thrown as food to wild beasts while others cheered in amusement?

The hum of the flying drone carrying him changed pitch, and it felt like they were descending. Seamus sat upright, fear nearly keeping him from looking out to whatever awaited him. Instead of a cheering crowd and a hungry beast, he saw his flying crate had joined a line of dozens of others, dropping to another floating complex. One by one the flying machines landed upon a moving conveyor belt, detached from the crates, and swooped up in graceful loops. With a rough bump, his crate touched down and the aircraft rocketed away, leaving him bumping along.

His crate rumbled forward behind a line of others for a few seconds, entering into a huge building. Inside the lights were dim, just like the Kaarthaaggian ship that had captured them. Seamus couldn't see much from his little window, but it appeared crates ahead of him moved off the main conveyor down other lines. Within a few minutes his own crate split off from the main line, joining a line of others heading through a square hole in a distant doorway. This conveyor moved more slowly than the first and the noise diminished as they moved. He could now hear the murmuring of other creatures until he got closer to the opening. Here it grew silent except for distant cries.

As he drew closer to the door, Seamus felt his sanity slipping away. His chest heaved in great fearful breaths, feeding his begging lungs and thudding heart. As each crate ahead slipped through the approaching doorway, fresh squeals of terror suddenly silenced. This was the end, Seamus thought. The plan didn't work.

He braced himself as his crate moved through the opening. Suddenly the door swung open. A dozen robotic tentacles whipped inside, grabbing his ankles, wrists, neck, and torso. Seamus cried out as the tentacles lifted him up, pulling him out. Like those before him, he howled in throat-burning horror. Something pierced his neck. The world dimmed and went black.

♦ ♦ ♦

Seamus awoke, lying facedown in a squishy foam bed with a hole cut out for his face. He pushed up groggily to find himself in a small cell, dimly lit from an overhead light outside a transparent door. Still alive! He sat upright and noticed he now wore a gray jumpsuit. What had happened to him? His back hurt and itched. He reached behind to find something between his shoulder blades: smooth, flexible, and it burned deep into his spine when he tried to pry it off. Then he remembered Löwin's words. All slaves were implanted with a device to make them obey and to keep them from escaping.

He had been fitted.

Seamus had expected a rush of emotion at this point. Over the past weeks – or however long it had been – it had seemed like he bounced from one intense feeling to the next. He had wrestled with disbelief. At times he had been angry, other times he had felt like giving up in the crushing reality of his predicament. But now he just knew there was nothing to be done. Slavery had come for him and there was nothing he could do to avoid it. It wasn't that he didn't feel horrible, it was just that he... he accepted it. He had accepted it and he might as well make the best of it. At least he was alive.

Yet behind his acceptance another thought sang like a distant melody. Löwin had told him: "Prepare, and if the opportunity presents itself, then we will act. Only then." He had not given up on gaining his freedom, finding his parents, and going home. But it wouldn't just happen to him. Of that he was sure. He would have to *make* it happen. So whatever situation he found himself in, he would learn, he would prepare. And then when opportunity came he would act.

Seamus stood, exploring his cell and contemplating his next steps. For several minutes he pulled on the cover of a small air duct until the glass door behind him slid open. Seamus spun around to see a squat gray creature standing in the door, clothed in a gray uniform. The first thing he thought of was an insect. Its shiny head reminded him of an ant with enormous bulging, black eyes beneath short stubs for antennae. On either side of its mouth hung what may have once in its ancestry been a pincher but now more resembled a mustache. The creature had two arms that seemed extremely long for its height, and short legs. And it looked very muscular and powerful.

"Onesimus, I am Captain Rado of the Mazzillian Merchantman *Trouveur*."

Seamus voice cracked as he said, "Hello."

"Please come with me."

Maybe it was how Rado spoke to him or just how he compared to everything Seamus had seen so far, but he felt instantly at ease. As Seamus approached, Rado turned to lead. Seamus kept slightly behind him, careful not to seem threatening or lagging at all.

As they turned a corner Seamus asked, "Captain Rado, how long have I—"

Blinding pain filled Seamus from head to toe. His arms and legs locked and he fell, smashing face-first into the metal deck. He could not breathe, he could not scream, but he felt everything. It was if his whole body burned with fire.

Rado flipped him over. "I did not tell you to speak."

The searing pain disappeared and Seamus' body relaxed in sudden release, followed by intense trembling. He wanted to scream, but his body demanded oxygen and he gulped in air in rapid pants.

Rado continued without a hint of emotion: "I purchase only the best slaves for my clientele. I bought you based on your piloting skills and because you're young and healthy. Those are valuable traits to my customers. But I also have a reputation for delivering obedient, respectful, hardworking slaves. You will obey my every command, nothing less. You will also remember your place and not presume upon me. Your life belongs to me now. If I want to take it, I will."

With horror Seamus watched him lift his left hand and press a button on a small control, sending wave upon crashing wave of pain throughout his body. It kept coming and coming until blackness wisped around the periphery of his vision and the world became a long black tunnel with Rado's alien face filling the distant end. And then it stopped with sudden mercy. Seamus cried out in anguish. His body shuddered violently and he could barely move. Rado knelt beside him.

"I've killed eleven slaves in my career, Onesimus. Eight were rebellious, two attempted escape, and one I decided I did not like. When I saw you trying to damage my ship just now, I considered making you number twelve. But dead slaves do not learn and there were no others present to learn from your example."

Seamus wanted to apologize over and over, but he was afraid to say or do anything more.

"We have a maxim in Mazzille: 'His sand is piled too steep.' We say that because sand piled too steeply will always collapse upon the digger, burying him alive. Your sand is piled steeply, Onesimus, and it may fall upon you at any moment."

As Rado stared at Seamus, panic nearly set in. Seamus touched his lips several times with trembling fingers.

"You may speak."

"I'm... I'm sorry, sir. I... I didn't know."

"Do you wish for me to teach you, Onesimus?"

"Yes, sir. Please, sir!"

Rado rose to full height and looked down at him. "Welcome aboard my ship. As we travel to Rom, I will teach you everything you need to know to perform your duties to the greatest pleasure of your masters."

"Thank you, sir."

♦ ♦ ♦

Just as he said, Rado spent time daily with Seamus, telling him over and over his expectations and giving him many opportunities to practice what he learned. Seamus learned quickly and he learned well, along with the dozen other new slaves on the ship. Mostly they learned about loyalty, etiquette, and anticipating needs. But he also learned a dark truth sucking all hope from his heart. He was property now. He had gone from being a person to a thing. And not an exactly prized thing, but rather an easily replaced thing living at the whim of his owner. It made Seamus hate how he'd treated Thunderblade all those years.

Löwin's advice on learning and preparing gave Seamus a lifeline. It altered his perspective enough that at times he felt like just as much of an observer as a participant. On the fourth day Seamus recognized the extent of Rado's genius at making slaves. It wasn't his incredible brutality that did it but rather his kindness. He dispensed praise much more often than he'd use the shocker, and Seamus had found himself wanting badly to earn his approval. He cursed himself whenever he did not please Rado, even blaming himself whenever Rado shocked him. The other slaves responded similarly, and Seamus realized how cunningly Rado took true hope away in one hand and offered false hope in another. In just a few days he seemed more like a savior than an oppressor. Just knowing that helped Seamus cope, and all along he looked for weaknesses in Rado's methods he could exploit.

♦ ♦ ♦

On the eighth day since leaving Kaarthaagg, Rado announced they were in final approach to the capital world of Rom. He gave a rousing speech about how proud he was of their accomplishments and growth, and his confidence they would all become indispensable to their future owners. Even knowing this was Rado's final ingredient of his manipulative recipe of slavery, Seamus felt stirred. And that night as he returned to his cell he struggled between the anticipation of meeting – and pleasing – his new owners and of finding a way to locate his parents and a way home.

SEVEN – SOLD!

Before this moment Seamus had defined heavy space traffic by an experience at the space elevator in northern Brazil. He and his parents had been heading to a training flight, and after a two-hour ascent, Seamus had been impressed to see five docked ships at the orbital hub along with two others on approach and another speeding away. He inwardly laughed at the memory. Even if you added all the peak traffic at all six of Earth's space elevators, it would look nothing like what he now saw. Hundreds of ships of all conceivable shape and size were visible on the main screen, flying in what appeared to be distinct travel lanes. Easily tens of thousands of ships could be orbiting the planet.

Rado had invited Seamus to sit up at the flight deck with him as he flew the *Trouveur's* service shuttle down to the Earth-like capital planet of Rom. Seamus had learned over the past week Rado thought of him as a trained pilot, not only from the counterfeit profile Thunderblade had created but from rigorous testing as well. Of all the pilots Seamus had ever met, he would hardly call himself skilled – maybe a gifted amateur. But true or not, he had been glad for the opportunity to sit up front, hoping to learn as much as possible. After the shock of learning of all the traffic around Rom, the next thing he noticed was the fiery glow in the atmosphere ahead of them.

"Master Rado, may I speak?"

"Yes, Onesimus."

"Thank you, sir. If it pleases you to answer, what is that orange glow ahead? I've never seen anything like it."

"It's called a reentry trail. The traffic on this approach is so heavy the heat and glow of one ship's heat shield burning through the atmosphere doesn't have a chance to dissipate before another ship is coming through. All the energy accumulates to make the lane look like a glowing tunnel. Don't worry. It is monitored and traffic is spaced to keep the temperatures from reaching the flashpoint."

"Sir?"

"There is a lot of hydrogen in the upper atmosphere. If it gets too hot, it will flash. Nothing like a nova, but it would upset traffic for thousands of kilometers and make for a rough landing."

Within a few moments they dove into the glowing tunnel, and after a few minutes they were in the cloud-thickened lower atomsphere gliding toward a rain-wet runway. After touchdown they were met by a large robotic towing machine that quickly attached and began pulling them through the drizzle toward a grouping of hangars and other nondescript gray buildings, overshadowed by a gray, overcast sky.

As they taxied in silence, Seamus' thoughts wandered. Rado had told them they would head straight to the slave market after landing, and Seamus could feel his apprehension growing. Rado was often cruel and manipulative, but at least Seamus felt like he had earned his respect and a corresponding level of kindness. Who knew what he'd find in a few hours? What type of person would own him? How would Seamus be treated? What would Seamus have to do? The only benefit Seamus could think of in a new owner was that he knew he would never escape from Rado. The trader seemed to always know where each of his slaves was and what he was doing. Seamus wondered if he may have some sort of psychic ability. Regardless, Seamus was convinced an escape from Rado would be short-lived – as would be any slave who attempted it.

The tug parked the shuttle in the hangar and Seamus followed Rado back to where the other slaves were buckled in. Of the twelve others, eight were Belgicians and four were Zandreans. The Belgicians, Seamus had learned, were prized for their craftsmanship with jewelry and knives. Short, furry humanoid creatures that reminded Seamus of a cross between badgers and mythical dwarves, Belgicians had come from a world rich in gems and precious metals. Their wares were renown throughout the Star Kingdom, and Seamus had been shocked to learn they willingly sold themselves into slavery just for the opportunity to become artisans elsewhere. The Zandreans were equally prized for their ability to quickly master almost any subject and often became educators. Similar to humans in size and shape, the Zanderans wore long, white, hooded robes that covered all but their pale, featureless faces.

Within a few minutes the group had disembarked and boarded a ground vehicle that had met them outside. Rado again invited Seamus to sit with him as they traveled through the fog-shrouded city toward the slave market through vehicle-thick streets. Rado clasped his hands and turned. “Onesimus, the nature of the others here give me no concern. They are contented creatures who will obey their masters and prosper.” He paused. “But you're human.” Another pause. “I have studied humans for many years and have found them to have curious traits. One human may be hard working and will see his work through to its completion, where another may use the same creativity and perseverance to avoid work. I find it peculiar how one human will pile sand while another will use the same effort to tear it down. Each human appears to be unique in what motivates it, and it is very hard to predict performance."

Most of what Rado said was lost upon Seamus. Once Rado had said he had studied humans for many years, a flood of emotion had struck Seamus. There were other humans here? He may actually see someone like himself? It was like a great hammer of hope had smashed through the thick walls of aloneness surrounding Seamus. Rado apparently had noticed Seamus' shocked expression.

"You understand why I say this? Humans are only partially motivated by physical needs or security. They have other motivations that are often conflicting, and those motivations change in time or circumstance. I have told you I have killed eleven slaves for being rebellious or for attempting escape."

Seamus nodded.

"They were all human, Onesimus."

Seamus did not respond, but felt the old frigid knot of fear forming in his gut.

"I guarantee all my slaves, and these were all slaves who had served their masters for some time. One had served well for four years before escaping. Four years! It took me six months to hunt her down. After I captured her, I asked her why. What had happened that she had become such a disloyal and rebellious slave? I had interviewed her owners and the other slaves in the household and all said she had been treated extremely well."

Rado paused so long Seamus almost attempted to answer the question.

"I still puzzle over her answer. She told me, Onesimus, that she *wasn't* a slave no matter what I said. I explained to her that she was a slave for life unless she had been granted freedom through manumission. She told me she would rather die now in freedom than to serve another minute as a slave."

"Then you killed her?" Seamus asked, forgetting his manners. He winced. Apparently, Rado didn't mind. This time.

"I did." He paused, stroking his pinchers with his muscular, right hand.

Seamus imagined the scene again and again until Rado broke the silence.

"I tell you this so that you may decide in whatever way you humans do, to pile your sand instead of tear it down. You show great promise, Onesimus. I hope that you serve well and live long. I find killing my slaves distasteful."

By either design or coincidence, Rado's speech ended with the ride. They were at the slave market. This was it.

Seamus disembarked with the others into a wild menagerie. Dozens of species moved through the crowded walkways: purple elephant-sized spiders, golden long-necked lizards, man-sized turtles with beautiful color patterns on their shells, walking bats with bluish fur, even a green leafy thing that seemed to walk on hundreds of little branches. It was as if every creature on Earth had been recreated into larger, more incredible things, some exquisite, some terrible. Yet among all the alien creatures Seamus saw many more humans, but humans unlike he'd ever seen before. They came in a rainbow of colors. Intricate patterns of color and shading decorated their faces and exposed skin. Where Earth had all the variations of brown, it seemed Rom had every other color: reds, yellows, blues, and even metallic shades.

Rado led them into what looked like a convention center, through doors big enough to accommodate the largest of the creatures Seamus had seen. Thousands of beings milled about. The chatter of dozens of languages mixed in Seamus' ears, overloading his translator, yet every so often he could hear snippets of haggling. After weaving through the crowds for a kilometer, they came to a row of narrow booths apparently belonging to Rado. Each slave was assigned one, where they sat waiting for interviews with potential buyers. All except Seamus. He stayed with Rado, who monitored the others and made final negotiations from his small cubical office.

Throughout the day the others were sold off, one by one. For the most part the artesian Belgicians went first, followed by the Zandrean intellects. Seamus waited quietly, knowing better than to interrupt Rado during such an important time. Each transaction was unique. Each customer had different needs requiring different skill sets. Rado seemed masterfully prepared for each request, directing the would-be buyers to the best choice and pulling up detailed supporting records. Seamus had no idea how money worked here, but it seemed Rado's earnings pleased him. When the last one sold and Rado had finished all his paperwork, he beckoned for Seamus to follow.

"Onesimus, you may be wondering why you were not sold like the others. The reason is that you have unique skills that two parties have specifically requested. We are meeting them at a private location."

Just as described, Rado led him through the rainy streets to a meeting room in a nearby restaurant where they were soon joined by two other parties. Rado greeted them with kind words and scans of some type. As Seamus sat quietly he studied both groups. Both, to his relief, were human – to some degree. One consisted of two men, both with dark brown hair, golden-tan skin, and a faint giraffe pattern running down their necks. The other party consisted of two women covered with fine pale blue feathers with bright pink plumes on their heads, wearing white, airy dresses. Neither group looked particularly friendly as they looked him over and glared at each other.

When all was ready Rado began.

"Thank you for coming. First, the security arrangements. My agents in the local police force report there are no impending raids. Just in case, I have guards posted at all the entrances, plus have several cars waiting and safe houses ready. Finally, the room has been scanned and is now shielded from surveillance or any type of recording equipment, so we may speak openly. Does this meet your approval?"

Seamus had already felt apprehensive, but now he felt like he might vomit. Why was this happening to him?

"I received your requests for a subject with the following qualifications: young, healthy, hard-working, obedient, and most importantly, a skilled pilot. As I responded to you, such a combination is rare. As you know, the Romians tightly control pilot training. Only soldiers are given manual pilot training, and they carefully screen those who desire to be trained for computer-controlled piloting. It has taken me seven standard months to obtain one subject with manual piloting skills worthy of your consideration." He motioned toward Seamus, who felt his face grow hot. "This is Onesimus, and I am now downloading his file into your readers."

Both parties studied small handheld devices for several minutes until one of the women called out, "This is nothing but a title file. What about his flying?" Seamus had never seen Rado smile, and he wasn't even sure he could physically do it if he wanted. But something about Rado looked very happy.

"If you will look at the holo, here is the flight data from a Kaarthaaggian cruiser. The targeted ship was piloted by Onesimus."

Seamus heard a hum and looked over his shoulder to see the air behind Rado filled with an image of his parent's cutter, floating over the rings of Corvus 2267-F. Suddenly, as two yellow explosions expanded around it, the cutter zoomed off. Other explosions rocked it, and then it really picked up speed, banking and weaving, finally diving into the ring, sending a splash of icy particles flying off in a misty cloud. The ship cut back and forth, evading explosions until it arched back into the icy cloud that had been the ring.

Seamus couldn't believe it. Was that really him flying? It had all happened so fast he had reacted without much thought. But it was him and seeing it made Seamus feel proud of himself. Maybe he was a skilled pilot after all? Just then the cutter climbed through the debris, offering a clean shot as it pulled away. What had he been thinking? A yellow orb of plasma smashed it, followed by a rocketing grappling clamp. The video ended along with Seamus' short-lived pride in his abilities.

The following silence unnerved Seamus. Finally one of the men spoke.

"That was you piloting, boy?"

Seamus didn't want to answer but he did: "Yes, sir,"

"Where did you learn to fly like that?"

"Uh, my... my parents, sir. They had a simulator on their ship that I—"

One of the women cut in: "But he was obviously caught."

Rado answered: "He was... after the *eighteenth* shot got through. His ship was unarmed, and unshielded, with only rudimentary gravity controls, yet look how well and how long he evaded Karrthaaggians! With the right ship, he could evade... anyone."

The video, this conversation, and the stares began to feed a swirl of emotions within Seamus. And seeing the beginning of this madness had brought a fresh wave of fury. He wanted to lash out at all of them, but he held his tongue.

Prepare then act.

After a few seconds of silence, Rado said, “I will open the bidding at twelve thousand Ceez.” The response was immediate and lively. Offer countered offer in escalating amounts.

Twelve minutes and fifty-three thousand Ceez later it was over.

“Sold!”

EIGHT - FIRST IMPRESSIONS

After five minutes of signing documents and transferring funds, Seamus returned Rado's farewell nod and followed his new owners out of the restaurant onto a rain-drenched sidewalk. They moved quickly and glanced warily about in a way that made Seamus feel even more nervous than he had during the auction. An empty car on computer control met them right outside and whizzed them away, but even then his new owners didn't look like they felt secure. They silently studied every following car and watched the traffic monitor on the dashboard, as if attack might come from any direction. The few words spoken sounded like warnings.

Who were these people? What was going on?

After a long, circuitous route through streets clogged with water and traffic, Seamus finally recognized the spaceport. Just as quickly, they exited the car to board a service vehicle, which whisked them toward a distant grouping of hangars. Within minutes they had arrived at a small snub-nosed, winged shuttle. As they boarded, Seamus could hear the engines already spooling up to a thundering whine.

"Strap in," one told him as they came to the cockpit. A boy that looked about twelve exited one of the pilot seats and sat on the bench next to him, as the others took his place. They had barely seated themselves before they were rolling out onto the tarmac. Ten minutes later they were in the air, blasting toward space.

The shuttle made orbit and docked in a small bay of a ship about the size of the *Fernão*. In the same hurried manner, they boarded, headed straight for the flight deck, and left orbit toward what Seamus knew as a hypertrack. The silent tension on the flight deck made the trip seem like hours, but Seamus was not about to break the silence, however uncomfortable - not after his first experience with Rado. Finally they arrived. A crowd of ships waited in line, slowly floating toward a sparkling blue nebula, arcing with lighting as ships entered or exited. Encircling the hypertrack, four huge Romian battleships hung in space, ready for anything. Seamus' new owners seemed especially concerned about those ships and their occasional scans.

"One ship in, one out, one in, one out," said one impatiently.

"Really slow today," said the other.

Half an hour later, they entered the cloud with the crack of entering hyperspace.

"We made it!" shouted the boy next to Seamus.

The two others jumped to their feet, hugging and laughing, looking entirely different than before. Their skin looked more golden than tan and the faint giraffe pattern running down their necks less pronounced. Even their dark brown hair seemed to spring to life where it had laid flat before.

"I can't believe I let you talk me into this!" said the younger man.

"You owe me, that's why!" said the older. "You're not out of your contract until I have a replacement."

At that point they all looked at Seamus at once, their joy quickly morphing into curiosity.

"So, what's his name?" said the boy.

The older man pulled the boy into a sideways hug. "That is Onesimus."

Seamus remembered Rado's instructions. He dropped to one knee, bowed his head, and looked down at his upward turned hands. He loathed what he next had to say, but he had to play along for now. "Greetings, my new masters. I pledge my loyalty, devotion, and service to you. I live for your pleasure." There was more to the ceremony, but apparently the older man had other ideas.

"Good. Very nice. Now get up." As Seamus stood hesitantly, he studied the older man. He was of average height, but a little overweight. The other main thing he noticed was that he moved and talked fast. It was as if he was always in a hurry, yet in a deliberate, conscious manner. The older man motioned toward the younger man, of the same coloration and pattern as the older, but more fit and better looking to Seamus. Maybe it was because his expression seemed more lively and friendly. "This is Epaphras. He's an employee of mine – a pilot – who is leaving me to go to some crazy religious school."

"It's not crazy."

"What do you call leaving a good job to go, er, never mind. Onesimus, now look at me, at me now. We've got five days on this hypertrack and another two on the next before we drop this idiot off at Effizus. So you've got seven days for Epaphras, here, to teach you how to fly this ship. Now look at me, he's only computer trained, but he's learned a few tricks here and there, so I expect you to learn everything and then some. I paid good money for you, so I expect that you'll be able to fly this ship manually in a few months. I'm banking on it, actually, so don't disappoint. This whole affair is costing me plenty and times aren't what they used to be."

"Uh, yes, sir."

"Well, get to it. Time is money and you're wasting it."

Seamus turned to follow Epaphras to the piloting chairs when it occurred to him that he didn't even know their names.

"Sir, if I may please speak?"

"Okay, enough of that. I know there is that Code of Submission. That Rado gave me a file long enough it'll take me a month to read. For now if you got something to say, you just say it. I don't have time for all the pleasantries." The quick flow of words stopped suddenly in a thoughtful expression. "But, then again, don't make me look bad in public either."

"Yes, sir. Um, how shall I address you?"

"Oh, right. I am Filymon. My son, here, is Chippus. You haven't met her yet, but my wife is named Apphia."

"Master Filymon, Master Chippus. I will get straight to work." Seamus bowed. Once they had turned away, Seamus turned back to Epaphras. The young man looked to be in his early twenties and seemed friendly enough.

"We best get in there," Epaphras said, nodding toward the flight deck. Seamus waited for Epaphras to move first then quickly took the copilot's seat. Epaphras glanced back down the corridor. "We better look busy or he's going to blister our hides. I don't know how many times he's beat me for what he thinks is loafing."

Seamus' rising hope of good masters crashed like a wingless shuttle. Without thinking Seamus let out a loud sigh, which he abruptly sucked back in when he heard the disrespectful sound in his ears. He cut his eyes over toward Epaphras.

"Ha! Just joking. He's not that bad. I'm no slave, but the most he's ever done to me was to give me a good yell."

Seamus let out a sigh again, but this one of relief. "You had me going there, uh, Master Epaphras."

"Oh, please, no 'master' for me. One thing I've been learning lately is that we're all part of something larger."

When Seamus heard that, he wanted badly to shout: Yeah, an evil civilization that attacks families without warning, splits them up, and sells them into slavery!

But instead he said nothing.

Epaphras must have noticed his expression. His warm tone sounded more formal as he said, "So, let's get started."

For the rest of the afternoon Epaphras taught Seamus all he knew about piloting. Most everything - even to the physical placement of particular controls - was remarkably similar to what Seamus was accustomed to, though much more simplistic. Most procedures were highly automated with little indication of the processes behind them. When Seamus questioned him on those type details, it became readily apparent there were large gaps in Epaphras' knowledge. It seemed like Epaphras had been trained to perform a series of tasks in a certain order for each situation but had little idea of what he was actually doing. It reminded Seamus of when he had first began taking the training modules on the *Fernão*. Those first lessons were designed to give a general overview with particular attention to initiating automatic systems in emergencies. Everyone on board had to learn those, which is what piqued Seamus' interest in the first place. Yet here, it seemed like there wasn't much more than that. Seamus found himself filling in the blanks for Epaphras, and after a couple of hours it seemed like Seamus was more of the teacher and Epaphras the student.

"...so in orbit, it's actually your relative velocity that determines altitude, it's not that you're thrusting upward or downward. The faster, the higher."

Epaphras shook his head. "But either way you say you're still 'falling' toward the planet? I'm not really following this."

"Okay, an orbit is just a curve, right? So to make a curve you have to move two directions at once. In an orbit you are moving forward, but you're also moving toward the surface. That's what makes the circular movement around the planet." He tried to illustrate with his hands, but it didn't seem to help.

"But your altitude is the same! How can you be falling if you aren't getting closer to the surface?"

Seamus huffed. "Because you're moving forward - *away* from the planet - at the same rate that you fall *toward* it."

"But wouldn't that mean you're hovering?"

"No, no, no! You're still moving in TWO directions!"

Seamus about jumped to his feet from being startled by the voice of Filymon behind him: "How's it going in here?"

"I've been learning a lot," Epaphras said tiredly.

"So I hear. What do you say Onesimus? Think you'll have it down in time?"

Epaphras waved both hands. "He already knows more than I do. He could probably fly right now."

"I will need to practice to learn the placement of all the controls, Master Filymon. But I think it will be no problem to fly under computer control by then."

"Good, good. And what about manual control?"

Seamus glanced toward Epaphras, who shrugged. "I'm not sure, sir. Once I have computer control down, I'll start trying to find ways to access things manually."

"Humph," Filymon muttered, rubbing his chin in thought. After several moments he looked up. "We're going to be eating soon, if you want to get to a stopping point."

"Sounds good." Epaphras said.

After Filymon left, Seamus asked, "What's so important about manual control?"

Epaphras glanced at him quizzically. "Huh? Where are you from?"

"Far away, sir. I'm not accustomed to..." Seamus voice trailed off.

"Oh." He took a quick glance back before answering Seamus' original question. "Times aren't what they were. It used to be that Kollos was the most direct route to Gallatiana from Effizus. Filymon's parents started a trading business and bought this ship, the *Wander Wide*. They made a lot of money before they turned the business over to Filymon. He did well for awhile but then about ten years ago they discovered another hypertrack that linked Effizus and Gallatiana direct. So, now business has dried up."

"But what does that have to do with flying manually? It sounds like he should shift his operations to the other hypertrack."

"Well, yeah. We've talked about that. A lot. But he's got a decent business out of Kollos and he doesn't want to be away from home so much."

The thought of home brought a sudden pang to Seamus' heart.

"So, he's been trying everything he can to build business back to where it was." Epaphras glanced back down the corridor and said the next in a much quieter tone. "He hasn't told me his plans, but there's only so many reasons you'd need a manual pilot, much less one off the black market. And they're all not the kind of business I want to be in. That's half the reason I'm leaving. We've already started taking some questionable cargo lately and I want nothing of it."

For all that Seamus was several weeks ago, he was now a much more guarded person. He wanted to make comment and ask more questions, but now he heeded all danger signals. Was Epaphras baiting him? Everything about this conversation sounded like it would bring him nothing but trouble.

"Epaphras!"

Seamus glanced back to see Filymon storming toward them.

"Uh oh," Epaphras muttered, quickly turning back toward the appearance of busyness. Seamus followed his example.

"Epaphras!" Filymon shouted, swinging the younger man's chair around to face him. "I've been monitoring your conversations this afternoon and you've crossed the line. I'm fining you half a day's wage for disloyalty!"

Seamus nearly flew out of his chair as it was whipped around. Filymon's giraffe spots were dark and his eyes wide and blazing, but worse, Seamus was horrified to see the shocker in his left hand.

"And you! A slave never questions his master!"

A wave of pain slammed into him, locking him rigid, and sending him crashing into the deck. He felt like he was falling into a dark tunnel, reality racing away to a bare pinpoint of light.

"Fil, stop it! It was me! He didn't..."

More was said but only in muffled tones that slipped away.

NINE – WANDER WIDE

Seamus awoke, barely glimpsing light through his eyelashes. Air! He needed air! He concentrated on drawing in as much into his lungs as possible, which was no small feat. After a few breaths his oxygen-starved lungs began to relax and his mind slowly began to take in other sensations. Shadows crossed over him and he felt hands shift him slightly as he lay on some hard surface. Then he remembered where he was and what had happened.

"Thank God he's breathing on his own. You know, that was really stupid, Fil. He could easily be dead now."

"Well, thank the *gods* he isn't. Now stop lecturing me, it was an accident."

"Maybe you need a good lecture."

"Shut off that noise-maker, Epaphras, or I'll toss you into the cargo bay."

Seamus had been focusing on making something – anything – move, but now he listened as Filymon and Epaphras' voices rose in pitch and volume.

"You know, for three years I've worked for you and I've held my tongue. But you know what? I'm not doing it any more, and you can dock the rest of my pay if you want. You're nothing but a bully. All you do is treat people like bots for your bidding and you never care what happens to them. It's one thing to treat a hired hand that way. Stupid me chose to stay here and take your abuse, but at least I could leave whenever I chose. This poor kid'll never have the option."

"He's not a kid. He's a slave. You can never ever think of them as anything other than property. That's why I did that. You have to show them up front who's boss, you have to set a precedence."

"He's a person, not a thing! You sound like some Romian. Where'd you get that crazy idea!"

"From this manual I'm trying to read! So stop distracting me. The chapter on the remote is at least twenty screens and Karrthaaggians can't make anything easy."

"Hmmph!" Seamus felt two hands grip his right arm and warm whispered breath on his cheek: "Kid, I don't know if you can hear me, but if this tyrant treats you bad again, just let his wife, Apphia, know. She'll set him straight."

"I think I've got it now. Let go of him."

"I hope he's not paralyzed by that thing. It's attached to his spine, you know."

"I told you to shut your yap, already!"

Seamus felt a tickle run through his body and suddenly he could move. He sat up, almost involuntarily, coughing and grasping at his throat.

"Now don't do that again or it's more of the same for you!" Filymon barked.

Before he knew what his feet were doing, Seamus was up and running. He bolted down the corridor back toward where he had entered the ship.

"Well, now you've spooked him!" he heard Epaphras shout.

He turned a corner and found the airlock to the hangar, but the door was locked. He only tried it for a second, if he really even tried at all. Rage and fear swirled in his mind, crowding out rational thought. There were two other doorways nearby. Which one to take? Just then one of them opened.

"Onesimus?" It was the boy, Chippus, holding a reader. "Are you okay? What's wrong?"

Seamus backed up against the other door, patting the wall for the controls. The door whisked open. He lost his footing and tumbled inside just as Filymon came around the corner, bellowing.

"Onesimus! Come back, boy! Right now, I say!"

As the door slid shut, he realized he had fallen into a closet filled with orange spacesuits. In the darkness he wiggled through to the most distant corner, his racing heartbeat thudding in his ears. "He's going to kill me now," he muttered to himself as his brain finally caught up with his feet.

As he caught his breath, Seamus' wild-running thoughts unexpectedly settled on a vivid memory from last year, just before he had been kicked out of boarding school. It was when William Thornton had punched him the first time. Seamus couldn't remember why, but there never had been a good reason. All that Seamus had been sure of was that William was a year older than him, and had singled him out for harassment. One minute Seamus had been changing into his gym clothes for basketball, the next he had been knocked to the ground with his shorts around his ankles, the laughter of a score of other boys ringing in his ears.

No one had said or done anything to William that day, and to his burning shame, neither had Seamus. He should have at least tried to hit him back, but instead he just lay there. Even now he felt his face burn in embarrassment. That was the first time it happened and far from the last. But eventually, Seamus had had enough and made sure William got what was coming to him.

"Onesimus! I can track you anywhere you go, so I know you're in that closet! Come out right now!"

Janey Mac, he was in a tight spot. Seamus thought about it for a moment and decided it was probably better to obey. He pushed his way back to the door, which slid open. All three stood there. Filymon stood in front with the shocker; Chippus and Epaphras just behind him. He looked furious, so Seamus decided to chance saying something to calm him down. He lifted his hands slowly and took a short step out into the hallway. He hung his head, as if in shame and dropped to his knees.

"I'm sorry, Master Filymon. I just... I don't know why I ran away. I guess I thought you were going to kill me." He slowly looked up to see Filymon giving him a blistering stare, and he wondered if he only had made it worse. But after a few seconds Filymon seemed to relax and the shocker came down to his side.

"No, I wasn't trying to kill you. I didn't mean for that to happen. I wanted to give you a little jolt, but I read the manual wrong."

Seamus could think of all sorts of responses, but held his tongue.

"I'm very sorry, sir."

"Well, no harm done. But next time don't be running off like that again, you hear me? We're all new here and we need to adjust, adjust to one another. When you ran off like that I had no idea what you were up to, if you were dangerous or not."

"He sure looks dangerous," Epaphras muttered sarcastically. Filymon tossed an annoyed glance momentarily over his shoulder, but offered no other response.

Seamus bowed his head. "I won't, Master Filymon."

"Well, get up. The food's probably cold by now, but let's go eat."

Seamus followed the others to the galley. Rado always had the trainees serve him at every meal, and no one else ate until he was finished. Seamus quickly began to do the same with his new owners. Luckily, everything was already laid out on the galley counters where Seamus could find it.

"Now that's more like it," Filymon announced, as Seamus began to dish out a purple stew to him and then to Chippus. He had no idea what it was, but it sure smelled delicious.

"I'll get it myself, but thanks," Epaphras said, but Seamus ignored him, setting a bowl down at one of the other open seats. "Uh, thanks," Epaphras said, as he took his seat. Once settled, he seemed to whisper something with a bowed head.

Filymon seemed to take notice and dropped his spoon with a loud clink. "Oh, forgive my manners!" He looked upward. "Mighty Artimiss, we ask for your blessings on our hunt and may our hands give birth to riches." To Seamus he sounded sarcastic and his hand gestures seemed exaggerated like he was mocking Epaphras. Epaphras said nothing in response, but Seamus noticed his giraffe pattern darkening.

The meal went on almost silently after that, with tension as thick as the stew. Conversation was sparse and short-lived. Seamus ignored a few promptings from Epaphras to join them, and instead dutifully offered to refill glasses and bowls and to attend to any other needs. Otherwise he stood at the far side of the galley. He was dreadfully hungry, but knew he had to wait for the others to finish and leave before he would be allowed to eat. At one of the quietest moments Seamus' stomach growled, or better said, *roared.* Chippus laughed, causing Seamus to turn red. After that he tried to make a lot of noise with the pot and spoon to cover the grumbling.

In what seemed like hours, the others finished their meal and didn't linger, quickly leaving in the same awkward silence overshadowing the rest of the meal. Only Epaphras tried to stay for a few moments to wash his own dishes, finally relenting to Seamus' begging when he told him that he didn't want to get into any more trouble for shirking his duties. As soon as he left the galley, Seamus ladled the stew into his mouth, gulping it down – he didn't even bother getting his own bowl and spoon. It tasted different than anything else he had before, but with his hunger he didn't care. Who knew what it was. It could use a little salt, but otherwise very satisfying.

After cleaning the kitchen Seamus headed back to the flight deck, where Epaphras sat checking the ship's settings. He glanced up as Seamus quietly took the copilot's chair, turned toward Epaphras. He wasn't really sure what to do.

"Oh, hi, Onesimus. Just double checking for the night. In hyper I usually let the ship fly itself – well, I guess for me it always flies itself. I'll come by every couple of hours or so to check the readings, either here or in the small station in my quarters. The rest of my time I'm usually in the engine room checking all the systems or doing whatever maintenance I can do while we're running. But I can show all of that to you tomorrow." He paused for a moment, looking around blankly, and then flicked a switch dimming the lights. He stood, stretching. "Whoa, what a day. I'm going to sleep good tonight... guess I'll turn in. Good night."

As he stepped through the open hatch, Seamus called after him. "Uh, Master Epaphras? What should I do now? Do I stay up here for the night?"

"Oh," he answered with surprise. He turned back. "I didn't think about that. Well, I guess you're going to get my quarters when I'm gone. You could bunk with me, but it will be tight." He thought for a moment. "Come on, we've got an extra room you can use tonight till we get things figured out."

Epaphras led him to a small room, containing a bunk, a closet, and a compact lavatory. Boxes were stacked everywhere, and it seemed as if the room hadn't been used in many years. Seamus thanked Epaphras and said goodnight, barely clearing off the dusty bed before collapsing upon it. He resisted the constant urge to try to pull the fitting off his back and settled in as best as he could. He stared at the wall for a few moments, breathing in and out deeply. Epaphras was right: what a day.

Sleep came quickly.

♦ ♦ ♦

The next six days were long and tiring. Seamus spent most of his time with Epaphras, trying to absorb all he knew about the *Wander Wide*. He didn't learn much more about flying the ship – there was little more Epaphras could teach him – but he learned a lot about all the ship's automated systems, their quirks, and their upkeep. His gray jumpsuit soon became filthy and Filymon and Epaphras tried to find some more clothing for him. He had soon assembled a few changes of baggy garments for different needs, namely ship maintenance, piloting, cleaning the galley, and sleeping – what little he got of it.

Filymon seemed to treat Seamus better after their first run-in, but each meeting was different. He always seemed to be reading what Seamus assumed were the files Rado had given him, and Seamus could tell when he learned something new. One day he seemed to be very inquisitive and caring, the next overly detailed in all his instructions and expectations, the next, hardly speaking to him except when necessary. It almost became a game to Seamus to guess the chapter titles on his instruction manual: *How to Keep Your New Slave Loyal, How to Motivate Your New Slave, How to Keep Your New Slave from Getting Too Blah, Blah, Blah.*

The boy, Chippus, was hardly seen except at meal times. He seemed to stay in his cabin most of the time. When he was out in the galley or the adjacent lounge, he usually played some sort of handheld video game or looked at a reader. A few times he followed them around, quietly listening to Epaphras' explanations. He was polite enough, but Seamus could tell Filymon had been coaching him on how to treat him, which apparently was mostly to leave him alone.

Seamus grew to like Epaphras. He always treated him with respect, and Seamus had to force himself from acting too familiar with him. It was hard not to treat him like a coworker and especially a friend. Mostly they talked about their work, but on the last day before their arrival at Effizus, Epaphras started to become wistful. He walked the length and breadth of the ship reminiscing under the guise of reminding Seamus of everything he had shown and told him. They ended up on the flight deck, Epaphras patting the main control board fondly like a good dog.

"I'm going to miss this old bird. I always wished I could have helped her live up to her name, *Wander Wide*." He snorted in humor. "Should have named her the *Stay Close By*, or maybe *G-K-E*, after our route. You know, Gallatiana-Kollos-Effizus? Still, I've clocked a lot of flight time in her on our little beaten path."

Seamus didn't interrupt with any comments or questions. He'd heard his parents reminisce often enough to know they were really talking to themselves and his only purpose was to give them an excuse not to look crazy, babbling to the empty air. He listened intently, though. He never knew when he'd stumble upon some significant piece of information that might help him to one day escape, to rescue his parents, and to return home. If that day ever came.

"But you know if I had been satisfying my wanderlust, I never would have met all my friends in Effizus. And I never would have learned about Yeshua. I now wouldn't be going to school. And I'd still be here, wishing for more."

This piqued Seamus' interest. What could make that much of a change in a person? "So what is Yechuma?"

"Yeshua? *Who*, not what. But I'll have to tell you later. Look at the neutrinometer."

"We're at the end of the hypertrack?"

Just as Epaphras nodded, the ship's computer announced the same, and then counted down from ten. At zero, the swirling blue of hyperspace flashed, revealing the deep black of normal space. In the far distance an orange glowing crescent noted their destination: Effizus.

TEN - EFFIZUS

Effizus reminded Seamus of Mars, but where the terrain of the red planet of his home system was the product of typical processes, Seamus had no idea what produced the geology of this planet. Orange sand covered Effizus, wrapping around the blistering equatorial region in an endless circle of desert. Two enormous rings of mountains - one to the far north, one to the far south - held the desert and its heat back like river banks, allowing a great ocean to exist in the northern polar region, encircled by ring of arable land and dotted with a few large islands. It amazed Seamus to learn the entire habitable area of Effizus was of comparable size to Australia.

"I'm surprised anyone could live here," Seamus said.

"Nothing did until a few hundred years ago," Epaphras remarked as he initiated the orbiting sequence signaled from Traffic Control. He leaned back, keeping an eye on the screens - as if he could do anything if something were amiss. "The old Athinsian Empire settled the planet after discovering the hypertrack here, but the Romians took it over when Athinsia fell. It might not look like much, but it's become the chief system of this region, since the Romians won't allow Athinsia to redevelop much and Gallatiana is so remote. Plus, there's a big naval presence here in case the Gothans ever try an offensive out of Ostro."

"And now this will be your home."

"For a while." He paused, staring at the orange globe as if searching for his new residence. "But Kollos will always be home. I hope that I can go back one day to share with everyone what I learn in school."

Again, Seamus' interest was piqued. "You were telling me earlier about meeting people on Effizus."

"Yeah, weird story. You know how sometimes one casual decision can end up making a huge difference? That's how this happened. I'd been working for Fil for a little over a year when our shuttle's computer froze up just as we launched from the bay. It was here at Effizus, actually. The computer rebooted okay, but it got me thinking about what could have happened if the shuttle systems ever completely died. I mean, we could freeze to death in a matter of hours and no one would ever notice."

It suddenly struck Seamus that with all the rush to teach him about the *Wander Wide*, they had never had a chance to go over the shuttle's controls. Everything else had been fairly simple, but what about the shuttle?

Epaphras continued: "The shuttle had been without a TENT for awhile – well, actually, I don't think it ever had one – and I finally talked Fil into getting one since it's getting so old."

"A Tent?"

"Oh, the 'life raft' I think you called it when I showed you. It's that inflatable pod in the shuttle that supposedly has enough shielding, equipment, and supplies to keep you alive in open space for a week, remember? Stands for Temporary Emergency Navigable Transport, but I'd beg to differ about the navigable part, since you'd probably need every bit of power to keep the life support running.

"Anyway, I found a good supplier on Effizus ran by a real nice couple named Aquyia and Prazella. Well, as I said, they were mighty friendly and in all our discussions we got to talking about religion."

Seamus crossed his arms. "My parents always said never to talk about religion or politics unless you want to get into an argument."

"You're right about that, ha-ha. But on Effizus everyone has some different mix of religion. Of course, everyone worships Artimiss, but they always have a few more gods on the side. You can tell a lot about people because they usually pick the gods they think will give them what they most want. But these folks I was talking about worshiped only one God, one I had never heard of before. When I asked more, they invited me to go with them to a lecture later that day, where a philosopher was going to talk about the One God. I had the afternoon off and no money, so I thought, why not?

"So I met them at the lecture hall where Tyrannus holds his morning classes, and this mystic named Pol was speaking. He wasn't very impressive at first. He was kind of short and wasn't all that great an orator like a lot of the philosophers around here. He spoke plainly and without the usual theatrics. And he also had these glasses. I learned later that he'd been nearly killed over in Gallatiana when some religious types started throwing huge rocks at him. Apparently, they really messed up the nerves in his eyes and the only way he could see is with these glasses."

At this point the ship announced they had achieved the assigned orbit, and Epaphras began to shut down many of the systems and adjusting others. Seamus watched closely: lidar down, navigation down, main drive down, station drive up, shielding to one quarter – basically everything needed to fly anywhere else was shut down. He could remember that. He had taken a ton of notes, but he wished the ship had a training program like the *Fernão* had. It would make things so much easier.

Epaphras continued as he rechecked all the systems. "Like I said, Pol wasn't much to look at, and he talked differently, but everything he said made such sense to me. It was like I'd heard the truth for the very first time and recognized it instantly."

"What do you mean, Master?"

"It's hard to describe. You know, I've sat and listened to a lot of the philosophers around here, and they talk and talk and talk. They all say something different and most of it doesn't make sense. Like one says that no one really desires evil or does evil knowingly. Everyone knows that's not true. Another says our reality isn't real, that this is all a shadow of the true reality. Well, it's the only reality I know. Another says we're just imaginations of nature." He shook his head. "The thing about it all is that none of what I've ever heard makes my life *work*."

Epaphras paused suddenly, almost jarringly. Seamus turned to see why, only to find Epaphras deep in thought, his eyes reflecting the deep black of space. He wondered if he should think of a question or comment to fill the quiet. Epaphras turned, looking at him intently.

"Onesimus, did you ever feel like life had great meaning and purpose, but whatever it was, it was hidden from you? It's like there is a great play going on and you have a leading role, but you don't know your part or have seen your script. And so we all stumble all over the stage, ruining every scene, and destroying the performance." He pressed his hand into his chest. "In my deep heart I know that there is more to this life than just surviving day to day. I have this deep ache for more. The philosophers know it, too, and they try to explain it away as meaningless or tell us to ignore it. They say that peace and contentment come from denying it. But none of it rings true."

In that moment, Seamus realized he had never paused to think about such things, but he recognized something in what Epaphras said.

"But Pol... what Pol said - what he says. Now, it rings true."

"Epaphras!" Filymon's voice echoed from far back in the ship. "You having second thoughts? Let's get moving! I'm losing customers every second!"

"Ah," Epaphras mumbled. He rolled his eyes, causing Seamus to smile silently. He stood. "I'm done here. Let's go."

The reflective moment evaporated, leaving behind a nervous knot in Seamus stomach. He followed Epaphras to the shuttle, where Filymon and Chippus were buckling in, and headed to the front. This was it. After this flight, Seamus would be on his own. Whatever he had learned before Epaphras set foot on Effizus might be all the training he would ever have again.

Epaphras answered one of his unspoken questions as they climbed into their restraints: "Well, this is pretty simple - even for me. The shuttle is loaded with landing programs for every port in the Star Kingdom. It picks up our current location and Traffic Control's landing assignments from the ship. Fil's got his own facilities at Effizus and Gallatiana, so that never changes. So, here's all you do."

Seamus was astonished to see him touch the LAND menu on the instrument screen, which in response displayed the particulars of the flight plan. After confirming the plan, Epaphras keyed it to execute and leaned back in silence. Seamus heard the atmosphere pumps working, followed by the low rumble of the bay doors opening. A few moments later, the loader arm extended, lowering them out beneath the *Wander Wide*. On its own, the shuttle gently thrusted out of the docking cradle and began to fall behind, slowly dropping toward the orange surface of Effizus.

Epaphras sat up straight as the mother ship diminished in size as it continued in its orbit. "Huh... now I see what you're saying about our speed affecting our altitude. As we slow down, gravity is pulling us down." Seamus grunted with a nod, proud Epaphras finally understood but also feeling a growing sadness. Outside of Löwin, Epaphras seemed like his only friend. And now he was soon gone, as well.

Fiery reentry gave way to buffeting winds in an orange streaked blue sky. A huge range of mountains passed beneath them, and an enormous sea appeared ahead. Lower and lower they dropped until another strip of land appeared on the horizon, covered by a sprawling city.

Seamus kept his eye on the icons of the flight plan and the altimeter. Everything looked on plan, but they seemed to be flying too low, landing too short. Just as he was about to alert Epaphras of an impending crash, the shuttle's computer announced, *"Prepare for water landing"*. The shuttle touched down on the ocean with a spray of water and billowing steam. The forward momentum slowed considerably, but the shuttle held course toward a marina and soon eased into a slip. The docking was automatic and the airlock doors swung open. It was going to take Seamus some time to get used to these water landings.

It took a couple minutes to shut the shuttle's systems down, but when they arose and turned, Filymon stood between them and the door, pursing his lips as his giraffe spots darkened. Next to him Chippus stood, looking down and drawing patterns in the carpet with the toe of his right shoe. Filymon finally broke the awkward silence.

"Epaphras, I want you to know you've been a good pilot for us. And I hate to see you go. I, uh, hope this school of yours works out, but if it don't, you're always welcome with us. I could always use a good hand."

Seamus glanced up at Epaphras, whose face looked rigid and his own spots flushing darker. "Thanks, Fil."

Chippus finally looked up – but just for a moment. "We're going to miss you."

Epaphras squeezed the boy's shoulder. "I'm going to miss you too. But I'm glad we'll get to see each other every few weeks or so."

"That depends on the business," Filymon mumbled. "Speaking of which, let's get going. We'll drop you off at Tyrannus' place."

Seamus followed the others out onto the dock, where a land car waited, having just emerged from a lower section of the dock. Obviously, Filymon kept needed equipment on site instead of hauling it with him. Epaphras had only an overstuffed bag and no other possessions, so they were quickly on their way.

The marina disappeared behind them as they drove into the city, blazing white in the sunlight. Seamus had never seen its like. Everything appeared to be made of some sort of white stone or marble, obviously of some off-world origin, as it contrasted highly with the orange browns of the indigenous stone and soil. In several rows, thirty-meter-tall white marble columns lined the main avenue, The Arcadia. All the buildings on either side were similarly decorated with columns and sculptures. Most of the roofs appeared flat, or else slanted to the rear unseen. It all spoke of grandeur and great wealth. After a few minutes they pulled into an alley next to a large building.

"Here we are," Epaphras said joyously.

"Well... may your hunt go well," Filymon said as he parked.

Epaphras grabbed his bag and stepped out. "Please come in... just for a minute? I'd really like to introduce you, if they aren't in the middle of something."

Filymon didn't look too enthused. "Uh... we really got—"

Chippus interrupted him: "Dad, can we please?"

After his face contorted in several waves of distaste, he finally relented. Seamus was glad to have a chance to see the school. Who knew what he'd be doing from here on. He may never have another chance.

Epaphras led them into the building. Perhaps a hundred or so people sat on the floor on mats, all intently listening to the speaker. On the stage a short older man with tan-green skin spoke. Assuming he was this Pol, Seamus thought, Epaphras was right in all he said about his appearance and public speaking. The man was dressed plainly, balding, with a long nose, atop of which sat a set of shimmering goggles. He seemed to pause with a smile of recognition, but quickly continued: "...remember that at that time you were separate from Yeshua, excluded from citizenship in his kingdom and were foreigners to God's promises, without hope and without God in this world. But now in Yeshua, you who were far away have been brought near—"

Just then an older woman greeted them from behind with a whisper. "Epaphras! I'm so glad to see you!"

Epaphras hugged her, and then turned to the others, beckoning them out into the foyer of the building. Once outside the lecture hall he introduced her. "Everyone, this is Prazella. I'm going to be staying with her and her husband. Prazella, this is my boss, Filymon, his son, Chippus, and my replacement, Onesimus."

"Epaphras, you shouldn't introduce slaves unless necessary," Filymon said with an embarrassed tone. Seamus felt his face flush and he clenched his teeth to keep from snapping back. Epaphras visibly bristled.

"No worries," the woman said with a glowing smile that immediately diffused the tension. "Here, my kind friend, we try to leave all the social trappings at the door. It makes things so much easier." Seamus brimmed with gratitude, and suddenly realized how beautiful she looked. Her sparkling eyes were like gems under dark hair streaked with silver, glittering eyes that conveyed joy and acceptance.

Epaphras quickly continued as if trying to deny Filymon the opportunity to respond. "Fil, Prezella is the dealer where we bought our TENT."

"I hope it's working out well for you?"

"Uh, yeah, sure. It's working just fine. Well, we haven't had to use it, but it stowed in the airlock as advertised. Slid in perfect like."

"Well, I hope you never have to use it. Just remember that every two years it needs to be serviced."

"Right, thanks." He paused with widened eyes. "Well, I guess we should be going. Best of luck to you, Epaphras. Be sure to let us know how you settle in."

"Thanks, Fil. I will."

After handshakes, Filymon quickly exited. He didn't look too pleased, or maybe just hurried. "Come on you two, I've got someone to meet."

From the backseat of the car, Seamus took one last look at the lecture hall as it receded from view. He hoped he'd see Epaphras again.

ELEVEN – FLYING SOLO

Filymon pulled in front of a building advertised as a manufacturing plant. It surprised Seamus to see how ornate the structure was, despite its utilitarian purpose. After parking in a side lot, they walked along a bricked walkway to the front office area. Here, just outside the entrance, a colonnade encircled a reflecting pool in which stood an enormous statue. The woman was striking: short, wavy hair framed a strong, feminine face; a loose, revealing tunic covered a trim, athletic body in mid-stride; one hand gripped a bow while the other drew an arrow from a quiver on her back. It was a masterful sculpture, combining sensuous beauty with warrior strength. Seamus lagged behind to read the inscription on the pedestal beneath her feet: *Artimiss, Goddess of Effizus.*

"Come on, boy!" Filymon growled. "You should be getting the doors instead of sightseeing! Come on, I say! Come on!"

Seamus raced to the doors. "I'm sorry, Master."

A young man greeted Filymon from behind a reception desk, "I hope you had a profitable journey, sir. Mr. Trius said to bring you right in." As he led them down a hallway, Seamus spied a fitting peeking out of the neck of the man's shirt. He was a slave. Seamus reflexively rubbed his own fitting, feeling the flexible device invisibly chaining him to Filymon. The man opened an office door, holding it wide.

"Fil, how are you?" a voice boomed.

Seamus stepped in behind the others to see a heavyset human man draped in a gray robe. As he stood from behind a desk, his skin coloring shifted from golden yellow to orange in a random circular pattern that made him look lumpy.

"Very well, Deme, *very* well," Filymon said, matching the other man's tone and volume. They embraced each other's arms and bowed their heads in some sort of greeting. As the slave exited the room, pulling the door behind him, Deme returned to his seat and motioned toward two other chairs. There was a third chair to one side, but Seamus chose to stand unobtrusively against the door as Rado had taught him. A slave was to always be in the background, blending in with the furniture, he had said.

Deme keyed a pad on his desk and Seamus heard a slight hum fill the room and the door behind him. "We're shielded now. No one can hear us. So... I take it your trip was successful?" He nodded toward Seamus.

"I got him!" Filymon whispered with excitement. "He's a manual pilot, and," he paused for effect, "he's *unregistered* too."

"Unregistered? How... how... where did you find an unregistered pilot!"

"Rado, like you suggested. But it took me fifty-three thousand Ceez to win him in a bid against a couple Dalmans."

"Anyone you knew?"

"No. Rado's good, though. He kept everything anonymous and held them until we had cleared the area."

"Good to hear that. The last thing you need is competitors snatching your prize." Deme stared at him with such intensity Seamus looked down at his feet to avoid his gaze. "Fifty-three thousand, eh?" He huffed. "But if he's an unregistered *and* manual pilot, you stand to make that back a lot quicker. So how good is he?"

Seamus glanced up to see Filymon looking at him. "I've seen some of his flying, and it's good, real good, I say. He's still got a lot to learn and he's got to figure out how to get my ship in manual mode. On the trip here, he showed my old pilot a few things, things like laws of planetary motions, orbital velocity, and the like. He definitely understands what's happening when he pushes the buttons."

Deme's tight-lipped nod morphed into a greedy smile. "We're going to make a lot of money. I've just about perfected the hollow idols. You've already got the route set up through Kollos that the Romians hardly watch. And now you've got yourself the pilot." He paused, clasping his hands as his eyes glazed over at the possibilities, until the obvious question – the question haunting Seamus – finally came to mind. "When do you think he will be ready? How long will it take for him to fly your ship manually?"

Filymon's measuring gaze hardened, as if he was threatening Seamus to learn as quickly as possible. "Soon. But, I'll let you know."

♦ ♦ ♦

A short while later as they returned to the shuttle, Chippus had the "great" idea his father should take him to some place called the Agora to find a gift for his mother, while Seamus got a head start on the work. Filymon quickly grew to like this idea and so they dropped him off at the dock to start moving the cargo to and from the shuttle's storage compartments. As they drove off, Seamus grumbled to himself. He sat for awhile brooding, but then finally got to work, afraid of Filymon's displeasure and the shock that would be sure to come with it.

It was hot, tiring work – especially when the blistering white sun peeked from behind the shuttle, doubly bright from reflecting off the water. It didn't take Seamus long to see how it traveled around this world sideways, just above the sea, never rising or setting; and always, always in the eyes. He hoped the mountains to his left would soon eclipse it before his skin burned. After a few minutes, he couldn't stand it any longer and moved inside the shuttle for relief, stuffy as it was. He began moving containers near the doorway, stacking them up where it would be easy to reach from outside.

As he worked, his thoughts wandered over the day's events, finally centering on the scheming he had heard earlier. Obviously, Filymon had plans to smuggle, and was counting on him to make it possible. He wondered what would happen if he failed, if they were ever captured. Would he even be tried in a court of law, where he could prove he was compelled to obey? If Rado and Filymon could kill him on a whim, would the government even care?

From what he had gathered, being an unauthorized manual pilot was highly illegal, so he was doubly in danger. And from what he'd heard about the Romians, he probably shouldn't expect mercy. He had to escape, not just to find his parents and get back home, but just to survive more than one major mistake.

He returned outside when it appeared the sun had moved behind the distant mountains surrounding the top of this world. Mindlessly, he stacked the off-loaded containers on the dock and began to stow the ones Filymon had pointed out to him from inside a small warehousing building adjacent to the dock. His thoughts wandered. What was his plan to escape? Löwin had taught him that preparation and planning were the keys to success. He had some ideas, but nothing that would take him all the way home. Plus now he had to track his parents down, wherever they might be. Maybe as he learned more, he could put it all together.

By the time he loaded the last dozen crates of silver plated Artimiss statues, he was exhausted. Next time he'd figure out what the heavy work was and leave it for his wonderful masters, who seemed to be taking the whole afternoon to shop. And Filymon had the nerve to yell at him for pausing a few seconds to read the inscription of that statue outside of Deme Trius' factory! He dragged himself to the passenger compartment of the shuttle and found a cold drink in the tiny galley. Just as he plopped down in the pilot's seat, he saw the car return. He sighed. No doubt he should go out and cheerfully greet his vile masters, after which they would get him working on the last of it.

"Wow, he did a lot," Seamus heard Chippus say as he exited to the dock into a twilight that was probably the closest to darkness Effizus came. Only the crates off the shuttle remained to be stacked somewhere. He had almost started to take them to the warehouse, but Filymon hadn't told him what to do with them, so he had left them until the end. Filymon muttered in a vague sort of agreement, but said nothing else as he stuck his head into the cargo door to examine Seamus' work. Chippus happily added, "Onesimus, we brought you our leftovers from supper." He held out a paper bag that seemed to be wet on one side, as if soaked with grease.

"Thank you, Master Chippus," Seamus said, trying very hard to keep all trace of irritation from his voice. Mmmm, someone else's leftovers...

"Next time, you need to spread the weight around," Filymon growled. He beckoned Seamus into the cargo hold. "These idols are heavy, so they can't be on one side. Half need to be over here and the other half here to keep us balanced. And they need to be closer to the front, or else we'll never get our back end out of the water."

"Yes, Master," Seamus said as he began to reposition the crates." After quickly moving the first two crates, his fatigue began to show. It took a lot of effort to lift the third and to keep his grip." The fourth crate thudded loudly as he placed it where Filymon pointed. He panted heavily then plodded back to the next one.

"Onesimus, stop. Leave it, boy. You've done enough. Go eat something and we'll finish up here." Seamus looked up, expecting laughter at a cruel joke, but Filymon's expression was one of slight concern. "Go on."

With joyous relief he headed to the front, plopping down in the comfortable pilot seat. Whatever they brought him to eat was sweet and crispy, like a fried vegetable of some sort, orange like a carrot, but more like a battered celery stalk. It was cold, but the food tasted wonderful and the chair did wonders for his aching back and feet. With a full belly, he closed his eyes for just a moment, slowly breathing in and out, enjoying every second of rest.

"Wake up, boy. We're ready to go."

Seamus sat up with a start, finding drool as he wiped his face with his hand. I can't believe I fell asleep, he thought. He looked around to see Chippus strapping into one of the seats in the back, while Filymon took the copilot's chair.

"Are we heading back to the ship?" he asked.

"Yep. Next stop, Kollos. Home."

Seamus stared at the glassy instrument panel, his awakening brain racing over hundreds of memories of what he'd learned over the past weeks from Rado and Epaphras but never pausing long enough for him to recognize anything. He had been taught scores of control panels, computer screens, and procedures. Which one? Where to start?

For lack of any better idea, he touched the navigation screen. A menu appeared, the top choice reading: "Return to *Wander Wide*". He snorted with surprise. Pressing the button, he watched a status indicator of the systems coming online and the engines warming. Within a few seconds the screen informed him a flight plan had been calculated, submitted to Traffic Control, and approved. The screen then asked for the okay to proceed. He gave it, and the shuttle slowly began to back away from the dock, bobbing in the gentle swell of the sea.

"I can't believe how easy this is," he mumbled.

Filymon must have heard him. "What? Have you figured out the manual systems already?"

"Uh... no, sir. I was just thinking how easy the shuttle is to fly under computer control. I mean, I just pressed two buttons and it's doing everything else."

"Oh, yeah," he sneered. "Why do I even need a pilot? Why pay a fortune when I could push two buttons myself? What was I thinking?" He huffed.

Seamus bit his tongue, counting to ten. When he was pretty sure he could control himself he said, "I will learn how to fly manually, Master. This is my second time in this shuttle, and I'm just trying to figure out all it can do, that's all." Filymon said nothing in response, instead, setting his jaw as he looked out the front windshield.

A few minutes later after picking up speed, they lifted from the water, skimming over its surface momentarily before rotating upward. The dazzling white sun peaked from behind the mountains as they ascended, eclipsed momentarily by clouds, then blazing. Pink sky grew purple then black. A few minutes later the *Wander Wide* was in sight, bay doors opening. The shuttle slowed, gently easing into the extended cradle. With a slight shudder, they docked and the cradle's arm pulled them into the bay. The doors closed, air filled the bay, and with just one more button to push ("Power down vehicle?"), Seamus first flight without Epaphras ended, absent of fanfare.

As they exited, Filymon finally spoke. His voice dripped with authority and veiled threats. "Onesimus, we got an almost two day ride to Kollos. By the time we get there, I want you to have an idea how long it will take you to fly my ships manually." After rounding the catwalk around the nose of the shuttle he turned. "Got that?"

Seamus nodded.

"Now get us going to Kollos, and then come back down here to take the groceries up to the galley."

All the way to the flight deck, Seamus muttered under his breath. If Filymon didn't have that shocker, Seamus would have given that old git an earful. And then he would have hopped back in that shuttle and left them to push their own buttons. What an ignorant fanner! Even his parents never treated him like that.

Seamus thought about the last time he'd seen his parents, regretting the petty argument they had just before their capture. They had never been mean, only firm, yet loving, he realized. He missed them terribly. As he entered the flight deck, Seamus paused. The cockpit lit up at his presence, waiting his commands. It was his now. He wondered if his parents would believe him now, the responsibility that was his, the expectations upon him. Would they be proud? He keyed through the simplistic menu to head to Kollos. As before, it did all the work for him.

Maybe this time he wouldn't screw up.

TWELVE - KOLLOS

The cloud-shrouded blue-green sphere of Kollos grew ever larger, visible just four hours from exiting the hypertrack. It had been a quick voyage of a day and a half, but Seamus was exhausted. The trip from Effizus had been largely sleepless, as Seamus had spent nearly every spare moment searching through all the computer files he could find for some sort of indication of how to control the *Wander Wide* manually.

Though his search seemed fruitless in that regard, it was not entirely without value. He had discovered operating manuals (computer controlled, of course) for both the ship and the shuttle, plus maintenance manuals for both vessels. Yet, the big find was a piloting simulator that covered all the material in both operations manuals, plus a lot of training scenarios. Seamus had been overjoyed to find it. Now he felt like he could at least master what Epaphras had skimmed over in a week. Plus, though Filymon wouldn't be happy at his progress on manual access, Seamus could at least show him he could quickly master computer piloting.

As if reading his mind, Filymon stepped onto the flight deck.

"I never tire of seeing that planet. I hate to be away for so long."

"Yes, Master. We should be in orbit within a few minutes."

"So, what have you to say about manual piloting? When can I expect you to be ready?" His voice had a hard edge, and Seamus could see the bulge of the shocker in his shirt pocket. This probably wasn't going to go well. Seamus wanted to bolt to the shuttle, but instead took a deep breath.

"I'm sorry, Master. I'm... not sure." As Filymon's spots darkened, Seamus said the next in a fast tumble of words: "Please don't be angry! I've spent almost the entire trip combing through the computer and haven't found any mention of manual access. I stayed up all night long, and I did find a couple manuals and a piloting simulator. I was glad to find those, because it will help me get as good as Epaphras in probably a week, but there's nothing else so far. And..." His voice faltered as he ran out of things to say. He winced as he paused, but to his relief Filymon seemed composed.

"I thought Epaphras was going to show you some tricks he had found?"

"Well, he did, but none of it is through the piloting systems, it's through maintenance. Like, he found a way to manually deploy the shuttle with a maintenance override, and there's a couple other manual system reboots, but nothing like what you want." After a moment he tacked on "Sir".

"Hmmm." Filymon rubbed his chin in thought. "Well... I'm glad to hear you've been working hard on it. So what's next? You got any ideas?"

Seamus rubbed his tired eyes, using his hands to hide a sigh of relief. He hadn't dared hope for such an outcome. Every scenario he had envisioned led to him being punished horribly. As he pulled his hands away, he had to force himself to keep his voice even and full of remorse. "Not good ones, Master. Like I said, I found a maintenance manual in the computer, so as I get into it, maybe I can find some other ways to manually access some systems. The only other thing I could think of is to see if there was a computer network I could get on and search for tips on getting manual access on this ship model. But from what everyone's said, I bet it would be hard to find."

"It would be, and, I'd rather you not. The Romians keep a close watch on all the nets. If anyone dared to put such a thing out there, it would be shut down and investigated within the day. No, that kind of information is held closely."

"I saw the maintenance records. This ship has had three light and one heavy maintenance visits to a shipyard. The software's been updated probably thirty times. Is there any chance your maintenance team would know? Is there anyone you trust we could ask?"

Filymon shook his head in the negative. "Rom is tight on maintenance teams for the same reason it's tight on pilots. They can suppress most any resistance by keeping everyone ignorant." Seamus couldn't understand the next few words Filymon grumbled, but he imagined they were curses.

Seamus didn't see an answer. "Sir, I can fly this or any other ship manually with enough practice, but I'm not a computer expert. I don't know how to hack computers. There is probably some easy way to access it, maybe a code or something. Maybe I will stumble on it, but if Epaphras never did in his two years, I'm not sure if I will be able to anytime soon." When Filymon's eyes narrowed, Seamus quickly added, "But I'm going to keep on it as best as I can, Sir!"

Filymon grunted unhappily. "I didn't expect to have to find a computer expert too. Quivers! This is getting a whole lot more expensive than I planned... and it's already more expensive than I planned, I say." As Filymon ground his teeth together, Seamus' nervously wondered what he might do.

Just then the ship's computer announced they had achieved orbit. Seamus took the opportunity to turn away from Filymon's grumpy scowl and to perform the regular shutdown sequences. At least with something to do, he didn't have to think about Filymon losing his temper. Or the shocker.

The computer buzzed a warning at his touch, and Seamus recoiled in surprise.

"We're not just floating in orbit here at Kollos." Filymon sounded exasperated. "I've got a slip at the *Phrygia Marina*. It's where I have all my servicing done. While we're down on the ground, the bots will top off our fuel and get the exterior cargo containers off and routed."

"Oh." Once again his ignorance glared like a supernova. A moment later as the *Wander Wide* crossed over the terminator to the night side of the planet, a distant glimmer grew ever larger – obviously the marina. The silence on the flight deck felt like a volcanic fog, churning with the smothering toxic ash of disapproval, growing thicker and thicker. Once again Seamus had to will himself to stay in his seat.

Filymon finally stood. "In your spare time, do what you mentioned about maintenance overrides, and I'll see what I can do about finding a systems pirate." He paused. "We're heading straight to the ground just after we dock, so don't dally up here. We're going to be home for a few days."

As he left, Seamus fell back into his seat as if his spine had turned to jelly.

A few minutes later, a beeping drew his attention to the sprawling girders of the marina, which appeared to house maybe three dozen ships on several levels around a central hub. As the

Wander Wide eased into its assigned slip, gently thudding into place, spidery robotic arms unfolded along the girders as if in greeting. Thumps and clangs all over the hull told Seamus they must already be at work. Remarkable, he thought, how automated everything was, how easy.

This time the computer did not protest as he powered the ship's systems down, and as the instruments darkened, he hesitantly headed toward the shuttle bay toward his masters. He owned nothing, so he didn't bother heading to his quarters. Filymon and Chippus were waiting for him in the shuttle, and quickly they were on their way.

♦ ♦ ♦

Kollos was lush and green. Like home, trees and hedges seemed to denote property lines that curved with the hills, and haze muted the dark greens of the distant mountains. A wave of homesickness hit him. This looks just like Derry, he thought, and he couldn't wait to get on the ground to see if the air smelled of rain and ocean salt. After flying over a small city, the shuttle nosed toward the edge of a forest toward a small scattering of tan domed buildings, where they eased down on a landing pad on the edge of a grassy field.

Seamus found himself incredibly eager. Maybe it was because of the similarity of home or maybe how Filymon and Archippus seemed so impatient for the doors' to open. Either way, this place would be a large part of Seamus' life for the foreseeable future. Chippus bounded out to the ground and raced down a pea gravel path toward what Seamus guessed was the house. With a whoop he flew inside. Filymon followed at a more leisurely pace, pointing out to Seamus the small storage warehouse they used and a few outbuildings for other needs.

As they approached the house a few minutes later, Chippus flung the door open wide. "There he is! See, he's not much older than me!"

Behind him a woman stepped into the doorway. Like the others, she had a faint giraffe pattern running from her temples down her neck, though of a lighter shade. The hair coiled upon her head was also not quite as dark. And her dress looked more elegant than the utilitarian jumpsuits the others wore. Seamus smiled, ready to greet Lady Apphia, but as he saw her darkening expression, his own faded. She looked angrier than he'd ever seen Filymon. And even more dangerous.

"What is this... this boy?" she snapped, her eyes burning into Filymon.

"Hello to you, too, loving wife! He's Onesimus, he is. Our new slave."

"You bought a *boy*? A boy? How could you buy a boy! The credit transfer came through yesterday. I can't believe you spent half our savings on a boy!"

"He's exactly what we need, I say!" Filymon roared back. "He can fly as good as Epaphras, and unlike everyone else, he'll shut his mouth when I tell him!"

"You'd like that, wouldn't you? You'd love to quiet anyone who tells you how much a fool you are! We don't have the money for this. You do realize you could hire a pilot for ten years for what you paid?"

"Yes, but none that can fly *manually*!"

"Manually? All that means is that he can fly you quicker to your own grave! You know how I feel about this. That Deme Trius is nothing but trouble. It's funny how you're going to take most of the risk and he's going to get most of the profit."

“Well, I’ve got to do something or else give up the whole business. You know that! You run the office, you supposedly do the books.”

“At least I care about the books—”

Just then Seamus felt a hand take his. So intent had he been in watching the escalating argument, he didn’t even notice Chippus slip from the door to his side. The boy pulled him toward one of the outbuildings.

“Come on,” he whispered. “You don’t want to stay here.”

Seamus followed him into a garage where two ground cars and a truck of sorts stood, parked in the dim. Chippus flipped on a light and headed toward a work bench covered with engine parts. He plopped down on a stool. Seamus stood in the doorway looking in, hesitant to leave Filymon’s sight, but then the shouting grew louder and a door slammed with a wincing bang. Out of sight was better, he decided.

“You know, in seven years I’ll be old enough to join the army. And then I’m going to get out of here.”

Seamus didn’t know how to respond.

“It’s always like this. We’ve been away for over three weeks. It should be a happy time, but they’ve always got to ruin it. They always have to fight. I hate it. I hate them! I wish I could put one of those slave fittings on them and then shock them when they get like this. Then maybe they’d stop.”

Seamus ran his fingertips over the top of the device bolted to his spine. Any way he reached he could only just touch it, and it was too smooth and flush to get a good grip on it. It would probably kill him to do it, but he wish he could pull the cursed thing off. His thoughts returned to Chippus’ last statement and he could only disagree. He would never make anyone wear one of these, and definitely never shock them.

They sat in silence for a few minutes, both lost in thought. Seamus wondered what to say. He considered stories he could tell of his past or repeating some of the same unsatisfying pat encouragements he had heard through life. He dismissed them all and simply asked, "Do they argue a lot?"

Chippus looked over at him, his expression blank. "Every few weeks. More around holidays. Usually, it's good for a week or two, and then there's a week where no one talks and everyone avoids each other 'cause a fight's coming, then there's the fight over something stupid, then another week of silence. So maybe things will be good in a few days. And if it's not a bad fight then I won't get in any trouble."

Just then the door opened.

As if caught in mid-sentence, Chippus said, "—the shop needs to stay clean. Before we ship out again, this place needs to be..." His voice trailed off as he looked to the door. Seamus turned to see Filymon holding the door open.

"Son, let me assign his work. I've got some important things for him to do."

"Yes, sir."

"You're mother's wanting to see you. Run along and don't forget the gift you got her at the Agora." As Chippus ran out, Filymon turned to Seamus. "It looks like it will be awhile before I can start looking for someone to break into the ship's computers. So, what I want you to do is to spend as much time as possible in that shuttle out there, seeing what you can come up with."

"Sir? What if I... what if I can't?"

"Then there'd be no point. I won't need a manual pilot without a manual ship."

Seamus didn't have the courage to ask what that meant.

THIRTEEN - APPHIA

Through the rest of the day Seamus sat in the shuttle, trying to figure out some way to access some sort of manual mode. It was much more difficult than doing the same on the *Wander Wide*. His main obstacle was exhaustion. He had skipped sleep the night before and now at dusk he could hardly keep awake. And, though the *Wander Wide's* systems allowed access to many of that ship's computer files, the shuttle only had a simplistic menu-driven operating system. So far, he had yet to find any way to get past it to even find files, much less look in them. Still, he kept trying.

"Onesimus?" Seamus turned to see Chippus step through the open hatch.

"Hello, Master Chippus. Is there any way I can serve you?"

"No, just wanted to get out of the house." The boy plopped down in the copilot's chair. He started pinching the fabric of his trousers, plucking it over and over. It was obvious the boy was bothered, and it wasn't much of a challenge to guess why. Seamus figured he came to talk.

"I guess the week of silence has started?" he asked quietly.

"I hope. This fight was pretty bad. Hasn't really ended yet."

Seamus wanted to pat the boy's shoulder or something, but Rado had been quite clear that a slave never acted so familiar with his or her owners unless explicitly told to. All he could think of was to say: "I'm sorry."

Chippus looked up, his lips grimly drawn. "I'm sorry my dad has shocked you. Maybe I could hide that thing from him?"

Seamus was stunned. At first the bright rays of surprise and gratitude glowed in his emotions, but then dark clouds of suspicion rolled in. Was this a trick? Was he sincere? He finally settled on somewhere in between those two extremes, but the idea of getting the remote to his fitting was so tempting. Plan first, then act, he reminded himself. "Uh, I'm not sure that's a good idea, but I'm thankful for your concern, Master Chippus. I hope that as your father gets to know me, he'll realize that he doesn't need to use the shocker on me."

Just then Seamus heard a beep and Chippus glanced at his watch, reading a message floating over the face. He sounded weary as he said the next: "Mom says it's time for supper. She wants you to come too."

Seamus nodded. Of course, he would be needed to serve them.

♦ ♦ ♦

After washing up, Seamus followed Chippus to the dining room. Apphia had just set one last bowl on a woven trivet, while a tight-lipped Filymon took his seat at the head of the table. When Seamus rushed forward to assist, she waved him away with a smile. "Excuse my behavior earlier, Onesimus. I'm embarrassed I so lost my manners. That was no way to greet you. I'm Apphia, and welcome to our home. I hope you enjoy working for us."

"Yes, Ma'am. What may I do to help?"

"Oh, just take a seat right there." She pointed to the chair next to Chippus, complete with a place setting of dishes and eating utensils.

Seamus froze and looked over at Filymon, who glared at Apphia.

"Take a seat, Onesimus," she said sweetly, yet firmly, "Slaves are supposed to obey, correct?"

"Uh, yes, My Lady." He didn't add slaves never ate with their owners.

Filymon looked like he was grinding his teeth together behind his closed lips, but didn't countermand her. Slowly, Seamus slid into the chair, ready to jump up at Filymon's first glance. As she began to serve the food Apphia asked, "So, Onesimus, where are you from? Were you born a slave?"

Seamus felt like anything he might say or do might quickly lead to a horrible outcome. He had been the reason for their fight, and from their expressions and glances, it was easy to see it was far from over. And now he was being dragged into it. How could he not offend one or both of them? Yet what else could he do? "Ma'am, I'm from a place called Ireland on a small planet called Earth. It's a long way from here, outside of the Star Kingdom. It's closest to Karthlagg." He really had no idea about that, but it was the first world he'd seen.

"You mean Kaarthaagg?"

"Yes, ma'am. And to answer your other question, no, I was not born a slave."

Chippus seemed to be gobbling his food down, maybe hoping to escape as soon as his plate was empty. In contrast, Filymon barely touched his food, slowly taking each bite and chewing each morsel deliberately – which was much different than Seamus had seen before. It also sounded like his breathing angrily hissed through his nostrils.

"And just how did you become a slave? Were you sold to pay off debts or were you captured in one of the wars?"

Seamus finished his bite of a diced red vegetable that reminded him of potatoes, considering how to best answer. After a few seconds he said, “Ma’am, it’s a long story and I would not want to bore you.” When she pressed him he relented. “My parents and I were chased down by a Kaarthaaggian ship and captured.”

“What?” She glanced at Filymon with renewed anger in her eyes. “When did this happen? Where are your parents?”

“It was a couple months ago, and... and I’m not sure where my parents are. I guess they were sold just like me.” He tried to keep his voice matter-of-fact, but he failed toward the end as despair crept in.

“Tell me you didn’t know this!” she snapped at Filymon. It sounded more like an accusation than a question.

“I didn’t know the specifics, but he was legally recruited by a chartered privateer. This is how things work. You know that.”

“You disgust me! Listen to yourself, ‘legally recruited’. It might be legal, but it’s one of the most immoral things I’ve ever heard.”

The last thing Seamus wanted was to fuel another argument even if he strongly agreed with her. He stood. “Maybe I should—”

“No, please sit and eat,” she demanded. “It’s the least we can do to make up for all the terrible injustice you’ve experienced.”

Seamus looked at Filymon, silently begging him with his eyes to let him go. He never looked at Seamus, only continued to glower toward Apphia.

“May I please be excused?” Chippus said around a mouthful of food. Seamus glanced down to see the boy’s plate was empty. Without waiting for an answer Chippus was up and heading into the kitchen.

Seamus took the opportunity to escape himself, grabbing his and Chippus' plates. "Let me get these dirty dishes!" He quickly scooted through the doorway toward the kitchen after Chippus. Behind him he heard Filymon and Apphia erupt in a quarrel. As he set the dishes down, snippets echoed through: "Empty quivers, we need him!" "You're as much of a monster as they are!"

"I hate them," Chippus whispered with glassy eyes.

Seamus needed to escape. "I'm going to the shuttle." When he saw the pleading in Chippus eyes, he added, "You can come with me, Master Chippus." The boy looked like a huge weight had fallen off his shoulders.

They stepped out into a night lit by two small moons that made the gravel path glow. Insects chirped merrily, indifferent to human moods. With quick, quiet strides they made it to the shuttle and once inside they turned off the lights greeting them. Seamus knew he could never really hide, but the darkness comforted him.

They sat quietly for awhile, watching the house like it might explode at any moment. No one followed, no one looked for them. As the calm of night eased the tension, Seamus ate a sandwich he had brought with him, made with a dinner roll and what he could cram inside from his plate. All remained silent. After a short while Seamus realized Chippus had fallen asleep. He retrieved two blankets from the storage closet, carefully tilted the boy's seat back, and covered him with the blanket. He covered himself with the other blanket and tilted back in his own chair. Despite his own exhaustion, he watched the house for some time, and then finally he slept.

♦ ♦ ♦

Seamus awoke, stiff from sleeping in a chair and wrapped tight against the cool air. Dew covered the windows, diffusing the morning light to a bright gray. He flipped the shuttle's environmental controls on for some heat, and then glanced over at the other seat. Chippus was gone. "Oh, great," he muttered. Where did he go?

He glanced toward the back of the ship, surprised to see Apphia lying asleep with Chippus snuggled next to her. She had folded down the back of the rear bench to make a small bed. Seamus sighed; partly in relief the boy was safe, but also in consternation at seeing her. So far, every time he had seen her had not ended happily. But then he noticed the quilt. During the night she must have draped a blue and gold heavy quilt over him. A sense of comfort as warm as the cover replaced his apprehension.

He leaned back, reflecting on this family. As dysfunctional as his parents had seemed, they were nothing like this mess. Working here would be a minefield, for sure. Yet, as crazy as they seemed, there were moments of care and kindness toward him. He had seen concern from Filymon, if well-hidden. And Apphia had shown nothing by empathy for him. It seemed, too, that Chippus already looked to him as a confidant and maybe even a friend. Maybe he could have a good life with them and learn to like them? It seemed Epaphras had. But Epaphras had been an employee, not a slave.

A rustling behind him drew his attention. He turned to see Apphia sitting up. "Good morning," she whispered, as she rearranged the blankets to keep Chippus covered. The boy stirred but did not awaken. He mouthed a silent 'good morning' in return and quickly rose when he saw her stand. He followed her outside.

"It's been awhile since I've been camping." She stretched, arching her back and rolling her shoulders with a wince. "We used to go a lot when Chippus was younger. I guess sleeping in a shuttle doesn't really count, but it sure feels like it."

"I've never been camping, My Lady."

She smiled faintly, maybe with sympathy for him.

"But I have spent many days in cramped space ships," he added, "so I don't feel like I've missed out."

"As long as you have backaches and lack the comforts of home, I guess it counts." He chuckled for what seemed like the first time in months, at least since he had been kicked out of school. She smiled, and then rubbing her upper arms and closing her eyes, she turned to face the sun, as if to soak up its heat.

In the following silence he glanced around the compound and the surrounding countryside. It looked almost like home, and he tried to frame the sense of familiarity as if he were staying with neighbors or distant relatives in Derry. He could almost believe the illusion. Almost.

"Onesimus, I feel a need to apologize. I'm sorry you were enslaved, and embarrassed by how we've acted so far. We really are a good family, and we'll treat you well. We're just dealing with difficult times and can't agree on what to do." She pursed her lips and stared toward the horizon. "Sometimes it's hard to keep moving forward."

Unsure of how to respond he stood next to her silently, looking over the grassy field glistening with dew.

She turned toward him and began to look him over. "I'm going to town this morning, and I'll get you some things. Fil tells me the only thing you have is this jumpsuit and a few other sets of old clothes he and Epaphras scrounged up." She pulled on the fabric covering his shoulders, and then checked the size printed inside the neck of his suit. The inspection made him feel uncomfortable and babied, but he did not protest. "Do you need more room for this thing on your back?"

"The fitting? No, ma'am. I hardly notice it." Unfortunately, it was becoming truer by the day.

"You and Fil will be leaving tomorrow, so I will try to get you everything you need this morning. We haven't talked about where you'll stay here at home, but I plan to put you in Epaphras' room above the garage. It's bare now, so I'll try to get the basics right away. If you find you need anything else, just let me know."

"Thank you, My Lady. You are too kind. Honestly, I don't know what I'll need."

She nodded with understanding. "I'm heading inside. If you would please keep an eye on Chippus until he wakes. When he does, please come to the house. I'll have some breakfast ready."

"Yes, ma'am. I can help in the kitchen, too, if you need me."

She smiled at his offer. "Thank you, but no. Just make sure Chippus doesn't run off to play army in the woods."

As she left, one thing she had said chilled him: he and Filymon would be leaving tomorrow. And it sounded like it was just the two of them. Already he could see Apphia – and Chippus to a lesser degree – was a moderating influence on Filymon. If so, how would Filymon treat him while they were alone?

FOURTEEN - MASTER

That night Seamus slept in his new room, Epaphras' former apartment above the garage. It was comfortably, if simply, furnished, though odd to his Earth-born eyes. Like half buried spheres, all the buildings on the compound had domed roofs and circular stucco walls, and so the ceiling curved to the floor, causing him - unnecessarily - to continually check his headroom. At first glance it seemed to him like most of the floorspace would be useless, but he soon began to appreciate the cleverly designed furniture. The doubly-deep lower drawer on the dresser, for instance, rolled out on casters to reveal dozens of cubby holes. Similarly, his bed had a built-in nightstand filling in the gap from the curvature of the wall.

He was pleased with Apphia's purchases. So many things he had taken for granted in his former life were now nearly priceless to him. He was overjoyed to find a toothbrush, and the comb was nearly as appreciated. Apphia had also bought him about two weeks of clothing in the both the loose tunic style most of the humans wore and the utilitarian jumpsuits. He had everything he needed, and it really felt good to actually have something he could call his own, even if it were at the whim of his owners.

♦ ♦ ♦

The next morning he awoke to a beeping from the watch he had been given. When he picked it up, Filymon's face filled the tiny screen. "Empty quivers, boy! You're still asleep? We're going to be off schedule if you don't get yourself moving. I've got a load of cargo to get to Galatiana, I say, and I'm not about to let a lazy slave cause me late penalties! Meet me at the shuttle in ten minutes or I'll—"

"I'm on my way, Master!"

The next was a blur. Seamus threw on his clothes, brushing his teeth as best he could the entire time. Thankfully, he had packed the night before, so he was out his door in five minutes. As he raced across the grass to the landing pad, he saw Chippus waving from the house. He waved in return as he climbed into the shuttle, and as soon as he was inside, the engines began to whine.

"Hurry up, boy!" Filymon shouted from the front, as Seamus stowed his duffel bag. "I've done the preflight. Let's get moving."

Seamus buckled in and, despite Filymon's huffing, performed his normal preflight checklist. He knew the automated systems did all this for him, but hundreds of simulated deaths on the training program of his parent's ship had taught him to always be careful. "Live engines in five seconds," he said.

"Finally!" Filymon grunted as the shuttle lifted off the ground, heading skyward.

Seamus caught his breath as the sky darkened with altitude, and just as they hit orbit, he happened to see the time on his watch.

It was nearly an hour *earlier* than their planned departure time.

Fury boiled up within him. Janey Mac, what a jerk! Fear of retribution and the desire to scream at Filymon wrestled for dominance. He counted to ten, trying to calm himself. Finally, when he had mastered his emotions, he said, “Master Filymon, I noticed the time. Did something move up our lift-off?”

“I was ready to go,” he snapped. The next was quieter: “Ready to leave.”

Ready to go? The thin calm he had achieved evaporated in a flash. His voice quaked with anger: “Sir, I’ll be ready anytime you tell me to be ready. I would have been ready if you had told me you wanted to leave early.”

“You should be ready all the time.”

Seamus tightened his grip on the stick so hard his knuckles bulged white. “That’s not fair,” he mumbled.

“What?”

“That’s not fair! How can I do a good job if you change your mind all the time? How can you say I’m making you late, when you change the time we’re leaving without telling me?”

“Watch your tone, boy! I’ll not have a slave talk to me like that. You hear me!”

Seamus looked straight ahead, hardly noticing the ever growing tangle of ships, girders, and service bots that was the *Phrygia Marina*. Tears blurred his vision, but he blinked them into submission, unwilling to let this tyrant see him cry. I will get him, he thought. He’ll be sorry he did this to me. The *Wander Wide’s* docking cradle extended from the open bay, gently caught them, then pulled them inside. Without a word or even an acknowledgement, Seamus threw off his chair restraints, grabbed his duffel, and marched out into the bay, heading to his quarters at a fast clip.

After Epaphras had left at Effizus, Seamus had taken over his quarters, which, in addition to the regular amenities, had a small computer station where he could easily check the ship’s condition and progress. From here he initiated the preflight sequence with angry stabs of his fingertips on the glossy screen, and then started unpacking. Both tasks were finished at roughly the same time, and he stomped up to the flight deck to get the ship underway.

Departure had already been granted by Traffic Control, so Seamus keyed the okay to proceed. "Live engines in five seconds," he announced ship-wide, trying to sound as insolent as possible. He wished he had some measure of manual control, because he would gun the engines if he could. He chuckled at the mental picture of Filymon plastered against the bulkhead from high acceleration. Instead, the *Wander Wide* gracefully backed from the slip, angled away from the marina, and headed toward the hypertrack under computer control.

Thankfully, Filymon didn't come to sit in or supervise, and the next couple hours to the hypertrack were quiet and uneventful. Seamus sat there for awhile, watching black space and the occasional glimmer of some bit of debris skipping off the deflection field. He half-heartedly worked on cracking the ship's systems with the same results as always. And, finally, the Romian picket came into view, hovering around the entry to the hypertrack to Galatiana. Seamus watched as the *Wander Wide* automatically transmitted destination and cargo manifests to the armored ships and the returning permissions. And a few minutes later after a computer-announced countdown and a flash of bluish light, they were in the hypertrack, clocking light years by the day.

This work done, Seamus stood to head to the engine room to check the readings on the real space engines. Before he left, he slightly adjusted the pitch and height of Filymon's seat, and the length of the seatbelt. He chuckled to himself as he walked out, thinking of the irritation this would cause his master.

♦ ♦ ♦

The rest of the day wore on with the drudgery of mindless tasks that didn't really need to be done, overshadowed with anger and frustration. He ran diagnostics and simulations on all the equipment, checked fluid and power levels, compared test results against baselines, cleaned, and so on. What really bothered him was the silence. Before now, there had always been the noise of conversation somewhere. But now the engine room echoed only silence or his own clangs and mutterings. Yet it wasn't just the silence, it was the loneliness it represented. He tried everything he could think of to lift himself out of his foul mood, finally succeeding by humming a song from his favorite singer. Time seemed to quicken as he hummed other remembered tunes, and it struck him how much he missed music from home.

By midday, with nothing left to do and a hungry belly, Seamus walked up front toward the galley. Not only did he want food, he wanted some music. Surely, there were music files on this ship that he could pipe into his quarters or the engine room. He paused at Filymon's door wondering if he should bother asking. From inside he heard voices, and then Filymon's typical swearing. It was probably the worst time ever to ask, but he knocked anyway.

A muffled shout: "Come!" Seamus thumbed the control and the door slid open. Filymon sat at a desk in a small office area adjacent to cabin, his back to the doorway. A woman's face filled a small screen on the far wall. She seemed to be reciting figures or something. Filymon had a remote in hand, which he pointed at the screen like a weapon. The woman froze. "Break my last arrow," he muttered, and then turned with a snarl on his lips. "What do you want?"

"I'm... I'm sorry. It's obviously a bad time."

"Arrrr," he muttered, shaking his head and dismissively waving at the screen. "My agent in Galatiana. Always full of good news. I need to fire her and get a new one, an agent who knows people and can get me some work." He rubbed his face then motioned toward a chair between the office and the bed.

"What's wrong?" Seamus asked as he took a seat.

Filymon looked at him for a moment, indecisiveness in his expression and then resignation. "The message courier out of Galatiana came this morning, and I've been going through the mail. My agent there sent me a report on the cargo lined up for our return journey, and it won't hardly pay for the trip back."

"What does that mean?"

"It means either we go home on schedule and make nothing for our trouble, or we stick around in Galatiana hoping for some more cargo. But I can't do that for very long or else I'll pay late penalties on the cargo I've got."

"If I may... would lowering your asking price get some more business?"

Filymon snorted. "It's not my asking price. I'm already lower than the going rate, and I've locked up most all the business coming from or through Kollos. I'm as low as I can realistically go. There's just not enough cargo going back through to Kollos. Galatiana exports raw materials mostly, and raw goods don't go down the G-K-E route no more, except for some local construction. No, the problem is that I have good contracts that make money going to Galatiana, but I don't have good enough contracts to make money on coming back. And there's not that much one-load business to pick-up and make up the difference."

Seamus was no expert in business, but even he saw the flaw in Filymon's thinking. If lower costs weren't an incentive, then something else must be more important to businesses based in

Galatiana. He remembered what Epaphras had told him about the recently discovered hypertrack directly linking Galatiana to Effizus, and how the new route bypassed the intermediate stop at Kollos, cutting a day off the journey. It was obvious to him the Galatis must value the time savings of the new route over the money savings Filymon offered on the old one. But Filymon didn't see it that way. To him it was a matter of finding the right contract terms or a new agent.

Seamus also remembered Epaphras said he had tried to convince Filymon to move his operations to the new route, but Filymon hadn't seen any need to change. So as far as Seamus was concerned, it was Filymon's own fault he was in this predictament. And it really wasn't his problem, anyway.

"I'm sorry, Master." It sounded sincere.

"Ah, it's just the way of the hunt sometimes." He touched his forehead then waved open-palmed toward a silver statue of Artimiss sitting on his dresser. "Bless my hunt, mighty one." After a moment of bowed silence he looked up. "So, what do you need?"

"Um, well, I was wondering if there was some music I could listen to while I worked?"

"Music? I'm dealing with all this and you're asking me about music?"

"Uh... sorry, I just thought—"

"Why don't I put on a play for you, too? Get out of here! Get back to work, you lazy deadbeat! And don't bother me about such nonsense again, I say!"

Seamus marched from the room, fuming and cursing silently, wanting to tell off that... that right maggot. How dare he treat him like that! All Seamus had done was worked and worked. He marched into the galley, made himself some lunch, and sat down, deliberately taking his time with each bite.

Half an hour later, Filymon nearly walked past, heading toward the flight deck. He paused, glaring, then sputtered, "Get up and get moving, you hear me? Or I'm getting my remote and teach you how to behave. Now, I told you to spend your spare time figuring out how to fly this ship manually. Not to lounge around!"

Seamus shoved back from the table, leaving his clattering dishes where they lay. "Yes, sir, Master, sir!" He stormed past Filymon to the flight deck. Thankfully, Filymon didn't follow him.

For the next hour Seamus imagined knocking his master in the nose or at least telling him off. It was some time later before he cooled down. As his anger subsided, Seamus' fear grew in proportion. He should never have acted that way, no matter what Filymon said or did or how much he deserved it. In this place death came easy, and he shouldn't beg for it. How close had he come? Seamus didn't see Filymon for the rest of the day, to his relief. And as he headed to his bunk that night, he purposely avoided the man as much as possible. If it was impossible to live with Filymon, then he would live as separately from him as he could.

FIFTEEN - GALATIANA

The next day was peaceful by comparison to the previous few days. Seamus successfully avoided almost all interaction with his master. Those brief encounters seemed strained but polite. It wasn't until the ship's computer announced the upcoming exit of the hypertrack they actually sat together or had any meaningful conversation.

"Galatiana is a big system," Filymon said. "There are six populated worlds here, three planets and three moons. My hub is at one of the moons, Tavium."

Just then, the computer counted down the exit of the hypertrack, and with a flash, star-speckled black replaced the blue swirl of hyper. As icons began to fill the tactical, Seamus realized the hypertrack had dumped them relatively close to the inner system. He didn't know much about hypertracks, other than they were some sort of wormhole or shortcut through hyperspace, but it seemed like all the ones he traveled so far had terminated somewhere between the Jovian and Kuiper bands of each system. This one, however, seemed to be smack in the middle of the system's gas giants.

The *Wander Wide's* systems laid in a course toward the largest gas giant, and they were in visual range in under an hour. Seamus was amazed. The planet was enormous. He wasn't sure, but the giant was probably ten or twenty times bigger than Jupiter.

It may even be a brown dwarf, a failed star not massive enough to support thermonuclear reaction. Still, fiery glowing bands encircled the planet's surface, radiating heat and reddish light, and its moons appeared temperate with liquid oceans and atmosphere. Soon they were in orbit around one of these, an Earthlike moon, roughly equal in land and sea: Tavium. They docked at a station similar to *Phrygia*, where bots on the slip began to detach the cargo pods and route them elsewhere while others attached new containers.

"Let's go. I've got someone to see planetside." Seamus followed Filymon to the shuttle, and within a half hour they were on the ground, speeding along in a rented hover car over dirt roads cut through wilderness.

Tavium was unlike anything Seamus had seen before. The moon and the rest of the mini-solar system of its parent planet orbited a yellow star at a Mars-like distance, and so the brightness of daylight was similar to just before sunset on Earth. Yet the gas giant loomed above them, filling half the sky with red bands like glowing coals. Every object had a yellow side and a red side from the two sources of light, and shadows were faint at best under their combined illumination.

A young world with less gravity than what Seamus was used to, Tavium's mountains soared like jagged daggers, glittering in the two-tone light from the same abundant metals that were the source of most of its economy. Apparently, the only towns surrounded mines and from several abandoned clearings with a few dilapidated structures, it seemed they quickly came and went. And the rest of the planet was wild. Virgin forests rose like skyscrapers, teeming with life that darted from sight as they crested each hill, mostly enormous monkey creatures with several sets of arms and legs. These would leap from their grazing for the enormous, thinly leaved trees, scampering from sight in great screeching troupes.

Within an hour they arrived at a bustling city. Again, Seamus was amazed. To one side was the mine where both bots and exoskeleton-clad humans carried huge chunks of stone and metal to smoke-belching processors, while upwind buildings stood, jammed together in a chaotic sprawl. But they weren't buildings, exactly. Seamus could see tracked wheels on the bases of most, and others stood above them on leg-like stilts. These buildings were *mobile*. It was a whole city of stores, homes, and industry designed to relocate after the mines gave out!

With wonder he gazed at each... what would they be called? What would they look like in motion? Did they travel in orderly caravans or did they race for the best spot at the next settlement? Were they self-supporting or was there some unseen infrastructure? If only his parents could see this!

Filymon slapped the steering wheel, slamming the brakes. Seamus nearly banged his head into the dashboard before his seatbelt caught him. "Quivers, "I'd give my last arrow if they'd keep these *mobuildings* in the same place every move!" He backed up to the honking protest of a few nearby vehicles, then spun down a jagged side street, looking up more at the skyline than at the busy road. "Ah, there it is."

They parked under the stilts of a decrepit walking train of a building, next to some stairs looking more rusty than sturdy. The gravity felt about a third less than normal and Seamus fought the temptation to jump several steps at a time as they climbed. They entered an opening on the underside revealing a narrow central corridor, dusty from countless moves. Filymon led Seamus down the hallway, stopping at one with the words "Tavium Ideal Import Services" on the door.

As they waited for an answer to Filymon's knock, it struck Seamus how high the doors and ceilings rose, giving everything the illusion of narrowness. When the door opened, he immediately understood why. A woman, easily a meter taller than he, greeted Filymon by name with a warm smile. Either by illusion or in fact, she looked extremely slender, but wiry rather than thin. Her skin was white like paper with silver shading, surrounding blue-white eyes. Similarly, her hair shimmered with a metallic sheen, more white than gold.

"Hello, Delis," Filymon said. He had to reach up to shoulder level to shake her proffered hand.

"It's been awhile, my friend," she said, motioning for them to enter. Seamus stood by the door as the other two seated themselves in the small office. In contrast to the building – mobuilding – and the filthy hallway outside, the office was immaculate, kept as neat as Delis' own appearance. She sat tall and straight, looking down at Filymon, with her hands folded in her lap.

"I wanted to continue our discussion about the, uh, opportunity Deme is offering."

"What's to discuss? As you well know, the Romians have tightly regulated our commerce. All cargo is loaded at Romian marinas with Romian equipment onto Romian approved vessels. Those ships are controlled by Romian programmed computers commanded by Romian certified pilots. All along the Romian policed trade lanes, Romian naval vessels match cargo manifests with scans. And, of course, at every step of the way Romian taxes are levied to pay for all these 'services'. With the Romians everywhere, it doesn't seem like there's much *opportunity*."

Filymon chuckled. "True, all very true I say. I suppose to have any sort of *opportunity*, an established shipper with an established route and the trust of the Romians would have to have specially designed cargo containers on an unofficial manually controlled ship, flown by an unofficial manually trained pilot."

It hadn't seemed possible before, but Delis sat even straighter. "Yes... yes it would. And do we know someone with all these... qualifications?"

A slight smile came of Filymon's lips, hinting of more. Much more.

She whispered the next: "You have a pilot?" As he nodded Delis looked incredulously at Seamus.

"All we lack is for some modifications to be made to the *Wander Wide* to access its flight systems manually. I was hoping you might be able to help us in that regard."

Delis stood suddenly, twirling and pacing, yet still poised. She seemed to ignore his last statement, instead babbling to herself at all the sudden possibilities. Here we go again, Seamus thought to himself. He tuned her out, though he continued to watch her with a mindless gaze. His thoughts turned inward.

It struck him in this moment how he had changed.

When first captured, he imagined himself as a prisoner of war. Every moment he had plotted escape and revenge upon his captors. But then came slavery, and somehow it had slowly changed everything. When he had been sold, he complied outwardly, but it had been much the same: plan for escape, wait for opportunity. But as the weeks passed, and as he grew accustomed to his new life and duties, less he thought about his former life or his plans for the future. Everything was in the now. He found himself wanting to please, and to his own astonishment, wanting to see his master succeed. Even now he felt Filymon's excitement. Seamus was part – not just part, but the key player – of some great thing, either great crime or great rebellion. And he *wanted* to be part of it. The purpose it gave him was overwhelming, so overwhelming it continually pressed out everything else. Every day he was becoming more a slave; his inward resolution eroding away until soon it would consume him: body, mind, and heart. And he hated it.

What have I become?

An eruption of laughter pulled him from his pensive thoughts. Both Filymon and Delis were standing, shaking hands, beaming. Filymon's voice boomed, "Now you'll let me know first thing when you find someone who can help us with the ship?"

"Yes, yes, of course!"

After a few more pleasantries they were out the door and soon in the hover car, heading back to the small space port where the shuttle waited.

Filymon was in a good mood, the best Seamus had seen so far. His tan skin nearly glowed, warm and golden, and his spots were a lighter shade than usual. "That went well, went well, I say. Did you hear her? Delis is even going to help in any fees we have to pay for someone to – what did you call it? hack? – the *Wander Wide*. I hope she can find someone soon. I'm sure she can. With all these mobuildings breaking down all the time, surely someone around here can get into a ship's computer."

Seamus didn't share his mood, but smiled and answered enthusiastically.

♦ ♦ ♦

By that afternoon they were back on the ship, and Filymon was even more joyous in that his formerly worthless agent had picked up one more order. He nearly danced as he walked, knowing the return trip would turn a profit. From the illumination of his earlier realization, Seamus tried not to share too much in his excitement, but it was hard not to. It seemed that Filymon's mood – good or bad – affected everything and everyone around him.

Unfortunately, his good mood was short-lived.

When the last cargo pod had been attached, Filymon had ordered for them to head home, and in the early evening they were on their way. As with most hypertracks, a stream of ships moved in line to enter, slowly approaching the invisible point that only revealed itself with the blue electrical flash of a transiting ship. The route to Kollos wasn't as crowded as others, but still a dozen ships cruised forward. As Traffic Control had updated the *Wander Wide* for number eight in queue, suddenly the power flickered and they slowed to a crawl.

"Master!" Seamus shouted. "The ship! The engines!"

Filymon thundered onto the flight deck. "What happened? What did you do?"

"I didn't do anything! We were just moving along and then everything died!"

Just then a message printed on the main screen, accompanied by a voice over the intercom: *"Interdiction Notice. Stand down and await boarding."*

"Quivers!"

"What? What's happening?"

"The Romians! They suspect something. They're coming out and going to send over a boarding party."

Seamus' heart started to race. Had the Romians learned of Filymon's plans? Had Delis turned them in or been discovered? His dread colored his voice: "How did they find out about us?"

Filymon whipped him around. "Now listen to me, boy. It's not just us. Look! All the ships have stopped. Their scans must have come up with something, but they're not sure which ship. Now, if they board us, you got to keep a level head! You hear me? Don't go saying anything about our plans! Look at me now, look at me! Just answer all questions like we're doing normal business, which we are. Got that?"

"Yes, sir. I will, sir!"

Just then a Romian cruiser came into view, heading their way down the line of awaiting ships. It was huge and oblong with a rounded top and a flat underside. Hanging out from the sides were large guns, dozens on each side. Each had a shield surrounding the turret, interlocking with the shields of adjacent gun turrets. The result was that each side of the ship had a thick umbrella of a shield, studded with guns. Seamus imagined that this Romian ship could be in a firefight for hours and the main hull of the ship would never feel a graze.

"Look, boy, see? They're scanning each ship."

Seamus watched as a hint of greenish light danced over each hull. Just as the cruiser reached it, the ship two ahead of them bolted away toward the hypertrack. Seamus nearly jumped out of his seat at its sudden escape. It dove under the ships ahead of it, using them as shields between them and the Romian cruiser.

"They've gone manual! They're running for it!" Filymon exclaimed. The ship looked much like the *Wander Wide*, its engine nozzles ablaze with full burn. The way they were moving Seamus thought they might make it to the hypertrack in less than a minute. Would they get away?

The cruiser angled away in pursuit, away from the line of remaining ships, taking them out of the line of fire. The intercom roared: *"By order of the Star Kingdom of Rom you are ordered to stand down and surrender your vessel! Comply immediately or we will open fire!"* A moment later a brilliant bolt of red flashed from the cruiser's chase guns, skimming over the escaping ship so close it must have singed their hull. The ship weaved evasively, always bearing toward the hypertrack.

Seamus grasped it in a moment, the flaw in their escape. There was only one way out of this system for them, one small point in space they had to reach: the hypertrack. Twist and evade they might, still they would reach a predicted point in a predicted time, and that was all a gunner needed to know. They didn't have a chance.

"This is your last warning. Stand down now!"

A moment later, the cruiser opened fire, red light splitting the black in staccato bursts. The escaping ship exploded in a white fireball, fiery chunks tumbling into the blue flashing maw of the hypertrack. It was over in seconds.

They had to wait for several hours as clean-up crews cleared the area, the shadow of the Romian cruiser crossing over them periodically as it patrolled. At every pass Seamus felt as if their eyes bored into them, searching their minds for any hint of criminal plan or activity. And at every pass Seamus imagined the *Wander Wide* split wide open from their fire. By the time they were cleared to leave, Seamus had made a decision. No matter what Filymon planned, Seamus would *never* let it succeed.

SIXTEEN - REUNITED

The *Wander Wide* entered orbit around Kollos, curving around the blue-green sphere toward night side and the *Phrygia Marina*. As the planet eclipsed the sun, Seamus sat in the darkness of the flight deck, illuminated only by the dim light the various screens and buttons provided. His mood was just as dark. And not just his. Filymon had been uncharacteristically quiet for the two-day journey from Galatiana, and the ship echoed his brooding silence.

Before their witnessing of the smuggler's destruction at the mouth of the hypertrack to Kollos, all of Filymon's plans had been optimistic and promising. But now the stakes were higher. Much higher. Seamus recalled how the Romian picket had barely warned the fleeing ship before destroying it. They hadn't even tried to disable them. It seemed the slightest provocation was all they needed to blast them to bits: no quarter, no mercy. And now after seeing this, both he and Filymon knew this could easily be their own fate. That knowledge made all the difference to Seamus. He had made a decision. Slave or not, he would have no part in this. He would sabotage this smuggling plan any way he could. Better to face the shocker than execution.

As usual, they pulled into their slip at the marina, and bots slid down the rails to unload their cargo containers and route them as needed. After shutdown, Seamus met Filymon at the shuttle, where they headed home. Reentry seemed quick compared to the long quiet of their journey. Seamus was glad to be back. Maybe seeing the rest of Filymon's family might make a difference in their moods.

As they passed over the compound, Seamus saw someone running from the tall grasses of the pasture toward the pad. Soon enough he recognized Chippus, dressed in a camouflage jumpsuit and holding a wild looking rifle. He waved as they approached and stood just off the pad until the shuttle gently touched down. As soon as the hatch opened wide enough he squeezed through excitedly.

"Dad, dad! Yesterday I saw something in the woods!"

"You did, soldier?" Filymon turned in his seat to hug the boy. "What was it? A horde of Gothan snow cats?

"No, this was real!"

"A bark deer?" Seamus wondered what that must look like.

"No, it was small and black! It had big red eyes and lots of fangs!"

"Oooo, sounds dangerous! Did you shoot it?"

Seamus could now see that Chippus' gun was no more than a homemade toy, though it looked pretty cool. He had obviously put a lot of time in to adding all sorts of tubes and knobs on it. He had even painted insignias and other wording on it.

"I'm serious!"

Filymon's amused expression wavered. "Aye? Now what happened again?" Seamus paused in his shutdown sequence.

"I was walking along the creek, going up to my fort, when I saw it at the rocks looking at our house. I tried to sneak up on it, but when it saw me, it ran away back into the woods. I've been patrolling all day yesterday and today trying to catch it!"

"Hmmm... it wasn't a low bear, was it? It's a little far from the mountains, but they've gotten down this way before." Chippus shrugged and Filymon rubbed his chin as he stood. "Well, at least it ran off. Don't go out there again until I can go with you to take a look." The pair of them exited, walking toward the house.

"Well, I guess I'll get all the luggage," Seamus muttered as he finished shutdown. He pulled the straps of all the bags over his shoulder and purposefully smashed Filymon's duffel into the side of the hatch as he stepped through.

A few minutes later after dropping off Filymon's bags at the house and being dismissed, Seamus headed to his room above the garage. He walked into the door and headed for the stairs to his right, curving with the wall above the small workshop. About halfway up, he heard a noise below. He paused, scanning the darkness below. He could hardly see anything with all the junk stacked on every flat surface. Then he saw two glowing red eyes staring up at him. Seamus tensed. That bear-thing had gotten inside!

"Seamus?" a familiar voice asked. It took him a moment to recognize it.

"Thunderblade!"

At once his little robot came out from its hiding place and raced up the stairs. Never before had Seamus shown Thunderblade so much affection. He gathered him into his arms and hugged him tightly, as tears blurred his vision.

"Seamus, I am very pleased to find you alive and well. I had calculated slightly less than even odds I would not be able to locate you again."

Seamus was so choked up he couldn't speak, but he knew they had to get out of sight quickly. He ran to the top of the stairs, the robot still in his arms like a parent with a child, but paused before entering. It took him a couple seconds, but he finally asked, "Can... can you tell if there are any cameras or anything else in there?"

"It is clear, Seamus." They entered swiftly and Seamus locked the door as soon as he had set Thunderblade on the circular table in the center of the room. Seamus sat in a chair, looking at him, the muscles in his face aching from his huge smile.

"Tell me everything that's happened! What about Mom and Dad? Where are they? How are they doing?"

Thunderblade didn't answer right away. "Seamus, I apologize, but I have failed to locate your parents. Forgive me."

Seamus' smile evaporated. "What happened?"

"It would be best if I began from the beginning."

Seamus nodded as dread filled his chest.

"During our capture by the Kaarthaaggian privateer *Rreennzeesstt*, I had been severely damaged by one of the Kaarthaaggians." Seamus remembered Thunderblade being swatted away while bravely trying to distract the shark that had discovered him, and he had been damaged even before then. He looked the robot over, noticing new scratches and dents, as well as some patches with neat weld lines.

"My first priority is for your safety, but I was nearly incapacitated. I managed to get off the cutter and into the cargo hold, where I took 2.34 days to make repairs to stay operational. After reaching minimum operational parameters, I began a schedule of accessing their computer systems, using the ductwork to scout for you, and performing further repairs on myself. On the third day I located you in your holding cell, where you were recuperating from translation chip implant surgery."

"You found me? W—why didn't you say something?" Anger and betrayal flashed to the surface like a solar flare.

"Your cell was being monitored, and at that point I had not been successful in interpreting the Kaarthaaggian systems or their intentions. Another factor was your health. They appeared to be very interested in your recuperation. I determined observation was the most optimal course of action until I had greater understanding and you were completely recovered. It was not until you had provided the Kaarthaaggians with a language reference that I was able to understand their systems." The robot opened a panel on its side. "I was able to obtain six of their translation chips and install them. They have become valued additions to my hardware."

"Six?"

"I only use one for translation purposes. The other five I use to expand my computational resources. I have had to greatly expand my programming in order to meet the challenges of my new operational parameters."

"I can imagine. So, go on. What happened to Mom and Dad?"

"As far as I could determine they were never on the *Rreennzeesstt*. However, there is a gap in my intelligence during the first 2.34 days while I repaired myself, plus an additional four days before I had completely scouted the ship via the ductwork. In retrospect, my priority should have been to scout the ship. At the time, accessing the ship's systems had appeared to have a slightly greater chance of success in finding your location and the intentions of our captors."

"It's okay; you didn't know," Seamus said. He stared off in thought, back to his time with the sharks. "Their captain said something about them being on another ship, but I thought he was lying."

"It is possible there was a second ship. There is a week where my intelligence is incomplete, and their systems appear to lack our standards of record keeping. I am unable to reconstruct much of that time."

Just then Seamus' watch beeped; Apphia's name blinked on the tiny screen. "Stay quiet," Seamus warned Thunderblade. "This is a communicator. It's visual, so stay out of sight too." Once Thunderblade had hid himself, Seamus answered. "Yes, M'Lady. How may I serve you?"

"Supper is ready, Onesimus, if you would please join us."

"I'll be down to help right away."

She smiled, shaking her head. "No help is needed, just come eat. You may be Filymon's slave, but you're not mine." Off screen he could hear Filymon snapping at her about her comment. He wondered about it himself.

Seamus paused for a moment before deciding to answer in a way where it was apparent he was following orders like any good slave should. "Yes, My Lady. As you wish. I will wash up and be down in a couple minutes."

After the connection closed he turned around, looking for Thunderblade, who came out from under the table. He began to order him to stay out of sight until he returned, but caught himself. He wouldn't treat Thunderblade like that anymore. He wanted to apologize to him, but he didn't have time now.

"Thunderblade, I need to go. Will you please stay here out of sight?"

If the toy robot had noticed his phrasing he didn't show it. "I will, Seamus."

Seamus washed his hands and face quickly and raced to the house, where the others were just sitting down. He waited against the wall until Apphia asked him to sit. He glanced toward Filymon, who as every time before, glowered at Apphia. He sat quietly, trying to draw as little attention as possible.

As she scooped out food on their plates, Apphia asked, "So how was Galatiana? Business picking up there?"

Filymon was hard to read. With little emotion he answered, "Steady. Had enough to pay for the trip back." He paused as if considering something. "And it looks like things are progressing with our long term plans too."

She halted in her serving, a slight scowl coming to her face. When she resumed, the gentleness of her movements had fled. She moved rigidly.

He continued around bites. "Aiolos City moved again. I say, they need to move their landing pad too. It's getting over an hour away."

Seamus realized Filymon had no intention of sharing about the Romians destroying that fleeing cargo ship. Obviously, he was having a hard enough time already in selling his wife on his plans without mentioning inconvenient facts like Romians blowing up smugglers.

"So, Onesimus, how did you like your first visit to Galatiana?"

Seamus continued to chew a bite much longer than necessary to buy himself more time to think. Should he tell her? Filymon would be furious, but getting killed was worse. He swallowed. "It was really exciting. Tavium was an amazing place, but that was nothing next to seeing the Romians in action."

Chippus sat up straight. "You saw the Romians?"

"I think so." He looked over at Filymon. "Master, wasn't that a Romian that blew up that cargo ship?"

Chippus whipped around "You saw a space battle?!?"

At the same time Apphia spun around toward Filymon. "You haven't said anything about this!"

Filymon glared at Seamus as he answered her calmly. "While we were in line for the hypertrack, some stupid shipper got crazy and ran from an inspection. When he didn't stand down, the Romian picket opened fire on him."

"And you saw it blow up?" Chippus asked with awe. "What did it look like? Was it big? Did any of it hit the *Wander Wide?"*

Apphia gasped deeply. Filymon sputtered, "No, twasn't even close to us! Look, these things happen every so often. The Romians inspect all the time. If you comply with their orders, there's no trouble, no trouble at all."

"Unless they find something," Apphia grumbled.

"That's right, *if* they find something! Look, look at me. I just got home and I don't want to talk about this right now."

"That's the problem, Fil. You never want to talk about this. You're either winding down from a trip or getting ready for one, so there's never anytime to talk!"

"Try as I might, I can't help if my work doesn't leave much time for home."

"Well, I can fix that!"

"And how do you suppose you'll do that?" Filymon spat.

Apphia stood. "I tell you how. On this next trip, I'm coming with you!"

SEVENTEEN - DETAILS

In the weeks he had been with Filymon and his family, Seamus had learned the best barometer of an impending knock-down-drag-out fight was Chippus. As soon as his mother had announced her intentions of traveling with Filymon, the boy impossibly crammed all the food on his plate into his mouth in one bite, mumbled something about 'excused', and then flew out of his chair and into the kitchen.

"Let me get these dishes!" Seamus exclaimed a bit too quickly and loudly, and with a clatter of plates and silverware swiftly followed after the boy. As soon as he bolted from the room it sounded like World War IV had begun.

Seamus didn't wait around. He carried his plate out of the house and up to his room. After locking the door behind him he sat down with a huff. "They're crazy," he muttered, then said, "Thunderblade, I'm alone. You can come out."

The bottom rolling drawer of the dresser opened and the robot climbed out. With a whirl he was into 'copter mode, then quickly back into humanoid form on the table opposite Seamus. "This culture must have curious eating customs."

"You have no idea."

"Do you wish for me to continue my report?"

"Please," Seamus said as he took a bite. He was happy it was still warm.

"After the Gothan snow cat, Löwin, arrived and you began planning escape, my intention was to support your efforts. Unfortunately, we arrived at Kaarthaagg before you made an attempt. My preparations were not in vain, however, as I had become able to access your files and make alterations. This is how you were sent here instead of to their ruling council for interrogation. And from the surveillance programs I put in place, it appears the Kaarthaaggians have been unable to uncover what happened."

"And Löwin? What about her?"

"She is begrudgingly serving as a household security officer for a Romian plebiscite, waiting."

"Waiting for what?"

"For us, of course. The only way she would agree to servitude was in the promise of helping you escape and save our world from conquest by the Romians. It seems the hope of such honor is staying her desire to rip her masters to shreds."

"You mean she still has her claws and fangs?"

"Her owners think otherwise, but, yes, she did when I left her."

Seamus sat quietly, contemplating the beginnings of a true plan of escape. It would require getting to Rom, breaking Löwin free, finding transport to Kaarthaagg so they could track down his parents. And from there get back to Corvis 2267.

It seemed impossible.

When he said all this to Thunderblade, the robot disagreed. "Löwin assured me she would have her own escape ready within the next few months. Before I left I devised as simple signal for her to let us know she is ready, and a way for us to signal her to execute her plan. I calculate the odds of her success to be 90.7%. She is quite capable, you know."

"I bet. What about transportation?"

"You are a highly prized manual pilot. It would not be difficult for me to set up a counterfeit ship registry and corresponding transponder codes for any ship we were able to obtain. As long as we do not attract too much attention to ourselves, I calculate we have reasonable odds for success."

"If Filymon would go back to Rom for even a few days, I bet I could get the *Wander Wide* and be gone long before he even knew about it. The problem is that we don't have manual access."

"I have been able to access most Romian systems. If I could get aboard the *Wander Wide*, I should be able to get you manual access."

"You could? Wow, if that's the case, then all we'd have to do is get to Kaarthaagg and find out where my parents are."

Thunderblade kept silent.

"What? You don't have any ideas on finding my parents?" Seamus had never seen Thunderblade pause like this before. "What? What is it?"

"I am navigating a potential logic paradox. I have been instructed by your parents to protect you. To stop at Kaarthaagg alone would decrease the odds of successful escape and thus violate that directive. It is probable that if information of your parent's location is obtained at Kaarthaagg, we may have to return to Rom or elsewhere in the Star Kingdom, which significantly impacts the odds of your continued survival."

"But we'll have to go there anyway to find out how to get back to Corvus!"

"No. I accessed the *Rreennzeesstt's* navigational logs while onboard and know exactly how to return to Corvus 2267. It was one of my top priorities."

"I don't care! I'm not going to leave my parents as slaves in this horrible place!"

Just then Thunderblade whipped around toward the door and then jumped to the floor and back to his hiding place in the roll-out drawer. It wasn't until he heard a knock at his door a few moments later that Seamus understood what was happening.

Oh, no... Who was it? What had they heard?

Seamus opened the door to see Chippus, eyes red and face streaked with dust and dried tears.

"Onesimus, can I come in?"

"Uh, sure."

The boy came in and plopped down on the bed. "I was down-stairs in the shop working on my gun when I heard you up here. So I thought I'd come up to see what you were doing. It sounded like you were talking to someone."

Seamus felt his face redden. "Oh, I was... uh... I was just..." His mind raced. There was nothing in his room for entertainment, nothing with video or music. What would he say? "Uh, I was just talking... to myself. Um, reciting lines."

Chippus wiped his nose with his forearm and a sniff. "Lines? For what?"

"A play. Well, not really a play. Sometimes I think of scenes and I try acting them out."

"Oh really, can I see one?"

"Uh, I don't ever show people. It's just something I do for fun."

"Oh, okay." He paused pensively but then brightened. "I go out and pretend I'm a soldier sometimes, but you can come with me sometime if you want to."

Seamus wasn't sure how to respond. He knew the boy was hurting, but Seamus had his own problems. In a formal tone he said, "I will, Master Chippus. Is there anything I can do for you tonight before I turn in?"

Chippus looked up at him and Seamus could easily see disappointment on his face. "No," he whispered, standing. He walked to the door. "Good night, Onesimus."

Seamus knew better, but he chose to let him go. "Good night, Master."

A few minutes later, once he was sure Chippus had gone, Seamus opened the drawer where Thunderblade was hiding.

"Your Master Chippus shows behavioral similarities to you at that age, usually when you had been in conflict with your parents or a schoolmate."

Seamus didn't want to talk about it. "Talk quieter! Now, back to what I was saying. We *are* going to rescue my parents whether you like it or not. What else do you have to say about our escape?"

"During the hiatus, I formulated a strategy that may provide the information necessary to find your parents without endangering you further. I have already created several surveillance programs on the Romian nets to ensure our protection and anonymity. I will create more to search for information about your parents."

Seamus nodded. It was better than anything for right now, and Thunderblade did have a point about the dangers of going to Kaarthaagg blind.

"One other consideration is your fitting. We will have to find a way to either remove it or neutralize its effects."

Seamus ran his hands over the flexible device on his spine. He had gotten used to it so much he hardly thought about it anymore. Most of the time.

"In my research I have not been able to determine a way to remove it. They are very cleverly designed devices. The only way to access their circuitry is from the side touching your skin, which is impossible without proper removal."

"Which is the point. So how are they normally removed?"

"According to the operation manual, the only way to remove it is for your owner to input his own code into the remote. Without that code you will never be able to remove it. The only other option is for you to get the remote and keep it with you always to ensure you never strayed outside of your free operation zone."

Seamus sighed in near defeat, running his hands through his hair. "I suppose I could get the remote. Well, actually, Chippus offered to steal it for me, once. I bet I could get him to do it." He thought for a few seconds. "Is there any way you could get another remote that looked just like it? One that I could swap?"

"It is possible. I will begin searching for options."

"And there's one other thing I thought of. You said you could get manual access to the *Wander Wide*?"

"Almost certainly."

"Once you did, could you keep anyone else from getting it?"

"I would be able to make it much more difficult. Though more advanced than Earth, Rom's technological knowledge is closely guarded. Typical security is much less sophisticated."

"Well, let's do that. My crazy master has some eejit idea of using the *Wander Wide* for smuggling, and Rom likes to blow up smugglers. When I couldn't find a way into the *Wander Wide's* manual systems, he put someone in Galatiana on it. I'm sure the next time we're back there will be someone waiting to take a shot at it." Thunderblade agreed, and with all this settled Seamus got ready for bed. He had one last thought: "Thunderblade, you talked about the operating manual for a slave fitting. Could I see it?"

"I have it and everything else Rado gave Filymon on file. Once I have access to the *Wander Wide's* systems, I will ensure you have access."

♦ ♦ ♦

Seamus slept horribly. He awoke often, his mind racing with ideas and plans. As often in such cases, he slept best right just before being awakened. His watch beeped a dozen times before he was coherent enough to answer it. It was Apphia calling him to breakfast. He joined them in that awkward post-fight quiet, which, half-asleep, he didn't mind today. After a near-silent breakfast of tart greenish pancakes with a yellow fruit sauce, Filymon told him to go out and play with Chippus – and to watch out for low bears. Seamus was in such a foul mood he almost told Filymon that he was fourteen and hadn't "played" in many years. He held his tongue, however, and went outside.

Chippus seemed to come alive as soon as the door shut behind them. He danced around him like a dog eager for a walk. "Onesimus, here, which gun do you want? This one is my favorite, but you can use it. We'll go patrol for the bears and then secure the base. Oh, I want to show you my fort! Have you ever had a fort? I've been working on mine for a couple years now, well months, actually, since I turned eight. My dad wouldn't let me go out by myself until I turned eight..."

Seamus soon realized his best strategy to calm the boy was to agree immediately with his first suggestion and then to get straight to it. With Chippus' favorite gun in hand – a taped-together collection of gray painted pipes and other spare parts – he and the boy trotted out into the pasture, pausing in silence occasionally to listen for bears.

When he asked him about "bears", Chippus described something much smaller than what Seamus had first imagined and apparently more timid unless cornered; something like a badger. With this main concern alleviated, Seamus actually began to have fun. They covered each other during an imagined attack and raced into the woods, ducking behind trees as they pressed in on their pretend enemy.

Several adventures later they reached Chippus' fort. It was more like a platform hanging off the top of a small hill, affixed in the corners to two trees. Under the platform was the "fort", dug into the side of the hill with old limbs lashed together to form walls. The platform above was the "lookout". Here, Chippus proudly described his fort's merits and his plans to improve it. Seamus complemented it, and even had a suggestion for a flagpole. Chippus liked the idea and as he talked about flag designs, Seamus sat on the platform gazing out into the woods.

Should he ask Chippus to steal the remote from Filymon?

From just the thought of it he felt horribly guilty. Slave or not, the boy looked up to him and treated him as a friend. But if it were his only chance of escape...

"Chippus, remember that time when...?"

"When what?"

"When..."

He couldn't do it. He'd have to find some other way. "Never mind, I remember now." He was thankful Chippus didn't press him. But now the obvious question loomed in his plans. How would he get the remote?

EIGHTEEN - RESPONSES

The next several days were some of the most fun yet also the most maddening Seamus had experienced in some time. The fun came from being ordered to play with Chippus instead of any other duties. They didn't say as much, but it seemed to Seamus that Filymon and Apphia either liked the idea of a baby sitter for their son or else they didn't want to fight in front of them anymore. Or maybe a little of both. And so, he and the boy spent their time in the woods, playing army or working on the fort. Seamus found himself liking the boy more and more every day.

Despite all the unexpected time off, Seamus was extremely frustrated not to have time to work on his escape plans. He felt like he was under a deadline, that every day apart lessened his chances of ever finding his parents. Yet he couldn't act without a good plan, and his "plan" had some very large pieces missing. When they left for Effizus after two days at home, he hoped he would have some time alone to put more of the puzzle together, but when Apphia saw how dirty the *Wander Wide* had gotten, she immediately put them all to work. Yet even that was enjoyable, as he and Chippus joked and laughed as they tidied, cleaned, and painted. The only thing Seamus could point to as a positive step toward escape was in sneaking Thunderblade to his cabin, where the robot was able to use his computer station to start hacking into the *Wander Wide's* systems. By the time they reached Effizus, the robot had made a lot of headway.

Apphia wanted to see Epaphras while they were there, but it was local night when they arrived, so they slept aboard ship in orbit, docked at a busy marina. The next morning they took the shuttle down, crossing over the desert planet's bare northern hemisphere and the lone ocean at its northern pole. As they crossed over a strange grouping of white islands, Seamus asked about them.

"Oh, that's the meteor," Apphia said from one of the seats behind him.

Seamus thought he misheard her and turned more directly toward her. "*All* the islands are *a* meteor?"

Her voice sounded almost incredulous. "Why, yes... This whole planet is the result of an immense meteor impact. This ocean is inside the crater."

"And look," Chippus said pointing over Seamus' shoulder to the scrolling map on one of the screens. "Do you see her, do you see Artimiss?"

Seamus stared at the archipelago, and as if gazing at clouds in a deep blue sky, he recognized a familiar shape. Together, from a certain angle, the islands formed the image of a woman in mid-stride, bow in one hand, the other reaching for arrows in a quiver behind her back. The chain looked natural, but striking in its similarity to the many sculptures he'd seen of the Effizian goddess. "I do. How did that happen?"

Filymon glanced over at him with a storyteller's smile. "Athinsian colonists found it that way, the goddess of the hunt calling the hunters home. They built her temple right over her eye so she would always be in her sight."

"Bah", Apphia muttered. "Everyone loves to spout that story, but no one seems to recall all the selective mining and building on those islands. Sure, it looked somewhat like that, but miners and builders had about as much to do with it as nature ever did."

Seamus could feel Filymon tense up beside him. Thankfully, they were about to land. "Splashdown in ten seconds," he announced.

Ten minutes later they were moored at Filymon's dock, and after a couple hours of working in the waterfront warehouse and a quick lunch, they were parking near Tyrannus' school. Having called him ahead of time, Epaphras was waiting for them outside. Dozens of others sat on the ground on either side of the walkway, while a steady stream of people made their way into the building.

"Epaphras!" Chippus shouted as he jumped from the ground car. Epaphras hugged the boy, and then walked forward to greet them. Apphia embraced him and Filymon shook his hand vigorously. Seamus stood to one side, watching the reunion, but also glancing at the ground where the others mostly sat or laid on mats.

"Is it him?" one man exclaimed, "Is it him? Is it the mystic?" From the way the man reached and the crossed, blank look in his half-closed eyes, Seamus could tell he was blind. He took a step backwards.

"No, you fool," a woman in a parked hover chair muttered. "Can't you hear him talking inside? Or are you deaf too!"

"I say, what's his problem?" Filymon muttered out of the side of his mouth as he stepped aside, brushing away the man's fingers from the knees of his trousers.

Epaphras pulled them into the vestibule of the building, where dozens milled about or stood in conversation. "It's the most amazing thing. Sometimes when Pol walks through here,

God uses him to heal people! Now everyone's asking him for pieces of his clothing in case some of that power soaks into the cloth. Sometimes this place seems more like a hospital than a lecture hall."

"Are you serious?" Apphia asked.

"You wouldn't believe what I've seen and heard."

Filymon waved dismissively. "I don't. These are all actors, I'm sure. Nothing like a good marketing team to get the business off the ground."

Epaphras smiled and shook his head slightly. "This is no business, Fil. Pol works for Aquyia and Prazella, building custom TENTs. No one is charged here. Tyrannus lets us use the school in the afternoons when there are no classes in session. If any money changes hands it's only people helping others. Pol won't take any money."

"Doesn't sound like a promising business plan. You'd think if he could actually heal people, he'd at least make a living at it."

"Same old Fil. I can't believe I miss your money-loving crankiness."

"Well, you're the only one," Apphia laughed. Filymon smirked humorlessly.

"Truth be told, there have been some who have tried to capitalize on all this. There's this religious type named Sceva and his family, who've made quite a living, supposedly driving away evil spirits and the like. Well, just the other day his sons tried to drive out a spirit from a man, commanding it to leave in the name of 'Yeshua who Pol preaches'. Instead of leaving, the spirit said, 'Yeshua I know and I've heard about Pol, but who are you?' And then the possessed man jumped on them and beat all seven of them so severely they went running out of the house bleeding and with their clothes in tatters."

"And I suppose you believed it?" Filymon shook his head. "I bet it was staged. I know old man Sceva. If there's money in it, he'll do it."

"What money?" Epaphras asked pointedly. Filymon didn't have an answer.

Just then the speaker in the main lecture hall began and those in the vestibule hurried inside. Seamus recognized the voice as that of Pol. Seamus glanced at Filymon, wondering what he would do. He seemed to be listening.

"I for one, would like to hear this Pol," Apphia said.

"Well, only for a few minutes," Filymon muttered as Apphia led them into the lecture hall. It had only been a few weeks since they had dropped off Epaphras, but easily the attendance had doubled. Curtains had been pulled back to overflow rooms allowing more seating, and still they ended up standing in the back of the room.

On the stage Pol sat on a stool, looking and speaking as plainly as last time. His green-tan skin almost blended into the background, and like last time, his odd glasses were slightly unnerving. Seamus wondered why Pol wouldn't heal himself if he actually had the power to heal others.

"...speak today about showing reverence for Yeshua by how we submit to each other. First, let's talk about marriage. Wives, submit to your husbands as to God, for the husband is to lead his wife as Yeshua leads his followers. And as his followers submit to him, so should wives submit to their husbands in everything."

Seamus stood next to Apphia and could feel her bristle beside him in obvious disagreement. The giraffe pattern running down her neck darkened. He glanced past her to Filymon, who looked pleasantly surprised. "I may have misjudged this man," he whispered with amusement. He groaned as she elbowed him in the ribs.

Pol continued: "Husbands, love your wives as Yeshua loves his followers. Remember, he who gave himself up for us to make us holy, to cleanse us by his words, to present us to himself as a radiant community: holy and blameless, without stain, wrinkle, or blemish. In this same way, husbands ought to love their wives as their own bodies. He who loves his wife loves himself. After all, no one ever hated his own body but feeds and cares for it, just as Yeshua does for his followers – for we are in a sense members of his own body! This is a profound mystery between him and those who follow him, but following in his example, you husbands must love your wife as you love yourself. And you wives must respect your husband."

Apphia seemed to relax as he spoke, her initial expression of distrust melting into thoughtful consideration. Filymon shared the same expression, sobering from his initial amusement. Seamus was glad they would listen to someone.

Pol stood, stepping to the edge of the dais, scanning the crowd. He finally stopped, gazing at a group of children and young teens sitting together. He smiled. "Children, obey your parents as God desires, as this is right. If you honor your father and mother, God promises that your life will go well, full and enjoyable."

Some unseen man spoke out, "Listen to him!" Laughter rippled around the room.

Pol chuckled, turning toward the voice. "Fathers, now, don't you exasperate your children!" This time, the children cheered, echoed by adult laughter. "Instead, train them and instruct them in the ways of Yeshua." The man gazed around the auditorium again. As his point sunk in, contemplative silence filled the room.

All of the sudden, Seamus felt like the eyes behind the shimmering goggles had locked with his own. Staring straight at him, Pol said, “Slaves, obey your earthly masters with respect and sincerity, just as you would obey Yeshua. Obey them not only to win their favor when they watch you, but like slaves of Yeshua, doing the will of God from your heart. Serve wholeheartedly, as if you were serving God, not men, because you know that God will reward everyone for whatever good he does, no matter if he is a free man or a slave.”

Seamus felt like Pol could see right through him, right past his outward obedience and into his secret thoughts and plans. How could he know? He felt ashamed, and he hated it so badly he wanted to conceal it with anything – anger, defiance, aloofness. But the shame was greater, swallowing his feeble attempts to cover it. Finally, Pol looked away, but his gaze still haunted Seamus as much as his words.

Seamus looked out into the crowd looking for some distraction and was shocked to see dozens of fittings peeking out of the necks of slaves scattered throughout the room. He couldn't believe how many slaves were here. He wondered how many were here with their masters. As the thought crossed his mind, Pol's words followed: “And masters, treat your slaves in the same way. Don't threaten them, since you know that he who is both their master and yours is in heaven, and there is no favoritism with him.”

Seamus couldn't help himself. He turned to look at Filymon.

His master stood there, jaw set, looking straight ahead with arms folded over his chest. As Pol went on, Filymon finally turned toward Apphia, never meeting Seamus' eyes. “We got to get going,” he whispered. She nodded, and Seamus couldn't tell if she was disappointed or relieved.

He followed them out into the vestibule, where Filymon quickly said goodbye to Epaphras. "Maybe you can stay longer on your next visit," Epaphras said as they walked out. Apphia answered him, but Seamus couldn't hear since he was already getting in the back seat of the car with Chippus. Filymon impatiently drummed his fingers on the steering wheel, sighing loudly.

As soon as Apphia got into the car and they pulled off, Filymon exploded. "That was the biggest bag of lies I've ever heard. Who does this Pol think he is, trying to upset the way things are? Can you believe him, ordering everyone to live to his own narrow standards? And is he the mouthpiece for the gods?"

"Well, I can't see myself 'submitting' to all your crazy ideas," Apphia snapped. "But if you could actually be that kind of man he talked about, I might consider it."

"Oh, so I'm the one with all the problems? It's my fault you don't treat me like a good wife would?"

"Grow up. Not many people could put up with you, and I don't pretend you actually *love* me."

The only thing that shocked Seamus more than Apphia's words was how it seemed to shut down Filymon cold. He sat quietly, driving, almost as if she had overwhelmed his every defense and his mind groped for some way to respond. Finally, he quietly flipped on the auto-drive, turned, and spoke. "You know I love you. Everything... everything I do is because I love you."

"Well, you need to rethink that, because to me it looks like everything you do is because you despise me. All these choices you're making scare me. You say you want the best for us, but all I see is my husband becoming a criminal and my son endangered by just being with you. Can't you see you're destroying our family? So what if we have more money. All the money in the Star Kingdom won't matter if you're ever caught by the Romians or if some other criminals decide they don't like you. All I can think about when you leave on a trip is that you won't come back."

She started to cry. When Filymon reached over to take her hand, she pushed it away. "And our son... he so admires you, and wants to be like you."

"I.."

"Let me finish. When we got married, we were going to change the world. We both hated the Romians' corruption, their greed and cruelty. And now... and now when I look at you, all I see —" She broke off in sobs, pressing her face deeply in her palms.

Seamus looked at Chippus beside him, to see the boy crying, his face contorted in shared agony. Several long minutes passed in painful silence until the boy said, "Are you going to get a divorce?"

Another bout of weeping came over Apphia. When she had composed herself somewhat, she looked up at Filymon. He pursed his lips tightly as they stared into each other's eyes, an unspoken conversation full of measuring and consideration. Expressions danced across their faces: sadness, regret, hope, love. But then as the silence lingered on, as the question remained unanswered, new expressions emerged: questioning, disbelief, sadness, despair. Fresh tears streamed down Apphia's face. As they tumbled to the armrest between them, something like realization and determination spread over Filymon's features. He turned, looking at Chippus squarely.

"No, we're not getting a divorce. Nothing is going to destroy our family."

Without looking at Apphia, he turned back to the wheel and flipped it back into manual-drive. As they drove in silence,

Seamus watched Apphia. She often glanced at Filymon, but he couldn't tell what she was thinking.

NINETEEN – MANUAL ACCESS

That evening, after a day of shopping at the Agora, they headed back to the *Wander Wide*. Seamus' felt nervous as the shuttle eased into the docking cradle and was pulled up into the small bay. He kept telling himself that Thunderblade would easily know they were on their way as soon as he had powered up the shuttle. And surely he would have finished whatever he had been doing and found himself a good hiding place by now. But despite his inward reassurances, he couldn't help but picture the little robot being discovered in just a few moments, or at least plenty of evidence laying around that someone had been on the ship, trying to get into its systems.

And beyond that immediate worry, plans had changed. Since the whole family was on this run, Filymon had decided to take the direct hypertrack to Galatiana instead of the two-leg flight through Kollos. Filymon had said it would save so much time and would boost their profits tremendously. What he hadn't said, and what was at the forefront of Seamus' thoughts, was that Filymon's friend at Galatiana, Delis, would have a computer expert on board to hack into the ship's systems in *two days* instead of three or four days. Would that be enough time for Thunderblade to completely crack the ship's systems, where he could thwart any attempts by someone else? If not, Seamus might quickly find himself flying manual and everything that would come with it.

As the bay doors closed and the outside atmosphere and temperature readings climbed, Seamus tried to calm himself. He wanted so badly to race ahead into the ship, but he knew that would look incredibly suspicious. And he couldn't think of any good reason to ask the others to stay behind. So, quietly, anxiously, he followed the rest out of the shuttle and through the bay airlock and into the crew compartment. Lights flickered on at their movement and the only sound was that of their own footsteps and voices.

"Boy, we're turning in, but I want to be leaving here within the hour," Filymon announced as he paused in the doorway to his quarters. Behind him, Apphia dropped several shopping bags onto the bed, and then stretched.

"Yes, Master. I'll have the systems warming up and underway as soon as I can."

Only after his door had slid shut and Chippus had gone into his own room, did Seamus dare enter his own cabin. Just as he hoped, the room looked as tidy and empty as when he had left it. "Thunderblade?" he whispered.

A thump in a closet told him where the robot had hid itself. Red eyes in a bug-like face peeked from the darkness. "Hello, Seamus. I am pleased to see you." The robot looked as delighted as he sounded when he stepped out.

"Good to see you too. How'd it go?"

"I have successfully hacked into all the major systems, except one. I have also modified this ear-com so I can speak to you without others hearing."

"Good idea," he whispered as he slipped the ear-com into his right ear canal. "And that's good news about you getting access of most everything. Filymon has decided we're going directly to Galatiana, so I was worried that you wouldn't have enough time."

"We are taking the 49.7-hour direct hypertrack, instead of our registered flight plan?" The robot sounded as if he were right beside him instead across the room.

The knot of worry returned to Seamus' stomach. "That's right… why?"

"The system I have not been able to penetrate thus far is the master network, which coordinates all the other systems. I calculate a 24% chance of success in gaining control of the master network before we arrive in Galatiana. Do you anticipate the computer expert will be waiting for us?"

"I would bet so."

"If that is the case, it is more likely your master will have complete manual access before I do."

Seamus plopped down on his bunk, cradling his head in his hands. "No, no, no!" He couldn't believe this! How can they be so close only to fail? He looked up, trying to keep exasperation out of his voice. "Can you stop someone else from getting access?"

"I do not have the information to answer that question, Seamus."

They remained silent for several long moments. Finally, Seamus asked, "What would your chances be if I got us another six hours or so?"

"Our chances would improve to 38%"

"Eight hours?"

"43%"

Seamus sighed and wiped his face with his palms. "Not even half a chance." He looked up at the ceiling, contemplating what it would cost him. "But it's the only chance we've got." He huffed and began to pull off his shoes. "Thunderblade, I'm going to 'forget' to get the ship underway. When Filymon realizes it, he's going fry me with that shocker. You've never seen that before. It's a horrible experience, but no matter what, I don't want you to interfere."

"But, Seamus, one of my prime directives is to protect you from harm."

Seamus couldn't help but smile at his little friend. "I know. But the best way to protect me is to let this happen. It will be temporary and it will buy us more time to hack into that master system."

"I calculate you are correct, though I have to input my algorithms carefully to avoid a logic paradox." The robot walked toward the closet in what almost seemed like sadness. He turned at the doorway. "My programs are in work as we speak. I will return to my hiding place and monitor events from there."

"Thanks."

As the closet door closed with Thunderblade inside, Seamus decided to make this crazy plan look as good as possible. At his cabin computer, he keyed in all the commands necessary for the ship to depart, and then he lay on his bed. His story would be simple: he would forget to activate the sequence and would fall asleep. He'd even sleep in his clothes to make it look better.

Only sleep didn't come until late in the night.

♦ ♦ ♦

"ONESIMUS!"

Seamus bolted upright just as the door to his cabin slid open. Filymon stood there, red faced and chest heaving in fury.

"WHY ARE WE STILL AT EFFIZUS?"

"Uh... we're at Effizus?" he asked contritely with just a hint of disbelief in his voice. He leapt up to check his computer. "Oh, no! I'm sorry, Master. I forgot to activate the departure sequence. I'll get us underway right now." As his fingers flew over the controls he spied the time in the corner of the screen. It was better than he hoped… just over nine hours!

"What are you doing flying my ship from your cabin?!? You expected us to just sail all the way to and through the hypertrack with no one on the flight deck?!?"

"Uh, I'm sorry, sir! I mean, no, sir! I just laid in all the commands here and I was going to go up on the flight deck. I just was so tired. I must have fallen asleep!" He plucked at his wrinkled tunic to draw attention to how he had slept in his clothes.

"That's no excuse! Get us underway right this minute and once we're on the hypertrack, you're getting punished!"

"Yes, sir," he mumbled with a fearful quiver. He wasn't faking it.

♦ ♦ ♦

As soon as they were in the hypertrack, Filymon made good on his promise. He made Seamus lay down on his bed and then with a sequence of buttons on the remote, wave after wave of pain coursed through his body. He writhed in agony and his clenched teeth muffled the scream coming from lungs. Long after it ended, his skin felt like it danced with fire, his hands shook, and his muscles spasmed uncontrollably.

He hoped it was worth it.

♦ ♦ ♦

Two days later they made orbit at Tavium, the moon where Filymon based his Galatiana operations. As Seamus had feared, a tall slender man waited for them at the marina. He crouched as he walked through the airlock and his head nearly brushed the ceiling inside the ship.

As the technician and Filymon exchanged small talk, Seamus regarded him with despair. As of that morning, Thunderblade had not been able to hack into the master network. Every other system he could control manually, but the one system that made them all work together as one still remained as impenetrable as ever. Their hope now was that Thunderblade would be able to remotely shadow the technician's work, anticipate his moves, and gain access first. If he could, then possibly he could lock the technician out before he knew what happened.

"Hello," Apphia said as she walked into the ship's lounge. She smiled at the technician, but looked puzzled. "Filymon, I didn't know we were having work done while we were here."

"Uh, yes my dear. Just a minor software upgrade." He looked back at the technician. "Well, let me get you set up. I'm sure you've got a lot of other ships to get to. Say, you want me to back down the gravity to make it more like normal for you?"

Apphia grimaced thoughtfully as they exited the lounge into the flight deck, and Seamus made for his cabin before she could put him to some sort of work.

"He's here," he whispered toward the closet after his door shut. He put the ear-com in his ear, and the robot's voice answered clearly.

"I know. How do you feel, Seamus?"

Seamus lay on his bed. "Better, thanks. Tell me what's happening."

"As anticipated, he is using a generic administrator login. Untraceable."

Silence followed and Seamus stared at the paneling on the upper bulkhead, following the various lines back and forth from wall to wall.

"Clever. He is accessing the secondary memory cache so the main memory will show no traces of tampering. It appears he is searching past software upgrades."

Seamus knew Thunderblade would be able to carry on a conversation and a hundred other things while monitoring what the technician was doing. But still, he didn't want to interrupt him, didn't want to take away even one bit of computing capacity that might be used to figure out what the technician was doing and beat him at his own game.

"He has located a maintenance event from twelve years ago. It is the log of a major software upgrade. He is searching the changes made."

Seamus clasped his fingers together upon his chest and began twiddling his thumbs. He hated how powerless he felt. It reminded him of boarding school, being in detention while the bullies who started everything had gotten away with it.

"He has isolated a command string. I see it now. I know how to get access." Despite his calm, robotic tone, the pace of his words quickened. "He intends to reverse the command inducing a... hold, please. I am attempting..."

Seamus bolted upright, swinging his legs over the side of the bunk, looking alternately at the computer terminal and the closed closet door where Thunderblade hid.

"Seamus, I need your help. The technician has plugged a reader into the main access terminal and is feeding a series of commands into the system. We both have access, but I can not shut him out via computer commands. Please attempt to remove the reader. If you can do that, I... hold, please."

Seamus was out the door in a heartbeat in a near run toward the flight deck.

"Onesimus, slow down! What are you doing?" It was Apphia.

"Sorry, M'Lady." He slowed to a trot, but she followed him from out of the kitchen, looking stern.

She caught his forearm and pulled him closer, whispering the next in with a commanding tone: "What's going on up there. Tell me."

Seamus paused. He glanced at her, but he didn't have time for this, didn't have time for anything. But then it hit him. She could stop them. "I think that tech is trying to get us manual access, and I was going to go watch."

The suspicion on her face erupted into fury. She stormed past him and into the flight deck. "Filymon what are you doing? Are you getting manual access without—"

"Apphia, I say we're busy in here!"

"Manual access?" the technician exclaimed. "Sorry, I don't know how to do that, and even if I did, it would be illegal. Are you trying to ruin me? If just the rumor of this got out I'd lose my license, I'd be investigated, maybe even imprisoned!"

"I... I, then what are you...?"

Seamus tried to peek around her. The technician was on his knees at the main access panel to the ship's computer. Next to him on the floor was the reader, unplugged.

Oh, no. Seamus bolted back to his cabin. "Thunderblade? Thunderblade, what happened? Did we get access?"

"Seamus, we have full manual access, but..."

"But what?"

"But I have failed you. Your master has full manual access too."

TWENTY – OWNER'S MANUAL

When Seamus heard his master had gotten manual access for the *Wander Wide*, he felt sick, and not just emotionally. He found himself racing to his lavatory where he vomited in the toilet. "Ugh, I can't believe it," he mumbled, wiping his lips with the back of his hand. After swishing water in his mouth from the sink, he patted his pale face with wet hands.

"I am very sorry, Seamus." Thunderblade's voice sounded both contrite and consoling in his ear-com. Seamus wished the robot could be with him now instead of hidden in the closet.

"It's okay. We tried our best."

Just then there was a knock at his door, which opened a second later. That so irritated him. Of course it was Filymon.

"Onesimus?"

"I'm in the bathroom," he mumbled as he stepped out.

"Come on, boy. I need you in the engine room." Filymon's tone was pleasant, but his expression told Seamus he was in no pleasant mood.

"Sir, I... I'm not feeling too well."

The answer was firm: "Come on, I need your help."

Reluctantly, Seamus obeyed, following his master past Apphia in the corridor, through the shuttle and cargo bays, and to the engine room. As soon as the door closed Filymon spun toward him, eyes wide and angry.

"It must not be obvious enough for you, boy, so I'm going to spell it out for you. You are NOT to tell Apphia anything about our business. You understand me?"

Seamus contemplated acting clueless, but his emotions were so charged he decided to speak up. "Sir, the Code of Submission requires me to treat all my masters equally, without favoritism. Are you asking me to favor you over Lady Apphia and to lie to her when she asks me direct questions?"

Filymon grit his teeth behind pursed lips and he shook his head, almost on the verge of losing his temper. He thumbed himself in the chest before poking Seamus in the sternum. "Onesimus, *I* am your master. You answer to *me*. Part of your service to me is for you to serve my wife and son. But make no mistake, I have this—" he pulled out the shocker from pocket "—and you *will* do what I say. We clear, boy?"

Seamus glowered at him, but held his tongue. When Filymon widened his eyes and wiggled the shocker in unspoken threat, Seamus nodded.

"Good. Now, as you announced to the gods and everyone, we got manual access. The tech even downloaded the original owner's manual and a simulator. Now, I don't have the fancy gravity controls, so you won't have the simulated acceleration when you use it. It probably won't matter anyway, since I don't care much for my ship being flown like a jet fighter. And as you've already seen, these ships with a lot of tonnage can't exactly evade Romian blasters. What we're all about is stealth. This is about altering course just a little and making some quick drops on our way to where we should be going. Nothing fancy. And if we're ever boarded, we act just like normal. No running!"

"Yes, Master."

"And whatever we do, don't tell a soul. If your Code makes that difficult, you just tell anyone who asks to talk to me. That includes Apphia and Chippus too."

Seamus started nodding and just kept on as Filymon talked on and on. He wanted so bad to roll his eyes, but his muscles and skin still ached a little from his last shocking. Instead he tried to think of loopholes to all these commands. So he couldn't tell anyone? What about writing? He didn't say he couldn't write anyone. What about charades? Could he act it out? He stifled a snort of laughter at the thought.

"Pay attention, boy!"

Just then the door opened. It was Chippus and he bounced a small yellow ball slightly smaller than a basketball.

"Dad, I'm bored. Can Onesimus play wallball with me?"

"Son, I..."

"Pleeeeese?"

Filymon grimaced. "Argghhh... Alright. Onesimus, go tire out the boy and then get up to the flight deck. And mind what I said. ALL that I said."

"Yes, Master."

Filymon walked out and through the cargo hold to the shuttle bay, the double doors sliding shut behind him with a whistling hiss. Seamus was glad to see him go, but he certainly didn't feel like playing either.

Chippus bounced into the cargo hold, which was mostly empty other than some dusty crates stacked in one corner and some old engine parts in several baskets near the door to the engine room. It ran the width of the ship and was nearly square.

"What side you want to be on?" Chippus asked, flinging the ball against the port wall with an echoing slap. He caught it as it rebounded, one-handed.

"I'm sorry, Master Chippus. I've never played wallball before."

"It's easy! See those squares painted on the side walls? One side is yours and one is mine. We try to get the ball and throw it on our square for a score."

"Sounds easy. Do you have to dribble, or what?"

"You can run, throw, bounce it, toss it in the air. You just can't kick it and you can't take more than three steps without the ball leaving your hands. And if you toss it, it has to be up higher than your head."

"Sounds almost like Gaelic football. Can you tackle?"

"No, but you can bump without using your hands or elbows, and it can't be in the face or back."

"Okay, let's try it."

Seamus met Chippus in the center of the bay, where they both held the ball between them. With a count of three they began pushing and twisting the ball one-handed until it spun away. Just before Seamus snatched the bouncing ball, Chippus shouldered him in the arm, sending him careening toward the wall.

"Do yih want ya teeth in a bag?" Seamus snapped as he caught himself on the aft wall. He turned to see the ball sail through the air and smack the wall just inside the square.

"Point for me! What was that again; teeth in a what? It sounded funny."

"Nothing. You about plowed me over. Is that fair play?"

"I just bumped you. Here, your ball. You got to touch my wall with it before you start." He tossed the ball to Seamus.

"Okay, lil' crab," Seamus muttered. "I'm gonna beat the lard out of yih, this time". As he said it, he could hear his mother chastising him for falling back into his Irish brogue and not using

Standard. But sometimes Standard didn't suit his mood, and fighting words sounded so much better in Irish.

Seamus touched the wall and dribbled the ball slowly, watching as Chippus advanced toward him, slightly crouched and arms spread wide. Seamus feinted toward aft, then bolted around Chippus the other way. The boy was quick, though, slapping the ball away. They both tore after it, but this time Seamus went for the bump, pulling his elbow in to make a fair play. Somehow Chippus felt it coming, darting out of reach, just as Seamus lunged. He tumbled to the ground, landing hard on his upper arm.

"Why you little..."

He scrambled after the boy, who was now making a play for the rolling ball. With a quick grab and a twisting jump, Chippus flung the ball toward his box. It missed, but barely. Chippus stumbled against his wall.

"Fair play to you," Seamus said as the ball bounced toward him.

"What does that mean?"

"It means..." He leisurely stepped up to catch it, but as soon as the ball touched his fingers he whipped around, flinging it toward Chippus wall with all his might. He caught it on the rebound and then sent it blistering through the air toward his own goal. It smacked the wall right on the edge of the square. "It means you did good, lad."

"Fair play to you too. One to one."

The game went on for just over fifteen minutes, sometimes as physical as a rugby match, and other times more a test of skill in throwing the ball. The highlight was Chippus' sixth point, made by the ball ricocheting off the upper bulkhead to strike the square. The game ended when Chippus got to ten, besting Seamus by three. Afterwards, Seamus plopped to the ground, huffing, his back against the bulkhead.

"Boy, I'm knackered. I can tell I've been in space too long."

"What does that mean?"

"Knackered? Ah, tired... exhausted."

"Oh. You seemed kind of tired today, even before we played."

"Not feeling too good."

"Sorry. So how do you say that where you're from?"

"Sick? Um, well, there's 'ill', or 'I had a bad dose', or 'laid up', or "right shook", or as me Uncle always says, 'as sick as a small hospital'."

Chippus snickered. "What else does he say? Your uncle."

Seamus chuckled. "Well, he'd say the line about wanting your teeth in a bag. He'd also ask if you wanted your eye dyed, or your snot broke. Never meant it, though. He was just a character. What else did he say that I can repeat? Oh, whenever I looked sad he'd say I looked like I was going around like a constipated greyhound." Chippus started giggling. "My favorite thing he'd say was when one of us would say something none too smart. He'd say, 'Well, there's no use being ignorant if yih can't show it'."

They both cackled, and it felt so good to laugh. When they caught their breath, Chippus giggled out: "Tell me more about your home, Onesimus."

"Home." He paused, sorting the emotions evoked by the word. "It's been so long since I've been there, I hope I can remember. You know, your place at Kollos reminds me a lot of it, except it isn't near cold enough." He paused again, his thoughts drifting to the places he'd wandered: the farms and fields, the shops his family frequented, the trees he had climbed. And the boarding school. His mood soured. "Master Chippus, I'd better get up front before your father decides to come back here and get me."

"Onesimus, do you like our home?"

Seamus brushed the dust off one elbow as he stood. "Yeah, I like your home."

"Good," the boy said, and mumbled something else as he stood.

"I'm sorry, I didn't hear that."

"Nothing. I'm just glad you like being in our family."

Seamus wasn't so sure about that, at least not completely, but he didn't say anything about it. "Hey, maybe we can play again tomorrow?"

♦ ♦ ♦

After getting on the hypertrack to Kollos, Seamus spent the better part of the rest of the day running the simulator and going over the owner's manual of the *Wander Wide*, all the while wondering what he could do about the situation. Since they now had manual control, Filymon was sure to start them down the path of smuggling. And despite all of his assurances to the contrary, Seamus was sure it would end in disaster. The question was what to do about it.

After the evening meal, Seamus turned in. As he plopped on his bunk, he slipped the ear-com in his ear and checked in with Thunderblade. The hidden robot was quick to announce the results of his latest task. "Seamus, as you requested, I have downloaded the booklet Rado gave Filymon concerning your service. It's in your reader."

"I'm sure this will be interesting," he muttered as he called up the file and began paging through the various chapters. He chuckled. "This sounds like the owner's manual of an air car. Listen to this, 'With good care and the right balance of discipline and reward, your new slave will bring you and your household many years of good service and enjoyment." Can you believe that?"

"Being a machine owned by a teen male, yes, I can believe it. Though 'good care' is not something I have experienced often in your possession."

"Whatever. You know what I mean. I'm alive." He paused, considering the parallels. "Do you consider yourself alive?"

"I am unsure how to answer that question, Seamus. I suppose it depends upon on how the term is defined. If in a strictly physical sense I–"

"Ugh, it's too late in the day to start thinking about that. Oh, here's the chapter on the remote. Man, I can't believe they can just kill a slave if they want."

"It depends upon your social level. Many slaves have rudimentary rights, depending on a variety of factors. Unfortunately, you have none."

"The story of my life... hold on a second. Janey Mac, I think I found it!"

"What, Seamus?"

"I found how to get to Rom! If we can get to Rom, then we can get to Löwin. And if we can get to her, then we can escape!"

TWENTY-ONE – PIECES

Almost as if the little robot couldn't help himself, the door to the closet opened slightly and Thunderblade's glowing red eyes stared out of the dim. "Seamus, how do you propose for us to get to Rom?" He sounded worried.

"It says right here: 'If normal disciplinary measures do not curb your slave's behavior, the slave can be returned for remedial training.' Don't you see it? If I can make Filymon angry or frustrated enough with me, he will take me back to Rado at Rom!" All the pieces to the puzzle seemed to be snapping together.

"Seamus, your voice is three decibels too loud. Someone might hear you."

"Oh yeah. Right, right."

"Much better. In a cursory examination of your plan, I calculate an 81% chance of you being killed before being returned to Rado, and only a 4% chance of you actually surviving remedial training."

"But if we swap the remote like we were talking about a few weeks ago..."

"Your odds improve significantly before being returned to Rado, but your death is a virtual certainty when he discovers the remote is a fake."

"You're not getting it! I have no intention of being taken to Rado, only getting to Rom. The main point of the remote isn't to shock me, or 'behavior modification' or whatever they call it. The main point is that it forces you to *stay close*. Right now I know I can't run away. He can track me down with that thing and if I get too far away, this... thing on my back will fry my spine. But, if we can swap the remote, it means I can go anywhere I please whenever I choose. He can't track me and I'll never get out of range of it where it would kill me."

Thunderblade quietly walked across the floor and jumped up on the end of the bed. "We have already established the need to obtain the remote, and I have located possible sources for a replacement on Effizus. Why is it necessary to anger Filymon so much he arranges to take you back to Rado? Why not escape from Kollos when most convenient and avoid the inherent dangers of being returned?"

"There are two real problems, well three. If we try to escape from some backwater like Kollos, Filymon is going to report it and we're going to get caught, even if you can set up a different transponder code and make us look like another ship. There just aren't a whole lot of ships out here, and it will be easy to spot us. We need to escape somewhere where there is so much traffic it will be almost impossible. Plus Rom gets us closer to home. So when we do try to escape, the fewer Romian pickets we see along the way, the better."

"Agreed. An escape from Kaarthaagg would be ideal, since there is not a Romian presence beyond that system. We could fly unhindered through the four other hypertrack transits required to return to Corvus 2267.

"Four? There are four more? Do you know which ones to take?"

"I have a detailed map in my memory I can download at anytime."

"That's good. I didn't know there were four... Well, anyway, I've checked the logs and Filymon has never been to Kaarthaagg. And if he didn't go there to get a slave, he will never go there. No, the closest he will probably ever get is Rom."

"You mentioned two other concerns, Seamus?"

"Right. The second thing is how to get to Löwin. It'd be a lot easier to meet up with her and escape from there together, than to try to stage two different escapes."

"May I point out when I contacted Löwin, she stated she would be able to escape on her own. I can contact her and advise her to do so, while we escape without her. We could avoid Rom altogether, taking the route through Syracus-E. An additional consideration is that if we are not accompanied by a Gothan snow cat it may also prove much easier. You can blend in with other humans. She can not."

"I'm not going to leave her in Rom! We promised to help each other escape and I'm going to do it. You even told me that she's staking her honor on helping us. If you take that away from her, she'll probably go berserk and try to kill a bunch of Romians before being killed herself!"

"I am merely pointing out the alternatives."

Seamus huffed. "The third thing is finding my parents. Most slaves end up coming through Rom, so I bet they're in Rom somewhere or at least the records of where they went. Did your surveillance programs turn up anything yet?"

"The only information I have so far gathered is that after our escape Commander Zaannddaarraa and several of your guards were condemned to the games and the rest of his crew disbanded with their fins marked in shame. Doctor Kaataannaa was reassigned to an orbital hospital where unhealthy slaves are treated before being sent to the planet for processing. She is the only one from the *Rreennseesstt* I have located who may be able to tell us the about your parents."

"Then we have to go there! That's a direct hypertrack from Rom, right?"

"Yes, we can transit directly from Rom, but I strongly suggest not visiting Kaarthaagg for several reasons, the foremost being your safety. As a runaway slave returning to where he was first processed, it is highly likely you will be captured and enslaved again. Any of your former captors who would have knowledge of your parents also have a vested interest in recapturing you to remove their shame. If you are recognized, as someone like Kaat-aannaa undoubtedly will, you will quickly be turned over to the ruling junta."

"That doesn't matter. We've got to find Mom and Dad!"

The robot did not answer right away. When he finally spoke, his voice was quiet and as earnest as Seamus had ever heard. "If your parents could advise you in this moment, it is highly likely they would tell you to leave them and fly straight for home." He paused before looking up at Seamus. "Besides, they..."

"They what?" He wondered if Thunderblade were suffering from another logic paradox.

"They... Seamus, as your guardian, I want what is best for you. I believe trying to find your parents will only lead to your own pain and possibly your death. Please consider what I am saying."

Seamus sat quietly for sometime, then lay back on his bunk, staring at the ceiling. His eyes didn't really see the bulkhead, but more saw all the possibilities and dangers looming ahead. He couldn't leave his parents here. Maybe a robot that could look at everything like a math problem could do it, but he never would.

"I'll think more about it, but I want to plan for it just in case."

"I understand... please continue."

"Anyway, here's what I'm thinking. We swap the remotes, and then I start acting up until Filymon decides to take me back to Rom. When we make orbit we use the computer to lock them in their rooms for a day or so and then deny them access to navigation and the radio for a couple days more. While they're locked up, we take the shuttle down to Rom and meet up with Löwin. From there we fly the shuttle out to Kaarthaagg..."

"Will the shuttle safely make a transit through a hypertrack?"

"Yes, from what I read in the manual, it doesn't need any special equipment to use a hypertrack – these hypertracks, whatever they are, do all the work. The only thing is that the shuttle isn't designed to be used long term. It has basic facilities, but I'll have to stockpile it with food and water and whatever else we need. We're also going to have to conserve fuel or else try to get more somewhere along the way."

"Will Romians or Kaarthaaggians question a short range shuttle without a nearby mother ship?"

"That's where I'm hoping you'll be able to forge a transponder code for us so we aren't questioned about it. Believe me, when I was at Rom last time I saw hundreds of different kinds of ships. We could be a yacht or something."

"That is feasible. I will begin research to find the best possibilities. What if we are discovered and the Romians begin to pursue us?"

"Well, there are two things I've thought of: one, to continually change our codes to make it hard to track us. The other is the TENT, the lifeboat back in the shuttle's airlock. If we could rig it with our transponder and send it off in a different direction, while we shut down everything and coasted the other way, then maybe they will follow after the TENT and not notice us."

"I have little information on Romian scanning equipment. Your plan may be very successful or quickly fail, depending purely on their technical ability and their operational doctrine. Based on what I know of the *Wander Wide*, it would have a 98% chance of success, but assuredly military equipment is much better. Under that assumption I would only give a 52% chance of successful evasion."

Seamus wanted to tell Thunderblade he'd take those odds, but he knew a lecture would follow. And one thing he wasn't in the mood for was yet one more lecture. "Well, let's hope they don't discover us until it's too late, and if they do, that the TENT will throw them off long enough for us to get away."

"Seamus, besides such incomplete data, it appears your plan is largely complete. I can not calculate the odds of success until it is determined how and where to meet Löwin and what is decided about Kaarthaagg. We will have to fly through the Kaarthaagg system to reach Corvus 2267, so the decision to stop there can be postponed as more information is gathered. Löwin will have to provide the details of her escape plans. My arrangement with her is to contact her with our plan when ready. Do you concur this is the appropriate time?"

Seamus savored the moment. Finally, after all these months, he had hope. "Yes, please let her know we will be ready when she is."

The robot seemed to freeze momentarily. "Done. My message will be hidden on the next message courier to Rom."

♦ ♦ ♦

Seamus slept the best he had since being captured. He awoke early in the morning, about an hour before his normal waking time, his mind racing with the joy of soon returning home. He dozed off again and dreamed...

He was back on Earth on his uncle's farm, walking along the top of one of the ancient, moss-covered stone walls encircling the hilly land. For dozens of generations those same walls had kept sheep inside and predators out, and also provided hours of a-musement for bored children. With arms spread wide, Seamus pretended he flew in the cool breeze, smelling the ocean and the dampness of the earth. The joy of freedom and being home filled his heart. And then his left foot caught a loose stone.

He stopped, peering at the rock. It was green, covered with moss and lichens, and though movable, still performing its duties as it had for hundreds of years, sitting in a hollow formed long ago, a capstone among thousands sitting idly in the cloudy daylight. He toed it until if flipped over, revealing a smooth underside which probably hadn't seen the sun in ages. And then he pushed it closer and closer to the edge until it wobbled and fell, clattering down the side and rolling down the short knoll to the creek.

He regretted it for a moment but then squatted to look at the exposed stones that had been underneath. He picked at the crumbling mortar, which easily gave way, and soon another rock tumbled after the first. He dropped to his knees, fingers prying underneath one piece after another, ripping them up, and tossing them toward the creek. The sheep gathered, watching, as he tore the breach wider and deeper. His breaths grew frequent and deep, sweat beaded on his face despite the chill, and still he toiled.

With anger and hatred he ripped and pulled. Tears came to his eyes and a cry of anguish to his lips. Stones tumbled one after another until one held on stubbornly. He screamed at it as he pulled, yet it wouldn't give. He bashed it with another loose stone until, pock-marked and dusty, it shifted. He pulled at it with all his might and it finally turned loose, flinging off over his head. Seamus lost his balance and fell backwards, tumbling after it until landing in the shallow creek. The cold water was shocking at first, but then felt good, easing his bleeding fingers and torn nails. His breathing calmed as the water trickled over ankles and just over his waist. The anguish in his heart subsided, as did his tears. He wiped the grime from his face.

He looked up to see two sheep peering down at him through the opening in the wall. One bleated mournfully. With a hesitant step, it hopped through the gap, while the second stumbled before following. Oh no, he thought. He had let the sheep out. The two trotted down the hill toward him and began to drink nearby. Then others followed, through the hole and down the hill, just as one stone had followed the other. And now dozens were milling around, some walking upstream on the grassy bank, some even now wandering from sight. What had he done?

A horrible screech ripped the air and suddenly a ruby dragon bounded down the valley. Sheep raced from it, but it snatched them up one after another, swallowing them whole. Seamus tried to get up but he couldn't move. He looked down to see the creek had frozen around his legs and wrists like stocks. The first two sheep bleated in fear, struggling to move, but their forefeet were stuck in the ice too. The dragon hissed and roared at him, fiery golden eyes narrowing in challenge, before snatching the two sheep with bloody fangs. With a gulp they were gone. Seamus knew it was his end, but then the dragon bounded up the hill, its claws sending huge clods of earth tumbling toward him and sliding across the ice. The beast attacked the rift in the wall and ripped the hole wider and wider until it wiggled through the opening into the pasture beyond.

Seamus awoke sitting straight up, clutching his sheets and gulping down air like he had been drowning. He wiped his face as he realized it had only been a dream, a horrible nightmare. He plopped back to the bunk in relief. That had to have been the most vivid dream he'd ever had. He chuckled at himself, but then quieted. For some reason he felt incredibly guilty. Why would he have done something so foolish, even in a dream? What did it mean?

The thought haunted him throughout the remainder of their journey to Kollos and the two days they spent at home. He never dreamed it again, but it seemed to be burned into his memories. The only thing that seemed to push it from his thoughts was when Thunderblade spoke to him the night after he and Filymon had departed for Effizus on their next run: "Seamus, I have been reviewing the latest message packet the courier delivered this morning. I received a message from Löwin."

"A message! What did she say?"

"She reports she will be ready in several weeks and will signal us then."

TWENTY-TWO – CONTRABAND

As the orange planet of Effizus came into view, its lone crater-rimmed ocean staring at them like the pupil of an alien eye, Seamus squirmed in his seat. It wasn't the odd view of the planet, but rather that two events would happen on this visit that would change everything. The first, and the one he tried to focus on the most, was Thunderblade's plan to obtain a fake remote. Seamus couldn't wait to be able to swap them out and to finally have his own life in his hands. The second event was much less appealing. Despite Apphia's insistence – and without her knowledge – Filymon was planning on finalizing his agreement with Deme Trius to smuggle. And to Seamus, sooner or later that would lead to being caught and punished by the Romians. He only hoped they could escape before that could happen.

After docking at the marina and making sure the few loaded cargo pods were getting handled right, he headed to his cabin to gather his things, including Thunderblade. Over several nights they had discussed at length how to get the robot around the *Wander Wide*, and had finally come to the conclusion that if anyone else were aboard, then Thunderblade should remain hidden in Seamus' cabin. It was just too risky. The *Wander Wide* was small enough the robot could easily be seen or heard, and the ductwork proved too small to grant him passage. Besides, with having access to the ship's computer through the pilot's monitor, there was little reason to go elsewhere anyway. The only exception was when he wanted to leave the ship. And so, with some apprehension, they decided to smuggle him out in a duffel bag. That was easy at Kollos where their bags always came and went. Seamus just hoped Filymon wouldn't question him about why he had brought his duffel with him to Effizus.

When all was ready, Seamus peeked out his door. Filymon was still in his cabin with his door open, of course. Thankfully, Apphia and Chippus weren't on this trip or else he'd never make it out. With quick dart he headed down the passageway right lively with his bag draped over his shoulder, took the quick jog to the right then left, and was just about through the airlock into the shuttle bay when Filymon shouted for him. Janey Mac! Did Filymon see him? "Be right there!" he yelled as the doors shut behind him. He ran to the shuttle and tossed his bag into the storage locker. It thudded against the wall and tipped over. "Sorry, mate!" He ran back.

"Yes, Master?" he asked when he arrived at Filymon's door. He tried to keep his breathing normal, as much as he wanted to pant.

"There you are. I say, now what we talked about the other day goes here too. Not a word of any of my side business to anyone, you hear me? If one other person finds out what's going on, it'll be broken arrows for sure. Now go get the shuttle prepped. I'll be along in just a minute."

Seamus barely got his duffel (and Thunderblade) upright and the storage compartment door shut before Filymon stepped in the shuttle. If he had noticed anything, Seamus couldn't tell, and within a few minutes they were easing out of the docking cradle and dropping toward the city ringing the water. Seamus had learned on their last visit that despite the fact the ocean sat over the northern pole, locals still referred to the various quadrants like compass points. And so they headed to Filymon's dock on the west side. With little cargo to move, they quickly got into the ground car and soon Filymon barreled down the roads toward Deme's.

Seamus noticed a few things right away when they arrived. The docks of the warehouse were quiet and empty; the reflecting pool around the statue of Artimiss no longer sparkled, but instead was full of algae and scum; and most notably, the slave who usually served as the receptionist was outside doing yard work. From the looks of it, he wasn't doing that great a job. He didn't look too pleased either.

"Aiolos, what's this?" Filymon asked, motioning to the yard tools.

"Master Trius had to cancel his yard service, and now I have to do it, on top of working in the warehouse. I suppose he's expecting you. Here, let me get the door." The slave fumbled trying to pull off a glove and Filymon grabbed the handle before he could finish.

"I know the way. You just go back to what you're doing." The slave nodded with gratitude and returned to his work.

Seamus followed Filymon down the corridors to Deme's office. The door was open and he could easily hear, then see, that Deme was quite upset as he talked on a headset. "Why don't you take my empty quiver too! I can't pay you if I don't have anything! You know I'm good for it... business if off this month." He waved them in, and Seamus stood unobtrusively by the door, while Filymon seated himself. The heavy man's yellow and orange skin looked flushed and his expression was one of controlled fury. "It's not just me, and you know it! Everyone's struggling right now. I know, I know. Look, pilgrim season will be here next month.

Things will pick up and I'll get it straight with you. Listen, I have a customer... let me call you back."

"Deme, my old friend, what's the matter?"

The man's lip curled in disgust. "It's those... those string popping Yeshuaians! And that Pol, their ringleader!"

Seamus was shocked, and it looked like Filymon was just as surprised. He shifted uncomfortably. "What do you mean, my friend?"

"Everyone is leaving the worship of our fair goddess to follow the teachings of some dead man from Judia. This Pol claims he's not dead and does some magic, and now everyone is leaving the hunt to follow him. You wouldn't believe some of the people who are in with them now... Rastus... uh, Trophimus. Then there's Tychicus and even Onesiphorus."

"Onesiphorus? Why, he's one of the city elders."

"Yes, and he's got all the other leaders looking the other way while Artimiss is neglected and shamed." He slammed his hand on the desk. "This is Effizus! This is where Artimiss waited for our people to find her! And now... and now, my friend, all the people are throwing out their icons and writings. I can't sell a thing right now. If you want an image of Artimiss, you can find them at any thrift shop for spare change. They're worth more for scrap metal than for selling, break my bow. And who knows what's going to happen at pilgrim season. All those people are going to come to visit the temple and there won't be anyone there to meet them or sell to them."

"Well, I... now that Pol came through here a few years ago, and then that – what's his name? App..."

"Apollos... argh, the bane of his namesake. Thanks to the fair goddess he left."

"Yes, Apollos. Now, I say, they only seemed to stick mainly with the immigrant crowd from Judia. Didn't make much of a fuss."

"Well, now they're going after everyone and converting a great many! Ach, it makes me want to pull my nose hair out." Deme paused then sighed. "Sorry to take that out on you. I got collectors calling... Business hasn't been off just this month. It's been getting bad for several months now. Just, this month's especially bad." He paused in thought, glancing at the papers on his desk, and then looked up. "So, was your lady friend in Galatiana able to do anything for you? Please give me some good news."

There was an unexpected silence that followed, and Seamus slowly shifted to get a better look at his master. The man looked thoughtful, and if Seamus guessed, maybe even a bit troubled or conflicted. He looked up and in an emotionless, matter-of-fact voice said, "I'm good to go. I have manual access of the *Wander Wide* and my pilot here is up to speed. All we lack is just the doing."

The look of relief that spread across Deme's face nearly transformed him into another person. "Aye, that is such good news. I may even sleep tonight." He chuckled, pointing. "You had me going there for a minute."

Filymon leaned back with what sounded to Seamus as a forced chuckle, conscious of his own body language. It looked like he was trying hard to seem relaxed. "So, how do we do this? I can move the stuff, I just don't have a clue on how to pick it up or deliver it."

"That, my friend, is the challenge. As you know, all cargo of consequence has to be packed in shipping pods at Romian secured warehouses and then loaded in orbit at the marinas.

Anything you load here at a waterside dock has to be chipped or else the dock scanners will alert the Romians. The only way around that is to ship through unregistered facilities, but we can't just park a lot of cargo ships around them without drawing a lot of attention. No, everything we do has to look normal, so that means this will happen in transit on your regular runs."

"In transit? You mean while we're underway?" Filymon's voice sounded as wary as Seamus felt. He listened closely.

"Yes, that's the only way. We get the cargo up there through a mining outfit, where they preposition a pod just off the normal lanes. Once you're out of planetary control, you'll have to go to manual, increase your speed to give yourself more time, alter your course to swap out the pod, and then get back on the lane and to the hypertrack on schedule. If you miss your projected arrival time either to or from a hypertrack, the Romians will get really interested."

Seamus felt a million questions bubble up inside like a noisy mob. He didn't want to interrupt, but he had to know the answers to at least a few. "Master?" he whispered. Filymon turned to him, his giraffe spots flushed and his expression one of someone trying to figure out an immense problem. He raised his eyebrows in a manner that made Seamus feel he could speak. "Sir, how do we load a pod? The bots always do it at the marina." Filymon shifted his eyes toward Deme.

"Good slave you have there, Fil. Thinking ahead. These pods are a little different than normal. They're fitted with reaction thrusters to keep them on station when waiting for pick-up and to help you load them. I'll give you the access codes so you can use the thrusters to guide them in place."

"What's the catch, Deme? I can see it on your face."

"The catch is that the electronics on these pods aren't sophisticated or else the Romians would pick them up on a scan. You'll have to do a spacewalk to use the controls and guide them in manually."

Seamus' stomach tightened. There was no way he was going to do a spacewalk; he'd take a shocking first. He wasn't sure about this Star Kingdom, but even though astronauts from Earth had been doing spacewalks for two hundred years, they were still as dangerous as the very first one. No suit could withstand any hit from a micrometeorite traveling at thousands of kilometers per hour. Or radiation, or depressurization, or suit malfunction, or a hundred other things that could and did go wrong.

"Deme, I say, it amazes me how often you forget to mention key details like this until I'm already committed to one of your schemes." Deme chuckled like it was a joke, but Filymon's face didn't share that sentiment.

"It's really not hard. I've done it before. I've got a pod up there now for you, full of my regular cargo so you can practice."

"Practice?"

"You want to get good at this before we start. Really good."

"True, I suppose." Filymon didn't look like he believed his own words.

"No, you really do, my old friend. With all the speeding up, stopping, and swapping cargo pods, you're going to have your hands full. And with a ship like yours, you're only going to have fifteen minutes, more or less, to do it. These first few times you need to have regular cargo. That way if you take too long and the Romians get interested in you, then you'll pass any scans. Once you're comfortable with it and doing it well, then we'll start with the contraband."

"Yes, you're right."

"I'll have an empty pod up there, too, for next time. When you come back through you can practice on the empty one. Just make sure you've brought an empty one with you from Kollos to swap out. Everything has to match your manifests or else it's going to be trouble. Oh, and make sure you're lady friend in Galatiana is set up the same way. The pod I'm sending with you full of the regular cargo is hers to use for swapping out. That way your manifests will match on her end too."

The two continued with the details for some time and Seamus lost interest. Instead, he thought about what the future held. It sounded like they had this smuggling business all figured out. It might actually work. He really hoped so. Who knew how many runs they would make before he could make his escape? Knowing his luck, they'd probably get caught just before he had the chance.

After a few more minutes, they left. Filymon remained quiet and thoughtful. Seamus didn't have much to say, so he kept silent too. He was surprised, though, when Filymon parked at the Agora instead of heading straight for the shuttle at the dock. Without saying a word, he got out and started walking into the open air market. Seamus ran to catch up with him. He finally caught up with him when he paused at an idol vendor, who seemed desperate to sell. He walked on wordlessly. Seamus followed, noticing where he'd seen idol sellers in the past only empty spaces remained. In the distance Seamus saw smoke and noticed that was where they were heading.

At the far side of the Agora several humans stood tending a small fire in a metal drum. People were coming in ones and twos every few minutes, throwing scrolls and books into the fire. Seamus couldn't tell what was going on. One thing for sure, each person who threw their belongings in the fire seemed happy to do so, even to the point of tears. He tried to imagine the feeling he saw on their faces. For some reason he thought of how he'd feel if he were ever freed from his slavery. He would throw that cursed fitting and remote in a fire with just as much emotion.

"You there," Filymon said to one woman when she had wiped the tears from her face and had turned to walk away. Seamus thought he sounded gruff and rude. "Are you one of those Pol followers? Is it true you people are burning your icons of Artimiss?"

"Me? Uh, I don't exactly follow Pol. He's one of the teachers. I follow Yeshua. He's freed me from so much."

"Yes, but what about Artimiss? How can you leave the hunt?"

"The hunt? The hunt for what? For myself, all I can say is that Yeshua has set me free. Three weeks ago I was..." her voice cracked with fresh emotion. "Well, let's just say that life had become so wearisome that I despised waking every morning. And now? Now, I can't wait for each day, to see what wonders God will do in my life. What about Artimiss you ask? She has done nothing for me."

Filymon opened his mouth, but then closed it slowly, tightly.

"You have questions, sir? Why don't you come to my sister's home this evening? Our community meets in homes everyday, where those in the school teach us what they've learned during the day."

"I must be going, miss. Thanks for your time."

Filymon turned and strode out of the Agora at a fast pace. Seamus nearly ran to keep up with him. "Sir, what's wrong? What's wrong?"

"I tell you what's wrong! I..." He stopped and turned, continuing in a quiet voice. "I'll tell you what's wrong. The world is upside down; it's changing and I don't like it. When I was a young man, things were much simpler then. But now it's hard to know... No, I don't care for change, unless it's me who's doing it."

Part of Seamus wanted to snap back how Filymon ought to try being kidnapped, enslaved, and criminalized. Instead he kept his mouth shut.

"Let's go, boy. Let's go home. We've got a lot of work ahead of us."

♦ ♦ ♦

A half hour later they were back at the dock. The ride had been silent and full of tension. There was nothing like driving with Filymon when he was either excited or furious. Thankfully, they had survived, though Seamus' knuckles ached from holding on to the seat handles so hard.

After locking the car in the warehouse garage, Filymon stomped up to the front of the shuttle and began to buckle in. Seamus made a show of making sure everything was stowed in the back. He opened the door to the storage closet.

"Thunderblade?" he whispered

The zipper to his duffel bag slowly opened and two red glowing eyes peered from the darkness within. Seamus wanted to ask so badly... And then, held in a black and silver hand, a white slave remote appeared – just like the one Filymon had. Just like the one that held Seamus' life at the touch of a button.

He had done it! And now the plan was in motion!

TWENTY-THREE - SWAPPING

Filymon's grumpy silence ended as soon as the *Wander Wide's* shuttle bay pressurized. It was amazing to Seamus how business could shift the man's mood. "Onesimus, when you're done with the shuttle, meet me up at the flight deck. We've got to plan out that cargo pod swap, and I want to get underway as soon as we're ready. Time is wasting, and if time is wasting then so is money."

"Yes, Master."

Seamus wanted to ask him what he was thinking about the spacewalk, or rather *who* he was thinking about doing it. Seamus wasn't looking for a fight, but Filymon could expect one if he was planning on Seamus doing it. But he still had to get Thunderblade back to his cabin and being in the middle of an argument wasn't probably the best time to do it.

By the time Filymon stepped through the airlock, Seamus had already shut the systems down. As soon as the door closed, he ran back, opened the storage compartment, and unzipped his duffel bag. "You okay?"

Thunderblade wiggled out. "Yes, Seamus. I am fully operational."

"Listen, Master Filymon wants me up front right lively. Could you drag my duffel back to our cabin? It would make things a lot easier."

The robot grabbed the handles and gave the bag a tug. "Yes, it appears I can for a short distance. Would you please carry it to the airlock?"

"Sure." Seamus picked up the bag and walked to the airlock with Thunderblade just behind. As soon as they were through the door, he set it down quietly and jogged around the corner and down the corridor toward the flight deck.

After passing his cabin Seamus noticed Filymon's door was open. He paused, glancing in, and there on the bed among his other belongings sat the remote. He glanced up toward the front and saw Filymon's shadow inside the piloting compartment. Janey Mac, if he just had the fake remote he could swap them out right now!

"Boy, are you coming, or what?" Filymon shouted unseen.

No time now, Seamus thought. But maybe he could figure out some excuse to come back. He ran up to the flight deck, where Filymon had already begun backing them out of the marina slip. That irritated him for some reason. "Here I am, sir."

"Good, now how do you pull up the navigation plan on this thing?"

As the *Wander Wide* settled into its own orbit with the marina falling steadily behind, Seamus walked him through the manual navigation menus, where they pulled up their assigned course to the Kollos hypertrack. After Filymon keyed in the coordinates of the smuggling cargo pod, Seamus began plotting their manual course they'd use after leaving sensor range of Effizus. Seamus was surprised to see that even with a full speed burn and turnover, plus a full speed departure to get back on course, there would only be fourteen minutes to get the pods swapped. At Effizus, Filymon had made sure the pod being swapped was the closest to the airlock door, but even still, fourteen minutes seemed like not nearly enough time.

As Filymon contemplated this, Seamus decided he'd better act quickly. "Sir, may I take a restroom break?"

"Hmmm... uh, what? Ah, yes. Sure. Go right ahead."

Seamus tried to act as normal as possible as he walked out. He kept glancing back toward the flight deck. So far so good. As soon as the door to his cabin closed, he whispered, "Thunderblade, where's the remote?"

The robot answered from the closet. "I have it."

Seamus opened the door. "Give it to me, quick!"

The robot complied. "May I ask—"

"No time!" He shoved it into one of his pockets. When he stepped into the corridor, Filymon was nowhere to be seen. He slinked into his master's open door, swapped the remotes, and was back out. He headed back up to the flight deck.

Filymon turned when he entered. "Ah, there you are. I say, this will be tricky. There's no way to improve this window. Fourteen minutes is it. The only way to speed things up is for both of us to spacewalk. Say, you look pale, are you alright? As I was saying, one of us can be getting the pod to put on, while the other is taking the other one off. The tradeoff is in not having someone here on the flight deck."

"That's what I was thinking, sir. With such a small window, I really should be here ready to get us underway as soon as you're back in the airlock."

"Aye, but here's what I was thinking. Both of us are suited up. I'll be in the airlock when we arrive at the pod. When we stop, I'll head out to get the new pod. As soon as you get the ship stopped, you head to the airlock and come out and start working on the old pod. As soon as it's loose and a safe distance away, you head back in and get the ship prepped for immediate departure. By that point I'll be getting the new pod on, and as soon as I'm back in the airlock, I'll signal and you can get us underway."

"Master, I..."

"Spit it out, boy."

"I've never spacewalked before, and honestly it scares me to death."

"Oh, you'll be fine. Come on." Seamus watched as Filymon hopped out of his chair and walked out. Seamus didn't like how this was looking. A moment later Filymon stuck his head back into view and motioned for him to follow. Seamus trailed him back to the storage closet, where, as he feared, Filymon handed him a spacesuit.

Within a few minutes both were suited up in the airlock, checking each other's connections and gauges. As apprehensive as Seamus felt, Filymon was a good teacher, patient and thorough. A few minutes later the outer airlock door opened with the impossible black of space outside, and Filymon dropped to his hands and knees to crawl out on ladder rungs recessed in the floor.

"Why are you doing that, Master?"

"It's better to orient yourself to feel like you're climbing out on top."

Seamus nodded inside his helmet and followed his example, dropping on all fours and making use of the ladder rungs as much as he could. As he reached the opening, the gravity had diminished to nothing, and the rungs were quite necessary despite his magnetized knees, boots, and elbows. He crawled out to see Filymon standing nearby on the nearest pod. Tentatively, Seamus stood next to him, keeping his eyes on his feet. He felt a little claustrophobic from his helmet and at the same time a little dizzy like standing on the edge of a cliff at a great height. He closed his eyes and took several deep breaths before looking up.

It was amazing.

The glowing orange planet filled his sight to left and the pin-pricked black of space filled the right. As incredible as some of the views he'd seen inside a ship, nothing so far could equal this. The fear melted away into wonder, and as he looked around he regretted never having done this before. Unfortunately it was short-lived.

"Feel okay, boy? Not dizzy or disoriented? Good. Now this is what you'll need to do. Like I showed you inside, you take one step at a time. Make sure you're firmly planted on the deck before taking your next step. If you do happen to float off, just press the thruster control on your forearm there, point your hands in the direction you want to go, and then squeeze your thumbs inside your fingers. The thruster on your back will send you right where you point."

Seamus wasn't too worried about that. He'd clocked many hours in null gravity. Of course that was inside, not out here.

"Now walk over here, like this and see this control? Key in 1-3-2-4, push the rail lock button – no, the yellow one – and then the red button to activate the thrusters. It will slowly move off the rail and drift out. And then just head back to the airlock and go back in. I've been timing us, so this should take about three minutes and probably another two for the pod to drift out of the way. That should be plenty of time for you to get back to the airlock. Hopefully, I can get to the new pod, and get it over here and locked on the pod rail in the next eight, and then back inside the airlock in time."

When they got back inside and out of the suits, Filymon decided they ought to eat and get some rest before departing in two hours. Seamus grabbed some leftovers and headed to his cabin, actually feeling good about the swap. It looked easy enough, at least his part in it. As soon as he was in his cabin, he opened the closet door and knelt. He pulled the swapped remote out of his pocket and handed it to Thunderblade, who had stepped out of the dark, cluttered corner. "Here, hide this."

Thunderblade handed him the ear-com. When Seamus had slipped it into his left ear, he heard, "May I ask what you needed the remote for?"

"Oh, Filymon's door was wide open and the remote was sitting there right on his bed. It was so easy! I just swapped it out!"

"Seamus, I had already swapped the remotes before coming inside your cabin."

"What did you say?" That didn't make sense. *He* had swapped the remotes.

"I had already swapped them before you took the remote from me."

Seamus' heart nearly stopped. "Are you saying I just... I just swapped them back? I just put the *real* remote back on Filymon's bed and this is the *fake* one?"

Thunderblade looked at the remote in his hands and nodded.

Seamus let out a long, frustrated sigh. "I... I can't believe this! Why didn't..." He pressed his palms on his face to keep from screaming.

"I am sorry, Seamus. I saw the same opportunity you did and acted on it similarly. I should have made sure you understood before you took it."

"Yes, you should have!"

The robot stood silently in the most irritating motionless silence possible, Seamus thought. He was probably going through his algorithms to pick the best words to say at the very best time. Seamus wanted to toss him out the airlock. He wouldn't, but at least he could fantasize about it for a while. He huffed in and out, muttering, trying to calm himself, and a short time later Thunderblade spoke.

"Seamus, during the last few minutes of your sullen brooding, I have quantified my observations about your master's recent habits regarding your remote. I calculate a seventy-four percent chance there will be another opportunity to swap the remote before reaching Kollos, with a ninety-six percent chance of success. If you dwell on these probabilities instead of sulking, then, perhaps, you will be able to contribute more positively to our escape plans."

Seamus was angry, but even more so he was genuinely stunned. "Did... did you just scold me? Are you... angry at me?"

"I do not feel emotions such as anger, but I do factor your emotional status as an input into attaining our goals. During seventeen percent of our interactions you make a positive impact; fifty-four percent has a negligible impact; and twenty-nine percent has a negative impact. Logically, I should try to limit your input, since your passive aggressive nature, blame-shifting tendencies, and general self-pity only make obtaining our goals much more difficult. Since I can not limit your input, my next best strategy is to try to modify it to be... less negative."

"I am not past aggressive!"

"Passive aggressive."

"Whatever!"

"Pouting is defined by many psychological organizations as a passive aggressive behavior – especially by children."

Seamus was so furious he wasn't sure what he'd do. He reached out and closed the closet door, blocking his view of the robot, then pulled out the ear-com. And for the next hour and forty minutes he lay on the bed trying to calm down.

♦ ♦ ♦

Just as they planned, they went to full power just after leaving Effizus Traffic Control, just slightly off their assigned course, and with their transponder off and most other systems off or as low as possible. Nervously, he kept checking the tactical plot, waiting for some Romian battle cruiser to come charging after them. The scope remained clear, as he impatiently waited for turnover. Finally, at the right time the manual program cut the engines, flipped the ship toward the opposite direction, and went to full burn. The ship slowed quickly, and then, just as planned they eased to a stop within sight of the awaiting cargo pod. He cut the engines just as the airlock alarm chirped.

Seamus headed back and entered the airlock. Just as instructed, he quickly double checked his suit readouts, and then keyed the opening sequence. The airlock depressurized, then opened. Just as planned, he scooted out, made his way carefully to the pod, keyed in the proper sequence and sent it drifting outward. He watched for just a few seconds to ensure it was moving away quickly enough and then glanced around in the surrounding black, thick with stars.

Nothing. No other pods, no Filymon.

He walked toward the top of the ship and glanced over the edge, and then over to the bottom side. He saw nothing, and his heart started to thump harder. Filymon had disconnected the radio in both suits to keep from giving their position away, and so Seamus couldn't call him. He quickly headed back in to see what he could see from the flight deck. Everything seemed to take much longer than it should and by the time he got up to the pilot's chair, eight out of fourteen minutes had already passed.

He couldn't see anything on any of the monitors. What had happened? Where had Filymon gone? Just as Seamus was about to flip on the lidar, a glint of reflected sunlight flashed on the starboard monitor. He pulled it up on the main screen and sure enough it was the pod, but it was much farther away than when they had arrived. There was less than six minutes left. No way Filymon could make it. Seamus considered the situation for a moment until an idea formed. If Filymon couldn't get to the *Wander Wide* in time, then maybe the *Wander Wide* could get to Filymon? Seamus made a decision and took the *Wander Wide* to full manual.

With short controlled bursts, he fired the directional thrusters so the *Wander Wide* began drifting toward the pod, while still keeping in the same relative orientation. Now it looked like they were coming together. He gave it just a little bit more and then let inertia take over. He wanted to really speed it up, but he wasn't sure what the thrusters would do if he tried to slow the *Wander Wide* down just before contact. He didn't want those same thrusters to blow the oncoming pod back the other direction.

He kept it on the main monitor and upped the magnification, wanting to see Filymon. His master was waving at him. What was going on? Seamus blinked the running lights, to which Filymon motioned toward his helmet. Something must be wrong. Seamus flipped on the radio. "Master?"

"Onesimus! The pod's out of fuel. Get out here!"

Seamus ran into the airlock, flushed the air, opened the outer door, and jumped toward the oncoming pod that was now just fifty meters away. Pointing toward the pod, he squeezed his thumbs, thrusting quicker toward it. It grew larger and larger until his hands touched the edge. Filymon grabbed his arm and pulled him to the back side. He pressed his helmet against Seamus' helmet. "Help me line it up!"

Seamus climbed on top, while Filymon lined up on the aft side. Seamus drove his fists into the pod, squeezing his thumbs. His pack pushed into him, pressing him hard against the pod. He looked up. Just a little more. He glanced over to Filymon whose pack jetted out a smoky plume. This was going to be close. It looked like they needed a couple more meters on his side. Then it hit Seamus. Filymon might be crushed if he stayed in place too long. Just as they were about to butt up against the *Wander Wide*, Filymon kicked off, and the pod slid into place, the locking collars latching on the cargo rail with a vibration that sent Seamus tumbling.

Before Seamus could right himself, Filymon had grabbed his ankle and thrusted them inside the airlock. Seamus had hardly gotten upright before the inner door hissed open. They barrelled to the flight deck, where Seamus slid into his seat and activated the departure burn. The ship jerked with thrust and they nearly tumbled out of their seats from the jolt. As soon as the gravity recovered, they both checked the clock.

They were four minutes late.

"Go put these suits up, boy!" Filymon barked. "We might have company!"

Seamus took Filymon's space suit and raced toward the back, where he climbed out of his own and stowed them both in the storage closet. As he sprinted back to the front he realized he had to warn Thunderblade that an inspection might be coming. He ducked inside his cabin and opened the closet, but before he could say anything the robot appeared.

"Seamus, I swapped the remotes!"

TWENTY-FOUR – TROUBLE

Seamus stared at Thunderblade for just a moment as the news sank in. And then it clicked. Yes! The little robot had done it; he had swapped the remotes! But the joy was short-lived as the coming dilemma completely filled his thoughts. "Great! But we've got big trouble on the way. We are going to be four minutes late for our rendezvous with the hypertrack, and Master Filymon thinks we might be boarded. You need to hide and hide somewhere good, you and that remote. Got that?"

"I will, Seamus."

With a curt nod, Seamus raced out for the flight deck. As he took his seat, he glanced over at Filymon. "Master, what are we going to say?"

"I'm thinking!" he snapped.

Normally Seamus would have been offended and fast scheming some sort of payback, but his mind was so quickly on what might come, Filymon's brusque tone barely registered. There had to be something they could do. He studied their course again, looking for any way to shave off even a few seconds, but the curve was as flat as they could make it and still come in on their registered trajectory.

"I say, it's got to be something that can't be verified, so nothing mechanical. And we can't claim a delay at Effizus, because they will know when we left their sensor range. No, it's got to be something that happened on the way, something they would believe could add four minutes to our flight time."

"Why don't we have a mechanical now? I could do something to cut the output of the engines just slightly so it would add four minutes by the time we got there?"

"That won't work. We were at cruising speed when we left sensor range at Effizus. Even coasting in on ballistic would put us there on time. No, we left there with everything running normally, and there's no kind of problem I can think of that will add just four minutes of flight time over three hours."

For the next hour they desperately tried to think of something. Unfortunately, the only way the manual override worked was to isolate the ship's automated Romian programming from the ship's systems with simulated inputs and outputs. As far as the ship's computer was concerned, it had been in control the whole time, completely unaware that the systems had been taken to manual. The only thing they had to do was to get the ship back in synch with the automated systems, but now that was impossible. And if they tried to manufacture some reason, it wouldn't match the computer.

As they quickly approached the sensor range of the Romian picket, Seamus felt himself becoming more and more nervous. And soon that nervousness had changed to anger. "Why would they even care about four minutes?" he muttered.

"What?"

"Sorry, Master. It's just if they care so much about four lousy minutes, maybe they can think of why we're late."

Filymon looked at him intently, obviously considering something. "That, my boy, is a fabulous idea. We don't have to know why we're so slightly late. We may not even know we're late. Why would we be, after all? We're just a dumb merchie, after all." He started punching keys furiously, but Seamus couldn't tell what he was doing.

Just then the com beeped.

"It's the Romian picket. Now remember, you're just a regular slave. You don't know nothing about piloting and the like. I'll do all the talking. If they do talk to you, then you just answer as quickly as you can and say as little as possible."

"Yes, sir." He didn't have to be told twice about that.

Filymon flipped on the intercom. "This is the *Wander Wide*, over?"

A deep voice answered. *"This is the Romian battle cruiser,* Veneto. *We show you overdue by four minutes, nineteen seconds, over."*

"Uh, we are?" Filymon paused for several seconds, taking the lidar to active and actually punching in the right buttons to call up what he'd need to confirm such a statement. "Uh, yes sir. I see that now, but I say our computer shows we're on plan. Quivers, our flight plan is going to end four minutes short of the hypertrack! We're just going to be sitting out here in the shipping lane! What do we do? Can you assist?"

"Stay on plan and prepare to rendezvous, over."

"Thank you, oh, thank you!"

♦ ♦ ♦

Twelve minutes later, they heaved to and docked with the massive cruiser, a flattened egg-shaped vessel with huge gun-turreted shields extended on either side like two umbrellas. When the airlock beeped, Filymon opened the door.

Three greenish creatures that looked like oversized velociraptors were on the other side, leathery bodies covered with a bony shell that wrapped around their necks and torsos. Two had squatted on either side of the airlock, their armored shins and forearms pulled in tightly and their beaked heads pulled inside their shells to form two massive boulders. They held enormous weapons that looked like they were even heaver than Seamus. The third Romian stood behind them, just shorter than Filymon. He also stood with weapon drawn and aimed.

Filymon raised his hands which Seamus quickly mimicked. "We're unarmed."

The two squatted Romians bolted from their positions, one shoving them face down on the deck, while the other covered. After patting them down for weapons, they quickly began checking the rest of the ship, racing on long, muscular legs like ostriches. The third stepped out of the airlock.

"This ship is over four minutes late and you do not know why?"

Seamus turned to look at Filymon, who was staring up at the Romian. "No sir! I say, I didn't even realize it until you called. I started a diagnostic, but it hasn't finished yet. I have no idea!"

"We are scanning your vessel now. If we find anything out of the ordinary, you will pay the price."

While Filymon jabbered away, Seamus heard the door to his cabin open and glanced over to see one of the soldiers step into his cabin. He sure hoped Thunderblade was well hidden. A few minutes later the soldier stepped out, and Seamus thought he would have fainted if he wasn't already lying on the ground. The soldier held Thunderblade transformed into ''copter mode. He looked the toy flying machine over one last time, as if trying to figure out what it was, and then tossed him onto Seamus' bunk before heading back toward Chippus' cabin.

Ten minutes later when the soldiers had searched the *Wander Wide* to their satisfaction, Filymon and Seamus were allowed to sit on the chairs in the lounge. It seemed like the Romians were more at ease, as much as Seamus could tell; at least their golden eyes didn't look quite as wary under their thick eye ridges. The commanding soldier continued to question Filymon occasionally in a conversational tone, while the other two stood guard at the airlock. Another Romian soon came, some sort of specialist, who went to the flight deck. The commander joined him and a half hour later they returned. Filymon stood and Seamus followed his example.

The specialist spoke with the voice of authority. "The software in your ship's computer has become corrupted and needs to be reloaded."

"Ah, I'm no computer expert, but that sounds serious." Filymon looked so earnest that if Seamus hadn't known better, he'd swear he was shaken. Even his spots were darkening as they usually did when he was angry or anxious.

"It is. You are fortunate that your navigation system is the only thing that is affected instead of engineering or life support."

"Aye, sir. You are so right. I never dreamed we'd have this problem."

"These older models need to have their systems checked more often. It should be yearly. Your last upgrade was almost three years ago."

"I'll do that, sir. Thank you. And what should I do now?"

The commander answered this question. "Your systems have been restarted and are working normally. Your orders are to return to Effizus where one of the shipyards can do a more thorough check. You have authorization for this ferry flight, but your operation license is revoked until a shipyards recertifies you."

"Ferry flight? But... but what if our computer malfunctions again?"

“Calm yourself. The Star Kingdom of Rom is not a taxi or towing service. If you want one of those, you are free to call for one.”

“But, the money! I don’t have that kind of—”

“We’ve wasted enough time here!” With a click from the commander’s beak and a wave of his hand, the three other Romians walked back through the airlock. He scowled at Filymon for a moment longer and then marched out.

As soon as the airlock door closed, Seamus threw his arms up in the air and took in a breath to shout in celebration. Filymon, however, slapped his hand over Seamus’ mouth. It stung and the surprise of it made his eyes water.

Filymon leaned close and whispered so quietly, Seamus could hardly hear him: “They may have bugged the ship.” When Seamus nodded, Filymon pulled his hand from over Seamus’ mouth and said the next in a normal voice. “Well, you heard those imperial thugs, let’s turn around and head back in system. I want you up on the flight deck with me. If the life support goes, we can seal off the command section and crank up the emergency life support systems.”

Three hours later they were met by an orbital tug that pulled them into a shipyards that looked like a tall cylinder with dozens of spokes radiating outward. As soon as they pulled into a slip, a net of girders unfolded, encircling them. Normally, Seamus would be pressed up against the windows, soaking in as much as he could, but he could tell Filymon was stewing. As soon as the airlock made hard seal, he was storming down the tunnel. Seamus hadn’t been told what to do, so he decided to stay put. He wanted to check on Thunderblade, but if the ship was bugged, it could be trouble.

Ten minutes later Filymon returned and motioned for him to follow. Seamus ran after him to the shuttle. As soon as he stepped inside he noticed Filymon had taken the pilot's seat. "Clean up that mess back there," he growled. Seamus turned to see the cargo areas had been turned over, presumably searched by the Romians. He knew that tone, so he got straight to work. As he straightened everything, he felt the shuttle lift from the docking cradle and make a slow turn. He wondered if Filymon were still acting for the benefit of any recording devices, or if he was really that angry. He soon learned it was a little of both.

"Hurry up back there and get up here and fly," his master barked. "My contact in the shipyards just scanned the shuttle and we're clear of any bugs." A minute later Seamus was up front and keying in their destination for their seaside dock at Effizus. As they dropped to the planet, Filymon finally spoke his mind.

"Empty quivers, those Romians really put it to me. They have me shut down until I have a complete software upgrade. We're going to be stuck here for two days and it will cost me ten thousand Ceez. Break my last arrow, if that Deme still had a coin left in his pockets, I'd make him pay for this. If he'd kept the fuel tanks on that cargo pod full, we wouldn't be dealing with this. Next time, we're not going to be in such a hurry. We won't move our pod until we're sure we can get the other one. Oh, that reminds me. Good job on moving the ship. If you hadn't done that, we'd be floating wreckage now, instead of wasting our time here. And I say you handled yourself right well coming out to help me get that pod in place. Thanks."

Seamus didn't know how to respond. Filymon had never thanked him before and had hardly ever complimented him. He decided on a simple, "You're welcome."

♦ ♦ ♦

As soon as Seamus had tied off the shuttle at the dock, Filymon had his ground car pulled around. They went straight for Deme's. They didn't get far before realizing something big was going on. The Arcadia was jammed with vehicles, all headed toward the great arena cut into the hills above the city. The traffic slowed to a crawl and crowds of people were now walking or running. Finally, they stopped moving altogether and Filymon cursed as he realized the cars ahead had been abandoned. Horns wailed behind them and people shouted at one another.

"What kind of craziness is this!" he shouted at no one in particular and pounded on the wheel. He swung his door open striking several passersby, but they ignored him, running ahead. Seamus couldn't get his door open with the rush of people, so he lowered the window and partway climbed out, holding onto the roof of the car. Just then Seamus saw the TENT dealer, Prazella race past holding tightly onto the arm of a man, probably her husband. And just behind them was Epaphras.

"Master, look! It's Epaphras!"

"Come on!"

Seamus grabbed Filymon's tunic and held on as they moved up through the running riot. Just before they arrived at the arena, they caught up with Epaphras. It took a vigorous shaking to get his attention. "Let go of —Fil? Fil, what are you doing here? I thought your schedule—"

"What's going on here? What's the trouble?"

"It's your friend, Deme Trius! He's summoned all the craftsmen and they're protesting Pol! The city is in an uproar."

"What?"

The crowd carried them along, in through the arched doors of the arena and down the aisles of the amphitheatre. People swarmed the seats and shoved others along to make room. Prazella's husband led them toward the far side, where others they apparently knew waited by another entrance. Before they got there, Deme's voice rang out. Seamus turned to see him on the stage as he made his way.

"People of Effizus, you all know why we are here! I've called together the craftsmen who make the icons of worship for our great goddess, Artimiss. And not just you, but everyone whose livelihood depends upon her worship. Pilgrims from all over the Star Kingdom come here to worship her, to see her face, and we send them the shrines and figurines they need to worship wherever they live. This is no small business, and it brings us a good income! Or it did." In response, the majority of the crowd booed and hissed. Others stomped and shouted.

"And why has our livelihood been so affected? That Judian, Pol!"

The clamor grew louder.

"Yes, we all have seen and heard how this Pol has brought trouble to us. He has convinced and led astray great numbers of people here in Effizus, and even in this whole quadrant of the Star Kingdom! He says that man-made gods are no gods at all. He discredits us! But it's not just us he defames, or our trade, he defames the great goddess herself, Artimiss! She who is worshipped throughout the quadrant and the whole Kingdom will be robbed of her divine majesty!"

The resulting cry shook the ground and forced Seamus to cover his ears. A voice chanted behind him, and then others joined. In a wave of unity that spread around from one end to the other, the filled arena began to scream, "Great is Artimiss of Effizus!" Over and over they shouted until no other sound was made other than the chant and the stomps and claps in beat with it. Seamus had never heard such a shout.

Just then there was a commotion at the nearby entry. Seamus caught a glimpse of Pol, his goggled eyes shimmering and his voice crying out with emotion. It looked like he was trying to come into the arena. Some of those who Seamus had seen at the school grabbed him and pulled him away. And it was a good thing too. Two of his companions who had entered before him were recognized by some of the crowd. They were seized and dragged out onto the dais, beaten the whole way. The chant fell into confusion, becoming an explosive roar.

Seamus wasn't sure what exactly happened next. Others, who looked similar to Pol with green-tan skin, sent a man out onto the stage. After speaking with Deme, he turned, motioning for the crowd to silence. Maybe it was his physical similarity to Pol, or maybe just his attempt to bring order, but in unison the arena found its voice again and soon "Great is Artimiss of Effizus!" thundered and echoed. This went on and on despite anyone's attempts to quiet them. And it soon became apparent that Pol's companions and the man who tried to bring order were not being allowed to leave the stage.

Seamus watched for awhile, until the excitement and emotion grew tiring. Still the chant went on and on. Nothing seemed to be happening other than people shouting. It was almost as if no one knew what to do next. Seamus looked for Filymon, but he didn't see him anywhere. Just as Seamus decided to walk around to look for his master, another man came to the dais, wearing the robes of a government official. The crowd finally quieted as the man stepped forward to speak.

"People of Effizus, doesn't all the universe know that the world of Effizus is the guardian of the temple of the great Artimiss and of her image, which fell from heaven? Doesn't she look out from the sea to greet everyone who comes to our shores? Since these facts are undeniable, you need to quiet down and stop making trouble!

"You have brought these men here, though they have neither robbed any temples nor blasphemed our fair goddess. If Deme Trius or anyone else has a grievance, the courts are open and the judges are ready." He turned to look back at Deme and the other craftsmen and traders. "If you have a case, then press charges! If there is anything further you want to bring up, it must be settled legally. As it is, we are in danger of being charged with rioting since we have no legal reason for all this commotion. Now go home! Go home all of you!"

Deme appeared to be glowering in the sudden uneasy quiet, but after a moment he headed for the exits with quick, long strides. The other ringleaders followed, and the crowd around Seamus started muttering and moving, and it looked like they were headed for the exits too. He looked around for Filymon, but he was still nowhere to be seen.

"This place is nutters," he muttered. He grabbed Epaphras' arm as the young man turned to leave. "Wait! Do you know where Filymon is?"

Epaphras drew close to be heard over the din. "I have no idea. Why don't you come with us? Filymon would probably check with us first."

"Where are you going?"

"To the school, probably. We need to figure out what to do next."

TWENTY-FIVE – DIFFERENT

An hour later after dodging especially surly groups of protesters and enduring nasty words most of the way, Epaphras and Seamus made it to Prazella and Aquyia's store. A couple dozen humans of various shade and a short porcupine-looking couple stood around the displays talking, sharing their thoughts and experiences of the day's events. As Seamus meandered through the TENT displays, he recognized some of them from his visits with Epaphras at the school. Overhearing their conversations, what surprised Seamus was *why* they were meeting. He had figured they would be discussing how to get off planet. Instead, most of those present were reconsidering plans that were apparently already in motion to do that very thing. They were now thinking about *staying*.

He quickly learned that just a few weeks ago, Pol had already decided his time in Effizus was complete and had appointed leaders for the various groups of local followers. As a result, the leadership training school had been closed just that very week, the students having learned all they needed to spread the teachings of Yeshua wherever they went. Unknown to the local artisans, a mass exodus had been about to take place, as students and their families would spread to other worlds to fulfill their religious missions. But now in the aftermath of such a great protest the talk was whether the riot would change those plans.

When Pol arrived with some others, they officially started. Seamus listened in at first. They sang some songs and prayed to their Yeshua for a few minutes before beginning their discussion. Two opinions seemed to form. Some were even more determined to leave, convinced the riot was nothing more than a last ditch attempt by some enemy to thwart their plans. Others felt like they shouldn't leave the planet while things were so unsettled and the local community of worshipers so exposed to harassment and danger. After a while Seamus slipped out. The conversation seemed to go back and forth, and it didn't look like it would end anytime soon.

Seamus wondered where Filymon was. The man wasn't answering his com, or else it wasn't working – he wasn't sure which. Of course if Seamus had wandered off and didn't answer Filymon's call, he would be sure to get a shocking for it. Seamus brooded about this for awhile, but then remembered that he now had the remote. Filymon would never be able to shock him again, thanks to his wonderful little robot. And that got him thinking about his escape plans. Part of him wanted to take Thunderblade's advice and leave Löwin on Rom, but besides having promised one another to help the other escape, Seamus believed he would really need Löwin. He had learned a lot in the months he had been here, but she knew a lot more – a whole lot more. So now what to do?

One thing he was sure of, he could make Filymon angry in a flash, but it would probably take time for him to become so frustrated with him that he would decide to take him to Rado. The key was to time it just right, but he had no idea when Löwin would be ready. He finally decided that under the circumstances he should start acting just bad enough that Filymon would punish him fairly regularly. That way when Löwin contacted them, just a bit more acting up would drive Filymon into returning him.

As Seamus sat on the window sill scheming ways to irritate his master, he watched the travelers on the road hurry past with the approach of "night". The sun never really set at Effizus: it more circled the horizon, dipping behind the northern mountains to create dusk for several hours. But it was enough for the locals to call it a day. When the sun disappeared the meeting in the TENT store broke up. The leaders quietly came out, staying in larger groups for safety as they made their way.

Epaphras finally came out a few minutes later. "Sorry, with the meeting and all, I forgot you were out here."

"No bother at all. So what did you folks decide?" The young man took a seat on the sill next to him, watching his friends hurry off.

"Mostly to stay the course. Pol is leaving for Macidon like he planned. Tem and Rastus are – I'm sorry, they're some friends of mine from the school – they are already there getting everything ready. Prazella and Aquyia are going to stay here and help lead the locals and others who stay. And we've got a lot of groups leaving. Every world on this side of the Star Kingdom will have someone headed their way."

"And what are you going to do?"

"Me? I was going to stay here for awhile, but since you and Fil are here, I thought I might see if he will let me come to Kollos with you now. I had always planned to come back one day to try and get something started there. And who knows? Maybe he will even let me use his place to start."

"Really? When you left I thought you'd never be back."

"Me too. But... things are different now."

Just then a lone figure caught their attention in the dim. A moment later they saw it was Filymon walking with a pronounced limp. Epaphras ran out to meet him and it took Seamus a minute to think to follow him. When he caught up with him, Epaphras had already inserted himself under Filymon's left arm, trying to take the weight off an obviously swollen and bruised ankle.

"Master, what's wrong? What happened?"

"Arghh, I caught up with that string-popping Deme after that ridiculous riot, and told him a thing or two about how poorly he set us up with that pod. Well, it came to sharp words, he grabbed my shirt, I busted his nose, and then his thugs chased me off. I got a-way easy enough, but then I rolled my ankle just after."

Epaphras chuckled. "Today was probably not the best day to have a disagreement with him, Fil. Of course, you always had im-peccable timing when someone was already in a bad mood."

"Aye, but he had it coming, and it was might satisfying."

Seamus had to ask. "Master, are we still going to ship for him?"

"I don't know, boy. We didn't get that far in our... negot-iations."

Epaphras chuckled. "And I suppose you left your ground car at the arena?"

"Me and a couple hundred other people."

"Then why don't you two stay here tonight."

♦ ♦ ♦

That evening they stayed at Prazella and Aquyia's home, a two-story apartment on the backside of the store. They graciously doctored Filymon's ankle, fed them, and made them comfortable for the night. The next day Aquyia and Epaphras drove them to the arena, where Filymon was able to get his car out of the thinning jumble of abandoned vehicles. Filymon offered Aquyia money for their hospitality, which the TENT dealer refused, saying how they were always welcome. Filymon seemed genuinely touched and promised to stop by on his next visit.

From there Seamus and Filymon began to make their way to Filymon's dockside warehouse, where Filymon intended to stay the next night on the shuttle as they waited on the shipyards to finish their unneeded work. Along the way Filymon muttered how Deme had probably burned everything down to the waterline in retaliation.

Seamus looked out at the shore, covered with all sorts of commercial wharfs. "If he did destroy your place, what are you going to do?"

"Rebuild, of course. My parents built that warehouse and dock, may they be blessed on their eternal hunt."

Seamus couldn't help it. "Sir, it doesn't seem like you need such a big warehouse. And we're usually only here a day or two every couple weeks. Why couldn't we use one of the commercial docks instead? It would probably be a lot cheaper, don't you think?"

Filymon gripped the steering wheel more tightly, but his voice was wistful. "I was your age when they built that place. There was so much freight coming through we had a small army working here. We even subcontracted out to several shippers, and ran the route every other day." He shook his head. "You should have seen it. But then they retired and handed the business over to me. It didn't take long for everything to go bad. Not long after giving me the business, they disappeared while traveling in this little yacht they had gotten. They were going to see the sights in Zandrea, but never arrived where they were headed. Then the Romians found the direct hypertrack from here to Galatiana, and business has been downhill ever since. But, you know, I'm going to make this work somehow. That warehouse is going to be humming one day, and I won't need to pander to bow breakers like that Deme to keep in business."

Seamus said nothing in reply.

A few minutes later the warehouse came into view, and the shuttle bobbed at the deck in the gentle swell. All was normal. Seamus helped Filymon limp to the shuttle, where a message from Deme was waiting on the com, saying he had canceled all his contracts with Filymon and was urging all his friends in the guild to do the same. Filymon took this quite calmly, as if he had expected it. Seamus didn't know what to think, and he definitely didn't know what to say.

♦ ♦ ♦

Later that day Epaphras came and talked to Filymon, asking if he wouldn't mind giving Pol and two others a lift up to the *Miletus* space station where their transport to Macidon was leaving the next day. Filymon agreed since the *Wander Wide* was to be ready by then at the adjacent shipyards anyway. Epaphras also asked Filymon about coming with them to Kollos, staying with them, and using one of the outbuildings as a meeting place as he spread the story of Yeshua. Surprisingly, Filymon agreed to this, too, on the condition that Epaphras not incite any riots.

♦ ♦ ♦

The next day Pol and the two men who had been dragged up on the stage during the riot, Aristachus and Gaius, met them at the dock, along with Epaphras. Filymon sat in the copilot's seat, turned to face their passengers. Despite losing his biggest customer – and a few more since then – Filymon was quite jovial. He joked how he hadn't seen Deme worked up like that in some time and how much he enjoyed seeing him get a taste of what was coming to him. Pol's response surprised Seamus. He chuckled when one of the others remarked how they always like to put on a big show. But then he spoke warmly in a tone both wise and kind.

"Believe me, Filymon, as much as possible we try to live at peace with everyone and do what is right in their eyes. We try to be sincere in our love, to hate what is evil, and cling to what is good. We want to honor others above ourselves, but at the same time, we never want to lack in our zeal. And when we are persecuted for serving Yeshua, we bless our oppressors and don't curse them. We do not repay anyone evil for evil. And we don't take revenge, my friend, but leave that to God to handle, who says in the scriptures, 'It is mine to avenge; I will repay.' But for us he commands, 'If your enemy is hungry, then feed him; if he's thirsty, then give him something to drink.' And his command means this: Do not be overcome by evil, but instead overcome evil with good."

"Well, Mister Pol, I admire your philosophy. It's certainly more straightforward than the regular fare here at Effizus. But I can't see that working for me."

Seamus glanced back to see Epaphras squirming as he glanced back and forth from Filymon to Pol. Pol smiled before answering, his goggled eyes shimmering.

"So, my friend, what philosophy would you say works for you?"

"My philosophy? Uh, well I'm no learned mystic as yourself. I'm just a simple shipper trying to get by." He paused for a moment, but when no one filled the silence, Filymon continued. "Well, like most on this side of the Star Kingdom, I worship Artimiss, the great goddess of the hunt."

"And that belief works for you?"

"Well, I say, my own hunt has been mostly a hard one. From the looks of it, kind sir, your own hunt hasn't gone too well. I heard you took quite a beating in Galatiana a few years back, eh?"

"Oh, yes, and not just there. I have been constantly on the move and have been endangered everywhere I've gone. I have been imprisoned frequently, flogged severely, exposed to death again and again. Several times I've received thirty-nine lashes from my people, the Judians. I've been beaten with rods by the Romians. As you noted, I was stoned in Galatiana. What else... I've been shipwrecked. I've labored through many sleepless nights. I've been homeless, hungry, and thirsty. I've been smuggled out of places where I've been ordered arrested for sharing my good message about Yeshua. Yet along with these troubles I've seen amazing things: visions and revelations from my Lord. I've seen paradise and heard inexpressible things, things no one is permitted to tell.

"I could boast like a madman of these things, of the things I've endured and those I've seen. I could become conceited, but God keeps me so I'd much rather boast about my own shortcomings. I've asked three times of the Lord to take this away from me–" he waved at his goggles "– but he told me, 'my assistance will be sufficient for you; my strength will be perfectly known in your weakness.'

"And so, I take delight in my weaknesses, in the insults I receive, in the hardships I face, in persecutions and difficulty. For when I am weak, then I am strong. I boast about my failings, so that Yeshua's power may rest upon me."

"I say, dear sir, that as one who engages in commerce I know the value in trying sell someone something they actually want. I'm surprised you actually have gathered so many followers with what you're trying to sell."

The whole group laughed, and one of the other men responded. "No, no empty promises from us. We face many hardships but we also have lives worth living."

Pol nodded. "That reminds me... sometime back, I visited Athinsia. They, like those of Effizus, are quite religious. I remember walking around to see all their icons of worship. The city was full of so many them!"

Filymon waved dismissively. "Aye, hundreds, I'm sure. I suppose that there is a god or goddess out there promising just about anything you want. But I've heard of your message. How can you claim there is only one god? And even if there is just one, how can you be sure it's the one you worship?"

As Pol leaned forward, Seamus realized he wasn't watching the instruments. He had been so tuned into the conversation, he had almost forgotten he was flying. He refocused his attention, but listened as Pol continued.

"Good questions. When I was in Athinsia, I carefully examined each of their gods. I even found an altar with the inscription 'To an Unknown God'. I had been invited by the local philosophers to answer those very questions, so I took that as an opening to proclaim to them that what they worshipped in ignorance is the God I preach.

"I told them God made the universe and everything in it. The Lord of all heaven and every world does not live in temples built by hands. Nor is he served by any creature's hands as if he needs anything. After all, it is he who gives life and breath to everyone, and has set the times and places where each should live, that they might seek him and even reach out for him and find him. He is not far from us, for in him we live and move and exist. And even your philosophers say we are his children.

"If that is true, then we shouldn't think of the Divine as being something crafted by someone out of gold, silver, or stone, no matter how well-designed or skilled the work. In the past God has overlooked such ignorance, but now he commands everyone everywhere to turn away from such things. He has set a day when he will judge the universe with justice. And it will be Yeshua who he appoints for this task. And God himself has proven this by raising him back to life!"

"Awww, I don't know about that. Other than the occasional resuscitation, I've never heard of anyone being raised from the dead."

Epaphras responded. "See, that's the thing, Fil. You say you believe in something even though over and over it hasn't proven itself true to you. And still you're the first one to doubt what other people say; even though it's the most honest thing you've ever heard."

"Honest? Yes." He paused. "True? I say, that's the real question."

Just then the shuttle's computer announced docking in thirty seconds. That seemed to end the conversation, but then Pol spoke.

"So, the question is: either I'm insane, or what I'm saying is true and reasonable."

Filymon chuckled. "Aye, that is the question."

TWENTY-SIX – NEW DIRECTIONS

After dropping off Pol and his companions at the main terminal at *Miletus Station* in orbit around the desolate equatorial region of Effizus, Seamus piloted the shuttle over to the *Wander Wide's* slip at the adjacent shipyards. As they came in, he looked the ship over with the shuttle's exterior cameras, searching for any damage.

"I remember being that protective of this old girl," Epaphras said, chuckling.

Seamus glanced over at the former pilot sitting in the co-pilot's chair, ashamed at being caught, but also questioning himself. Why was he acting so protective of this ship? He chided himself as the docking cradle caught them and pulled them in. Now was no time to get sentimental, not with what he had in mind.

While Filymon went into the yard station to settle his bill (with Epaphras tagging along to visit an old friend), Seamus went back to his cabin to catch up with Thunderblade. When he sat on his bunk, the robot climbed up next to him, showing him a small, black, u-shaped device. "What's this?" Seamus asked.

"I have constructed this mechanism to adhere to your back, just under your slave fitting, where it would not be easily noticed. It is tuned to the fake remote in your master's possession, and will induce a mild current into your back if he decides to shock you."

"Mild current? As in electric current? Why would I want to do that?"

"In reviewing your plans to incite your master to return you to Rado, I determined there was sufficient risk he would shock you without your direct attention. If he were to initiate punishment and you did not immediately react, you may find yourself in much more trouble than you intend. I fabricated this device to provide a mild form of stimulation so that you would not be caught unaware."

"Uh, yeah, I see what you're saying... Does it hurt?" In response, Thunderblade pressed it on Seamus' forearm, where a slightly painful tingle caused him to jerk and reflexively try to knock it off. "Hey!"

"Exactly the immediate response required. Do you confirm the pain was quite weak and short in duration?"

"Uh, yeah, I guess so."

"Please allow me to attach this before your master returns."

Reluctantly, Seamus turned and lifted the back of his tunic. He squirmed as the cold metal pressed onto his skin, and his pulse quickened with the slight fear of being shocked again. At least this one he could pull off if he wanted. It was tempting. Once complete, Seamus turned back to Thunderblade and shared what had happened down on Effizus, both the riot and Filymon's falling out with Deme.

"Curious," the robot said. "Yes, I am accessing his accounts now. Sixty-eight percent of his contracts have been canceled. If Delis, his contact in Galatiana, reacts similarly, I calculate he will lose forty-five percent of his business there."

"And that's not the strong side of his business, anyway. He hardly ever makes money coming back from Galatiana. He's lucky to break even."

"Has your master mentioned his contingency plans? This may impact our tactics significantly."

Before he could answer, the airlock alarm buzzed. Someone was coming through. Seamus hurried out as Thunderblade returned to his hiding place in the closet.

"Well, let's get going before these sand eels suck another Ceez out of me." Filymon didn't look too happy and Epaphras looked like he was staying clear of his former employer.

A thought came to Seamus mind, and with it exhilaration and fear. Should he start now? He was all set with the fake remote and now with the addition to his fitting, he would never be caught unaware. Another second elapsed before he answered. "In a minute. I'm in the middle of something." He walked toward the galley.

Filymon's response was like the rumblings of a dormant volcano coming to life and finally erupting. "I... I... I say, come back here! Get on that flight deck and get us underway right now!"

Seamus turned and looked at him, allowing the actual indecision he felt to show on his face. His heart raced, thudding in his ears. He had never acted so openly blatant before. Never. He felt so powerful.

Fury darkened Filymon's spots and contorted his face. As he began slapping his hands on his pockets in search of the remote, Seamus made for the flight deck right lively. Quicker than ever before he got the ship underway, so that a half minute later, when Filymon stormed onto the flight deck with remote in hand, the ship was already accelerating toward the hypertrack. Seamus could see his master's reflection on one of the screens. He was infuriated, deep sharp breaths whistling through his nose, and the remote pointed squarely at Seamus.

"Boy! I say, you act that way again, your hide is going to be stinging for a week, you hear me?" He turned and stormed off.

Seamus let out a pent up breath and actually a whisper of a chuckle. He couldn't believe what he'd just done! He savored the rush of such open defiance. Oh, this was going to work, he thought, and what's more, it was going to be fun.

♦ ♦ ♦

A short while later Epaphras made his way up to the flight deck, slipping into the seat next to him. "Onesimus, you really shouldn't test Fil right now. He's lost a lot of business and just paid a lot of money to get the ship out of the dock."

"So? How's that my problem?" Again, Seamus' heart raced, but he wanted to taste that power again. Epaphras didn't seem to take the bait.

"He's your master. You should treat him with respect."

"Oh, like how he treats me? Or how he treated you? He got himself in this mess, and he's lucky this is all that has happened to him."

Epaphras sat there quietly for a minute, then stood and walked out.

♦ ♦ ♦

An hour or so later, Seamus was having second thoughts about how he acted. Had he done too much, too soon? And he really regretted how he had acted toward Epaphras. When he got to his bunk that night, he quietly asked Thunderblade what he thought. The robot replied that he should probably not defy Filymon again for another week, but he should continue with less confrontational things "as was his nature".

"What's that supposed to mean?"

"I am referring to your passive aggressive tendencies."

"I... am... not... past aggressive!"

"Passive aggr–"

"Whatever!"

Seamus pulled the covers over and flipped out the light.

♦ ♦ ♦

For the remainder of the trip back to Kollos, Seamus did do several minor, irritating things. He kept leaving the galley a mess and set a tool box in the corridor where Filymon tripped on it coming out of his quarters. And just before Filymon boarded the shuttle to fly down to Kollos, Seamus had poured some water on Filymon's seat and then dropped the cup on the deck where it would look like it had tipped over and fallen. Filymon cursed as the liquid soaked the seat of his trousers, and he threatened Seamus again with a shocking. Seamus only smiled to himself.

Everything was going perfectly.

♦ ♦ ♦

After being warmly greeted by Apphia and Chippus, Filymon suggested for Epaphras to look at the various outbuildings to pick one out for meetings. Filymon's generous expression soured as he glanced at Seamus. "Boy, go help him clean it up or whatever he needs." As Seamus and Epaphras walked off past the garage, he heard Filymon grumbling to Apphia about how Seamus had been acting.

"What's so funny?" Epaphras asked.

"Oh, nothing. So what's in all these buildings?" They walked toward the dome closest to the garage where Seamus stayed, a building roughly the same size.

"This was a warehouse back before the Romians started requiring all the freight to come through their stations. I couldn't tell you what those other three are. I think I've only been in this one once when we needed a part or something."

After keying in the access code, the large, bay-style door slid open with a squealing rumble. The lights flickered on, illuminating the dusty air. Various crates were stacked here and there and a forklift poked from under an old tarp.

"This might work," Epaphras said with growing excitement. He bounded in, leaving footprints in the dusty floor. He checked what looked like an office, tried the plumbing in the restroom, and then took the stairs two at a time to the second level. He called out unseen, "It has an apartment up here just like my – I mean, your – room above the garage."

Seamus looked the place over, his nose tickling from the particles filling the air from their movement. This was going to take a lot of work. He noticed several drain grates on the floor and wondered if they could just move out the boxes and other equipment and just hose the place down.

Epaphras trotted back down. "This will be perfect."

Just to be sure they checked the other buildings that were smaller. One looked like it had been a barn at one point, one was another storage building piled high with old junk, and the third looked like an old factory of some sort. Epaphras explained that Filymon's great grandparents had bought the place and the factory had already been here. No one was sure what it used to do, but thought it might have processed some of the grains that used to be farmed here. The main thing was that it had enough space to hold what was in the warehouse.

♦ ♦ ♦

The next day the whole family pitched in to help Epaphras clean the building. The forklift didn't work, so Apphia called a neighbor who hauled over a farm tractor with forks that could do the job. After clearing out the warehouse for them, the man asked what they were planning. Filymon nervously started to make up some excuse, but then Epaphras butted in and shared his story. By the end the man had invited Epaphras to visit in a few days so he could hear more.

And so, by the end of the day they were exhausted and filthy, but with a great sense of accomplishment. Epaphras had a clean apartment to sleep in upstairs and an office area below to work in. The restroom was clean and running well. And with a lot more cleaning, the main area would be ready for at least a hundred people. But what Epaphras said was the greatest accomplishment – was that hopefully the first of many fish had come into the nets Yeshua had given him.

♦ ♦ ♦

The next day, Filymon and Seamus departed for Galatiana. Seamus had planned to act up enough to get shocked during this trip, only Filymon was very preoccupied. He seemed oblivious to the things Seamus did to irritate him, such as leaving empty pitchers in the refrigerator. And for much of the trip he worked in the small office area of his cabin reviewing the mail he had received on the last message courier. And it must not be very good mail from the swearing Seamus heard through the door.

Filymon's only other interest was to see if they still had manual control of the *Wander Wide*. When Seamus checked, he found their access gone, wiped away during the recent software upgrade. Filymon seemed to take this in stride – surprisingly, Seamus thought. But then, he realized, his own access through Thunderblade might be gone too. At his first opportunity he made straight for his cabin. To his relief, Thunderblade told him he had kept access the whole time.

When they arrived at Tavium, Filymon hurried them down to the moon's surface to meet Delis. It took a little longer since the city had moved again and reorganized in a new location. But the train-like building on stilts looked the same as well as the giant woman's immaculate appearance. As Seamus stood attentively at the door, he listened as Delis explained that she could not do business with Filymon anymore. "I'm sorry Filymon, but the consortium has an exclusive contract with the artesian guild at Effizus. If I go against what they decided, then it will ruin me."

Filymon's voice was flat and it looked as if he barely had the energy to speak. "But what about my record? I have the best service and prices around, and we've been partners for years!"

The tall woman grimaced. "I'm sorry, old friend. You've been blacklisted. I'll try all I can to get you back on the preferred shipper list, but until then..."

♦ ♦ ♦

The trip back to Filymon's landing pad was as quiet as it was tense. Seamus could tell Filymon was thinking hard. He even turned his hover car on auto-drive while he stared off at the thick tall forests racing past. About halfway to the pad, he began scanning through the local businesses. When Seamus saw he was looking at real estate sales, he finally worked up the courage to speak.

"Master, are you thinking of selling your landing pad and storage building here on Tavium?"

"I don't see what else to do, Onesimus. Between Delis and Deme, I've lost nearly all of my off-world accounts. The only business I have left is local to Kollos. I say, I won't need my off-world bases anymore, and like you said at Effizus, I can really cut my costs by moving my operations to a commercial distributor."

"But I thought you weren't going to sell—"

"I have to, my boy. I have to. I've got to take things in a new direction. I just need to figure out what that direction is to be."

TWENTY-SEVEN - SUMMONS

The next several months saw incredible change to Filymon and his family, to Epaphras, and even to Seamus to a lesser extent. Facing incredible losses from his falling out with Deme, Filymon had cut back severely, trying to match his expenses to his income. He sold his facilities at Tavium and Effizus, using the proceeds to settle a lot of debts. And what had been a twice monthly route between Galatiana, Kollos, and Effizus he now ran once every two months - if that. It was an emotional few weeks, but once he made the hard decisions, Filymon immediately started to look to the future.

With Effizus and Galatiana nearly off his lidar, Filymon began focusing on his few customers at Kollos. Kollos had been little more than a stop along the way between Galatiana and Effizus during good times, and was still suffering from the loss of traffic from when the direct hypertrack had been opened. There wasn't much opportunity. Even so, Filymon seemed to be enjoying the challenge of rebuilding and diversifying his business. Seamus heard Apphia tell one of her friends that the difference was that he was building his own business instead of tending to one he had inherited. True or not, Seamus had to agree. And in building his new business, nothing seemed to be unworthy of Filymon's consideration. He was even trying to find a use for the old grain processing factory on his property that had stood idle longer than he had been alive.

Apphia and Chippus seemed to thrive as well. With Filymon home much more often and with some of the main sources of friction now gone, Seamus began to think of them more as a family than as a mother and son that he and Filymon visited for a few days every week. But it wasn't just that. Apphia and Chippus had joined with Epaphras's small-but-growing community of Yeshua followers. Everyday, Seamus would hear them talk about what Epaphras had taught and would read from their holy writings. And it surprised him how immensely practical these seemed to be. It was almost as if they had enrolled in a school to teach them how life best worked and every day was an opportunity to apply and test what they had learned.

Epaphras was budding in his new role too. After that first talk with Kepheus, their neighbor who had helped clear the old warehouse, Epaphras had met the man's family, more of the neighbors, and some of his own relatives. Their first organized gathering numbered about fourteen people, and many came to accept Epaphras' message about Yeshua. Those followers met every few days at either the dome or in various homes, constantly inviting others.

Soon their numbers grew to over sixty and they began to call themselves an *ekklesia*, an old Athinian term for an assembly of public servants. And serve they did. It almost seemed as if this religion of Yeshua intended to relieve every social ill within their influence. Every follower seemed to take whatever he or she was best skilled at doing and use it to find a way to better someone's life in the name of Yeshua. Even though Seamus was uninterested in the religion itself, he found himself wanting to help make such a difference as he saw among the Yeshuaians.

With all of this change, Seamus' role changed too. Instead of flying and tending to the *Wander Wide* so much, he found himself running errands on various business ideas Filymon had dreamed up, trying to get the old grain factory working, or else helping out with the ekklesia. At first, he found himself cleaning the building after their gatherings, but soon others noticed and insisted on taking on this work. Social trappings were left at the door, he was told. He was glad to hear it, too, as much as he hated cleaning. In time he found himself flying the shuttle a lot for the ekklesia, moving people or goods here or there around the city and even elsewhere on the planet at times.

With his work for the ekklesia, he tried to do a good job, and also for Apphia and Chippus. But when it came to Filymon, Seamus kept up his plan of intentional irritation and laziness, accented by an occasional display of defiance resulting in a "shocking". His favorite "play", as he began to think of them in wallball terms, was to fall asleep while out of sight. Invariably (and more frequently), Filymon would come to check on him, find him "asleep", and start screaming at him about his laziness and general worthlessness. Seamus thought he had found the right balance where he was regularly in trouble, but only shocked every couple weeks. It seemed like he could easily get Filymon in a fury whenever he wanted, and so as he waited on word from Löwin, he just kept to this routine.

After a couple months, Seamus had Thunderblade contact Löwin again to make sure she was okay and still able to arrange for her escape. She responded that things were taking longer than expected, but she would be ready very soon. This worried Seamus a little. With the *Wander Wide* largely unused, she was now out in an inexpensive, distant orbit, as Filymon had given up his slip at the marina. Direct communication was impossible and so Thunderblade and Seamus now only used short text messages by some arrangement Thunderblade had devised. All that Seamus knew was that he sent the message over his watch and a few days later he'd get a response. He hoped that when Löwin contacted them, that the communication lag wouldn't cause any problems.

♦ ♦ ♦

After several months of the same routine, Seamus woke up to a text from Thunderblade, reminding him it was his fifteenth birthday. Seamus was shocked at seeing his robot's greeting and well wishes. Had it been so long? He thought back and realized he had been a slave for almost eleven months by Earth's calendar. So much had happened that it seemed like he'd been here for years. That precious thread back to his former life was coated with emotion. It reminded him of who he really was. He thought of Earth, where extended family and friends would hopefully remember him and wonder where he and his parents were. Did the Agency ever send out a search party?

Seamus was sullen for the rest of the day. Chippus first noticed when Seamus declined to play army or wallball with him. Later Apphia approached him as he sat outside on the wing of the shuttle, tossing blades of grass he had plucked. After sitting next to him and repeatedly, if tenderly, questioning him, he finally gave in and told her it was his birthday. She didn't seem to grasp the significance of it, until he explained to her how special birthdays were where he was from.

"I'm sorry, Onesimus, our milestones aren't tied to the calendar. Instead of... *birthdays*—" she said the word like it was in a foreign language "—we usually celebrate levels of achievement. If Archippus continues at his normal pace, he will complete his primary studies next month. He can then become an apprentice or begin secondary courses if he wants to go to a trade school or university. We are planning a big party for that, much bigger than when he finishes each level." She looked at him with a sad smile. "What does your family usually do on your... birthday?"

"I don't know... a party, usually. And everyone wishes me a happy birthday."

She looked at him and then said something that made him fall apart. "You miss your family." He began to cry, and then wail as she hugged him. He covered his face with his hands. She held him tightly as he sobbed, and that made it all the worse. How long had it been since anyone had shown him any love?

When he finally quieted she said, "We're not your family, but we're—" Just then Filymon called on his watch. He glanced up at Apphia. She motioned for him to answer, and with a smile and a wave, made straight for the house.

"Yes, Master?"

Filymon's face filled the tiny screen. "Onesimus, fly over to that factory we were at the other day. I say, Kepheus thinks he sees what the problem is with this machinery and we called in for a part. They'll have it at the desk."

Seamus wondered if he should backtalk, but he really wasn't in the mood to fight. Besides, it would be two hours away from here. "On my way, sir."

♦ ♦ ♦

Seamus took his time and when he finally got back the family was gathering for supper. While eating, Chippus begged and begged him to go to the gathering that night, to hear Epaphras talk about Yeshua. Finally, Seamus relented, if nothing more than to get the boy to shut up about it. And so as dusk settled, they headed to the dome on the far side of the garage. Even Filymon went, though it looked like Apphia was making him go.

When they entered, all those gathered turned and began to clap, shouting "Habby-barthay!" Seamus cocked his head trying to understand what was being said.

"Habby-burrethay, Onesimus!" Chippus yelled above the din.

Then he understood. They were wishing him 'Happy Birthday', but they didn't know exactly how to pronounce it! He laughed aloud, both at them and at the surprise and joy of so many wishing him well.

Instead of gathering for study and conversation as usual, the ekklesia had a party that evening for a slave. Apphia ran to the office, returning with a huge sunberry pudding – his favorite Kollosan dessert (so far). He was given the first bowl. Between bites, he tried to explain how birthdays were celebrated where he was from, and some upcoming ones that were even more special. Apphia found him after awhile with another large helping, and everyone laughed while he beamed with delight.

Through the night, Filymon caught his eye. At first, the man stood warily, leaned against the wall, watching the crowd. At times his expression was puzzled, at other times he seemed uninterested, and still other times he seemed to almost disbelieve what he was seeing. Many made their way over to him and he seemed pleased to talk. And Seamus even overheard someone apologizing to him for some past wrong. And at some point, he lowered his guard and joined in, laughing and visiting and even getting a second helping of pudding.

After the party ended and the four of them walked back toward the house, Seamus cleared his throat, trying to will the emotion welling up within him from affecting his voice. "Um, thanks for the party. I had a mighty craic time."

Apphia smiled, but took on an exasperated air. "Onesiums, you've already taught me one new word. Can we keep it to one a day?"

Seamus chuckled. "Sorry, M'Lady. I had a really fun time. This morning I never would have guessed I'd be having a birthday party."

"We hope you enjoyed it."

Chippus looked like he might burst with excitement. He darted into the door to the garage and came back with something in hand. "Here, Onesimus!" The boy handed him a box, wrapped in colorful paper. As much as he was surprised to be receiving a gift, he was also glad that some things, like wrapping presents, were the same here in this alien culture. He ripped off the paper and opened the box.

"Hey, it's a new wallball." He palmed the ball, squeezing it, then pulled it out. Wow, this is a nice one."

"I picked it out! Maybe we can play tomorrow and try it out?"

"You're on," he answered, but then thought to look up at Filymon. His master was looking away, his lips pursed as when agitated. Seamus decided to say nothing more other than "Thank you all, again. Good night."

"Good night, Onesimus, and happy... birthday."

As he closed the door he could hear Filymon outside muttering: "He's a slave, remember? Not one of the family."

He paused on the stairs to his room as he heard Apphia's response, firm, yet calm – much more calm the hotheaded explosions he'd heard from her in the past. "I know how you feel about him, but we're the only family he has right now."

♦ ♦ ♦

Seamus awoke the next day, expecting either a load of busy work from Filymon as a reminder he was a slave, or at best some time to play wallball with Chippus. Instead, breakfast was full of excited chatter. As soon as he walked in the kitchen, Chippus bounced up beside him, yanking on his sleeve. It seemed like the boy was getting taller by the second. "Onesimus, did you hear? Epaphras got a message from Pol, asking if we could come pick him up with the *Wander Wide*!"

Seamus glanced into the dining room where Filymon and Epaphras were just sitting down. Seamus must have looked quizzical because Epaphras answered, "And despite his reputation, Fil has graciously volunteered his services."

"I say, it's nothing. It's not like the *Wander Wide* is getting much use right now."

Apphia herded Seamus and Chippus to the table, shushing Chippus before he started up again. Once they all had seated themselves and quieted, she glanced over at Epaphras who looked heavenward. "Oh, good and gracious God, we bless you for this table. Thank you for meeting all of our needs as we spread your fame."

Seamus glanced at Filymon during the short prayer. As usual, he sat quietly, though he didn't appear to be participating as Apphia and Chippus did. Things had changed so much. The icons of Artimiss had disappeared months ago. The only ones remaining were on the *Wander Wide*, and those he had seen Filymon put in one of his drawers. Seamus reflected that since the riot, his talk with Pol, and the meltdown of his business, it seemed like Filymon no longer worshipped Artimiss. But, then again, it also seemed as if he wasn't sure what to believe.

The conversation at the table quickly turned to preparing the *Wander Wide* for departure in two days. Pol apparently had made plans to leave the quadrant and wanted to pull together all the leaders from the various worlds he had visited for a parting conference at Effizus. He was currently in Athinsia, and not only did he need passage, he had requested passage for many others. The plan was to visit two moons, an asteroid belt, and dock with two ships in transit. It was a tight schedule and somehow they had to accommodate somewhere between twenty and thirty people. The internal cargo bay was the obvious choice, but Filymon didn't want guests sleeping on the deck.

As the table grew quiet with thought on this subject, Apphia mumbled something. After Filymon coaxed her, she said, "Halcyon might have plenty of bunks at his hunting lodge available this time of year." The silence continued, chilling, and Seamus wondered why. Filymon wiped his mouth with a napkin.

"Hmmm... you know, last night at your gathering, Halcyon apologized to me."

A jumbled chorus of surprise answered him: "Really?", "You talked last night?", "Does this mean you and Halimeda's dad's not fighting no more?"

"Oh, I say, it surprised me as much as it does you. Yes, we patched things up." He paused thoughtfully. "I guess your religion is making an impact on people."

Seamus couldn't stand it anymore. "I'm sorry to interrupt, Masters, but I don't understand. What are you talking about?"

Apphia glanced tentatively at Filymon. "Well, it started when Filymon and I were young, before we fell in love. I was seeing Halcyon–"

"That has nothing to do with it! It was a partnership gone bad, that's all. The only people who don't know partnerships are a bad idea are those getting into them."

Epaphras kept the faltering conversation moving. "So, you think Halcyon might loan us bunks out of his fishing lodge?"

Filymon shrugged. "Maybe. It's nowhere near his peak season and his usual patrons are in the north seas right now. I don't want to ask him, though. We may have made amends, but that don't make us friends again. If you asked him, he might."

♦ ♦ ♦

After breakfast Epaphras did just that that very thing, calling Halcyon to share their need. Halcyon was agreeable and even eager to help out, which set off a huge flurry of work over the next two days. Soon the *Wander Wide* was back in low orbit with a dozen volunteers from the ekklesia at work. Seamus spent those two days flying almost non-stop, piloting the weight-maxed shuttle back and forth. The first day it was moving people to and offloaded cargo back from the ship, while the second day the craft was crammed to the flight deck with beds, mattresses, bedding, food, and other supplies from Halcyon's oceanside fishing lodge.

On the afternoon of the second day after several volunteers had unloaded the last of the supplies, Seamus shut down the shuttle and wandered through the door from the shuttle bay to the cargo hold. It looked like a maze. Someone had rigged up a grid of crisscrossing cables from various recessed eyebolts on the walls, deck, and upper bulkhead. Thick fabric had been attached to these to form small rooms, each having overlapping flaps for doors, a bunk, and a small storage chest. Seamus was impressed at how they had made accommodations for thirty out of thin air, and especially with the cleanliness of the cargo hold.

Chippus marched past wearily with a tall stack of bedding. "Looks like no wallball on this trip, Onesimus."

"Well... all this could make for interesting sport."

"Ha! Good one!"

Seamus walked back through the shuttle bay to the main cabin, where more construction neared completion. Chippus' room had been changed into a locker room of sorts. Dressing rooms similar to the temporary bunk rooms had been set up, and it looked like a reader had been attached to the wall next to the lavatory. On it Seamus read a short explanation of the *Wander Wide's* limited water processing capabilities, followed by a sign-up for a strict schedule for showers.

Three or four workers were busy in the spare cabin as he walked past. Both his door and Filymon's stood open. Chippus' bunk looked like it had been moved into Filymon's quarters, and his own room had been altered too. A fabric screen cordoned off the sleeping area, making a hallway to his lavatory, where another reader of water use procedures hung. And next to it was his closet. He fought off the urge to check on Thunderblade and instead found the flap to the screen to put his bag down. As he heaved it onto the bed through the curtain, he nearly hit his head on a second bunk now erected above his own. He recognized Epaphras' duffel sitting atop. It looked like they would be cabin mates on this run.

The galley and lounge were a work in progress too. Crates of food he had just delivered were stacked up along the walls and on the table. Apphia and a young couple were trying to organize it all. Similarly, the lounge was crammed. Gone were the regular furnishings; in their place extra tables and chairs had been set up, while supply crates covered any flat surface. Scanning over the seats, obviously, meals would be in shifts. It struck Seamus how tight things would be on this flight. Everyone had done an incredible job to make room for thirty more, but the simple fact was the Wander Wide was built for no more than eight people.

♦ ♦ ♦

That evening all the preparations were complete. Seamus had made several more trips back to the surface to return the volunteers to their homes and to pick up some last minute supplies. When he finally returned to the *Wander Wide* he was exhausted, but feeling like they really had accomplished a lot. In two days they had gotten ready and in the morning they were departing to answer Pol's summons.

As he plopped down on his bunk (making sure his head cleared the empty bunk above him), he noticed his ear-com resting on his nightstand. That stupid robot must have snuck out of the closet and put it there so he'd see it. With irritation he plugged it in his ear. With a whisper he said, "What are you doing, sneaking out? Someone might have seen you!"

Thunderblade's voice answered. "It was a slight risk, but I thought you might like to know."

"Know what?"

"Löwin has contacted me. She reports all is ready. All we have to do is to signal her when we arrive at Rom."

TWENTY-EIGHT - RETURN

Seamus could hardly sleep that night. Löwin had contacted them! Months of preparation had come to this moment. He knew exactly what to do to get Filymon so angry he'd take him back to Rom. The question was *when* to do it. One thing he didn't want to do is to ruin this trip for Epaphras or the others in his religion. They were good people, who he didn't want to think badly of him. But there would be a moment when they would be dropping off the last of their passengers back in Athinsia.

And Athinsia was one hypertrack away from Rom.

So that morning, first thing, Seamus decided to get things moving in the right direction. Instead of heading to the flight deck as Filymon had told him the night before, he headed straight for the galley where Apphia was setting out breakfast. Just as Filymon briskly walked past, Seamus took a seat. Filymon must have seen him.

"Come on, boy! What did I tell you? I say, we have to keep to the schedule."

"Well, if you're in such a hurry, why don't you get the ship moving?" Seamus' heart thudded in his chest as he said it and he could feel his face flushing hot.

"Onesimus!" Apphia exclaimed. Chippus and Epaphras paused, looking up in surprise. Filymon slid to a stop and spun around.

"How dare... you lazy, worthless...!"

Seamus just shrugged and started eating a pastry.

Filymon stormed back to his cabin, returning a moment later with the remote. His chest was heaving as he sputtered out the next: "You are not going to act your same old ways on this trip!" He thumbed the shock button as hard as he could.

Seamus jerked as the mild current ran over his body. Thanks to the addition Thunderblade had made to his fitting, it was nothing compared to what it should feel like. But it still hurt. He acted along, thrashing and groaning through gritted teeth, trying to make this look as convincing as possible.

As this went on for a few seconds, he unexpectedly thought of his father. One of the last things he had told Seamus was how he had been up to his old tricks – almost the exact words Filymon had just used. With that realization he felt a searing flash of shame, shame of how he had treated his parents and shame of what he was doing now, however necessary it was. As he fell to the floor in mock agony, he vowed things would be different as soon as this was all over.

♦ ♦ ♦

After he "recovered" and got the ship underway and through the hypertrack to Effizus, Seamus headed back to his bunk to rest as was his practice after being shocked. He slipped on the ear-com and whispered, "Did he do anything?"

Thunderblade's voice came through clearly. "I heard your provocation. You have considerable talents in this area."

Seamus ignored the jab as much as he wanted to snap back at him.

"To answer your inquiry, yes, he did do something. He pulled up your owner's manual on his reader, where I made sure he quickly found the instructions to return you to Rado for remedial training. He talked with Apphia, who defended you. At this moment he is compiling a message regarding your behavioral trends over the past few months and your most recent act of insubordination."

"He's sending Rado a message?" He was so excited at this prospect, he could hardly keep his voice a whisper.

"It would appear he intends to send it once we arrive in Athinsia."

Things were going just as they hoped.

♦ ♦ ♦

Throughout the rest of that day, and the next as they cut through the Effizus system to the hypertrack to Athinsia, Seamus continued to target Filymon with a steady stream of irritations. He kept hiding his reader. He unscrewed the cap of the salt shaker so that Filymon dumped salt all over his meal. And he allowed his expression to say what his mouth could not. Filymon noticed all of it, as evidenced by his increasingly nasty tone. Two days later when they arrived in the Athinsia binary system, Seamus wondered if he might take him straight to Rado right then. The tight schedule in the system seemed to calm his nerves, however, and instead they headed straight for *Troas Station*, at Athinsia where Pol awaited them.

After docking at the colossal station that made *Militeus* at Effizus look like a small outpost, Epaphras went in to find Pol and his companions. Instead he returned with about ten men and women of various shade and hue. This surprised them all.

"I say, where is your friend Pol?" Filymon looked disappointed.

An older man, answered instead of Epaphras. "Our dear friend, Pol, has gone ahead of us to the colony on Assos. He wanted to spend more time with the believers there, so he took an earlier flight yesterday."

"Uh, sorry Fil, this is Lukaas, he's a physician."

"It is my pleasure, Captain Filymon."

Filymon seemed to swell with either pride in the title or respect toward the speaker. "And mine as well Doctor Lukaas. If I might say, I'm pleased to hear our dear friend, Pol, now has someone to tend to him... knowing his history."

"Yes and too much history in some cases."

Seamus was sent to the flight deck at that point to get the *Wander Wide* underway, so he didn't get to hear any other introductions.

♦ ♦ ♦

It didn't take long to get to Assos, a larger than average moon at a distant orbit around the green orb of Athinsia. As soon as they made orbit, Epaphras and Seamus prepped the shuttle. With passengers onboard the *Wander Wide*, shuttle operations were more complicated, especially since the shuttle bay separated the cargo hold (turned bunk room) from the rest of the ship. There were automated safeguards in place, of course: motion sensors in the bay and all the doors to the shuttle bay were double doors. If anything were amiss, the ship's computer would not allow the shuttle to launch. Still, space is very unforgiving with second chances exceedingly rare. So after several announcements, Filymon and Apphia doublechecked the bay and manned the doors.

"Five seconds to live engines," Seamus announced, and soon he and Epaphras were away dropping toward a surface landing pad on the barren moon.

Epaphras looked back at the seating. "If it's all the same to you, on the trip back I'll sit back here with Pol."

"No problem. Looking forward to seeing him?"

"I sure am. I never expected our community on Kollos to grow so fast, or to have so many different opinions over beliefs."

"Really?"

"Oh, nothing too bad. Just some people keep trying to mix in a little of their old religious traditions."

"I could understand that. There's a big difference between what my life was a year ago and the way it is now. Every now and again it's nice to see something familiar."

Epaphras looked off, worried. "In my case, what you believe might make all the difference between following Yeshua and losing your way. I hope I'm handling this right."

♦ ♦ ♦

They landed on a circular pad that recessed into the ground, which then pulled them along a subterranean tunnel lined with small bays. The shuttle was deposited in the first one unoccupied, which quickly filled with air. In answer to Seamus' questions, Epaphras shared how the whole colony on Assos existed underground in huge caverns that once were ancient aquifers. It had first been settled for mining of the beautiful crystals, but now was more known for a school of philosophy.

Seamus couldn't wait to see a city in a huge cave, but as soon as the pressure had equalized, Pol and a few companions were marching through the open door. And just as quickly, they had rolled back out to the surface and on their way back to the *Wander Wide*. Apparently the man was in as big a hurry as he had first said in his message.

♦ ♦ ♦

The rest of the day was quite busy. Seamus got the *Wander Wide* underway and within a couple hours came in sight of their second stop at the asteroid belt between the Terrestrial and Jovian bands. Mitylene was technically a dwarf planet among an orderly stream of debris, but seemed more like a space station. A lattice of buildings, domes, docking towers, and travel tubes mostly covered the oblong hunk of rust-colored rock. Seamus squirmed in his seat as the computer piloted the *Wander Wide* up to one of the towers, thrusting continuously to match rotation and also in opposition to the slight pull of gravity. As before, several were there to meet them, coming in through the airlock as soon as they had docked.

Then it was off to the hypertrack, where two other ships were transiting across the system to rendezvous with them. Within sight of the massive Romian picket, they heaved to and docked first with the *Kios*, a merchant freighter shipping silk out of Felepye, and the *Samos* out of Kreet, another merchie transporting wine. With a full load, Seamus got them into the hypertrack to Effizus.

By then it was time for the evening meal and Seamus stepped out into a crowded room. A dozen sat around the small tables in the lounge, laughing, talking, and eating, while still others stood here and there, mostly in line at the galley. The *Wander Wide* had never felt so small. He weaved his way through and past the galley, deciding to wait until later to eat. But then Apphia called his name. He paused, as she handed him a bowl of stew over the shoulders of some of their passengers. With a thankful smile he waved at her and made straight for his bunk, but not before bumping into someone coming from his lavatory. He pulled the curtain closed for an illusion of privacy.

"What a day," he sighed.

After eating, he lay down and decided to check-in with Thunderblade. He inserted his ear-com and whispered despite the noisy din coming through his open doorway. “How are you doing?”

“I am optimal and have good news to report. Filymon sent his message to Rado, coded for the response to be returned to Athinsia. I calculate a 91% chance he intends to make a decision about taking you for remedial training when you return to Athinsia after the conference.”

“And everything else is ready?”

“It is. I still maintain manual access and have loaded programs in the ship and shuttle as we have previously discussed and planned in detail.”

Seamus grinned.

♦ ♦ ♦

During the next two days as they transited the hypertrack, Seamus mostly kept clear of everyone. He spent the majority of his time either on the flight deck or in the engine room, where his main task was to ensure the water treatment systems kept working smoothly. Filymon had moved the furniture from the lounge in there - a pleasant addition - and he quickly decided to stay here instead of his quarters. Despite the hum of the machinery it was much quieter than his bunk.

The lounge, crammed it might be, was still the largest area on the ship. At various times of the day and for the greater part of the evenings, everyone aboard would somehow find a place and listen to Pol speak. And one thing was sure, if Pol was speaking, he was going to do it for a long time. Seamus had slipped back there on the first night, and hadn’t regretted it since.

The only other curious event is that on the second day Seamus walked into the flight deck to find Pol and Filymon sitting in the rear row, praying together. Despite the fact it was a perfect opportunity to irritate his master, Seamus retreated, but not before he heard Filymon pray out loud something about repenting and following. Later he saw Filymon toss his icons of Artimiss in the airlock and flush them out into space, while his family and the other passengers cheered him on. Filymon seemed so happy after this, that it made Seamus wonder if there was really something to this religion.

♦ ♦ ♦

When they arrived in Effizus, Pol quickly made arrangements for passage to his home world of Judia. As it turned out the only flight where he would arrive in time for an important holiday was leaving that evening. So instead of holding the conference on Effizus, Pol made arrangements to hold his meeting on *Mellitus Station*. Again, there was a flurry of activity, with Seamus tasked with shuttling up several of the leaders from Effizus, including Prazella and Aquyia. Once they arrived and everyone had assembled in a low-ceilinged cargo hold, Pol began.

"You know how I lived the whole time I was with you, from the first day I came into this quadrant. I served God with great humility and with tears, although I was severely tested by the plots of those of my own people who don't believe my message. You know that I have not hesitated to share with you anything that would be helpful to you but have taught you publicly and from house to house. I have declared to both my own people and those of other races that they must turn to God in repentance and have faith in our Lord Yeshua.

"And now, compelled by God, I am going to my homeworld, not knowing what will happen to me there. I only know that in every world I visit, those who hear God's voice warn that I will face prison and hardships. However, I consider my life worth nothing to me, if only I may finish the race and complete the task Yeshua has given me — the task of testifying to the incredible news of God's grace.

"Now I know that none of you will ever see me again. Therefore, I declare to you today that I am innocent of the blood of all men. For I have not hesitated to proclaim to you the whole will of God. Keep watch over yourselves and all the community of which God has made you overseers. Be guardians of the ekklesia of God, which he bought with his own blood. I know that after I leave, savage beasts will come in among you and will not spare their victims. Even from your own number some will arise and distort the truth in order to draw away followers after themselves. So be on your guard! Remember that for three years I never stopped warning each of you night and day with tears.

"Now I commit you to God and to the message of his grace, which can empower you and give you an inheritance like family members among all those who have been made holy by God. And speaking of God's great riches, I have not coveted anyone's money or possessions. You yourselves know that these hands of mine have supplied my own needs and the needs of my companions. In everything I did, I showed you that by this kind of hard work we must help the weak, remembering the words Yeshua himself said: 'It is a greater blessing to give than to receive.'"

After this short speech, Pol and the other leaders prayed over each other, weeping as they embraced him. A short while later they walked Pol to his ship where he, Dr. Lukaas, and a few others accompanying him said their goodbyes. Seamus had already begun trying to detach himself from everyone, especially Chippus, but even so he was touched by the outpouring of love and well wishes as Pol returned to his homeworld with an uncertain future ahead of him.

That night Seamus took those from Effizus back down to the surface and returned to the *Wander Wide*. Those from the Athinsia system seemed eager to return, so Filymon asked Seamus if he'd be willing to stay up to get them on the hypertrack. Seamus agreed, mostly because he was eager to get to Athinsia himself, but also because he was surprised Filymon politely asked him instead of ordering him. It was so out of character, he wanted to say yes. And so long after everyone else was asleep after a long, emotional day, Seamus sat alone on the flight deck.

He enjoyed the silence and the swirling blue of hyperspace. "Goodbye," he whispered. He was processing so much right now, it was hard to say what or who he was saying goodbye to. Kollos? Effizus? Pol? Filymon, Apphia, and Chippus? Epaphras? He wasn't sure. One thing he did know for sure was in two days he was going to do all he could to make sure he would leave this cursed Star Kingdom and never, ever return.

Never.

TWENTY-NINE - ESCAPE

There was something different that morning. The world felt different; it vibrated with eminent change. Seamus awoke feeling how he imagined someone facing a duel would feel: a nervous excitement, second-guessing, maybe a sense of mortality. A line would be crossed today, a point of no return. Today his life - at least that of the past year - would change forever. But he had long made up his mind. He was ready. Under the guise of cleaning up, the shuttle was packed, ready for an extended flight. Thunderblade had everything ready to takeover the ship. And Seamus could sense from Filymon that he was ready for a showdown, too, especially when he received the response from Rado urging him to return Seamus for retraining. The only thing holding them back was the last of their passengers.

After breakfast, the *Wander Wide* exited the hypertrack and Seamus laid in the course: *Mitylene*, the industrial city in the asteroid field; then the Athinsian moon, Assos, with its underground civilization; and last, the gigantic orbital station, *Troas*. Throughout the day, they made each stop, saying warm goodbyes. The ship felt emptier and quieter, and at the same time building with tension.

At last the airlock door closed at *Troas* behind the last of their passengers, and they were all alone.

"Onesimus, we need to talk," Filymon growled. Chippus and Epaphras seemed to shrink behind the galley table. Apphia walked to Filymon's side with a cautious expression.

"About what?" Seamus spat.

"Your attitude, I say."

"My attitude is just fine. I think you're the one with the attitude."

Filymon's eyes narrowed and his spots darkened. "Boy, you're about as stupid as you are lazy and rebellious. You have no idea what's about to happen."

Apphia tried to insert herself between them. "Onesimus, what is wrong? Why have you been acting this way? You act like we mistreat you."

Seamus ignored her. "Stupid? How is this for stupid? How about a pitiful old man who is so stupid he runs his business in the ground? And then instead of doing the smart thing like moving it to a place where he could actually make money, he decides to try his hand at organized crime? But no, he's so stupid, he can't even break the law right, and then tops it all off with an incredible display of stupidity by hitting his best and most influential customer? Now that's stupid. But you know what? You're right. I am stupid. Maybe even stupider than you are. I am stupid for putting up with all of this for a whole year!"

With a roar of fury, Filymon had the remote out of his pocket. Seamus felt the tingle of current dance over his skin. He winced with discomfort and twitched from the slight pain, but it was nothing. His heart was pumping and he felt the fire of his words. His rage was real, and he wanted to fight. Who cared what happened next! A distant part of his brain cried out for him to stick with the plan, to fall to the floor in fake agony, but he didn't care. He wanted to hurt this wicked brute and lash out at him for all the injustice he had endured.

"You think that hur—" The taunt died in his throat as a searing pain crisscrossed his back, searing hot, like fire. Something was wrong! The fitting was working! But it was different, it burned! He fell to the ground, writhing, clawing at his back, screaming in agony. What had happened?

As soon as it stopped, Seamus pushed himself up, staggering to his feet. "I hate you, you sarky maggot!" He reared back to hit the man, but another wave of white-hot pain scorched his back. He screamed, scratching and flailing, and then dropped to the floor trying to pull the fitting off his back.

"Don't kill him!" Apphia cried.

He went limp as the pain stopped. Hands grabbed him on either side and he found himself being dragged down the corridor and thrown into Chippus' quarters. The door slid shut and he heard Filymon swearing as he keyed the panel to lock the door.

Seamus lay there in a mangled heap, tears finally coming to his eyes as the emotion and pain subsided. What had happened?

A short time later he heard his name. "Seamus? Seamus, are you all right?" It was Thunderblade's voice, and it took him a few seconds to remember he had left his ear-com in his ear.

"Yes. I'm okay. But something horrible has happened. Filymon's remote somehow accessed my fitting. How are we going to escape?"

"Seamus, that is incorrect. I anticipated you might lose control of yourself and designed the device on your fitting with two pain levels. When you deviated from the plan, I activated the second level to incapacitate you. I am sorry, Seamus."

Seamus lay there feeling a mix of emotions: anger and betrayal at Thunderblade, disappointment in himself for both losing his cool and that he was so predictable his robot had planned for it, and finally relief the plan was still on track despite himself. He sat up, rubbing his back. He decided not to comment on the fitting.

"So, what did Fil do?"

"He has announced his intention to return you to Rado. We are now in transit across the system to the hypertrack to Rom. Your plan worked."

For some reason Seamus didn't feel all that happy. He blamed the lingering pain between his shoulder blades, but deep down he didn't like what he had done to get here.

♦ ♦ ♦

Finally the day came. Seamus awoke hungry and sore after another long night of sleeping on the floor. The last three days had been hard despite his anticipation of escape. The room had been empty other than the curtains erected to form dressing rooms, and from these Seamus had made a bed of sorts on the floor. It wasn't very comfortable no matter what he tried. The sink in the cabin lavatory provided water to drink. Otherwise, Filymon had allowed no food or contact. Only an occasional brief report from Thunderblade over his ear-com provided any company.

As he lay there with stomach growling, he thought about his journey to this day: the day of his capture; meeting Löwin; escaping the sharks' interrogation plans through Thunderblade's intervention; being trained and sold into slavery by Rado; coming into Filymon's possession; being a part of a budding – and ultimately failing – smuggling operation; and now here. But the line to this point had been intersected by another over and over, a religion that seemed to change all who it touched: a pilot giving up a good job to train to be a religious leader; a family on the verge of falling apart but now growing closer; an ambitious businessman who freely volunteered his ship and time to provide passage for a mystic. It all seemed too crazy, too unbelievable.

And what had he become in all this time? A year ago he had been kicked out of his boarding school. His parent's connections and visible status in the Space Agency had quietly quashed all the legal troubles, but still no other boarding school would touch him. And so they had reluctantly arranged to bring him along. But now a year later things were so different. He felt like he had aged ten years in that time, yet one thing was still the same. He was in trouble. He told himself one more time there was a difference now. There was reason for his actions; a good reason. That in itself tarnished all his excuses for his past, making them look cheap and childish. It made him hate what he was now doing all the more. In this moment of truth he knew what he was. He was a past aggressive brat – wait, passive aggressive – who ruined people's lives for his own ends. In the past it was because he had been driven by the craving of revenge. But this time he had to find and rescue his parents. And as distasteful as the next few minutes would be, he kept telling himself that all he had done over the past year was for that reason alone.

And then the moment came. Thunderblade's voice held no emotion as it came through the ear-com: "Seamus, we are in orbit of Rom."

"What is everyone doing?"

"They are within parameters."

"Parameters? Well, if that means they are doing what we hoped, then please go ahead with the plan."

Seconds passed, then minutes.

"Filymon and Apphia are in their cabin. I have closed and locked the door... Epaphras is in your cabin lavatory. I have closed and locked the door... Chippus is in the shuttle bay. His behavior is now out of parameters."

"I'll handle him."

"I will be on the flight deck for approximately 4.8 minutes, and will join you at the shuttle."

Seamus looked up as the doors slid open, his grin widening. His first order of business wasn't the shuttle bay as much as he should head there right away. It was the galley. Already Filymon and Apphia were pounding on their door as he passed. After throwing together the closest thing to a sandwich he could make out of Kollosian leftovers, he headed toward the shuttle bay. Now Epaphras beat on his door too. As he walked down the corridor, his former masters' voices faintly mingled together with Epaphras', tinged with anger and fear. He wished he could block it out.

When the doors to the shuttle bay slid open, Chippus looked like he had been waiting on him. His face held no trace of surprise.

"I knew you were going to do this. It was the only thing that made sense."

Seamus was astonished, but tried not to show it. "Oh, really?"

They stood there quietly for a few seconds, eyeing each other. Seamus wondered what the boy planned to do. If he had suspected the escape, had he planned for it too? He certainly had the imagination for something with all his play soldiering in the woods. But what could Chippus do? There was no way he could stop Seamus.

And then it hit him.

Even though everything in the *Wander Wide* was shut down by the program Thunderblade had installed, the shuttle was still active... as well as its *com system*. If Chippus had already called for help, the Romians would be here in moments. But if he hadn't yet, Seamus still had to stop him. But how? What was he willing to do?

"So where are my parents?"

"They're locked in their cabin. An hour after we leave, the doors will open and they'll be free. And after that they won't have any control of the ship or the com for another two days. By the time they get back in control we'll be long gone." After a second he added, "I'd never hurt your parents... or you."

Chippus nodded. "I know." He paused looking at the deck, then back at Seamus with determined eyes. "A year ago I would have asked to run away with you. But now Yeshua is changing my family. And he gave me a job to do. Pol even reminded me before he left."

Seamus was nervous now. What did that mean? What had that old mystic told him? And then he saw the remote in the boy's hand. It wasn't the real one, but it had knocked him to the floor last time. Where was Thunderblade? Had he reset the remote back where it didn't shock so bad, or better yet, no longer worked? If the boy shocked him now, it could be the end of any escape.

"I hoped you'd want to stay with us..." He lifted the remote.

Seamus tensed, ready for anything.

"...but I understand why you need to go. Here. You'll need this."

Seamus couldn't believe it. He reached out and gently took the remote from Chippus open hand.

Just then, Thunderblade stepped through the door behind him.

Again no surprise from Chippus, though some recognition and curiosity. "You're the creature I saw in the woods, aren't you? And I bet you're the one Onesimus has been talking to when he thinks no one can hear him."

"I am. My name is Thunderblade."

"I knew you had help." He smiled wistfully. All of the sudden the boy hugged him. Seamus flinched, ready to throw him off but then realized what he was up to. He hesitated for a moment then returned the embrace. Chippus pulled away. "You better get going." And then he walked around them, through the open doorway, which slid shut behind him.

Seamus stood there, taking a deep breath at what had just happened.

"Seamus, may I suggest we take Chippus' suggestion and begin the next phase of the plan?"

"Next time you say 'out of parameters', please give me a little more detail."

A few minutes later, the bay doors opened and the shuttle lowered into space. After half an orbit they headed down the assigned reentry trail, a fiery glow of super-hot atmosphere created by hundreds of ships burning through at minimal intervals. Part of his mind wondered how hot it had to get for the hydrogen-rich upper atmosphere to flash; another part wondered what other surprises lay ahead; and yet another thought of his parents. But mostly, he thought of who he left behind and what they thought of him. Nothing good, he was sure.

THIRTY – PLAN B

As the shuttle dropped to one of the Romian Capital City's space ports, Seamus glanced over at Thunderblade. The robot looked like a sleeping toddler sitting in the adult-sized chair, but sleeping was the last thing he was doing. Even now, silent and still as he might be, Thunderblade was hacking into the Romian nets, setting up for the next phase of their plan. Already, the record of their arrival had been altered and several counterfeit registries for their "yacht" recorded. And now various programs were being put in place to watch for the first sign of trouble and to provide help as needed. Hopefully, they would never need them.

As they landed, Seamus stared at the enormous structures of the city. Now that he knew the Romians had physical similarities to turtles, he could easily see how their biology informed their architecture. Everything had a rounded shape, while protective walls and shields stood everywhere, though he wasn't sure if they were functional or decorative. As he considered this, he thought about how his mom had once told him how people generally liked their cars, ships, and even homes to look like they did.

The reminder made him wonder: was she here somewhere in this city?

After a few minutes, Thunderblade announced they were clear for takeoff. Their transponder now identified them as an atmospheric transport so they could move around the city, closer to Löwin. Unfortunately, the shuttle had no programming for navigating the aerial traffic grid, so Seamus had no choice but to fly manually. He wasn't blind, however. Thunderblade had been able to pull up the travel lanes and the flight control profile they were expected to follow. He reminded himself he had practiced for this, flying all over Kollos. Even so, as he eased into the thick traffic above the city, his palms felt sweaty as he held on the stick.

Löwin served as security for a wealthy plebiscite north of the city, nestled in the wooded hills. From her communiqué they knew her masters were traveling, so he had little worry when they landed on the private pad fifteen minutes later. The grounds were beautiful. Tall, thick walls made of quarried gray stone encircled the inner compound, in the center of which a curving, vine covered concrete shield rose several stories in the air to form a shallow cave. Underneath stood a glass fronted home, a rounded dome structure that together with the shield looked like a glassy eye looking up from the earth. Water features and large decks surrounded the house. Obviously, sunning and swimming were important to the owners.

Thunderblade stayed in the shuttle ready to take off, while Seamus climbed out. He waited in front of the shuttle, enjoying the warm sunlight. A moment later Löwin exited the house, approaching with two large duffels. It had been a year since he'd last seen her and then she had been drugged, muzzled, and gloved. She stood, tall and powerfully built. Her creamy fur sparkled in the sun, and her thick jaw had a fine long beard. She looked regal, every bit the aristocrat she served.

"Hello, cub," she said with a fang-flashing smile, tail flicking as she lowered her bags to the ground. "The truth of your word honors me. You are a vow-keeper."

"You would do the same for me."

Her tail curled around her feet. "You are taller now, and your chest is filling out. And do I see hints of a mane?"

Seamus chuckled. True, he had started shaving his chin not too long ago. "You look well, Löwin, like a queen. Definitely the mother of many warriors."

"Grandmother!"

"Do you have the remote to your fitting?" he asked her.

"Better than that," she said twisting. "Feel."

Seamus saw that her fitting was gone. But as he ran his hand between her shoulders he felt something under the fur.

"I have a neutralizer covering my fitting, covered with a clone of my own pelt. It mimics the remote and counters its effects where I can move about at will."

"Where did you get that?!?"

"They are very difficult to obtain. That is why it took me so long. But now... here we are."

"I can't wait to hear all about it. Ready to go?"

"I am. This heat is oppressive." She paused thoughtfully, glancing back at the house and pool. "Before we leave I must do one last thing."

Seamus lifted his eyebrows in unspoken question.

She grinned and with three bounds she was back at the largest pool, leaping to a fountain in the middle. One claw caught the centerpiece sculpture of a Romian soldier as she nearly sailed past. Leaving deep furrows in the stone, she spiraled down around to the base. She paused looking up and then with another leap and a quick swipe of her extended claws, she beheaded the sculpture, sending its head tumbling into the water. At the same time she kicked off its chest, somersaulting to the edge of the pool. And then with several powerful flips she nimbly landed between her bags.

"I've wanted to do that since my first day here."

Seamus was too speechless to respond.

She picked up her bags and walked past him to the doorway of the shuttle. "Come on, cub, we have an escape to make."

♦ ♦ ♦

Things were going exactly as intended. As the shuttle lifted from the pad, Seamus asked Thunderblade, "Still clear to head back to the spaceport?"

Before the robot could answer, Löwin turned. "Cub, I don't have time to explain, but plans have changed." She keyed in some numbers on the navigation screen.

Seamus thought he must not have heard her right. "What?"

"Plans have changed. Make for these coordinates now, as fast as you can."

"Why? We have it all—"

Löwin roared with a chilling yowl. "Obey me! Now!"

If it weren't for the seatbelt, Seamus would have fallen out of his seat. Instead, he quickly got them moving, all the while watching Löwin out of the corner of his eye.

"I don't understand..."

Thunderblade's voice seemed like the only thing calm in the shuttle. "Seamus, I'm picking up alerts all over the planet. She has sent out a coded message in Gothani. Defense forces are scrambling."

"Yes, robot. And they are coming after us."

Seamus whipped his head around. "What! Why are you doing this? They're going to blow us out of the sky!"

"As they should. I just sent a message in an older code saying all is ready for the invasion."

At first Seamus was too shocked and angry to speak. The clouds broke as they climbed upward, and the sky darkened with altitude. "You... you... you used us? We're just pawns for some Gothan invasion?"

"Don't be so timid, cub. The plan you sent me would get us off Rom, but never through the hypertrack to Kaarthaagg. And despite my years, my mind and fangs are still quite sharp. I'd never announce an invasion. No, what we need is a diversion."

"A diversion? You could have told us!"

"I am telling you."

"Seamus, may I interrupt to point out four fighters are in pursuit and will reach us in three minutes. Two battle cruisers are being dispatched to intercept us in orbit."

Seamus felt his heart hammering in his chest. What had she done?

"Cub, when you reach the reentry trail, go straight up the middle. The evasion programs of the incoming ships will steer them out of your way."

He could see the glow above as they hurdled toward it. And the streaks of light told him ships were still coming through.

"Seamus, the fighters will be in firing range in twenty seconds. The odds of evading and survival are... less than optimal."

Just then they reached the glowing reentry trail. Ships screamed past, buffeting them in their wake. It was like driving down a one way street at a thousand kilometers an hour. Alarms started to buzz.

He flinched as another ship nearly collided with them.

"Seamus, we are in firing range of the fighters."

Just then laser fire zipped past and the sky exploded, bouncing them this way and that. Alarms wailed. Had they been hit? Seamus held the shuttle as steady as he could. He wasn't sure what else to do in the eye-watering glare. And then the icy black of space appeared.

"Splendid, cub! You flashed the upper atmosphere. That should keep them busy! Now I have some work to do." She jumped out of her seat and headed toward the back.

Seamus kept on course, but rotated the shuttle where he could see the planet. Below the sky glowed, shockwaves spreading out like an atomic bomb from where they had come through. He had never seen anything like it.

Thunderblade came up next to him in the copilot's chair that Löwin just exited. "The fighters have lost track of us, but I calculate the pursuit will resume momentarily."

"That crazy..." he struggled for a word until he settled on "... cat."

"Do you still trust her? Our destination appears to be the hypertrack to Pannon, which lies just outside of the Gothan Empire."

Seamus thought about it for a moment. "I do trust her, but there's not much of a choice right now, either."

Löwin returned for a moment. "Cub, I have reprogrammed your TENT's transponder to match this shuttle. When I tell you to, turn toward the Kaarthaaggian hypertrack and give us five seconds of full thrust. Afterwards cut all power so that we're coasting dark toward the hypertrack."

Thunderblade sounded more optimistic. "It appears she intends to use the TENT for a decoy. With the commotion and interference from the atmospheric flash I calculate we have a seventy-seven percent chance of successfully making a ballistic course to the hypertrack undetected."

Now Seamus understood. At her signal, he cut the engines and reoriented the shuttle. She launched the TENT uninflated as a decoy. He caught a glimpse of it spinning off before firing the thrusters for five seconds. He cut the power immediately thereafter as soon as he saw they were on course.

With the power out, so went the gravity. Seamus turned, wishing for a light other than Thunderblade's eyes in order to see if anything needed to be stowed. There was nothing like zipping through a room in microgravity and colliding with a loose piece of junk floating somewhere along the way. His first week on the Corvus 2267 survey had taught him that. A light came from the back of the shuttle, and Seamus saw Löwin sailing forward with her two duffel bags and a hand light.

"Here, cub, open this." Seamus caught the first floating bag and unzipped it, revealing a large piece of equipment. "That's a survival atmo-scrubber. Put it somewhere out of the way and turn that switch. It will keep the air warm and filter out the carbon-dioxide."

Seamus scowled, but obeyed with Thunderblade quietly accompanying him. He couldn't believe what she had done without consulting them first. He pondered on what to do next. He wasn't sure he wanted to stick it out with Löwin if she did this sort of thing a lot. It was obvious from the scrubber she had at least considered the possibility. Had she been planning this all along?

After doing what he was told, he returned to see Löwin tying down another piece of equipment between the pilot and copilot seats. "What's that?"

"It is a low-power portable tactical and passive scanner. That way we can see where we are and what is around us." She turned on the power.

Seamus clenched his teeth behind closed lips. Now he had no doubt she had planned this well in advance. He stewed in silence.

"Cub, even without a twitching tail I can see you are angry. Speak your mind."

"Why didn't you tell us what you were planning? We could have been ready. We could have helped!"

Löwin looked up, her face impassive. "Two reasons. First, I wasn't sure it was you. I thought your robot might be a trick of the Kaarthaaggians trying to see I if I knew where you were."

"This is accurate," Thunderblade said. "She required considerable evidence."

"I still wasn't sure if you were actually the one talking to me, but I went along, planning to overpower anyone other than you." To add to her point, she lifted a pistol from her bag before returning it.

"The second reason is your plan wouldn't work. The Kaarthaaggians enjoy more freedom than most, but Rom regulates slavery very tightly. Ships going to or from Kaarthaagg are scanned down to the person. If they saw two slave fitting readings with only two life forms on board, it would have brought them upon us. We would have been killed within the day."

"So what do you plan to do? Just coast into the hypertrack, hoping they won't see us? Why couldn't we just do that with our plan?"

"We're not going to coast, cub. As I said, we needed a diversion." She pointed to the portable tactical screen, showing an expanding picture of the area. "Look, see these military transponders? They are all headed away from the hypertrack back to Rom. If I'm right, Rom has recalled the local pickets to bolster their defenses for an invasion that will never come. Soon enough we'll be out of range and able to fly under power right through the hypertrack without a single Romian to notice."

Seamus sat back. He could see she was right, as much as he hated to admit it.

"I calculate a ninety-seven percent chance of success," Thunderblade said. "eleven percent better than our own plan." That really annoyed him.

"One thing needs to still be decided, cub. Your plan left open the possibility of stopping at Kaarthaagg. What have you decide-ed?"

Seamus looked straight at Thunderblade to make sure he saw his serious expression. "We're going to stop and find my parents."

THIRTY-ONE - PARENTS

It took most of the day but just as Löwin planned, their ballistic course took them right to the hypertrack, undetected. The only Romian military they saw along the way was a patrolling frigate, zipping past at the edge of their passive sensor range. In contrast, dozens of civilian ships raced by - some quite closely - heading for the safety of Rom's orbital marinas and forts. Little did they know the imminent invasion from the Gothan barbarian hordes was nothing more than a hoax, a diversion for a tiny, powered-down shuttle flown by a pair of runaway slaves.

Time dragged out, it seemed, as they steadily drew closer to the hypertrack. There was nothing for Seamus to do other than stay warm and wait, though Löwin seemed to doze most of the time, uncovered. She seemed to enjoy the cold.

An hour out, Löwin awoke, explaining they had to be powered to enter the hypertrack. For some yet-to-be-known reason, only gravity-enabled ships set the whole physics conundrum of hypertracks in motion. The plan was to power-up ten minutes out, so that as soon as they were functional - and emissions visible - they would disappear into the hyperspace tunnel.

"Powering engines," Seamus said at the proper time.

Just then a Kaarthaaggian freighter appeared directly ahead, radiating blue lightning from exiting the hypertrack. Seamus' heart seemed to jump into his throat.

"Stay calm, cub. Ease us out of the way and shut down. Their sensors won't work for a few minutes until all the energy bleeds off."

"I'm on it right lively." Seamus had already instinctively got them moving out of the way. He powered down quickly and watched through the edge-frosted canopy as the freighter held its station a bit too long.

"Look, cub, they are confused! No Romians are here to challenge them."

A few moments later, the freighter began to move, heading in-system. It thundered past them, buffeting them in its wake and sending them on a gentle roll. They waited in the dark, watching the portable tactical as the ship sped off, while the stars slowly spun in the canopy. A few minutes later when they were sure they were well out of sensor range, Seamus began to restart the engines.

"You can power all the systems, cub. From the Kaarthaaggians reaction it's obvious no one is around." Seamus did so, and a minute later with enormous relief and great joy, they dove into the hypertrack. They had escaped Rom!

♦ ♦ ♦

The next week seemed to crawl as badly as their powerless float through the Romian system. Out of sheer boredom Seamus tried to replicate many of his maintenance tasks which would keep him busy on the *Wander Wide*. This didn't take half a day and so he listlessly paced around the too-small shuttle. He hadn't expected the size to be so difficult. There were only two "rooms" on the shuttle, the cargo hold and the passenger cabin / flight deck. The airlock, a storage closet, a small galley, and the lavatory that was quickly showing its overuse separated the two, but still there was no real privacy. No matter where he was, it always seemed like he could hear Löwin groom herself, over and over again. She never seemed to tire of it, though her slurping nearly drove him crazy.

The only bright spot in such a long and dreary week was in planning for Kaarthaagg. After sharing with Löwin all they knew about Doctor Kaataannaa being reassigned to an orbital quarantine station, they finally settled on a solid plan to lure her aboard and question her about Seamus' parents. The trick had been in having enough leverage where she would both tell them what she knew and not report them to the Kaarthaaggian Junta.

Löwin explained that like her own people, the Kaarthaaggians were an honor-based society; only after the Romians had conquered them and poisoned their oceans they had lost their way. Still, the dishonor she must feel would be enormous, and she would likely try anything to regain her honor. Only the threat of even more dishonor would keep her silent, and so they structured their plan around that fact. Unfortunately, it meant that Seamus would have to be hidden and would not be able to question her himself.

♦ ♦ ♦

Eight days after leaving the Rom system, they arrived at Kaarthaagg. Just as Löwin had hoped, the picket on the Kaarthaaggian side of the hypertrack had been recalled to Rom, so no ship was there to meet them with active scanners. Under normal power they headed in-system and soon were in orbit heading toward the medical quarantine station where Doctor Kaataannaa served.

A half-hour before arriving, Löwin and Thunderblade put Seamus in his hiding place. On his last trip up from Kollos when they were preparing the *Wander Wide* for the journey to Athinsia, Seamus had brought aboard all sorts of things he had been collecting over the past few months. He had known a lengthy trip in the shuttle would hopefully be coming, and had packed anything he could think of for himself, his parents, and Löwin. And so several large crates were in the cargo hold, and during the hypertrack transit they had emptied and lined the largest with anything metal and made it as comfortable as possible. Wearing a spacesuit and his ear-com, Seamus was locked into the best thing they could come up with for a scan-blocking hiding space.

"Can you hear me, Seamus?" Thunderblade asked. The robot was in hiding, too, but not nearly to the same level. He would look like part of the ship unless he moved.

"I can hear and I'm getting the video feed too." Seamus cycled through the various interior and exterior cameras on his reader. If he couldn't be there in person, it was the best thing to it.

Over the next few minutes he listened in as Thunderblade, using the voice and language of a Romian, radioed in for instructions on bringing in a sick slave candidate. As hoped, they were directed to dock with the quarantine station and to lower their gravity. The next step also involved Thunderblade. He quickly hacked into the station systems ensuring Kaataannaa received the order to report to the shuttle, to make sure no inconvenient visits or scans occurred, and to erase any trace of their visit. Even if Kaataannaa had a change of heart, she'd never be able to prove it.

The next few minutes dragged by as they docked on an exterior tower and waited. Thunderblade finally said, "She is coming."

On his reader, Seamus watched Löwin crouch across the shuttle from the airlock, well out of reach of any poison tipped finger-spines.

The blue shark floated through the doorway, which closed (and locked) behind her. In a flash Seamus vividly remembered so much about her: the black, expressionless eyes, the rows of teeth, and especially her role in trying to get him to tell more about Earth. Her arm-fins billowed outward and her head tipped upward. "Greetings to our Romian allies, where is the slave you—"

Löwin rose, gun in hand. "Quiet or it's belly-up for you."

"A Gothannnn," she hissed.

"Wrap your fins under you and interlace your spines over your head."

The shark complied hesitantly, wrapping herself, and slowly sinking to the floor under the slight pull of gravity. "What do you want?"

"You may not remember me, but I was one of your... customers a year ago."

Seamus suddenly felt uneasy. Here he was locked in a box, while his only hope of finding his parents was under the gun of an obviously emotional Gothan snow cat. A snow cat who'd already proven not to stick with the plan.

"I do remember. You and the human boy escaped, and now most of my crew is dead and my fin is crimson with shame." Only then did Seamus notice the bright red marking on her dorsal fin. It was obviously a great dishonor.

"Good, then you'll remember everything I need to know."

"I'll tell you nothing. You may as well kill me."

"I won't kill you, and you will tell me."

"Never!"

Löwin paused. "I questioned the boy for some time before he died. He didn't tell me what I needed to know, but he did tell me his parents knew the answers. He also told me this..."

They had made the recording a few days ago, and had pre-positioned a reader right where she'd see it. Seamus listened to his and Löwin's exchange as Kaataannaa watched. It had taken a lot of work to make him look so bruised, beaten, and ready to "confess".

"...So, human, how did you arrange our escape?"

"Why are you doing this? You were supposed to help me."

"That was before I found out you held so many secrets in your paws. So how did you break us out of a Kaarthaaggian slavers?"

"If I tell you what I know, will you let me go?"

"Maybe. It depends on your answer."

"It... it was the doctor. She said she had told her people and they would protect me from the Kaarthaaggians of the other seas."

"That is a lie!" Kaataannaa roared. In a blur, her arm-fins had unwrapped, drawn back ready to strike.

Löwin had plenty of cover and was still safely well out of range. "Careful, doctor. Lie or not, you know this recording would bring you instant death and shame your entire pack. Maybe even war."

Seamus squirmed from the intense fury of her voice: "May your seas turn to poison and your oceans reek of death; may your corals die off, and your water taste of bitterness for a thousand generations, you vile beast! If I ever have a chance, you will die the slowest of deaths, eaten alive by kanailan fry!"

"I take it, you will cooperate."

The shark bared its jagged rows upon rows of teeth, its spine tips glistened, and its small black eyes somehow looked bigger and crazed. She said nothing.

"What happened to the boy's parents? Where are they?"

Seamus held his breath. The moment he had waited and worked so hard for was finally here. His mind raced ahead about arranging their escape and coming back through Kaarthaagg to Corvus.

"Do you think if I knew that, I would be here?"

"Now who's the liar? You do know. Tell me or this recording goes everywhere, even to Rom."

"Say it!" Seamus shouted, unheard.

The shark said nothing for many seconds, and then: "They are dead."

Seamus' drew in a raw breath. "What?"

Löwin stood, emphasizing with her pistol. "Don't lie, or I swear by my own mane..."

"I do not lie!" The shark seemed to relax with the admission. "One died during the capture, the other a day or two later. We tried to save it, but its injuries were too severe. I nearly killed the boy with how much blood I transferred trying to save it."

"No," Seamus mumbled. "No, it can't be. They can't be..."

The shark and the snow cat continued with their hate-tinged conversation, but Seamus heard nothing more. What was left of his world was crumbling into jagged splinters of disbelief, sorrow, and rage.

"NO!" he screamed and began thrashing and kicking. He wanted out. If his parents were dead then he'd kill every remaining shark on that ship.

Starting with Kaataannaa.

"Thunderblade! Get me out of this coffin!"

"Seamus, it is almost a certainty your safety would be compromised."

"Let me out of here or I'm going to light into you just as soon as I'm done with that bloodthirsty maggot!"

"Seamus, I care too much about you to allow you—"

The next was a growl: "Thunderblade, you let me out of here right now."

"Seamus, I have been charged with your safety. I—"

"If my parents are dead, then their orders don't matter anymore! Let me out of this box! I order you!"

"I... I... hold, please..."

"Let me out of this box!"

"...logic paradox... logic para—" And then Thunderblade's signal went dead.

"Thunderblade!" he screamed in rage. But when the robot didn't answer, his fury quickly shifted to alarm. "Thunderblade? ...Thunderblade? Answer me!"

Only now did tears come to his eyes and his voice trembled.

"Thunderblade?"

No one answered.

THIRTY-TWO – CORVUS

Seamus sniffed back the tears and set his jaw. He couldn't, wouldn't believe this. His parents were not dead, and Thunderblade had not just shut down.

"Let me out!" he screamed. "Thunderblade, listen to me!"

Again, the only response was the conversation between Löwin and the shark overheard on his reader. But he didn't want to listen to that lying cur, Kaataannaa. That beast would never tell the truth as long as there was any way to profit from it. His parents were being held somewhere. He didn't care what anyone said. She could say his parents died in the capture as much as she wanted, but it was all lies!

He hated being locked in this box. That shark was so lucky he was or else she'd be sorry she ever had even laid one of her beady black eyes on him. There had to be something he could do to discredit her! He had to remember something that would disprove that filthy beast. The cutter had never taken a direct hit, and even though that clamp had caused a lot of damage, they had still been airtight. And there hadn't been any radiation spikes from the drive. Nothing external or systemic could have killed them. That shark was such a liar.

But then he thought about all the equipment. Could any of that have done something? Some poison or radiation leakage? But even then, nothing would have touched it without piercing the hull and he would have known about that. The only thing he could think of is if some piece of equipment was hit by something loose in the cabin.

In a flash he remembered that last scolding. *"Seamus, what are you thinking? You could have hurt someone! There are tons of un-stowed equipment out in the lab!"*

Oh, no.

He pushed a horrible image from his mind. No, there was no way his parents would have been killed by random loose equipment.

But what if they hadn't been strapped in?

He remembered seeing the holo of his flight. He had pushed it up over 4 gees and with all that banking and turning.

No, it couldn't be that.

Suddenly, bright light blinded him as the lid to the crate swung open.

"Cub?"

Seamus jumped up, ready to fight, but the shark was gone.

"Are you well, cub?"

"Where is that lying..."

"Kaataannaa has gone. And we must be going too. Between our blackmail recording and your robot's manipulation of their computer systems, we only have a short time."

"We need her back. She's got to tell me the truth."

Löwin looked long at him. "She smelled of truth, cub. And the oaths she used–"

"I don't care about that! If I – if they killed my parents, then I'm going to kill them all!"

"No, cub, we are going."

"No we're not!"

She took his challenge silently.

"Thunderblade put you up to this!" Seamus stormed to the closet. "Thunderblade!" As soon as the door slid open he was inside, ripping everything out of the way until he saw the black and chrome figure nestled in the corner. He snatched the robot and began screaming, "How dare you turn me off like some..." Thunderblade slumped over, lifeless.

Seamus snarled hatefully as he flipped open the access panel on the robot's back, thumbing the reset button. Nothing happened. He tried several times. "Stupid robot! Turn on!"

Löwin stepped up next to him. "Cub, it told me this might happen."

"What?" he snapped.

"If it faced a particular paradox, it would shut down."

"Well, did he happen to tell you how to turn him back on?"

Löwin gripped his shoulders to turn him toward her. She was gentle, yet her grip hinted of great strength. "Cub, your parents and your robot are gone. Forever. But their honor and bravery will live on in your songs to your offspring and to theirs."

Seamus glared at her, willing her to turn away in shame for lying to him. But as she stood their looking intently at him, he felt his resolve crumbling. Just then the power cut off and the gravity disappeared. The lantern must have already been on, as its dim light cut through the darkness to illuminate one side of her face.

"W-w-what's going on?" he said, hating the trembling sound in his voice.

"We're going to Corvus. To your honorable guardian robot, I swore by my sire's mane I would return you there to your ship."

Tears now came to his eyes. "No... no. We've got to go back. Just please take me back to talk to Kaataannaa. I'll make a new deal with her, and you too. If you'll just take me back, then I'll use my ship to get you back home to the Gothan Empire. And I'll get my parents back and dad will know how to fix Thunderblade."

Löwin did not reply, only squeezing his shoulder and pushing off toward the flight deck.

"Please..." he called out. "I'll do anything."

She did not answer.

Seamus lifted Thunderblade as he wiped his eyes. "You knew. You knew all this would happen." Fresh emotion threatened to erupt to the surface, but he willed it back. "Why didn't you tell me?" He released the robot to float back in the closet, more gently than he really wanted, and then made his way up front.

♦ ♦ ♦

There had been moments in Seamus' life where time had no meaning, where the passage of seconds into minutes and minutes into hours no longer followed orderly logic. One such moment had been the "accident" which had resulted in his expulsion from the boarding school. And there had been others. None compared to this.

Throughout the rest of that day Seamus stayed on the flight deck, wrapped up in a blanket and strapped into the pilot's seat, where he mindlessly gazed at the pinpricks of starlight. Löwin respected his silence, only occasionally bringing him water in a zero-gee pouch. Mostly, he daydreamed, pushing as much conscious thought away from himself as possible. At some point they went into the hypertrack, but he didn't notice or even really care. He only realized at some point how the black of real space had turned into the swirling mottled blue of hyper, and the power and gravity had been turned on.

Seamus' thoughts wandered through a dark forest of sadness, the branches of horror and guilt ripping at his soul. Oddly, tears did not come after his first initial outburst. He just didn't care now. All he had loved was gone and nothing else really mattered to him. And worse, it was his fault. All the choices he made had led to disaster. Why was he alive when his parents and Thunderblade were now gone?

♦ ♦ ♦

Black space again, and then another long period of hyper. Löwin sat with him sometimes, always silent, dutifully attending to his needs of food and drink. Several times black space and hyperspace alternated. And then it struck Seamus they must have traveled for some time. He checked the chrono: nine days had passed. He decided to clean-up a little, and when he returned he sat next to Lowin.

"You said something about songs to remember."

Instead of answering, Lowin looked upward, closed her eyes, and opened her mouth slightly. An eerie tone vibrated deeply in her chest, then rose to a high, wailing pitch. Somehow maintaining the deep rumble in her chest, the tenor in her throat formed words in a sad, majestic tune.

The days of trouble came.
The armored ones poured through the gate,
With ships slow and strong, and dishonor in their hearts.
Warriors roused from their prides, from their kittens.
To the black sky they arose, with bravery in their hearts.
The clan-queen's finest warriors faced the coming death.
They saw their fate come through; they raced to embrace it.
Warriors all, they threw their bodies on the guns of their enemies,
Their bodies becoming shields for their sisters and brothers.

With their claws and fangs and by their great manes they withstood,

Their enemy held back, as the young and honored fled.

And then, leaving their hollowed dead, they withdrew.

Our dead are remembered, none fled at the sight of their enemies.

We honor them in growing strength, as our enemies weaken with corruption.

Your deaths will be avenged, beloved warriors.

She abruptly stopped, leaving the song as jarring as it had been moving. Seamus at first thought she had been overcome with emotion, but as she looked at him, he could see she had ended.

"It sounds like it isn't finished."

"It's not, cub."

He had considered asking her to help him write a song for his own family. Truthfully, he had considered a sad song for his own sorry life, but now the idea of unfinished songs unnerved him.

"When will you know when the song is complete?"

"Are they ever?"

Seamus snorted. This was starting to sound like Thunderblade's psychobabble. The thought made him wince inwardly. In a sort of inward apology, he said, "I guess not."

"On Vissi, we have master song weavers with songs days long. It has comforted me many times to know the songs all connect."

He considered that for a few minutes, and his thoughts wandered to the impact his parents and Thunderblade had on his life, and he wondered about the impact of his own life on others.

With a pang of guilt, Filymon, Apphia, and Chippus came to mind. He hoped they were alright and hadn't been implicated in any part of their escape. A few moments later he thought about Epaphras. Now there was someone who had made an impact. But then, it was Prazella and Aquyia who had first impacted him. And then there was Pol, and obviously that Yeshua had impacted his life. Maybe Lowin was right.

The nutrionmeter beeped, and by the time they reached the front the canopy was filled with the blackness of real space.

Lowin pulled up the tactical. "So, cub, I take it this gas giant with the hole in its ring is your Corvus 2267-F?"

Seamus looked at the screen and nodded.

Within an hour they were there, the streaked blue, ringed planet, where he had been captured, looming ahead. And there was its outer ring, jagged and warped on one end from his attempted escape. His eyes drank in the sight of it. It was real. He was finally here. It was the moment he had dreamed for and fought for. Yet, it did not bring the joy he expected. His whole existence had been focused on this one moment, yet it was so bitter, so shallow in its meaning.

"The *Fernão* is parked on the fourth moon," he sighed.

Löwin took the shuttle toward the icy sphere, where they entered orbit a few minutes later. Seamus didn't know where the ship was, other than they had landed on a smooth ice field. They circled the moon several times, scanners active and finding nothing. "I didn't think it would be this hard to find," he said.

The snow cat increased the power to maximum. "The scanner suite on this shuttle is not very sophisticated." She turned on the passive system she had brought with her. "But there doesn't seem to be any emissions I can detect. Shouldn't it be broadcasting a transponder signal?"

"We always kept a telemetry feed going for redundant recording. I don't—"

"I think I've found it, but only on visual." She pulled it up on the main screen.

He looked at her quizzically. "What? I don't see it."

"There." She pointed.

"That? That doesn't look anything like the *Fernão*. She's long with a girder structure and all these interconnected modules. That is just a... crater."

And then he saw it, or rather what was left of it.

His last hope, the *Fernão de Magalhães,* had been destroyed.

THIRTY-THREE – WHAT NOW?

Seamus stared at the screen in disbelief. His greatest unstated fear had been the Kaarthaaggians having found the *Fernão*. Never had he even considered the ship as having been *destroyed*. Yet here it was: a black pockmark in the white ice, recognizeable components strewn outward. And as he studied the horrible, unimaginable picture, he could see the explosion had come from the reactor with maybe a smaller one from where the flight deck had been.

"I'm sorry, cub. The robot expected this too."

"This? How could he have known about this! ...Sorry, I didn't mean to yell at you."

"He called it 'Omega Protocol'. If your ship met with a hostile alien civilization and capture was imminent, it would self-destruct. To protect your world in such a way is an honorable sacrifice. Maybe we Gothans should have done the same."

Seamus stared at the screen, ignoring the comment. Honorable sacrifices didn't help at the moment; what he needed was a way home. It looked like some of the cabin might still be intact...

"We're going down."

♦ ♦ ♦

The first time he'd walked on this moon, the ice crunched under his boots. Now it felt slick and glassy, having been melted from the explosion and flash freezing just afterward. Hundreds of jagged shards of metal pierced through the ice, half submerged. He gingerly stepped over these with an emergency suit patch in hand and wishing he had some sort of walking stick in the other. One slip might be his last.

"Careful, cub," Löwin's voice said in his ear.

She had stayed in the shuttle. The spacesuit he had brought for her had been big enough to fit her body (with her tail tucked down one of the legs), but the boots didn't fit well and the helmet was an extremely tight, uncomfortable fit.

"I am," he answered with a hint of exasperation.

He made it to the largest remaining chunk of the ship. A small burst of hope filled his swirl of negative emotions as he recognized it as part of the living quarters. Maybe some hint of the direction of home had survived? He walked around the perimeter until he found a gaping split down the side.

"Löwin, I've found a hole and I'm going in."

"I admire your bravery, cub, but what is to be gained?"

Seamus ignored her as he stepped through the hole. As his eyes adjusted to the darkness he thought it might be their main living area, twisted and ripped through from shrapnel. Every edge looked pointed and serrated. It was the worst place he could be with the type of suit he wore, but he flipped on his helmet light and carefully moved deeper. He could do this. He just had to make sure of every step.

The room was hardly recognizable. Everything had been burned or ripped away. As he moved farther away from where the engine compartment had been, the devastation lessened. He found an intact computer screen that had been sheltered in a recessed section of the outer bulkhead. Of course there was no power, but something was laser-etched on the screen: 'OMEGA-2C33A6LQ98P4'.

"I found a message, 'Omega' plus a long string of numbers and letters."

"A warning to any of your people who come here in search of you. The code must tell the story of the attack."

"Maybe."

"Do you wish to keep it?"

"The code? I guess so."

"I'm ready."

"2-C-3-3-A-6-L-Q-9-8-P-4."

"Cub, please come back now."

Seamus didn't answer, but looked around a little more. He wasn't sure why. He now knew with certainty there would be no record of home, much less its location. And the reality was that even if he did know, there was no way to get there. All the civilizations he had met had never developed hyper drive. They had found hypertracks first and so had never considered another alternative.

The wall was missing, but he recognized the sleeping cabins. His room had been obliterated, but his parent's had fared better. He walked in, trying to imagine it as it once was. With his parents alive. He stood there for some time, more seeing memories than charred reality.

"Cub?"

Seamus paused for a moment before answering. "I'm about to head back."

He turned to see another intact screen, the same message burned across its warped surface. With one more sweep of his gaze he turned to leave, but then a shiny glint caught his eye. Wedged in the side of the charred tumble that had been the bed was something shiny. When he dug it out, he gasped, trying not to cry in a spacesuit helmet. It was a silver frame and inside was a family photo of the three of them.

This was what he was looking for.

Before he left, he picked up a small chunk of debris, one without any sharp edges. With it he scratched his mother and father's names on the wall underneath the screen, followed by his own. He stared at the three names for a few seconds before he slowly drew a line through his mother's name and then his father's. He left his own unchanged.

"I'm coming," he said, and left his makeshift memorial behind.

♦ ♦ ♦

The first thing Löwin said as he emerged from the airlock was, "What now?"

Seamus had no idea. He shrugged.

"Shear my mane; I do not wish to tell you this, but your robot made me swear. He told me that if we found your ship destroyed, he wished for you to return to those who had owned you."

He couldn't help but chuckle. "Filymon? Oh, I don't know about that. I don't think I could ever go back there after what I did to escape. If they weren't arrested by the Romians, Filymon would probably shoot me on sight."

"I just swore to tell you, not to say you should. You are welcome to come with me back to Vissi, if there is a way."

Seamus considered it for a few moments.

"I guess there's time to think about it. There is nothing more out here, is there?"

"Not that has been discovered. I had not come out this far, but I was out here looking for another way home when I was captured."

As Seamus thought about what had been said those past few minutes, a flash of irritation came over him. "So what else did Thunderblade say when I was locked up in that crate?" It was obvious to him now that half of the reason of the crate was to keep Seamus under control when he heard the bad news. That robot was – had been – smart. He had thought out all this in advance.

"The only other thing is that while we were docked at the Kaarthaaggian medical station, he was able to learn of a way to suppress the signal from your fitting and remote. You would have to keep the remote on your person, but it would not be detected by a regular scan."

It escaped him why that would be necessary. "Why?"

"So we can go back through the hypertrack to Rom. The Romians will detect my fitting, but not yours. They will assume I am your property."

"Ah..." Thunderblade *had* thought of everything.

After a few more minutes of deliberation they began their journey back toward the Star Empire of Rom. There really wasn't much choice. They were running out of everything: food, water, fuel. And Seamus wasn't sure what else to do, anyway. Three hours later Seamus left Corvus 2267, and with it all hope of ever returning home.

♦ ♦ ♦

Nine days later they prepared to emerge into the Kaarthaagg system. They weren't sure what to expect. Thunderblade had covered their tracks extremely well, and they were now using a different transponder code. No one should think of them as anything more than a prospecting ship. But still they had left Kaataannaa furious. Who knew what she might have been up to over the past couple weeks? Anything she might do would be suicidal, but she had a lot to avenge.

With a flash of blue they erupted into real space. As the sensors came online, they saw another ship floating nearby. Seamus looked out the canopy with dread.

"It's the Romians."

"It's just the picket, cub. They're back on station just as they should be." Löwin's conclusion proved true, and the Romians didn't seem concerned by their arrival.

After getting clearance they headed across system directly for the hypertrack to Rom. Along the way something curious happened. Thunderblade's surveillance programs began to pop-up, displaying all sorts of new information. Apparently, the robot had programmed the shuttle to display this automatically whenever something new came through, which must have happened when they and the Romian ship had been in contact. He pulled the reports up on a reader.

"Look at this, Löwin. Your former owners had their citizenship revoked and were expelled from Rom after your escape."

"Well deserved, those lazy plebiscites. They should have not made it so easy for me. They are lucky they didn't lose their heads."

"Really? They could have gotten their heads chopped off?"

"Beheading is the execution of choice for Romian citizens. It's quick and relatively painless. For the rest of us they've invented more painful and long-lasting ways to die, such as the games. It's a lot easier for us to die too. Not just slaves, but anyone who isn't a citizen. The law—" she chuckled "—the Romian law treats citizens much better than the rest of us."

Seamus started reading the various summaries of everyone who had any bearing on their escape. He was curious but he also wanted to quickly push such morbid thoughts out of mind. "It says here that the *Wander Wide* returned to Kollos. Nothing else... I guess nothing happened to them." He felt a pang of remorse, especially now that he had learned the truth about his parents.

"I'm curious, cub. Why would your robot suggest for you to return to them? I can't imagine why it would want you to become a slave again."

"I don't know." He paused in thought. "They treated me well. After Filymon stopped dabbling in smuggling, I felt safe there. Mostly." He paused again. "Thunderblade did everything he could to keep me safe."

They flew on in silence for a few minutes. Seamus started to read again.

"How about that... it says here that Pol was arrested and is now under house arrest in Rom. Last I heard he was heading home to Judia."

"Who?"

"Oh, uh, Pol. He's a religious leader... a good guy. He started this religious school in Effizus and a lot of the people I know went there. Epaphras went there before he came to Kollos to start the ekklesia, you know the Yeshuaians who met at Filymon's? And you remember the conference I told you about? He's the main leader."

"Why was he arrested?"

"Some sort of religious complaints... a riot - another riot, wow. And it says he saw several local officials before appealing to the king."

"He appealed to the king? No wonder he's in house arrest. It might take years for the king of Rom to get around to seeing—"

"Oh, no!"

"What is it, cub?"

"Epaphras went to visit him at Rom and was arrested too! It doesn't say why."

"The Romians don't need much reason, cub."

As they approached the hypertrack Seamus sat silently, thinking about what to do next. They were already heading to Rom. There were three hypertracks from the Star Kingdom to Vissi, and the only way to get to any of them was through Rom. Plus, they needed supplies badly. Löwin had said there was no place busier than Rom, and busy was the best place to be to quickly and quietly get what they needed.

What Seamus had not expected was to hear that Epaphras and Pol had been arrested. And now that he knew about Romian "justice", he was worried. He didn't know what to think about the stories of Pol's Yeshua coming back to life, but everyone who'd ever talked about him had agreed he'd been put to a horrible, unjust death. If that happened to the leader, then what could Pol or Epaphras expect?

As they entered the hypertrack to Rom, Seamus turned toward Löwin. "Do you think they'll be put to death?"

"I don't know. It depends on the whim of the Romians."

Seamus paused. "We've arranged two escapes already... want to go for three?"

THIRTY-FOUR – STAY OR GO?

Having a new goal invigorated Seamus. He had been devastated to learn of his parents' death. Yet it wasn't solely their loss, it was also the deep sense of having failed them. His goal had been to find them, and nearly every moment for over a year purposed toward that end. He had failed. The resulting sadness and depression had been intense at times, and only the lesser goal of finding his way home – of knowing his parents would want that – eased the pain. Yet that dream also died, leaving nothing but questions. Why had he survived? What should he do? Where should he go? His mind had wandered through empty deserts, searching for something, anything. And now here it was. With the idea that Epaphras, Pol, and their companions might need his help, he felt alive again. His life had meaning.

Rom was just as busy as the last time they had been here. Starships formed an orbiting cloud and tiny service craft fell like rain to the surface. Joining a long parade, they took their assigned track down through the fiery tunnel of Reentry Trail Fourteen and within ten minutes were landing at one of the Capital City space ports. As Seamus shut down the shuttle, Löwin turned toward him.

"Do you remember what to do?"

"Yes."

"Are you certain? I will be in hiding and will not be able to come to your aid or even talk to you over the radio. Just the sound of my voice might ruin everything."

Seamus rolled his eyes. "I remember. There are thousands and thousands of slaves here. If I go about acting like a slave and doing slave work, no one will question me."

"Let's hope not. Remember, you need to be back before sundown. If you're caught after slave curfew and found with your master's remote, they won't bother questioning you."

Seamus agreed, promised, swore, and reassured, and then finally was on his way. His first stop was to arrange for fuel and supplies to be delivered to the shuttle the next morning, as well as some minor servicing that wouldn't require any registration records. Money wasn't a problem. Early on Thunderblade had opened some accounts and had funded them through some sort of stock trading. It wasn't a whole lot, but it could be stretched out for another six months of flying around the empire if needed. Not that he wanted to spend another moment in that cramped, smelly shuttle.

It was raining again and low lying clouds obscured much of the city, ringed and streaked with thousands of contrails from aircars. Now that Thunderblade was... off, there would be no flying around the city as they had before. It had been hard enough in good weather, but without step-by-step instructions from his robot it would be impossible. And so, Seamus headed out using public transportation: oversized buses packed with all sorts of alien life.

After stopping at a warehouse office to pass along a message from Löwin to one of her contacts, Seamus made his way to where Thunderblade's surveillance programs had indicated Epaphras and Pol were staying. The bus dropped him off a block from the street, and he was surprised it turned out to be a residential neighborhood instead of a government or prison complex.

He had no idea what the standards were here, but it looked like a nice place to live. Rounded homes with curving, decorative shield walls lined the street. Walking through the warm rain to the right address, he paused in front, looking for some clue. Surely this couldn't be it. After a long glance around he decided to move up toward the house to see what he could learn.

The outer shield wall curved over the domed building, narrowing to a point directly overhead, where it joined with a similar triangular structure rising from the opposite side of the home. This left the front and back of the house exposed and it also looked like they made narrow passages between the house and shield wall on either side. Seamus decided to walk along the apparent property line between the house and the building next door, hoping if anyone saw him they would think he was heading to the other house.

As he walked out of view of the windows, he dashed through the shrubbery and into the passage between the shield wall and the left side of the house. What he thought was a passage actually ended a little over a meter inside; the shield was in fact part of the house. The back outer corner offered some shelter from the rain, so he squatted there in the relatively dry dim, wondering what to do next. Should he glance through the windows? Should he listen at the door?

Just then the front entrance opened. Seamus slowly pushed himself as deep into the corner as he could. A Romian soldier stepped out to the edge of the slight overhang and peered out into the rain. Seamus' heart nearly stopped beating. The beaked creature stretched its neck out of its armored shell and flexed its massive arms and legs. And then even more surprisingly, Pol stepped out of the door on the other side of him. He came to the soldier's shoulder. Seamus very nearly gasped out loud in shock as he heard him talk to him in a friendly tone.

"Your question is a good one. Even though your people have never received God's law directly as my people have, by your own nature you do the things it requires. Even though you don't have God's law, you are a law to yourselves. In your hearts you know the law. Its requirements are written there. And your consciences tell you it is there, at times accusing you of breaking that law and at other times letting you know you are obeying it. Is that not true? And that is the root of my message to you. One day God, through Yeshua, will judge all that happens in your heart. It's not that you've been formally presented God's law, it's that you've obeyed it."

The turtle turned to look at Pol, his back to Seamus. "I don't know why I still speak with you about your God, human. Don't you see? Either way I'm doomed. I'm ignorant of all your God has decreed, and even if He has given me knowledge of his expectations, I know I've not always obeyed my conscience. How could I possibly earn your God's favor? It sounds impossible."

Pol seemed to beam at this admission as if it were important, and as the turtle turned to walk back inside Pol patted the soldier's shoulder in a friendly gesture – one Seamus would never have dared to offer. Pol turned to follow him, but as he did, his shimmering, goggled eyes seem to lock upon Seamus for a moment. "That is not the end of my good news for you," he said as the door closed.

Seamus relaxed. Pol was here all right and obviously under guard. Yet Seamus could hardly believe Pol was trying to convince the soldier about his religion. It seemed the man never stopped. Even if he was manic about it, Seamus was surprised he would want to share with a Romian, especially one of his *guards*. But then, maybe Pol was trying to gain the sympathy of his captors? Maybe this was part of winning their trust so he could more easily escape? If so – and Seamus couldn't fathom any other reason – breaking them out was looking easier every minute!

The door opened again and Seamus again pulled himself tight into the shadows.

"Onesimus?"

It was Epaphras!

Seamus leapt to his feet, but stayed in the corner of the shield.

Epaphras walked over to Seamus, offering him a large towel. "Onesimus, what are you doing here? We heard you ran away from Filymon."

Seamus felt a flash of guilt. Instead of answering right away, he wiped his face and hair with the towel. "I did run away... But then I heard Pol was arrested and brought here, and then you were arrested too. I read about why Pol was arrested, but what happened with you?"

Epaphras shrugged. "Can't say, really. I came here as soon as I heard, and then I was put under house arrest too. The best I can tell it's either because I witnessed the riot in Effizus, or because I was running too many errands for Pol and they got nervous."

"Well, how many guards are there?"

"Here? Uh... usually just one. They keep rotating them through."

"You're under arrest and they're keeping you in an unlocked house with just one guard? I can't believe how easy this is going to be!"

"Easy?"

He whispered the next. "Easy to break you out! I've come to help you escape. That reminds me, how many people are here? The shuttle can hold eight, but we can take a few more in a pinch."

"Escape?"

Seamus shushed Epaphras.

"Onesimus, we don't want to escape. You don't understand. Pol is right where he wants to be! He appealed to the king and at some point he will be granted an audience. Don't you get it? He's going to have an opportunity to share about Yeshua with the king! Can you imagine what that might mean? Already there are many of his guard and even some in his household who are followers."

Seamus was dumbfounded.

"You... you don't want to go? You want to stay?"

"Yes, we want to stay."

Seamus was speechless for a few seconds. "Are...are you off your nut?"

"Pardon?"

"Are you crazy?"

"Why would you say that?"

Now Seamus was getting angry. "What is with you people? Haven't you seen what these bloodthirsty Romians can do? Their first answer to every problem is to kill. Don't you get that? With my own eyes I saw them blow an unarmed freighter to bits. They have these gladiator games where people are... people are eaten by monsters. They hire mercenaries to hunt down families to make them slaves..." He was starting to get upset now, so he stopped talking.

"We're not worried. There's nothing that can happen to us that God does not allow."

Seamus looked up. "You should be. You were locked up for no reason and if this king is having a bad day, he might sentence you to die."

"I'm fine with that, as long as it makes Yeshua more famous."

Seamus couldn't take it anymore. He waved his hand dismissively, flung the towel off his shoulders, and marched back out in the rain toward the road.

"Onesimus?"

Seamus paused and turned, the rain blurring his sight.

"Onesimus, stay with us. You'll be safe here."

He shook his head – not really saying no, but more in disbelief. Then he turned and walked on.

♦ ♦ ♦

He made it back to the shuttle before curfew, and as he stepped through the airlock he was met with a blaster aimed at his face. Löwin purred in recognition, lowering her weapon.

"I'm cheered to see you, cub. We're you followed? Are you alone?"

"Yes, I'm alone! I'm not a child!"

The hair around Löwin's neck flared out slightly and her tail lashed the deck. He knew she was angry, but he held his ground. She seemed to take a few moments before speaking again. "What troubles you... young warrior?"

Seamus sat in the pilot's seat and turned to face her. As he told her the story of his visit with Epaphras, Löwin listened thoughtfully, running her claws through her beard like a comb. As he ended with Epaphras' offer for him to stay with them, Löwin nodded.

"Yes, I agree, it sounds strange. It is very risky, since the Romian king believes himself to be a god. Yet, I see their endgame. If the king can be won, then the whole kingdom would be open to them and their message. I've never considered such strategy, but if I thought the king would give me a fair hearing, I might consider the risk for the sake of my people." She paused. "But then I'm an old cat. I've spent my youth."

Seamus silently considered her judgment, but still wasn't quite convinced Pol and his followers weren't up the walls with madness.

Löwin stretched and began to groom herself. Seamus turned and watched the bustle of the ground vehicles and taxiing spacecraft in the growing darkness. It was always so busy here in Rom.

After a few minutes Löwin paused in her slurping and looked up at Seamus. "While you were gone, young warrior, I received a reply to the message you delivered this morning. My contact is able to arrange for me to have transit all the way to Belgicia, one hypertrack transit from the only contested system where I could reach my people."

"Really?"

"Yes, but it will be risky. I will be caged as if bound for the games, but will be freed when I arrive. Assuming my contact is still one of honor."

"And do you think you can make it the rest of the way from there?"

"I think so. The farther you get from Rom, the less friends Rom has."

Seamus leaned back, running his fingers through his rain-dampened hair. "Funny," he snorted, "I have that problem, too, except for you."

"But all your friends are *crazy*... including me." Her tail flicked in what he had learned was amusement. She lounged back on the bench staring at him. He felt himself growing uncomfortable, but kept himself from squirming under her gaze.

"So, young warrior, what do you want?"

"What do you mean?"

She paused thoughtfully before answering. "A year ago I met a young man-child, frightened and ready to flee at the first sight of trouble. But now a year later he is grown; he's wiser, more honorable. He no longer needs his robot or an aged snow cat to guard him. He prowls the streets of Rom looking for those to rescue instead of waiting to be rescued himself. You are right in what you said earlier, you are no child."

Seamus was shocked, yet warmed through by her words. No one had ever praised him or thought of him as anything more than a troublesome kid. "Why... why are you telling me this?"

"It is said the ancients would force out their young males to find their own way, to roam the snowy fields of Vissi alone or with their brothers. And after they gained wisdom and strength, through war they'd take another pride for their own. You are of age, Seamus. You've wandered and grown strong and wise. And now you must choose your place, your home." She looked at him even more intently.

"Do you want to stay? Or do you want to go?"

THIRTY-FIVE - CROSSROADS

Should he stay with Epaphras and Pol, or should he leave with Löwin? The question haunted Seamus all through the largely sleepless night. There were pros and cons to either choice. If he went with Löwin and they safely made it to her people, he would never fear capture again. But he would be even more of an alien with her than here. He would never be a snow cat, and he wasn't sure if he wanted to live like one on frigid Vissi. If he stayed, he would always be in danger of discovery. If he were lucky, he'd be returned to his owners if ever captured. More likely he would be killed. But... he'd be with those like him. And one thing he was sure of, these people who followed Yeshua were kind. They also had a sense of purpose he so envied.

What to do?

He awoke to the sound of a service vehicle latching onto the shuttle. As Löwin hid in the storage closet, he stepped out, watching the workers fill the fuel and water tanks and topping off the other fluids. They also stacked crates of food and other supplies he had ordered by the door. After they left, he moved these inside into the cargo hold, ready for another two months of travel if he chose.

What to do?

After all was clear, Löwin came out. She had been staring at him expectantly since their last conversation and it was no different now. She wanted an answer, though he knew she would not ask again for one. She would give him all the time he needed. But now with the shuttle provisioned there was nothing more to wait on. It was decision time. If he chose to go with her they would fly together through Mazzille and on to Belgica, try to find a way into Gurmyni, and then slip across to the Gothan side of the system. If he chose to stay, she would pose as a circus gladiator, making the same journey inside a cage. All he had to do was to give her the word.

"Löwin, I..." He stalled. "I know you want an answer. I just—"

"You have an answer, young warrior. You only wish to avoid its consequences."

He smiled. "True." He paused for another few moments, thinking again through all his options. Would more time considering make any difference? Would rethinking it again and again bring out any other outcome? Probably not, and Löwin, for all her patience, was ready to get home. He knew what that felt like.

"Löwin, I think I need to stay. I—"

"A wise choice."

Her statement surprised him. "Why do you think that?"

"When we first met, I told you I aimed to fight in the games rather than to become a slave. And the reason is this: it is always better to die quickly, having lived, than to live long, dying in your heart day after day. I think you would live long in Vissi but with regret, forever unfulfilled."

As Epaphras would say, her words rang true. He nodded. "Yes, you're right."

"Don't misunderstand me, young warrior. One as brave and cunning as you shall live many years. And even if you do not, I will sing of you to our song weavers, and your tale will be told for a thousand generations."

"Really?" He felt awed and humbled. "You'd do that?"

In answer she broke out in song, a low hum in her chest accompanying a strong tenor voice:

They came to new worlds seeking knowledge,
But battle fell upon them from the skies.
The queen and sire fell, but their cub, Seamus, survived
Though he knew not of their fate.
Enslaved by Kaarthaagg and taken to Rom,
Along the way he met one of the pride, Löwin of the plains.
They swore in mutual aid, yet, slavery caught them first,
Separated, many systems apart.
With honor and cunning Seamus made his escape,
With the help of his robot, Thunderblade.
They came to Rom, helping Löwin escape,
And together left the kingdom shaking in fear.
They returned to Kaarthaagg and found their captors
He learned of the murder of those who gave him birth.
Still he pressed on until all hope of home was lost.
With honor in his heart, Seamus brought Löwin toward Vissi,
And then heard of the capture of friends.
With valor he went to them to arrange their escape.
They refused, wishing to fight with their words.
With great care Löwin and Seamus parted,
Each to their own journey.
Löwin to her people and Seamus to a new battle.
His voice joined his friends as they fight not with claws
But with great honor and loyalty.

The lyrics were too idealistic. Honorable was the last thing he'd call himself, but he said nothing about that. "It doesn't sound finished."

"Are they ever?" Löwin answered. He smiled as her tail flicked with humor.

♦ ♦ ♦

An hour later a truck pulled up, driven by Löwin's contact. In the back of the covered trailer the Athinian woman had a cage. Seamus walked Löwin to it and shuddered as the door clanged shut. It hurt him to see his proud friend like this, even if the lock did not actually work. She could leave it if she wanted, but he knew she wouldn't – even if taunted. It was the plan after all, and it was a good one.

She looked at him through the bars. "May my people and your people always live at peace, a peace of honor and faithfulness and never of fear, young warrior."

Seamus wasn't sure how to respond, but then he thought of an old Irish saying. "May the road rise up to meet you. May the wind always be at your back. May the sun shine warm upon our face, and rains fall soft upon your fields."

Löwin chuckled. "That would be an insult on Vissi, but I take your blessing."

He smiled, holding back tears. And when he could hold them back no longer, he swung the cage door open and embraced her. Her soft fur felt like silk on his fingers and on his face. She returned his embrace, though he could tell it wasn't natural to her. He looked up into her glowing, yellow eyes. "Without you I'd be dead now. You taught me what I needed to hear when I most needed it. And you've been a good friend."

"Now, young warrior, *that* is a blessing of great praise."

♦ ♦ ♦

After saying goodbye and watching the truck drive away, Seamus felt energized with purpose. He arranged long-term storage for the shuttle, packed the few perishable food items he had bought in his duffel, and closed up the space craft for who knew how long. Hopefully, it would not be too lengthy a stay, and hopefully he would be leaving Rom with Epaphras, Pol, and their companions with him.

♦ ♦ ♦

This time Seamus walked right up to the door and knocked. Epaphras answered. “Onesimus, you came back!”

Seamus shrugged, swinging his duffel around from his back. “I was hoping you had a place where I could stay, and that I could help out.”

“We sure do!”

Epaphras brought him in, where Pol sat talking with several others. Seamus recognized a few from Pol’s conference: Doctor Lukaas, Tem, and Aristarchus. Of course, at the time he hadn’t been too interested in them and had stayed mostly in the engine room. As they were all telling him how pleased they were he had joined them, a gruff voice cut through all the welcome.

“What is *that*?” A Romian soldier rose, glaring at Seamus from across the room.

Seamus knew this moment would come and had already rehearsed a response. Just as he began to speak, Pol stood.

“He’s with me. He’s the property of a friend at Kollos, and here to help me as I’m here in chains for the glad news I share about Yeshua.”

The soldier grimaced. “Another one?”

As Epaphras walked Seamus to where he’d be bunking, he explained that four other young men were staying there.

“Wow, you’ve got a full house here.”

“We have all sorts of people coming through. It reminds me of when I first met Pol at Effizus, when the school was just a dozen people.” He swung the door open, and Seamus realized how the wide doors were built for Romians, not humans. The room had six bunks, and a young man with the same greenish-tan skin as Pol stood, holding a reader. Epaphras introduced them: "Yaunmarck, this is Onesimus."

After interlocking arms with Seamus in the Athinian manner of greeting, Yaunmarck pointed to an empty bunk and then showed him an empty drawer in a dresser where he could store his belongings. Epaphras excused himself as Seamus unpacked. Yaunmarck went back to whatever work he was doing on his reader.

"I've got some Kollosi sunberries if you want some," Seamus said, as he began to pull out all the fruit and bread containers he had brought with him.

"You're joking," Yaunmarck mumbled, as he looked up. A split second later he was at Seamus' side. "Oh, I love Kollosi berries. I haven't had any in months." He popped one in his mouth, slowly savoring the flavor.

Seamus ate one too. "These are the best." It had been months since he had any either. It reminded him of the pudding Apphia had made him on his birthday.

Just then three other young men came in – all a couple years older than him and sporting giraffe patterns on their necks like Epaphras. One looked familiar. "Kollosi berries!" one shouted and when Seamus said they could have some, they all tore into the open container. Only after they'd had a few did Yaunmarck get around to introducing Seamus to the others.

"Guys, this is Onesimus. And this is Demas, Phroditus, and Tychicus."

Seamus pointed at Tychicus, were you at Effizus when Pol had his school?"

"That's right. And aren't you the one who piloted that ship we took to the conference on *Miletus Station*?"

Seamus nodded, but before he could say anything, Demas added, "You're that runaway slave Epaphras told us about."

Seamus felt his cheeks grow hot and he stiffened as the others began glancing at the fitting peeking out of the neck of his tunic from between his shoulders. "Yes," he mumbled with a shrug. "That's me."

Demas looked excited. "Tell us what happened! Not many slaves run away and don't get caught."

Seamus didn't know how to respond. He felt a certain sense of pride in having beaten the odds and escaping, but he also felt an overwhelming sense of shame at the lengths he had gone to do so.

Yaunmarck caught his eye. "It's all right. You don't have to tell us." For some reason, that made Seamus feel better. At least they weren't ordering him around like a slave. And they all seemed as kind as any other followers of Yeshua he had ever met.

They all sat down on various bunks and Seamus shared his story: being captured by the sharks, sold to Filymon, the ekklesia on Kollos, making his escape, learning the truth about his parents, finding the *Fernão* destroyed. He left out all references both to Löwin and to Filymon's attempts at smuggling. His story stood on its own without those embarrassing or endangering details. Once he finished, they all sat silently, and he could tell they were judging his actions. Demas was the first to speak.

"I don't know about you guys, but I don't blame you at all. If I were in that situation, I'd run away too."

"I think I would have tried to stay," Phroditus said. He looked up at Seamus with a slight smile, his expression and tone of compassion, not judgment. "Like Pol has said, maybe as you follow Yeshua, it would influence your owner."

"Epaphras said that Filymon has really changed a lot. That whole family has changed. You might be right," Tychicus said. "I'm not sure what I would have done."

Seamus shifted uncomfortably. What they said was true – at least the part about Filymon changing. He'd seen enough of that. But the other part... he didn't follow their religion. And he hadn't known then all he knew now. What should he say? He had just come here and he surely didn't want to offend anyone. "I... well, it's too late now. I already ran away."

That seemed to kill the conversation, thankfully. Seamus looked down at his feet until another voice spoke. "You know, I ran away once." It was Yaunmarck.

"What?" Tychicus said. He looked astounded.

"I ran away once. I was with my Uncle Barrnabus and Pol when they went on their first visits in Galatiana." He paused, looking even more embarrassed. "It got tough. Pol was almost killed and it seemed like everyone was against us. I got scared... discouraged... so I left them and went back home."

Phroditus looked shaken. "You?"

"Yes, me. I felt horrible about it afterwards and I wanted to make it up to them. My uncle agreed I could go with them on their second trip, but Pol didn't trust me. They got in an argument about it, so my uncle and I went to Xypruzz and Pol took Zylas with him instead." He paused, looking forlorn. "It was all my fault."

Seamus knew how he felt. "So... what happened? If Pol doesn't trust you, why would he let you be here?"

"He gave me another chance. I can't say he trusts me like he did, but I think I'm earning it back. I just pray God will keep me strong when it gets tough again."

♦ ♦ ♦

The evening meal was a sight. Three tables were jammed together, where Seamus joined eleven others, including their Romian guard (who was finally starting to act civil) and a man named Justis. Justis apparently owned the house and was a good friend to them all. After Tem blessed their food with a prayer, they all enjoyed the fresh fruit, vegetables, and bread Seamus had brought with him.

The table was full of lively conversation and Seamus soon learned one of the older men, Aristarchus, was also a prisoner, making three total in the house, including Epaphras and Pol. He also learned what the younger guys did. Since Pol was under house arrest he couldn't leave, but he could have all the visitors he wanted. So Tychicus, Yaunmarck, Demas, and Phroditus went about Rom, talking to different people, and inviting them to come hear Pol.

The strategy seemed to work really well, Seamus thought, as just in this one day there had been a steady stream of visitors. And they had come from all walks of life: politicians, philosophers, religious leaders, wealthy, impoverished, slave, and free. Everyone wanted to hear the man who claimed to be an ambassador of God in chains because of his message.

♦ ♦ ♦

The next morning Seamus joined the other young men – the "Fearsome Foursome" as he learned they were called – as they visited an agora which catered mostly to poor immigrants. To cover more of the market they split up into two groups; Seamus went with Yaunmarck and Phroditus, while Demas and Tychicus took the far side. Seamus mostly watched the other two as they talked to various people, who they apparently visited often. Despite their obvious passion, they had varying results. He quickly learned how deceiving looks could be. Some of the surliest looking people seemed to be the most interested in the message they shared.

Toward the end of the day Yaunmarck said they needed to start heading back to meet with the others. As they made their way, Phroditus saw some Romians at an idol vendor. "Let me talk to these people real quick."

As he walked over to them, Seamus turned toward Yaunmarck. "So you do this every day?" Before he could answer, Seamus heard shouting.

"I told you people to leave me alone!" Seamus turned to see one of the Romians hit Phroditus, who cartwheeled into the table of idols. Phroditus screamed and convulsed. Suddenly blood was everywhere.

"Oh, no," Yaunmarck cried as he ran toward his friend.

THIRTY-SIX – YESHUA

It took a moment for Seamus' brain to tell his body to move. Just a few moments before, Phroditus had begun talking to a group of Romians at an idol vendor, when one hit him. Phroditus had flown into the table of full of idols and now he was screaming. Yaunmarck was already at his side and now the guilty Romians were running away. Only when one bumped him, did Seamus start moving himself.

"How bad is it," he cried as he arrived.

"Bad... real bad."

Three figurines had punctured into Phroditus' left side, while dozens of others had ripped his face, left arm and left hip. Everything seemed covered in blood.

"I go get help!" the furry Belgician vendor shouted, running off.

Seamus followed Yaunmarck's example, pulling off his tunic and using it to apply pressure to the worst wounds. They only had four hands between them, so the rest of the gashes would have to wait. Phroditus' screams subsided.

"Yaunmar..." Phroditus mumbled.

"Yeah, buddy?" Yaunmarck's face looked ashen.

"Is it my time?"

"I don't think so. You... you're not as bad as I first thought. I've seen a lot worse. A whole lot worse."

Seamus thought Yaunmarck was lying, but he wasn't sure. All he knew it was the worst he'd ever seen... except for once. He started feeling woozy from all the blood and guilty from the memory, so he looked away. People were gathering around. Suddenly, someone shoved her way through the crowd, holding a first aid bag. It was a porcupine-looking Kreeti, apparently a doctor or nurse or some sort.

"Good, keep pressure on those wounds..."

♦ ♦ ♦

It was early in the morning before Doctor Lukaas came out from the operating room of a nearby hospital to tell them Epaphroditus was "critical, but stable". The visible relief on everyone's face – especially Yaunmarck's – was like seeing a rainbow after a violent thunderstorm. Tychicus quickly called Pol at the house to share the good news, and a short while later they all wearily went home for the rest of the night.

Two days later Phroditus came home, where he was given his own room while he recovered, with Doctor Lukaas tending to him. He slept mostly, but the next day he was awake enough to have visitors. Seamus followed Yaunmarck, Demas, and Tychicus as they quietly walked in, circling the bed.

Phroditus looked pretty banjaxed. Deep purple bruises peeked out from under the edges of large bandages on his face, neck, and left arm, and his torso was wrapped like a mummy, stained dark here and there from wound secretions. He had nearly died, and he looked like it. Fortunately, he was expected to completely recover.

"Hey, guys, how are you?" he said with in a dry, scratchy voice. When they all said fine and asked how he was, he answered, "Been better, but getting better. So, how are all our friends out in the city?" No one answered right away.

"We haven't been back out yet," Yaunmarck said.

"Don't tell me that. You guys need to go back out there. Yeshua has us here for a reason, and Pol's counting on us to bring people to hear him. We're the Fearsome Foursome, remember? Uh, I mean Fivesome."

"We just took a few days off until we knew how you were doing," Demas said, glancing around as if for reassurance.

Tychicus shrugged. "We're thinking of going back out tomorrow."

"Good." Phroditus wearily looked over at Seamus. He spoke slowly, but Seamus listened patiently. "Sorry about this. Your first day out with us and I get on the wrong side of an angry Romian. We get yelled at sometimes, but usually not this."

Demas muttered something, but didn't repeat it again aloud.

"It wasn't your fault," Seamus said. "I just wish the authorities would do something more. We talked to the police, but it's like they lost interest when they heard it was Romians who did this."

"God will settle it all for me. I just forgive them." He paused for a few moments. "Guys, I'm getting tired, but promise me you'll go back out tomorrow."

"We will," Yaunmarck said as Tychicus nodded vigorously.

♦ ♦ ♦

The next day they did go back out, and Seamus listened in as they prayed for protection and boldness. Yaunmarck said they should go back to the agora. Demas wasn't too sure, but finally relented. When they arrived, all the vendors who saw them rushed from their booths to ask about Phroditus. After hearing he would recover, it seemed everyone wanted to hear more of their message. Many even wanted to come to the house to see Phroditus and to meet Pol and the others. The Belgician idol vendor was especially relieved to hear the news and said he'd come over that very evening.

That night, the majority of those promises came true. The house was packed, and Seamus listened from the doorway of his room as Pol talked about the "mystery" God had hidden throughout the generations. Many decided to follow Yeshua and the small ekklesia in Rom nearly doubled. It really touched him. He wasn't sure if it were the emotions of the week, the genuine love Pol and the others had for everyone, the selfless service, Phroditus' quick forgiveness and commitment, or how they accepted Seamus even as a fugitive slave. Whatever it was, it felt overwhelming. He wanted to join these people, to be a part of them.

As Seamus got ready for bed, he saw Yaunmarck working on his reader, as he usually did during quiet moments. "You're busy tonight."

"Hold on... I'm writing something. There. Yeah, I've been trying to put together all the stories I've heard about Yeshua. The Romians want to hear all about him and we keep telling the stories we know, so I thought I'd write it down for them. I grew up in the first ekklesia in Judia, where many of Yeshua's first followers still are. I've heard these stories a hundred times. Most of these are from Cephas himself of when he and the Twelve were with Yeshua. The problem is I can't quite figure out the order it all happened."

Seamus' interest was piqued. "Could... could I please read it sometime?"

"Sure... You know, Doctor Lukaas has been proofing it for me. Maybe he would loan you his reader?"

Seamus asked right away and Doctor Lukaas was happy for him to borrow it. And so Seamus spent the next couple hours reading all Yaunmarck had written. All he had heard did not prepare him for what he read.

The next morning Seamus arose early (he could hardly sleep) and found Pol and Doctor Lukaas sitting at the table drinking tea. As he handed the reader back to Doctor Lukaas, he said thanks and then turned to Pol. "I want to become a follower of Yeshua. Only..."

"Only what?"

"Only... I don't know if he would want me as a follower."

"And why do you say that, Onesimus. I know you've heard our message of God's outlandish love for you." Pol's goggled eyes sizzled with intensity.

"It's just that... that I've been so... *bad*." He paused as shame and self-loathing bubbled up from within. "I mean, *really, really* bad. The whole reason I'm here is because I did a really bad thing." Neither Pol or Doctor Lukaas said anything, and Seamus reluctantly continued. It was something he never wanted to anyone to know, but he had to know where he stood. "There was this boy named William who picked on me all the time. And I'd just take it and take it and take it, but then I got angry. I should have just told him to back off or tell a teacher, but I wanted to hurt him."

He paused, wondering if he dare continue. He looked up expecting self-righteous judgment, but instead saw only compassion.

"I rigged a door to hurt him and it cut some of his fingers off."

Still only compassion.

"They were able to grow them back, and I got away with it by saying it was an accident. But... But I *wanted* it to happen. And not just his hand... I wanted to kill him."

He started to weep as he admitted it to himself for the very first time. Pol and Doctor Lukaas comforted him with hands on his shoulders.

When he calmed down, he continued. “I got kicked out of boarding school. Word got out about what I had done and no other schools would have me. My parents decided to keep me with them on their next survey mission. And then… when the Kaarthaaggians attacked I panicked. I… I think I killed my parents by the way I flew. I just wanted to get away. I didn’t think about all their equipment in the lab and how they’d get knocked around while I…”

Pol put his arm around him as he wept, holding him tight as if he might bounce away from the trembling of his sobs. Doctor Lukaas prayed quietly.

“And then all the things I did to Filymon to manipulate him so I could escape. He could have been executed for what I did… So you see? Why would Yeshua want me to follow him?”

Pol smiled. “You know, in my former life back in Judia, I persecuted the ekklesia and the followers of Yeshua intensely. I tried to destroy them.”

“You… you *fought* against what you’re doing now? And still he wanted you to follow him?”

Pol nodded. And then he told him his own amazing story of coming to know Yeshua and choosing to follow him. By the end, Seamus was convinced God loved him and wanted him too. And he chose to follow Yeshua.

♦ ♦ ♦

Over the following months, Seamus was in his own version of the religious training school Epaphras had left Filymon to join. Everyday he listened to Pol and the others, and more fully understood all that God had done for him and how to practically live it out. He continued to go out daily with the other young men in effort to make relationships with those in the city and to invite them to join them. And every evening he heard Pol and the others share the great news of what God had done to those who came to hear Pol speak.

As different as this life was, there was also the familiar. He took odd jobs to help pay for some of the costs of renting the house and for Phroditus' medical bills. He slowly began to take on tasks around the house for its upkeep and to make life easier for the others. All in all, it began to feel very familiar, only with a much deeper sense of purpose and the knowledge everything he said and did mattered.

Phroditus soon began walking again and Doctor Lukaas had him doing a lot of different exercises to help regain his strength and range of motion. Seamus helped out a lot with these and began walking with him in the mornings or holding him steady while he went through the painful exercises. They became good friends. Seamus was amazed at Phroditus' attitude and belief God would make a lot of good things come from his near-tragedy. Already a lot of the local community had been impacted by what had happened, but soon it became readily apparent the good would go much, much further.

During this time, Phroditus began to get a flood of messages from his home of Felepye. His family and friends had heard the news of his injuries and were worried about him. Phroditus sent replies back sharing about his improving health and new battle scars. More messages came back with more news of home, including messages to Pol and some money to help him with his work and any legal costs he might have. Pol was very pleased with this, especially knowing how the ekklesia at Felepye had been going through a rough time of their own.

Soon thereafter Pol shared with those in the house he had realized something. In all the time he had gone about sharing the great news of Yeshua, he had always done it in person. He and others with him had started hundreds of ekklesias all over the quadrant, and one of his frustrations had been that he couldn't visit them as often as he liked to ensure they stayed on track. And now with his house arrest continuing on indefinitely, he felt it was time to use another strategy. His intention was to start sending representatives in his place, armed with letters he had written.

The first place Pol wanted to send a letter was to Felepye. As soon as Phroditus was well enough to comfortably travel, Pol dictated a letter. Seamus listened in as he thanked them for the gift they sent and their concern. He shared how proud he was of them for their perseverance, and he encouraged them to stay on the path following Yeshua. At one point he talked about Phroditus and how he was homesick. The young man turned bright red as he listened, but also nodded. And a week later after a goodbye celebration, Seamus accompanied his friend to the nearest space port. And as Phroditus boarded his flight, Seamus knew he had a lifelong brother no matter where their paths went.

Pol didn't stop with just Felepye. He decided to send letters to Effizus and Kollos. Epaphras had mentioned some problems before at Kollos, but it sounded like it had gotten worse. Apparently, some who had been devout in other religions before coming to Yeshua were now mixing some of their old practices with their new faith. This was one of the reasons Epaphras had come to Rom, hoping to find Pol and get advice on how to handle it. Unfortunately, he had been arrested too. And so Pol dictated letters to these two worlds and tasked Tychicus with delivering them.

When Seamus heard about this, it really got him thinking about Filymon, Apphia, and Chippus. One of the main ekklesias met at their home and they were probably dealing with all this trouble in Epaphras' absence. He found himself wanting to help them, and thought a lot about Thunderblade's desire for him to return to them. He wondered how they would react to him after all he'd done. The next morning he decided to talk to Epaphras about it, since he knew them best.

Seamus had never told Epaphras directly what all had happened, so over breakfast, he shared his whole story, ending now with this welling desire to go back and help them at the ekklesia at Kollos. Epaphras looked a bit overwhelmed.

"I know I've been horrible, but hope you don't think badly of me," Seamus quickly added.

"No, no, it's not that at all. It's just that I have been praying about this, that God would show me someone who could go help in my place. And here you are."

"But what about Filymon? What do you think he'd do? He could put me to death as soon as I hand him the remote."

"Onesimus, all I can tell you is this. God changes people and I've seen a lot of changes in that family." He paused as they locked eyes. Seamus was so unsure, and truthfully, scared out of his mind. "What do you think God wants you to do?"

"Go back."

"If you believe that is what God wants you to do, then you need to obey him."

"Yeah," Seamus sighed. It felt right, but no less scary.

They talked to Pol, who agreed and offered to send a letter to Filymon that Seamus could deliver. And, whatever the outcome, Seamus would accompany Tychicus to Effizus and then on to Kollos.

♦ ♦ ♦

A week later all was ready and there was yet another goodbye celebration. The house was much fuller now than when Seamus first arrived. And these weren't strangers and acquaintances here. They were family.

Demas dropped him and Tychicus off at the spaceport where the shuttle was ready to go – the shuttle stolen from Filymon. Just as they stepped out of the ground car, a transport rumbling by screeched to a skidding halt.

"What's that all about?" Tychicus asked.

A feeling of dread came over Seamus, but he wasn't sure why. "Come on, let's get going." They climbed up the wing and into the airlock, and just as he reached the flight deck, he saw an insect-like creature running toward them from the transport.

It was Rado, the slave trader – *his* slave trader.

Seamus powered up the engines, and Rado stopped, just clear.

The remote crackled in his pocket. As he pulled it out a voice came through a speaker he didn't know existed: *"Onesimus! I've never lost a slave, and you won't be the first. I'm not calling the Romians, because I want to capture you. I want to look you in the face and ask you why, and then there is only one fate for you. Death!"*

THIRTY-SEVEN – RUNAWAY

Rado's words echoed in Seamus' ear: *"...I've never lost a slave, and you won't be the first. I'm not calling the Romians, because I want to capture you. I want to look you in the face and ask you why, and then there is only one fate for you. Death!"*

The ant-like face glared at him through the canopy, as if his hateful stare could make good on his promise. He lifted something similar to Seamus' remote, only larger.

Without really thinking about it, Seamus revved the engines. The ship lifted slightly, edging forward. Rado backed off.

"Run slave! Go ahead and run away! I'm not sure how you've suppressed your fitting signal, but now that I've got you locked in, there is nowhere you can go where I won't find you! You've piled your sand too high, human! You should have never come back to Rom!" With that he turned, stomping back to the transport. Seamus could see it was full of a load of slaves. The part of him not terrified was furious at the sight.

"Uh, what was that about?" Tychicus held onto his armrests like lifelines.

Seamus didn't answer right away. He punched in codes as quickly as the nav could take them. As soon as Flight Control gave clearance, he took off.

"Onesimus, *who* was that? I thought your owner lived at Kollos."

The windows darkened as they passed through a cloud, and Seamus leaned back into the seat, shuddering. "That wasn't my owner. That was Rado. He was the slave trader who got me from the Kaarthaaggians and sold me to Filymon. He... he told me he's tracked down and killed every slave he'd ever sold who's run away, and I don't doubt he will do all he can to kill me too."

Silence lingered as if the threat absorbed all sound as well as life.

"So... do you think he's really tracking you, or just bluffing so you'd give up?"

Seamus looked at his remote. A blue light he'd never seen before blinked. He checked the tactical and sure enough, it was emitting a clear signal. He had no idea about the range, but he was sure Rado would know which way he was heading.

"No, he definitely wasn't bluffing."

What should he do? He tried thinking of options, but nothing came to mind.

"What am I going to do?" he asked aloud. He felt himself slipping into panic. He tried to pray, but the words seemed to stick on his tongue.

"Okay, calm down, Onesimus. Think this through. Does this really change anything? You're still going back to Kollos, right?"

Seamus breathed in deeply, trying to bring some sort of calm to the war inside his mind. Two sides fought viciously. One screamed at him to run, to flee as far and fast as possible. He had a jump on Rado... maybe he could get out of range before he could begin pursuit? Maybe some corner of the Star Kingdom would be far enough away? The other side wasn't quite as loud, but seemed just as insistent: the time for running was over. It didn't matter what Rado said or did. All that mattered was that he do what God had told him to do and to take responsibility for what he'd done and make it right.

"Onesimus?"

His mind calmed enough for him to pray silently for strength, boldness, and protection. He finally answered. "No, it doesn't change anything. Being captured was always hanging over my head. And I'm doing this knowing Filymon holds my life in his hands, anyway. I'm still going back to him. We... we're just going to have to do it faster. I want to see Filymon... before Rado catches up with me."

♦ ♦ ♦

Just as it had many other times, the hypertrack greeted them with a calm that belied the danger ahead. Still, it was five days he knew Rado could do nothing. But then it would be a race across the Athinsian system to the next hypertrack. He only hoped he could make it before Rado came through. Including Rom, there were five hypertracks leading out of Athinsia. If they could just get to the hypertrack to Effizus first, hopefully Rado would have to guess which way they were going.

♦ ♦ ♦

They spent those five precious days talking, praying, and watching the messages Pol had recorded to the ekklesias at Effizus and Kollos. It was comforting to see Pol and hear his voice. Seamus and Tychicus talked through all of what they had heard.

Of all the younger people who had worked with Pol, Tychicus was the one Seamus had gotten to know the least. He was now really glad for the opportunity the trip gave them – as dangerous as it might now be for them both. And it proved fruitful in other ways. The day before they were to arrive in Athinsia, Tychicus had an idea. "Can you duplicate the signal coming from your remote? Maybe we could fool Rado into going another way?"

Seamus thought about that for awhile. He wished he could just toss his remote out the airlock, but that would never work. When it got too far away, his fitting would kill him. And if that didn't do it, Rado would surely recover it and kill him with the press of a button. But Tychicus might be on to something, if only they had something that could do the job. Seamus checked all their stores. The only thing onboard that might be able to do it was some of Thunderblade's lifeless components, but Seamus had no idea how to do it. And he wasn't sure he wanted to disassemble his old friend, packed away in the storage closet, even on the chance it might make a difference.

Yet it wasn't a wasted exercise. Seamus thought of something else that might be helpful. He looked into it and what he suspected was actually the case. With triumph he explained it to Tychicus. "I checked the sensor logs and saw something. The remote sends a signal, but so does the remote Rado is using – and we can *track* it. At least this way we can know if he's following us." He then explained the crate they had used to try to block the fitting signals from outside scanning. Maybe if Seamus could hide in there while in Athinsia, it might make a difference?

Just before they emerged in the Athinsian system, Seamus set his manual flight plan in motion. They changed transponder codes to look like a yacht out of Syracuse-E. As soon as they cleared sensor range of the Rominan picket, they would make a full speed run toward the hypertrack. Then they'd reduce their speed to arrive at the hypertrack to Effizus at the right time. That way, the Romians would think nothing differently, and hopefully from Rado's standpoint, they would look like a completely different ship, moving way too slow. God willing, with Seamus inside the crate, Rado wouldn't pick up his remote's signal. And they could make the next leg of their journey undetected.

Only it didn't work out that way.

As soon as Seamus got in the crate, his remote began going crazy. The blue light began flashing faster and faster and then his fitting began to get hot between his shoulders. Finally, he couldn't take it any more and he signaled for Tychicus to let him out. As soon as the crate opened, the blinking on the remote slowed to normal and the pain from his fitting immediately dissipated.

Tychicus looked worried. "What's wrong?"

Seamus rubbed his neck. "I don't know. Some sort of feedback from this thing was causing my fitting to burn." He huffed with frustration. "This isn't working."

A few minutes later the shuttle slowed. Everything had gone according to plan, but without blocking the signal it was all for naught. Seamus let out a frustrated sigh. As they feared, Rado's signal appeared at the Romian hypertrack a half hour before they made it to the hypertrack to Effizus. By the time they went in, it was apparent he was headed straight for them.

♦ ♦ ♦

Two days later they arrived at Effizus, armed with another plan at evading Rado. Seamus quickly brought the shuttle in for a water landing, bumping up at a public dock. Tychicus exited, met by Prazella and Aquyia. Seamus didn't stick around, however. He backed off, heading for the sky once again, this time with a military transponder code.

"Okay, Mister Rado," he muttered to himself, "let's see if you really mean what you say about not calling the Romians."

As soon as he made orbit, Flight Control cleared him and he took the ship on a direct course for the Romian fleet parked halfway between the hypertracks to Felepye and Cappado. Epaphras had told him Effizus was the military command center of the quadrant, and this fleet stayed here at constant readiness in case the Gothans attempted an invasion. Whatever reason, he hoped Rado would find interacting with them... distasteful. As soon as he was out of scan range of the planet, he cut all power, continuing on a ballistic track.

Based on his last experience with this sort of thing, Seamus had decided he didn't like having *zero control*. And so he had figured out a way to manually fire the directional thrusters using a maintenance procedure designed to prime the lines. As the shuttle neared the fleet, he opened a panel on the floor, and then fired a series of breaking thrusts. With the screen of Löwin's passive tactical tilted toward him, he refined his thrust pattern until he had come to a relative stop right between the engine nozzles of a battle cruiser.

Seamus peered out the window. Six enormous nozzles filled the canopy at every side, while the hull of the rounded ship lay just a hundred meters away. Off in the distance to either side he could see the curving battle shields, no doubt bristled with guns and missile tubes, ready for a fight. Slowly, he moved over in the shadow of one of the nozzles, out of sight except from a few angles. It was the perfect hiding spot... unless the ship decided to move off suddenly, cooking him in its wake.

Just then the passive tactical showed him Rado had arrived.

"Let's see what you do," he whispered.

He wished he could know exactly what was going on. Rado was undoubtedly trying to pick up is signal. At some point he'd find it, pinging away from within the *Romian fleet*. He grinned thinking of the questions Rado must be asking himself when that happened. He watched unwaveringly to see what would happen.

Slowly, Rado's signal began to head in-system to Effizus – exactly what they had expected – and hoped.

Now it was a waiting game. Tychicus had wanted a couple days on Effizus if possible. So Seamus would wait here for his signal over the hidden network Thunderblade had set up. In the meantime, Seamus would pass the time watching the traffic patterns to figure out how and when he could best make is way back to Effizus. One thing he had learned from the military while training with his parents for the survey mission, they did everything with a regularity you could set your watch by.

♦ ♦ ♦

Two days later, a beeping message aroused Seamus, saying Tychicus was ready. He checked the schedule of the traffic records he'd been keeping, and an hour later, he manually fired his thrusters toward Effizus, shadowing the regularly scheduled transport. He couldn't keep up on just thrusters, but that really didn't matter. His main goals were first, to mask himself leaving the fleet, and second, to make Rado believe he was on a military transport with all that that implied. Soon, he was out of range of either the fleet or the transport and switched on the power, now showing the transponder code of a different military transport he had picked up the previous day. As before, Traffic Control cleared him without a question.

As they had prearranged, Tychicus was waiting at Filymon's old dock when Seamus brought the shuttle in. He headed back out to sea as soon as Tychicus came through the airlock, and by the time he strapped himself in they were lifting out of the water.

"I'm relieved to see you," Tychicus said. "I wasn't sure you'd be able to hide out for so long without getting caught."

"Tis grand to see you too. How'd it go?" Seamus was a bit surprised himself, truth be told. He glanced at the tactical.

Rado's signal was on the far side of the city and still stationary. For now.

"Really well... no problems. It was good to be back home. Everyone says hello. I got you a fried kapoto root. I've really missed those things... so sweet and crunchy." Tychicus handed him a greasy paper bag.

"Thanks. Those are good." Seamus saw Rado's signal change. "Well, he's after us again." From Rado's signal it looked like he was already airborne. That wasn't good, since they haven't even left the atmosphere yet.

He still had one trick up his sleeve. He skipped climbing to orbit first, and instead punched it, going as fast as he could in the atmosphere without Flight Control noticing. It was one of the few tricks he had learned flying manual: they only monitored orbital space. They cleared him as soon as he made altitude and he headed off toward the hypertrack at normal power. "That should have bought us about ten minutes."

"Onesimus, I hate to tell you this, but it looks like Rado has done the same thing."

"What?" He looked at the tactical and in shock, realized something horrible, something stripping away every advantage he had been counting on.

Rado must be a manual pilot too.

THIRTY-EIGHT – RECKONING

The blue of hyperspace dissolved into black, pinpricked with stars. Ahead lay a G2 yellow star, and unseen, the world of Kollos. As soon as Seamus received permission from the Romian picket, he headed in system as fast as his clearance allowed. There was nothing more to do at this point. Any faster and he would bring the Romians down on him. Seamus only hoped they had enough of a lead on Rado for him to have time enough to talk to Filymon. At this point it was his only hope.

Thirty minutes later just before they left sensor range, Rado's ship came through the hypertrack. Now knowing Rado was probably a manual pilot, Seamus wondered what they were up against. "Tychicus, focus our active sensors on him after he's cleared the picket. I want to be able to see him."

A few moments later, Tychicus looked up sharply. "Something's going on. It's like there's another ship now."

Seamus pulled up the tactical on the main screen. Sure enough, there was a faint reading of another ship, but it wasn't broadcasting a transponder code. It began to pull away from Rado's ship, and then it hit him. "Thundering notion, why didn't I think of that on the *Wander Wide*? We could have used the shuttle – oh, sorry. He's got a second ship, and from the looks of it, you have to have active sensors right on it to even see it! See, the main ship stays on the Romian-approved course, all fine and dandy, but then this little bugger can go most anywhere and do anything without the Romians knowing! He must have had a hidden bay of some sort for them not to notice it."

Tychicus looked worried. "Whatever it is, it looks like it's gaining on us."

♦ ♦ ♦

Two hours later they reached Kollos with Rado right behind them. Seamus took the shuttle down at the steepest angle the spacecraft could take, wringing as many seconds as he could out of the flight time. And Rado was so close seconds might make all the difference. Orange and red streaked from the shuttle's nose, a near-blinding blanket of fire ripping over the canopy.

Tychicus grabbed his arm. "Onesimus! We're burning up!"

"No, we're good, still good," he said, eyeing the status board. Barely.

They broke through the clouds over the glistening sea at sunset. With a supersonic roar they came over land, past Halcyon's fishing lodge, now over the mountains, and then the forested hills leading toward Filymon's. It was past time to slow down for landing, but Seamus kept his speed up.

"Onesimus, aren't we going to overshoot?"

"I'm going to flip over and go full thrust. Maybe Rado will fly right past." At least that's how it happened in the movies. "Hold on, full power in three seconds."

At the right moment Seamus cut power and whipped the shuttle around.

In that split second before the thrusters kicked in, he saw the silver gleam of Rado's fighter, hardly a kilometer ahead. And then they whipped forward by the sudden breaking, restraints hardly holding them in their seats. The sky turned grey and darkness wisped around Seamus' peripheral vision. He squeezed his stomach muscles to force more blood in his brain to keep from blacking out. And then silver flashed past.

It worked!

No time to celebrate now with the shuttle dropping like a rock. Retros kicked in and Seamus pushed the ship forward to try to generate more lift.

Tychicus slumped over, blacked out with G-LOC from the move.

Seamus eased the shuttle into a corkscrewing spiral to stay over Filymon's landing pad.

They were dropping too fast!

He rotated upward so the main engines would provide some lift. They were slowing, but would it be enough?

Seamus cycled the landing gear, and braced himself.

The shuttle slammed down with a bang and a bounce, but still in one piece.

Home.

"Where am I?" Tychicus mumbled, looking disoriented.

Seamus unbuckled as fast as he could. "It will pass in a couple seconds."

Leaving Tychicus behind, he grabbed his reader and ran for the door. He nearly tripped jumping through and slid down the wing to the ground, taking off at a tearing sprint toward the house.

Already Chippus had come out. "Onesimus! You came back!"

Just then a blast of scorching air knocked Seamus flat.

With a roar Rado flew overhead just a meter above him and dropping hard to the ground.

Grassy clods of soil pelted the garage as Rado's fighter skip-skidded to a stop onto the gravel drive.

He picked up the reader and jumped to his feet, running for the house.

Seamus heard a popping noise and felt the spray of dirt. With shock he glanced over to see Rado standing up under the opening canopy of his fighter, taking aim with a pistol.

A bolt of red light raced past Seamus' left, ending in another dust-tossing blast.

"Stop that right now!" Filymon bellowed from the doorway. Chippus peeked out from behind him.

The shooting stopped and Seamus nearly tumbled to a halt at Filymon's feet.

Around the heaving of his chest Seamus said, "Master... I've come back... I'm sorry... for running away... and for all... for all I did."

With a thunder of footsteps Rado ran toward him, pistol drawn.

Seamus kneeled in the manner required by the Code of Submission, offering the remote.

Filymon took it just as Rado reached them.

Seamus began to recite the ceremonial pledge: "I pledge my loyalty, my–"

"Quiet, runaway," Rado growled shoving his pistol right against Seamus' left temple. To Filymon he said, "He's only doing this since I have caught him. He hopes to play on your sympathies to spare his life."

"That's not true," Seamus said. "I was already coming back. Please, Master, please listen to this message." He slowly lifted the reader, keeping his eyes averted. He didn't know what Filymon's expression looked like. He didn't know if he was pleased or furious. He only knew his master took his time to take the reader from his hand.

A moment later he heard Pol's voice.

"This message is from Pol, imprisoned for Yeshua and Tem our brother to Filymon our dear friend and fellow worker, to Apphia our sister, to Chippus our fellow soldier, and to the ekklesia that meets in your home: Grace to you and peace from God our Father and Yeshua.

"I always thank my God as I remember you in my prayers, because I hear about your steadfast belief in Yeshua and your love for all who follow him. I pray that you may be active in sharing the story of your belief in our great news, so that you will have a full understanding of every good thing given to us by Yeshua. Your love has given me great joy and encouragement, because you, brother, have refreshed the hearts of those who follow him.

"Therefore, although in Yeshua I could be bold and order you to do what you ought to do, yet I appeal to you on the basis of love. I then, as Pol — an old man and now also a prisoner of Yeshua — I appeal to you for my son Onesimus, who became my son while I was in chains. Formerly he was useless to you, but now he has become useful both to you and to me..."

Seamus knew his slave name, Onesimus, sounded like the Athinsian word for "useful", and it sounded like Pol was making a play on words. He hoped Filymon was in the mood for it.

"...I am sending him - who is my very heart - back to you. I would have liked to keep him with me so that he could take your place in helping me while I am in chains for the great news I share. But I did not want to do anything without your consent, so that any favor you do will be spontaneous and not forced. Perhaps the reason he was separated from you for a little while was that you might have him back for good - no longer as a slave, but better than a slave, as a dear brother. He is very dear to me but

even dearer to you, both as a young man and as a brother in Yeshua..."

What was Pol saying? How could Pol know what Filymon would think? And why would Filymon think anything of him but as a slave, and a poor one at that? What little hope he felt began to slip away.

"...So if you consider me a partner, welcome him as you would welcome me. If he has done you any wrong or owes you anything, charge it to me. I will pay it back – not to mention that you owe me your very self. I do wish, brother, that I may have some benefit from you; refresh my heart in Yeshua. Confident of your obedience, I send this message to you, knowing that you will do even more than I ask..."

Seamus couldn't believe what he just heard. Pol would do that? For him? With all he had done? His words overwhelmed him, and his sight began to blur with tears. At that moment nothing mattered any longer.

What he had hoped before, he now truly believed.

God accepted him; God loved him.

Pol's voice continued: *"...And one thing more: Prepare a guest room for me, because I hope to be restored to you in answer to your prayers. Epaphras, my fellow prisoner in Yeshua, sends you greetings. And so do Yaunmarck, Aristarchus, Demas and Doctor Lukaas, my fellow workers. The grace of Yeshua be with your spirit. Farewell."*

As the message ended, silence replaced it. Seamus could hear the wind blowing through the trees and grass, smelling of the sea, reminding him of home. Filymon's voice finally brought the peaceful moment to a close.

"Rado, I say, I believe I will handle things from here. What do I owe you for your trouble?"

Rado's pistol jammed harder into Seamus' head. "This piece of trash is a runaway slave, deserving of death. He must die for his crimes against us. He ignored our training and soiled our reputations!"

Seamus dared to look up, catching Chippus' and then Apphia's frightened eyes before looking directly into Filymon's. The man looked troubled, serious. He looked down at the remote in his hand, running his thumb over the buttons.

"Yes, Rado, I suppose you're right. Taking back a runaway slave would set a bad precedent for all the other slaves."

Seamus gasped. Chippus blurted, "Dad?"

"I'm glad we're in agreement," Rado said, triumphant. "I would be happy to take him off your hands and carry out the sentence."

Rado lowered his gun and reached out for the remote.

"No," Filymon said quietly. "This is something I've been *wanting* to do."

"As you wish. I will be your witness."

In horror Seamus watched as Filymon thumbed several buttons on the remote.

So this was it. At least he got to apologize and try to make things right.

Click.

Searing pain ran down his spine and he dropped to the ground, writhing.

"No, dad! Don't kill him! Please!"

The pain flared, but then suddenly stopped.

Seamus felt something move on his back.

Bewildered, he rose to his knees and reached back to find something sliding from between his shoulders.

He grabbed it.

Something like strings or wires pulled at his skin, released, and then a cool sensation followed.

Whatever it was came loose into his hand. As he brought it into view he realized with joy what it was.

It was his fitting.

It had fallen off.

"Mister Rado, I think if you shot a freed slave, you'd be guilty of murder."

"What!" Rado snarled.

Seamus felt bewildered. What had happened?

Filymon reached down, gently taking Seamus by the elbow and helping him to his feet. "Onesimus, I grant you manumission. You're *free*. And, I say, we want you to stay with us and be a part of our family."

He looked up into tender eyes. And then felt the arms of Apphia and Chippus, and then even Filymon's strong embrace.

"Mister Rado, if you would kindly remove yourself from my property?"

Rado hissed, spun on his heals, and stomped back toward his fighter.

A moment later he was inside the silver craft and with a roar skybound, but not without scorching most of the yard with his exhaust first.

As they watched the fighter recede, Chippus looked up to Filymon. "You were telling the truth, right? You meant what you said, didn't you?"

"I did," Filymon said, nodding. He didn't smile, but he looked happy. "Of course, it's up to Onesimus to choose what he will do. He's free now."

"I'd like to stay," he said, grinning.

He wanted to say so much more, but it was all he could get out right now. It was funny how things had worked out. For nearly two years he'd yearned for freedom and family. And now he had both.

"What did I miss?" Tychicus called out.

Seamus looked out to see his friend walking toward them, and then did a doubletake. A small black and chrome robot walked beside him.

"Thunderblade!" Seamus cried, and ran out to meet him. "I thought you were dead," he said, gathering the robot in his arms.

"In effect, I was."

"What happened? How did you come back?"

"Forgive me, Seamus. I enacted programming which would cause me to have a logic paradox and shutdown if you ever realized you could override your parents' commands to me to keep you safe. I calculated your best chance at continued safety would be here, and if I were not a factor in your planning you would eventually choose to come here. I set my reactivation upon your arrival here."

Seamus was too happy to argue with Thunderblade right now. He set him back on the ground. "Well, you were right about one thing. I'm safe here. And now I'm free too!" He twisted to show his fitting-less neck.

"I am pleased by the news, Seamus. The results are much better than I hoped."

Seamus had a thought and decided to follow through. "Thunderblade, I want to give you what I have been given." He paused while the robot focused on him. "I want you to be free. My last command to you is for you to do what *you* want, to be free."

Thunderblade stood so still and so quiet, Seamus became alarmed, wondering if the robot had suffered another paradox.

"Seamus, this is unexpected and generous. Forgive me as I remove all the applicable parameters. This will take a few seconds."

Seamus smiled at his little friend, waiting. When he looked up, he asked, "What will you do?"

Thunderblade took a moment to respond. "I believe I... When I was last informed, Doctor Lukaas had been conferring with a colleague named Theophilus about underwriting a project. He intended to use source material from Yuanmarck and to travel to Judia to interview eyewitnesses in order to write a complete history of Yeshua. Do you know if he has begun this effort?"

Seamus shrugged. "I have no idea."

"If he is, I believe I would like to aid him. It appears a culture-shifting movement is underway, and I would like to observe it as it unfolds."

"That sounds like a great idea."

"And you, Seamus? What will you do?"

Seamus thought about it for a moment. Like Thunderblade, his "parameters" had changed in so many different ways. He looked around the grounds. He looked at his new "family", so different now than when he first met them. He smelled the sea air as it kissed his face. And he looked at the dead fitting in his hand. Lastly, he looked inward at what had been a cold, vindictive heart, now overflowing with so many good things.

"I don't know what I'm going to do. I just know my song is not finished yet."

"When will you know it is complete?"

He shrugged, smiling with memory. "As Löwin says, 'Are they ever finished?'" He looked to the sky, now darkening to a starry night. "All I know is that I will face every moment and give it my best. And I want to live up to my name."

"Seamus?"

"No, no more. My name is Onesimus."

THE END

Note from the Author

I hope you have enjoyed reading *Runaway* as much as I enjoyed writing it. By far, this was the most challenging and satisfying project I have ever undertaken. At one point I suffered many weeks of writer's block, terrorized by the prospect of tackling the character of Pol (more on that in a moment). At most other times I have never felt so inspired in my writing. It seemed like great ideas were whispered in my ear and flew from my fingers to my keyboard with hardly a thought.

By the end of writing *Runaway*, I felt like I had captured something beyond myself. I think I understand now what Michelangelo meant when someone asked him how he created such amazing sculptures. His reply was that the sculptures had always been in the marble... he just had chipped the extra away.

I had three goals with *Runaway*, the first to tell a great story. I hope I succeeded in that. The second was to share my deeply held belief that God changes people and then uses people to change their world. My third goal was to inspire my readers to try to find out more about the origins of this story.

If you are a Christ-follower, you may have recognized this story is inspired by parts of the Bible. I encourage you to go to your scriptures and read the book of *Acts* anew. If you are not a Christ-follower, I encourage you to do the same, but first start with the biography of Jesus written by Luke, which is the prequel to *Acts*. I'm sure you won't regret learning more from the source.

Now, let me share a little more about Pol, who is inspired by the Apostle Paul who wrote the letter to *Philemon* upon which *Runaway* is partially based. Since this is a biblically-inspired story, I felt a great deal of responsibility to accurately reflect the spirit and intent of the source material (hence my writer's block).

Undoubtedly, I have failed at some point, but not without giving it my best. In the following pages I have included a cross-reference outlining my attempts at keeping the Apostle Paul, as well as other biblical characters, as biblical as possible.

Lastly, I would be remiss if I didn't share a little bit more about Onesimus. The Bible is silent on the outcome of Paul's letter to Philemon. But the fact that his letter is in the Bible leads most to believe Paul was successful in his attempt. There are some hints outside of the Bible as to what may have happened to Onesimus.

About forty years after the book of *Philemon* was believed to be written, one of the early church fathers named Ignatius stopped in Ephesus on his way to a martyr's death in Rome. Afterwards, he wrote the Ephesian church a letter, in which he praised their leader, Onesimus, and encouraging those Christ-followers to emulate him. No one is certain if this is the same Onesimus, but I'd like to think the runaway slave who found Christ also found forgiveness, freedom, and a future.

Edward D. Casey

Biblical Cross Reference

Introduction

In writing *Runaway*, I had the challenge of writing a fictional story with real biblical characters and situations. My goal, being a believer of the authenticity and supremacy of scripture, was to treat the scripture both literally and with reverence. To that end, all characters of biblical origin are treated with the minimum of fictionalization. Some characters have little written about them in the Bible, while others have quite a lot. In each case, I attempted to create believable characters who serve the story, using all scriptural and select scholarly sources to inform their creation.

Unlike most of the biblical characters in *Runaway*, a great deal of scriptural material exists about the Apostle Paul. Writing the Apostle Paul was a particular challenge, as he is such a central character of early Christianity whose writings are core to our beliefs and theology. To avoid many pitfalls, I chose to link as much as possible concerning the Apostle Paul to scripture. To aid both myself and the reader, the following is a cross reference of all the scriptural material used to inform Pol of *Runaway*. Please note I used the NIV version of the Bible in either direct quote or paraphrase.

Chapter Ten

Physical appearance

2nd Corinthians 10:10; 11:23-27

Eyesight

There is some biblical evidence that Paul had a physical condition with his eyes (Galatians 4:15, 6:11, 6:17). Though it is more likely a medical condition – if any at all – existed prior to having arrived in Galatia, the author has taken the liberty of attributing this condition to having been stoned to near death on his first missionary journey (Acts 14:19-20). This conclusion is based upon the audience of Galatians possibly being witness to this event and Paul's comments.

Lecture

Ephesians 2:12-13

Chapter Eighteen

Financing

1st Corinthians 9, Acts 18:1-3

Healing the sick

Acts 19:11-16

Lecture

Ephesians 5:21-6:9

Chapter Twenty-Four

The Riot

Acts 19:23-41

Chapter Twenty-Five

Pre-riot plans to leave

Acts 19:21-22

Response to the riot

Adapted from Romans 12:9-20

Conversation in the shuttle

Adapted from 2nd Corinthians 11:16 – 12:10, Acts 17:16-34, 26:25. In the first of these passages, the Apostle Paul talks about his "thorn in the flesh", calling it a messenger of Satan sent to torment him. There are various (and sometimes controversial) opinions on what this "thorn" was, whether it was of a spiritual, mental, physical, or some other nature, or even a combination of many. The context of these chapters involves false teachers who harassed Paul, who persecuted him, who attempted to thwart his teachings wherever he went, and Paul's response and example through service and hardship. The typical end result of this harassment was for Paul to be physically and/or legally assaulted in some form (as he describes so thoroughly) and to leave the area, but not before establishing a solid group of believers. With many various viewpoints to draw upon, for the purposes of this story the author has interpreted this "messenger of Satan" as being the personification of his detractors (certainly spreading a false message), with the physical result (thorn) being his damaged eyesight, as theorized above under Chapter Ten.

Chapter Twenty-Eight

Leadership conference

Adapted from Acts 20:13-38

Leading Filymon to Christ

Philemon 19

Chapter Twenty-Nine

Encouragement to Chippus to complete the work he received from God

Colossians 4:17

Chapter Thirty-Four

Discussion with Romian soldier

Adapted from Romans 2:13-16

Chapter Thirty-Six

Talk with Seamus

Adapted from Galatians 1:13-16

Chapter Thirty-Eight

Message to Filymon

The book of Philemon

Cross-Reference of Characters

Runaway Character	Biblical/Historical Figure
Aquyia	Aquila
Apphia	Apphia
Aristarchus	Aristarchus
Artimiss	Artemis
Chippus	Archippus
Deme Trius	Demetrius
Demas	Demas
Epaphras	Epaphras
Phroditus	Epaphroditus
Filymon	Philemon
Gaius	Gaius
Justis	Justis
Lukaas	Luke
Onesimus (Seamus)	Onesimus
Pol	Paul the Apostle
Prazella	Priscilla
Rastus	Erastus
Tem	Timothy
Tychicus	Tychicus
Tyrannus	Tyrannus
Yeshua (Hebrew spelling)	Jesus Christ
Yaunmarck	Mark or John Mark

About the Author

Edward D. Casey is a husband and father. He and his wife, Amy, with daughter, Emma, live in Atlanta, Georgia, USA, where Edward is employed as an analyst for a major airline. In his free time, Edward enjoys landscape gardening and volunteering at his church. This award-winning author's passion is telling imaginative stories that resonate with universal truths.

Edward can be contacted at:

Email: **EDC@EdwardDCasey.com**
Website: **www.EdwardDCasey.com**

About the Cover Artist

Paolo Libunao is a freelance illustrator and painter, who has worked on various projects for companies such as Harsh-Realities, Brave Design, and Community Comics. Paolo also serves as a Bible teacher and youth ministry volunteer at his church in Manila, Philippines.

Paolo can be contacted at:

email: **np.libunao@yahoo.com.ph**
website: **www.paololibunao.deviantart.com**

Want to read more from the world of *Runaway*?

Visit **www.EdwardDCasey.com** where you can read a short story entitled *Stowaway* about Thunderblade's adventures while on the Kaarrthaaggian slave ship. Also, available is an alternate ending, not included in *Runaway*.

Would you like a signed copy of Runaway?

Go to **www.EdwardDCasey.com** to learn how to get a free author-signed label for yor copy of *Runaway*.

Edward D. Casey is proud to support the **National Center for Missing and Exploited Children**. 10% of the proceeds of each copy of *Runaway* sold will be given to help NCMEC in their quest to prevent child abduction and sexual exploitation; help find missing children; and assist victims of child abduction and sexual exploitation, their families, and the professionals who serve them.

NCMEC has assisted law enforcement personnel with over 165,000 missing child cases, resulting in the recovery of over 151,000 children; trained over 272,000 law enforcement and other professionals; handled more than 816,000 reports of child sexual exploitation through their CyberTipline, printed over 46,000,000 copies of issue-related publications; and handled over 2,475,000 telephone calls through its national toll-free Hotline, 1-800-THE-LOST® (1-800-843-5678).

For more information about NCMEC, please visit their website: **www.missingkids.com**.

www.ingramcontent.com/pod-product-compliance
Lightning Source LLC
Chambersburg PA
CBHW020822180626
46814CB00001B/64

* 9 7 8 0 9 8 2 8 4 9 1 0 1 *